THE TRAVELER BOOK TWO:
THE HUNTER

THE TRAVELER BOOK TWO: THE HUNTER

KIM PRITEKEL

SAPPHIRE BOOKS

SALINAS, CALIFORNIA

The Traveler - Book Two: The Hunter
Copyright © 2020 by Kim Pritekel. All rights reserved.

ISBN - 978-1-948232-93-7

Editor - Tara Young
Book Design - LJ Reynolds
Cover Design - Fineline Cover Design

Sapphire Books Publishing, LLC
P.O. Box 8142
Salinas, CA 93912
www.sapphirebooks.com

Printed in the United States of America
First Edition – February 2020

This and other Sapphire Books titles can be found at
www.sapphirebooks.com

Dedication

To the love of my life.

Chapter One

The world looked different through the black lace that covered Sally Little's face. A sunny day was given a markedly cloudy feel looking through the millions of tiny spaces in the delicate material. As per usual, she had Tomlin drop her off, and she made her way down the street, enjoying her freedom, if only for a few hours. No responsibilities, no decisions, no shame.

As she always did, she glanced at every woman who looked to be in her early twenties who she passed. She knew it was futile but wondered if maybe, just maybe she was all grown up and somehow had ended up in Colorado from Pennsylvania. A fool's errand, she knew, but some wounds could never heal, and the loss was profound. In a face she passed, would she see herself? Her mother's eyes? Perhaps her father's gestures?

She reached her first destination, nodding her acknowledgment as a man held open the door for her so she could enter before him. The small store was as it had been the week before, shelves filled with basic staples such as bread, flour, cans of lard, and a few house accessories among other things such as medicines and sweet treats.

She reached inside the small pouch that dangled from a strap around her wrist and retrieved a folded piece of paper, which she carried to the counter where the store owner stood, stocking a cabinet with baby dolls and accessories for little girls.

"Well, the widow has returned," he said with a smile, looking at her through the glass case from behind where the door was opened.

She smiled at him, never correcting his assumption of why she was dressed in black from head to toe, the veil covering her face and hair. "Good morning, Mr. Wheeler. How's the new year treating you?"

"Well, nearly a month in, can't complain." He placed a tiny pair of handmade leather shoes next to the doll before closing the case and locking it.

"It won't do you any good," Sally provided, both chuckling at such an obvious fact.

"No truer words spoken." He stepped away from the doll cabinet to stand in front of Sally, the wide berth of the counter between them. "Got a list for me?" He nodded toward the paper in her gloved hand.

"I do." She handed it over. "My man will pick it up tomorrow. In the meantime, I have a small list of things I need dropped off at this address." She pulled a second folded piece of paper from her pouch, unfolding it and laying it flat on the counter. It consisted of a half dozen items such as fifty-pound bags of flour, sugar, and yeast, as well as several bolts of fabric.

The shopkeeper took the list and read it over before nodding at her. "Yes, ma'am. I'll send Hal over with it this afternoon. Good enough?"

"Good enough." She reached into her pouch again for her coin purse. "I'll also be needing two pounds of the hard candy," she said, indicating the large glass jar filled to the brim with colorful pieces of small candies in various shapes. "A random mix will do."

"Absolutely, Mrs....?" He eyed her from where he was opening a paper sack for the candy.

She smirked, though she knew he couldn't see it. The poor man had been trying to figure her out ever since she'd first arrived in town, hiding in plain sight. "And why do you assume I'm a married woman?" she asked, stepping over to where he fulfilled her order.

"Well, a woman with the beauty of your heart," he began, sparing her a shy glance before returning his focus to his task. "There's no man on earth that would allow you to get away. So, I assume you're mourning the passing of such a lucky man."

It was not the first time there had been assumptions about her marital status. After all, a woman at the doorstep of forty should have been married for decades already. Who was she to buck the system?

"Well," she said at length. "We all see what we wish to see at times, don't we?"

He smiled as he nodded, continuing to fill the bag with candy. "That we do."

"How's your wife?" she asked, not unkindly. "I hear she has the cancer."

"She's doing well," he said, clearing his throat, as he seemed to be blushing a bit.

Sally had seen it so many times. She'd come to the realization that there were two houses in the species that was men: those who looked at women not as a person, a partner, and equal, but a thing to collect, possess, and tack onto a list of acquisitions. Then there was the minority house, those who looked at a woman as his true better half, the one person who gave him the strength to do the impossible.

It shouldn't take more than a second or two to guess which group made up the majority of her clientele. In an instance like this, a man before her who was clearly looking for a little female attention, she would have found a way to convince him that all he needed was a Little Piece of Heaven, problem solved. Someone like Seth Wheeler, however, would never forgive himself for a moment of earthly pleasure while his wife was desperately trying to hold off the meeting of her maker. Unlike her mother, she could never corrupt a truly God-fearing, wife-loving man. So, instead, she offered him her gloved hand, giving his fingers a light squeeze.

"My thoughts and prayers are with her," she said softly.

The soft sobs of a child caught her attention. Glancing over her shoulder, she saw a young mother kneeling as she hugged a small boy, no older than four.

"I know, son," the mother murmured, rubbing his back. "I just ain't got the money right now for that. Maybe next time, huh?"

Sally gave the kneeling mother a small smile before turning back to Mr. Wheeler. "Add a scoop of sweets to their order, Mr. Wheeler," she said. "My man will pay you for all this tomorrow when he picks up my order."

✥ ✥ ✥ ✥

Sally couldn't help but smile at the sweet little face that looked up at her with so much confusion and awe. Once she'd entered the doors of the Denver Orphan's Home, she'd removed her veil, flipping it back over the black headpiece it was attached to. She knew she'd not be recognized within the walls.

"It pains my heart that so many children are abandoned by parents who can't afford them," she whispered, lightly running her fingers down the soft cheek of the child in her arms. She smiled when the move brought a natural smile to the cherubic face looking up at her. "Or who have no parents at all."

"It is tragic. Our numbers are high right now," Pamela Aiken said with a heavy sigh, taking a seat next to the chair Sally sat in. "Since opening this place ten years ago, the numbers of abandoned children have grown." She met Sally's gaze, her own sad. "Reminds me of the war thirty years ago."

Sally could feel the older woman's gaze on her, but she paid it no mind as she was focused on the precious one in her arms.

"Do you have any children of your own?" Mrs. Aiken asked softly. "You're so wonderful with our little ones on your weekly visits."

Sally gave the baby a sad smile, only to smile with joy when the tiny bundle blew bubbles from his lips. She'd been asked the question many times, and she responded as she always did. "It's never been the right situation for me to raise a baby," she said quietly.

"What a shame." The older woman stood. "Well, shall we go surprise our older children with the sweets you brought for them? And," she added, a hand going to Sally's shoulder. "I can't thank you enough for the supplies. We're forever grateful."

❧ ❧ ❧ ❧

The fire felt wonderful on Sally's face, and the slow fire building within from the bourbon felt even better. She sat in her bedroom, which made up the lion's share of her apartment. It was far more than a room that held a bed and bedroom furniture, however. The seating area—where she sat before the warm fireplace—took up a portion, replete with beautiful furniture to sit and enjoy quiet time reading or intimate conversation.

She stared into the flames, hands wrapped around her glass as she contemplated her day and all that she'd accomplished. A lot had been done, and it had been a very expensive day in doing so. She knew when she sat down to input everything into her ledgers, it wasn't going to be a fun time, but nothing had been arbitrary.

She raised the glass and took a sip of the liquid fire when she heard a knock on the outer door of her bedroom. Only one other person had the key to the main door of her apartment. "Come in, Lark." She felt fresh hurt pinch her guts from the younger woman's harsh words the last time they'd seen each other. She knew it was childish, but she was hurt and didn't look at her guest as she swished her way over to her.

"I didn't know you'd come back," Lark said softly from where she stood on the other side of the second chair placed before the fireplace. "You didn't come down for dinner."

"No," Sally replied, just as soft. "I haven't been back long."

"Do you want me to get Ginny to make you—"

"No. Not particularly hungry." She glanced briefly at Lark before returning her gaze to the popping flames. "Thank you, though."

After a moment of uncomfortable silence, Lark said, "Can I sit?"

Sally indicated the empty twin to her chair with a wave of her hand. "Help yourself. Bourbon?"

"No." Lark got herself seated and skirts situated around her. More awkward silence, then, "I heard what you did," she said, softness in her voice, perhaps tinged a bit with guilt.

Sally glanced at Lark, who was looking back at her. "Have you ever known me to not take care of my girls? Whether they are here, working for me," she said, indicating the house around them, "or have had to move on?"

Lark's gaze fell to her hands, which rested in her lap. "No," she nearly whispered.

"So, why would I start with Rebecca?"

Lark let out a sigh, her shoulders falling with the exhale. "I don't know. I'm sorry." She met Sally's gaze again. "Truly, I'm sorry. I guess I was just upset at what happened to her, and I lashed out."

Sally studied her profile for a long moment as Lark had looked away again. She was so lovely, skin like porcelain, eyes like the deepest pools of blue and hair like spun gold. She'd felt a connection instantly, as though she'd known her all her life. It scared her. In fact, one of the first things she'd said to Lark that rainy night was *Have we met before?*

She knew it wasn't easy for Lark to live there, work there, *be* there. She saw the sadness grow in her eyes by the day, it seemed. "Lark?" Sally said softly, reaching across the scant distance between their chairs and taking a warm, soft hand in her own. She waited until she had that soulful gaze on her. "I know you spend a lot of your life angry with me, and I don't pretend to always know why, but I know you are. Why do you stay here? Why don't you go out and find someone who can give you what you need? What you want?"

Lark intertwined their fingers, which Sally allowed, though she knew it was wrong and cruel. "You know what I want, Sally," she murmured, repeating, "You know what I want."

"Lark—"

"No!" Lark slid down from the chair and moved to her knees before Sally, looking up into her eyes, her own pleading. "Don't give me your usual excuses of everyone you've ever loved you lost or hurt, and you don't want to lose or hurt me. Isn't that for me to decide? To take the chance?"

Sally looked down at her, her heart swelling as much as it broke. She reached down with her free hand and cupped the side of Lark's face, so soft, so beautiful. "You are so lovely," she whispered, unaware that she'd spoken the words aloud until she saw Lark's eyes fall closed as she leaned into the touch. "We've been through this so many times," she murmured, her tone not unkind, yet filled with the hopelessness she felt. Her heart leapt when Lark reached up and covered her hand, sliding it around to leave a kiss in Sally's palm. "Please don't," Sally whispered, though her tone wasn't even believable to her own ears. She released a heavy sigh—part arousal, part annoyance— as Lark's lips moved to her wrist.

Feeling her willpower dwindling by the second, Sally was startled by the ringing of the bell, two tugs on the chain downstairs that rang in her apartment. Two tugs meant a very special meeting for a very special clientele.

Lark sighed, head falling before she released Sally's hand and got to her feet. "I'll get things ready," she said, sounding resigned. She walked to the doorway where she turned and met Sally's gaze. "Someday, Sally," she said. "Someday, you'll love me." With that, she was gone.

Sally's eyes closed as her head fell back against the chair in which she sat. "I already do," she whispered.

After a moment of stewing in her misery, she also got to her feet. She finished the bourbon, then made her way into her dressing room. She'd already changed out of her daytime garments when she'd returned from town, so now she simply had to fix her hair and change from her comfortable robe to one made of the finest of silks, a deep red color to contrast with her hair and eyes. She looked good, good enough to make a very profitable deal.

With her hair down and brushed to a midnight shine, she headed to a small parlor, where she knew Lark would have brought her guest. This area was for meetings with clients who had a very specific, often refined need: ladies looking for the company of a woman for the night and the rare man who came along who wished for company of a more phallic nature.

These clients had to remain hidden in the recesses of her apartments because, though she peddled in the currency of pleasure, fantasy, and countless indiscretions against the mother of their children, her mainstream clients held their God-given right as powerful, dominant Christian males to draw a line on what was carnal pleasure and what was godlessness.

She entered the small well-appointed room and ignored the fetching redhead who was seated casually on the settee nearest the fireplace. Instead, she walked to the small bar tucked into the corner and poured two glasses of red. She walked back toward the settee, feeling the icy stare of her guest on her the entire way.

"Thank you," the woman said, accepting the crystal goblet.

Sally said nothing as she sat next to the woman, dressed in powder blue to match her eyes. Her heart was racing, the instant attraction she had to this stranger palpable. That was a rare thing for her these days. Finally, she steeled her spine and resolve and met the woman's intense gaze. "Good evening, I'm Sally Little. What are you looking for?" she asked, all business.

"Right to it, hmm?" the woman asked, a fiery eyebrow raised as she took a small sip from her wine.

Sally smirked, taking her own drink. "That is why you're here, isn't it?"

"I hope you take a little more time in the bedroom to whet the palate than you do to organize a deal."

Sally burst into laughter, amused and charmed. "Well, since my prowess isn't on the block for examination, I guess you'll just have to hope."

The woman smiled, which made her all the more beautiful. "Fair enough. I'm Rachel, and I'm looking for a young woman to be brought to my home for an intimate evening."

"Any men?" Sally asked, getting an idea of what she'd be sending her girl into.

"No, just me," Rachel assured.

"Any potential for complications? Jealousies? Problems?"

"None."

"Wonderful. Well, then what are you looking for?" Sally asked again, crossing one elegant leg over the other, settling in for the fun part.

The woman locked her gaze on Sally as she took a slow, dramatic sip of her wine. "I want the little blonde that showed me in here," she said softly, indicating the room around them.

It wasn't the first time someone had their eye on Lark, and Sally knew it wouldn't be the last. All the same, she felt her spine stiffen. "She's not an option," she said curtly.

"Oh?" Rachel purred, raising her eyebrows in question. "Is she yours?"

"She's not available," Sally repeated.

"I see," Rachel said after a moment, studying Sally as she drank more wine. "You want her to be."

Sally grew unusually angry as the woman pushed. She set her wine glass aside and moved to stand. "Clearly, you're not here for business—"

"Wait," Rachel said, placing a warm hand on Sally's thigh. "I'm sorry. It was rude of me to assume and pry."

Sally met her gaze, Rachel's expression contrite. She relaxed again next to the woman, who had yet to remove her hand. Admittedly, the warmth of her hand was traveling farther up Sally's thigh.

"Is she your type then?" Sally asked, trying to get her anger to subside and get the train of her emotions back on the right track.

"She is, yes. She's absolutely beautiful. I love the almost..." Rachel glanced toward the door where likely she'd last seen Lark as she seemed to be organizing her thoughts. "...angelic quality to her. An innocence."

Sally nodded, reaching again for her wine glass. "Yes," she murmured. Sipping to clear her head, she removed her thoughts from mental images of Lark to the woman before her. "So, blonde? Blue eyes?

Delicate build? Are these things you're wanting for your night?"

Rachel let out a heavy sigh of contemplation until finally she spoke. "I don't care so much about hair or eye color." She met Sally's gaze with a penetrating one of her own. "I want the innocence, the aura of the newly emerged butterfly."

Sally nodded, understanding. "It will be done."

"And your girls know what they're doing?" Rachel asked.

Sally gave her another smirk. "Yes. My girls know how to touch a woman."

"Trained by you?" Rachel asked, her fingernails trailing tantalizingly across Sally's thigh, where her hand had remained.

Sally's smile grew as she remembered the smell of her hair, taste of her skin, and breathy pleas for release. Many nights had been spent with Sandra, who would go from student to teacher. "Indirectly."

"I see. Well, shall we discuss the terms?" Rachel asked.

Chapter Two

Sally watched Sheriff Cook carefully, amused as he seemed to be taking in every detail of her office. She followed him with her gaze as he popped up from the chair and walked over to the fireplace, his finger tracing the intricately carved decoration.

"You know," he said, "my father was a master carpenter." He smiled at her. "He was pretty upset when he realized his youngest son just didn't have the same talent as him and my three brothers."

"What did he say when you told him you wanted to be a lawman?" she asked, her guest retaking his seat across from her.

"He threatened to disown me," he said, followed by a burst of laughter. "So," he said, his tone back on business. "I'm impressed with what you've done here, Sally. These ladies seem to have a safe, healthy place to live, come and go as they please."

"Thank you," Sally said. "They're happy here, and I care about all of them." She reached for the silver tray with silver coffeepot and cups Ginny had provided. Pouring him a cup, she asked, "How's Mildred doing? I understand she's expecting again. Black, two sugars, right?" she asked, a fingernail tapping the bowl containing sugar cubes. She took his look of surprise as an affirmative. "This will be your fifth child, correct?" She glanced at him with a raised eyebrow and slight quirk to her lips. "My, my, Sheriff," she purred. "You've been a busy boy."

He accepted his coffee with a sheepish grin and slight blush crawling up from behind his heavy handlebar mustache, perfectly waxed to curled, upturned tips.

"Guessing you're hoping for a boy, finally?" she pushed, preparing her own cup. "I can't imagine it's easy to be the only man with four girls and your wife."

He chuckled, setting his cup down, the petite cup all but disappearing in the large man's hand. "Well, I'd be fibbin' if I said I wasn't hoping." He grinned. "Be nice to have an ally in the house when the little fella got older."

Sally returned the smile. "No doubt. Well," she said, pushing her chair back from the desk before standing to grab the small wrapped loaf that sat on a table beneath the window, a square of folded material next to it with gold ribbon snaking its way across. She grabbed the loaf, provided by Ginny just before the sheriff had arrived. She took the wrapped loaf and materials back to her desk. "My personal cook baked up a loaf of her sinfully good banana bread for your girls," she explained, opening the folded material and setting the loaf at the center. Reaching into one of the desk drawers, she pulled out another wrapped package, this one a pouch of the finest Tennessee tobacco soaked in Kentucky bourbon. "And," she added, glancing at him as she set the pouch atop the loaf before wrapping the entire thing up in the material, creating a bag. "A little something for the man of the house."

She artfully tied the whole thing shut with the ribbon, tying it in a dramatic bow. The tail was a tad too long, so she reached into the top drawer of her desk and retrieved a dagger, sharp as the devil's tongue as it ended in a wicked point. The gold handle was the body of a mermaid. She used it to swipe off the unneeded ribbon, dropping the excess into the wastebasket next to her desk.

"That's quite the piece." The sheriff reached across the table and took hold of the heavy dagger. He looked at it this way and that, lightly tapping the tip with his finger. "Where'd you get this?"

"It was a gift from a man who hailed all the way from India," she explained, finishing with his package and moving it to his side of the desk. "Exquisite, isn't it?"

"Certainly unique." He set the dagger down and rose to his feet, looking down at his gift. "This is awful kind of you, Sally. Mildred and the girls will love it."

"I hope they do." She extended her hand across the desk, which was taken in his much larger one, fingers lightly squeezed before her hand was released. He grabbed his hat from where he'd hung it on one of the decorative knobs of his chair and carried it with him as he headed to the door, followed by Sally. "Lark, will you see our guest out?" she called, surprised her assistant wasn't already there waiting for them. "Lark, honey, Sheriff Cook would like to leave." Still nothing. Hiding her irritation, Sally smiled up at the man who was easily a foot taller than she and took his arm. "Let me walk you out."

Sally chattered on like a monkey in a tree as she led the lawman back through the house to the main floor. They stopped here and there as she pointed out architectural details that she thought might be of particular interest for such a knowledgeable man, all the while keeping an eye out for Lark. It wasn't like her to be so rude to a guest, especially one as important as the sheriff.

Sally was pleased to see Tomlin had the sheriff's horse waiting for him and could hear the *tink tink* of his sledgehammer off in the distance as he was working to add stalls to the stables. She said her goodbyes, then turned to head back toward the stairs, skirts swishing around her. She stopped at the foot, hand on the balustrade. Glancing down the hall that ran alongside the stairs and led to the kitchen, she thought she heard voices.

Hand sliding off the smooth, polished wood, she headed in that direction, focusing on the voices. It was a man's voice, but it wasn't one of hers. He was talking with a female, which as she got closer, she realized was Lark.

Moving toward the door beneath the stairs that led to the basement, she saw that it was open, and the voices were coming from inside. She stood just outside the line of sight of the door and listened.

"...I'm thinking, don't you?" the man was asking.

"I don't know," Lark responded softly.

Uncomfortable with the situation, Sally stepped forward into the open doorway. The surprised pair, who stood in the small area at the top of the steep stairs, looked at her. She recognized the handsome man, likely just a tad younger than she was, with his dark wavy hair, intense blue eyes and fine suit.

"Mr. DeMarco, wasn't it?" she asked, remembering him as a new member, their soiree a few nights before his first with her business.

He turned away from Lark, who instantly looked down at her feet, stepping from the shadows of the stairwell to the lit hallway. "Montreal DeMarco." He took her hand and kissed her knuckles.

"Nice to see you again, Mr. DeMarco, but I have to wonder what you're doing in the stairwell to my basement. I don't recall hiring you on to man my boilers." She couldn't keep the irritation out of her voice, especially as she eyed Lark, who still refused to meet her gaze.

"My friends call my Monty," he said, the syrupy sweet tone of his Southern accent a bit unnerving. "Don't be sour with your assistant here. I came by to pick up my walking stick that I forgot when I was here the other night, and while wandering around looking for someone to talk to about my predicament, this fine young lady found me here. She was just so lovely," he added, glancing at her before turning back to Sally, "that I had to talk to her. And," he concluded with a wide flourish of his arms, "here we are."

"Well, Mr. DeMarco," Sally said, emphasizing the last name as opposed to his suggested shortened first name, "I can help you find your property." She stepped back into the hallway enough for the pair to exit the space at the top of the stairs. Lark scurried by her, holding her skirts so as not to trip as she headed for the stairs to go up.

"This way," she said, heading back down the hall toward the front of the house, only to cut in front of the stairs and into the great room. She pulled out a ring with long heavy brass keys hanging from it. Choosing one, she unlocked a closet and opened the door. Inside was a small variety of belongings: a white tie that once was part of a man's tuxedo, a black top hat, silver flask, and a walking stick leaned up against the wall. "I presume this is it." She reached in and grabbed the extravagant piece with its long cane part made of ebony and topped by a large sterling silver skull made to fit nicely in the palm of the user's hand. She noticed the small sapphires that were inlaid in the hollow eye sockets, as well.

"Thank you," he said, taking it from her with a smile.

"That's quite the cane, Mr. DeMarco."

"Indeed, it is," he agreed, holding it up to look it over. "A man made this for me in Savannah. Exquisite workmanship."

"Indeed. Quite intimidating." She chuckled, looking into the bejeweled eyes for a moment before meeting those of the cane's owner. "So, let me show you out."

As they headed toward the front door, each step punctuated by the tap of his walking stick, he asked, "What would you take for this house?"

Stunned, she was stopped in her tracks. She'd been told numerous times how much Whitney Grove was admired but never received such an offer. "Pardon me?"

"For the property, the house, the grounds, all of it. Just as it is," he added, as though that would sweeten the deal for a woman who'd spent her life's savings and work to build her own paradise.

"Well," she said, hand floating nervously up to rest on her chest for a moment as she was left uncharacteristically void of a quick response. Clearing her throat, she reached up and patted her hair, making sure it was still pulled up in its complex updo. "Your offer, though compelling, Mr. DeMarco, isn't something I'm interested in entertaining."

"Well, gosh," he said with a disappointed-sounding sigh. "That is unfortunate." He tapped his cane restlessly on the floor for a moment before he continued walking. Sally watched him for a second before following.

"Tomlin!" she called from the front door, which she'd opened for her unexpected guest. Tomlin glanced at her from where he worked on the stables. "Could you please see to it that Mr. DeMarco gets out safely?"

"Yes, ma'am," he called back, instantly putting his sledgehammer down before jumping to fulfill his new task.

"Good man," DeMarco said, watching him before turning back to Sally. "Loyal?"

She smirked. "In my line of work," she nearly purred, "loyalty isn't an option. It's a requirement. Good day, Mr. DeMarco."

Purposely not giving him a chance to respond or dominate their parting, Sally made her way to the main staircase and climbed to her floor. She fully expected to find Lark in her office cleaning up the remnants of the coffee she'd shared with Sheriff Cook, but Lark was nowhere to be found. Concerned and confused, she headed down to the second floor and Lark's room. The door was closed, so she raised her hand to knock when she heard something from within the room. Leaning her head in, she thought she heard muffled sniffling.

Ordinarily, she'd knock, but with Lark clearly upset, she tried the doorknob and, finding it unlocked, stepped inside the small room. Lark was sitting on the narrow bed, her back to Sally. She spared a glance over her shoulder and quickly wiped at her eyes and tried to sniffle her upset away.

"Sorry to just walk in on you," Sally said softly, closing the door behind her before walking over to the bed. "I heard you crying and was worried." Sitting next to Lark, Sally reached down into her cleavage and pulled out the kerchief she kept there for moments such as this. "Why are you crying, sweetheart?"

Lark accepted the offered kerchief and used it to dab at her eyes and face. She said nothing as she seemed to be trying to get her emotions under control.

"Did he hurt you?" Sally asked gently. She knew her little angel could be on the sensitive, emotional side, but there seemed to be something behind this. When Lark shook her head, Sally felt relief wash through her. She reached a hand up and ran her fingers down the blond strands that had been purposely loosed from her updo. "Do you know him?"

Lark let out a cleansing sigh as she wiped her nose and gave a one-shoulder shrug. "I saw him when he was here," she responded, meeting Sally's concerned gaze. "I just feel like I let you down."

Confused, Sally's hand dropped to rest on Lark's back, able to feel the heat of her skin through the material of her dress. "Sweetheart," she said softly, giving her an affectionate smile. "You could never let me down. If anything," she added with a rueful laugh, "I've let *you* down." Sally was surprised when Lark looked away from her at that admission. She continued. "I'm very selfish when it comes to relationships. I hate that about myself, but I'm well aware of it. If I gave you what you want, that line between give and take would be strictly take on my end, and you'd be left hurt and likely alone." Her hand slid down the length of Lark's back until she flopped gently to the bed behind where Lark sat. "I can't do that to you."

Lark met her gaze, her bright blue eyes filled with a wisdom that belied her age. "You sell yourself short, Sally. In the end, you'll be the one who ends up alone." With those sage words, she pushed to her feet and left her own room.

Sally remained where she was, filled with sadness. She knew Lark was probably right, but she had no idea what to do about it.

≈≈≈≈

Sally brought up a flour-covered hand, using her forearm to wipe at her tears, her belly hurting from the laughter she was sharing with Ginny. "And," she managed through her amusement, "remember how her face would get so red?" She wiped her eyes again before returning to her task of kneading the dough that would become bread. "Sally!" she shrieked, perfectly imitating her mother's voice. "I told you no steam-powered manipulators will be used in this house! That's what the goddamn clients are for!"

Ginny was bent over with her laughter, slapping at her knee. "Ginny!" she added, almost unintelligible through her laughter as she too imitated Sally's mother and her former boss. "You made that man grunt like a bleeding pig! Whatever did you do?"

Sally burst into a new round of laughter. "Maybe you used a steam-powered manipulator on his testicles," she said, which sent them both into more raucous laughter. She noticed that Ginny was glancing past her toward the archway that led to the pantry and one of the many back doors in the house. She glanced over her shoulder, and quickly sobering, she cleared her throat. "Tomlin, I honestly had no idea a black man could blush so deeply." She tried to keep it together as Ginny erupted into fresh giggles. She bit her lip, trying not to join her, as poor Tomlin looked like he was torn between uncertain laughter and simply turning around and bolting. "Just some girl talk," she said, waving off Ginny's laughter as she walked over to him.

"Yes, Miss Sally," he said, a twinkle of amusement in his dark eyes. "Got the post." He held up a handful of sealed envelopes.

"Thank you, darling." She took them from him with her fingertips, not wanting to cover them with flour.

With one final look to both women, Tomlin shook his head as he left the room.

Sally chuckled as she walked over to the table she'd been working on and tossed the pieces of mail onto a clean area so she could wash her hands and go through it. She wiped her hands on the apron tied around her waist before she picked through the missives, tossing aside those that were for her girls— to be delivered later—as well as those that needed an urgent reply from her.

"Ginny," she said, holding up a letter for her.

Wiping her hands on her apron, Ginny walked over and reached across the expanse of the table to take the letter. "Thank you much."

Sally went back to sorting through the rest when she heard Ginny announce it was a letter from Rebecca. She glanced over at her. "How is she?" she asked, the guilt staying with her when she had to remove one of her girls for something that was not her fault. "Did she end up going back to her mother's house? That's what she said she wanted the train ticket for."

"Don't know about that," Ginny muttered, reading over the letter she'd opened. "But she does hate you."

Sally let out a heavy sigh. "Of course she does," she muttered, sadness in her heart.

"Her mother was able to get the roof and fireplace fixed, however," Ginny continued. "Guessing you gave her money?"

"Don't I always give them means to start over?" Sally asked dryly, giving Ginny a side glance.

Ginny nodded, meeting the gaze. "You do. Sometimes, they use it for good, other times, for ill." She lowered the short missive in her hand. "I hope Rebecca is doing well. She's a good girl."

"They all are, Ginny," Sally said softly. "*We* all are." She looked down at the small square envelope in her hand that bore her name. A personal correspondence. She had no idea whom it was from. She tucked it in the pocket of her apron and continued sorting.

❧❧❧❧

"You sure 'bout this, Miss Sally?" Tomlin asked from his perch on the lazy board, reins in his gloved hands. "This the right place?"

Sally looked out through the mud-splattered glass of her carriage and had to admit she wasn't entirely sure. She knew she had the right address, but the old abandoned mill wasn't exactly what she'd been expecting. The brick and stone building was long ago stained black by the choking smoke from the coal fires that burned daily for production and heating purposes. The windows seemed to be blacked over, as well, though this seemed to be a current touch, likely with heavy black curtains. Sally had done the same at times in her previous business in Philadelphia. Sometimes, things were going on that prying eyes just didn't need to see.

She clutched the heavy black cloak a bit tighter

around her body, delivered to the house the day after the written invitation she'd received:

Dear Miss Little,
    You have been invited to an evening of the utmost secrecy. Drink and dining will be provided. You may bring a guest if you wish, but be sure they are of a trusted nature by you. Soon a "key" will be provided to allow you access.

    Rachel
    P.S. It will be my personal pleasure for you to attend, Sally.

The note included with the packaged cloak had stated she would need to wear it the night of the event to gain entrance. Though initially she'd been disappointed when Lark had turned down the offer of a potentially fun night out, looking at the building she was to enter, part of her was glad. She wasn't entirely sure she wanted the delicate young woman exposed to whatever lay within.

"I don't know, Miss Sally." Tomlin opened the carriage door after he'd hopped down from his position as driver. "I ain't so sure I'm wanting to leave you here."

"I appreciate your concern, Tomlin." Sally did her best to keep her voice even and calm, even as she had a tempest of uncertainty swirling inside her. "See you later." She left a brief touch to his muscled forearm before exiting the carriage and making her way to the building.

She looked up at the place, a knot in her stomach forming as she heard Tomlin mount the carriage, then the noisy departure of him and the two-horse team. Her breath left her lips in white puffs of steam as she made her way to the large wooden door at the center of the three-story building, which opened just enough for a dark-clad man to step through. He wore a black velvet mask over his face, leaving cutouts for his eyes and the lower portion of his face—mouth, chin, and jaw—revealed.

"Madam," he said, hand lifting to extend a similar mask to her, black ribbon to tie it on dangling freely.

She took it from him and quickly put it in place, though her hands were trembling slightly as she tied the ribbons tight at the back of her head. It was a rare thing for her to feel nervous or that a situation was over her head. But this mystique and dark secrecy made her feel unsettled and a bit off balance.

The man stepped aside and opened the door wider so she could enter. He followed, closing the door tight, then seeming to disappear in the dimness of the building innards, lit only by strategically placed candles and sconces. The naked brick walls acted as a screen for the eerie dancing shadows of objects and people caught in the light of the dozens of tiny flames.

From where she stood just inside the door, Sally was able to look down the narrow hallway that led from the small foyer to a larger room, likely the main belly of production when the building was still an operating mill. She could see shadowy figures moving in the larger room, all in similar cloaks as her own. There seemed to be a mixture of men and women. As she took a few steps into the hallway toward that larger room, she saw that everyone in attendance wore a mask like her own, making identifying anyone impossible.

This, of course, was likely the point.

"Have you ever heard of Sir Francis Dashwood?" a familiar female voice asked from behind her. Sally went to turn around, but hands at her waist kept her still. "Just watch them," the woman said, her voice soft and sultry in Sally's ear.

Sally returned her focus to those who were standing together talking, some off in the deeper shadows engaging in more intimate activities. Men mingled with men, women with women, and mixed company flirted and shared hors d'oeuvres.

"Who was Sir Francis Dashwood?" Sally asked, breath catching slightly as she felt the hot breath of the woman behind her on the side of her neck.

"He was a British aristocrat," the woman began. "More than a hundred years ago, he began a club in Britain for rich men with, shall we say, exotic tastes? It was called the Order of the Friars of St. Francis of Wycombe. You see," she continued, "Dashwood and his friends, men who were in government, wealthy landowners, royalty, and even our very own Benjamin Franklin had these caverns created in Wycombe in England. Over time, groups like his became known as the Hellfire Club."

"Why the Hellfire Club?" Sally whispered, her heart racing when she felt soft lips replace the hot breath.

"Because" came the soft response. "They named the caverns that housed their debauchery the Hellfire Caves," the woman whispered directly into Sally's ear, sending a shiver through her spine. "Welcome to my Hellfire Caves, Sally."

Sally's eyes closed as her stomach lurched along with her arousal. "Rachel."

Chapter Three

Pulling away just enough to turn around, Sally came face to face with the beautiful redhead who had been in her office mere weeks ago. She was dressed in a form-fitting black gown, unlike anything Sally had ever seen. It was almost as though Rachel were wearing a silhouette, not a dress.

Usually the woman in charge in the room, Sally wasn't comfortable with feeling like she was on the defense, it simply wouldn't do. She cleared her throat and raised her head slightly, chin lifted in defiance. "How did you know it was me? We all seem to be dressed alike here."

Rachel's smile was pure sex. "I told them to alert me when you arrived. So, here we are."

Sally returned the smile, her blood simmering as heat washed throughout her body. "Here we are."

Rachel looked beyond Sally down the remainder of the short hall to the festivities underway in the larger room. "Let's go upstairs." She reached out to take Sally's hand. "The music will be starting, and I want us to be able to talk. Besides," she added with a scorching look. "I want a bit of privacy."

Sally said nothing and allowed herself to be led back toward the door she'd entered and to a narrow stairwell she hadn't noticed. Her heart was racing as they climbed the uneven stone steps. Sure enough, muffled in the distance, sounds of cheerful music filtered up behind them. Reaching the second floor, Sally was led through another large room with huge windows. No doubt, the women and children who worked in this textile mill worked as late as the light the large windows would allow in.

It was a herculean task to make Sally Little blush with the life and business she'd run, but as they walked through the large room that was more dark than lit, she saw naked bodies everywhere—men, women, white and dark alike—tangled together in a writhing mass of pure, unabashed pleasure.

"Want to join them?" Rachel asked in Sally's ear above the symphony of moans, grunts, and cries of release.

"No." Sally shook her head.

"Come on," Rachel said, amusement in her voice as she continued their journey, the two forced to walk around—and in one instance over—a pair fornicating directly in the path. Finally, they arrived in a small room that was nothing more than a nest of pillows on the floor. A few candles were dotted around in holders on shelves, leaving most of the room in shadows, especially at the floor level. On one such shelf was a bottle of wine with two glasses and a long narrow pipe she knew well.

"Get comfortable." Rachel walked over to the wine and poured each of them a glass.

Sally took hers and lowered herself to the pillows after she reached up and untied her cloak, tossing it aside. She got herself settled before taking a careful sip of the wine, which was sweet on her tongue. She watched as Rachel joined her, her wine glass in one hand, the pipe in the other, the telltale smoke issuing from it following her downward progress in lazy swirls in the firelit air.

Seated across from Sally, Rachel carefully nudged the foot and stem of her glass through the spaces between layered pillows until the glass was supported upright, leaving her to focus on the pipe, which she brought to her lips. Her eyes closed as she inhaled, head falling back as the pipe was removed from her lips and absently held out toward Sally. A moment later, smoke billowed from Rachel's full, sensual lips.

Sally looked down at the ornately carved opium pipe, though it was too dim to see what the images were. Doing the same with her wine glass, she brought the pipe's mouthpiece to her lips, the lit contents warming her face as she closed her eyes and inhaled. Though she'd imbibed before, it wasn't something she did often. Being out of control for any reason was not an option she liked to explore.

The pipe was slowly lowered as the drug entered her lungs and ultimately her system. She felt the pipe taken from her fingers, so she let it go and rested back into the pile of softness, like a cloud enveloping her body, the inhaled smoke blown out between her lips.

"What did you want to talk about?" she asked at length, glancing over to see Rachel expelling more smoke. She accepted the pipe again.

"I wanted to tell you how much I enjoyed Sandra," Rachel said. "She was lovely, embodied everything I asked for."

Sally eyed her. "But?" Sally kept her gaze on the beautiful woman relaxing not more than a foot away from her as she brought the pipe back to her lips.

Rachel's smile was surprisingly sheepish. "Busted," she murmured, raising her glass of wine in salute. "But..." She sipped her wine, gaze on Sally over the rim of her glass as she did so.

Sally waited, handing the pipe back as she expelled the smoke from what she intended to be her final inhale. She could already feel the relaxing effects swimming through her body, warming her as it went.

"But," Rachel said again, lowering her glass and taking the pipe in her other hand. "I don't want an imitation. I want the real thing."

Sally watched as Rachel stood, placing her wine glass and the pipe on the shelf from whence they'd come. "I told you I wasn't an option," Sally said, surprised when her own glass was taken and placed with them.

Like a dream wrapped in black silk, Rachel lowered herself to her knees before Sally. "I don't want a transaction with you." She trailed a fingernail along Sally's jaw.

"Then what do you want?" Sally met Rachel's gaze with the ferocity of her own personality, even as any resolve she may have had begun to melt with the power of the opiate high that was consuming her.

Rachel leaned in, their lips mere inches apart. "A good old-fashioned seduction."

Sally accepted the kiss, her hand coming up to rest on the side of Rachel's face. She gave in fully when she felt herself being pushed back into the pillows, Rachel following. Her kiss was all-consuming and demanding, and with the added effect of the drug, Sally felt like she was being caressed from the inside out by a thousand hands. Every touch, every kiss, every whimper was amplified.

In the seconds that seemed to have been elongated into minutes, somehow, she found herself naked, as was Rachel. Their kiss resumed, Sally's hands coming up to bury themselves in long red hair, which had been released from its bindings. She pulled Rachel closer, their kiss deepening.

Confused, she gasped when she felt hot warmth envelop one of her nipples. She lifted her head to see a blond head at her chest. In the dimness of the room, she could make out little more than that the woman was naked and wore a similar mask to her own, though Rachel had removed it along with her clothes.

Sally's head fell back to the pillows, and her eyes closed as pleasure consumed her. Her mouth was taken by Rachel again with two leading fingers to her jaw. She moaned into the kiss as her legs were parted by the mystery woman, and the talented tongue that had tormented her breast was taking residence in a most needed place.

Her back arched into the intimate feasting, and she moaned into her kiss with Rachel. Her hand reached up and cupped a small breast, the nipple rock hard against her palm. Rachel returned her moan as that nipple was manipulated by Sally's fingers.

Rachel left her mouth as her lips explored Sally's neck; meanwhile, the mouth between her legs worked to bring her closer to her release. Her hand shot down to tangle in long hair as her hips bucked, and a loud gasp escaped her throat followed by a cry of intense pleasure.

Somewhere in her occupied brain, Sally sensed Rachel moving away as the mouth that had been between her legs was working its way up her body until she was covered by the blond woman who now lay atop her.

Sally wrapped her arms around the strange woman, their kiss deep and sensual, the woman's lips and tongue covered in Sally's warm desire. As they kissed, she felt a thigh move between hers, gasping as it pressed into her, hers returning the favor against volcanic wetness. They moved together; the room around them, Rachel, and the sounds of the group beyond disappeared. In Sally's state of mind, she felt as though she knew this woman's very soul, had many times. It wasn't like a random coupling in a sexually charged event, but like two women making love.

Her mystery lover held Sally to her as they continued to move together, their breathing too hard to continue kissing. She could feel and hear the quickening breaths and whimpers in her ear as the blonde buried her face in Sally's neck.

Sally's nails dug into the woman's shoulders as a new wave of climax washed over and through her. She felt the other woman's body tense, her hips grinding against Sally's partially raised thigh before she went rigid, a loud burst of sound in Sally's ear marked the moment of her release.

They remained where they were for a long moment before Sally felt a kiss to the side of her neck, then coldness. Opening her eyes, Sally looked through the dimness for the woman but saw only Rachel laid out beside her, her fingernails trailing lightly over Sally's stomach.

"Jesus, that was beautiful," Rachel murmured, leaning over and leaving a soft kiss on Sally's lips.

Sally blinked, looking around again for the woman who had just made love to her. All she saw was Rachel.

⁂

Sally's eyes blinked open a few times before they remained open. She found herself lying on her bed, wrapped only in the black cloak. She lay on her stomach, sprawled out diagonally across the expanse. The bedding beneath her was all jumbled, half of it spilled down to the floor.

Raising her head, she squinted as she looked around the room, the morning sunlight shining through the sheers that covered her windows. She groaned as she slowly turned over to rest on her elbows, cloak falling to expose naked breasts.

"Jesus Christ," she muttered, head more muddled and body sorer than it had been in years. She blew out a breath, which blew some long dark hair out of her face. It was then that she heard movement in her dressing room. "Lark?" The movement continued, sounds of clothes hangers sliding across the wooden bar of her wardrobe, then a thud followed by a hiss. "Lark?" she said, voice louder. "Can you bring me my robe, honey?" She rested her upper body weight on one elbow as she raised the hand of the other arm to wipe at the grains of sleep in her eyes. Suddenly, her world went dark, her satiny robe landing over her head with a material flop. "Thanks." Tugging the garment from her head, she was faced with an amused Ginny, who stood across the room, shoulder leaning against the wall with her arms crossed over her chest. "Where's Lark?" Sally grumbled.

"She ain't here, least far as I know."

Awkwardly tugging the robe on, Sally paused, right arm halfway through the sleeve. "What do you mean? Where is she?"

"After you left last night, that orphanage you're always at came a-callin'. Some issue," she explained, following the trail of the pieces to Sally's outfit the night before, from stockings to bustle to outer skirt and everything in between. "The girl went in your stead. So, now I'm here cleaning up after your lazy ass, so she don't get into trouble for not doing it." Ginny stood erect, arms full of clothing. She smirked. "Looks like you been rode hard and put away wet."

Suddenly, Sally had the image of being bent over her bed with Rachel standing behind her, grinding against her as she thrust three fingers inside of her. She shook the memory, fuzzy as it was, away. "Not too far from the truth," she muttered. She brought her robe in closer to cover her nakedness.

"What are you suddenly so shy about?" Ginny asked. "Ain't like I've never seen you before, Sal."

Sally looked at her, eyebrows drawn in confusion. "When?"

One of Ginny's eyebrows lazily rose. "You don't remember that fella from Billings? Liked 'double trouble,' as he called it back in Philly?"

Sally thought for a minute, then chuckled, letting the ends of the robe fall open freely. "Right."

"Don't let the girl see all them love bites all over you, though," Ginny warned, heading back toward the dressing room. "Break her heart."

Left alone, Sally let out a heavy, tired sigh as she climbed off the bed, allowing the robe to fall gracefully around her body, the silky material like heaven on her skin. She cleaned up the bed, making it properly. Her memories of the night before were spotty and mostly triggered by the soreness with each step. She figured she should probably strip the bed for proper washing of the linens but was just too tired to care.

"You planning to bathe this morning?" Ginny

called from the other room.

Sally reached up and pulled the robe ends apart and took a whiff. "Yes," she called back. "I am not appropriate for any type of human consumption at the moment," she muttered, smelling of sweat and sex.

Ginny chuckled. "I'll get it ready for you. Oh." She stepped into the room. "Margaret and a couple of the other girls are headed into town today. With it being Sunday and all, they want to go to services. Do you need Tomlin to pick up anything while he's in town?"

Sally considered the offer but shook her head. "No, I think we're good here. Do any of them need money?" She walked over to her vanity where she had a small bit of cash kept in a drawer. She rested her hand atop her silver brush, which lay on the vanity top while she waited for Ginny's response.

"They didn't mention that they did, but I'll ask before they leave," Ginny said, heading back into the dressing room. "Do you want me to send Lark up here when I see her?"

Sally looked at her disheveled reflection in the mirror for a moment, noting a "kiss" on the glass made with lips and lipstick. She shook her head and turned away, guilt filling her after her wild night with Rachel. "No."

"You need to let her go."

Sally looked up surprised to not only see Ginny once again standing in the entrance of the bedroom, but also by her tone. "It doesn't concern you, Ginny," she said defensively.

"No, technically, it doesn't. But what you're doing to that girl is unfair," Ginny said, eyeing Sally. "Either fuck her or let her go. If you do neither," she said, turning to head to the bathroom, "she's going to hate you."

"I hate it when you do that!" Sally called out after Ginny disappeared. "Never lets me get the damn last word," she muttered, heading to her dressing room to decide what to wear for the day.

⊰⊱⊰⊱

An hour later, Sally sat at her vanity wrapped in a clean robe. She watched her reflection in the mirror as she used that silver brush to lightly tug at some of the tangles in her hair. Her mind was in a hundred different directions, her long, hot bath helping to clean out the fuzz in her head, so she could focus on what needed to be done for her business and other ventures she was involved in. She knew she had meetings coming soon with some other investors for an incoming hotel.

"How was your, oh, what did you call it, 'soul debauchery'?"

Pulled from her thoughts, Sally looked up beyond her own reflection in the mirror to see Lark entering the room and walking up behind her. She looked tired. "It was all right, I suppose." Sally winced as the brush bristles snagged a particularly dense tangle.

"Let me." Lark reached around Sally to gently take the brush from her.

"One for the books, to be sure," Sally concluded, watching Lark work. She had such a calm, gentle energy to anything she did.

"Clearly, you brought the party home with you," she said, lovingly working out the knot of dark hair.

Sally watched Lark in her task for a moment

before her gaze floated up to meet bright blue eyes in the mirror. "Why do you say that?"

"You don't wear that color," Lark said pointedly. "And I don't wear lipstick."

Sally found the bright red kiss mark on the mirror, which she'd forgotten to remove before her bath. Feeling that guilt rise again, her gaze fell, but she said nothing. She cleared her throat as her guilt threatened to overtake her and cause her to offer an apology. Instead, she felt her defenses pricked.

"I understand you had your own late-night outing," she said, her voice much harsher and words sharper than she'd heard them in her head.

With her usual grace, Lark seemed to ignore the spiked tongue and replied evenly, "I did. I was saving your behind."

"Meaning?" Sally met Lark's reflected gaze.

"That orphanage you spend so much time with came calling. There was a train derailment last night, and several children were displaced for the night. They were taken to the orphanage while their parents were dealt with medically. They were calling for all hands on deck, anyone who was what they called a 'friend' of the orphanage." She held Sally's gaze. "Apparently, that meant you. So, I went for you."

Sally looked at her, incredulous. "Train derailment." She searched Lark's face for any change in expression. None was forthcoming. Moving away from Lark, she pushed up from her seat and turned to look at her. "You left in the late hours, not to return for many more, and you expect me to believe it was because you were playing the good Samaritan to a bunch of children at the orphanage?"

Lark handed over Sally's brush, which she

snatched from her fingers. "I don't owe you an explanation of where I go," Lark said softly. "But yes, that's what happened. Believe what you will."

Sally felt a rage fill her as she could see the distance in Lark's eyes. She was losing her, and that just wouldn't do. "You work for me, Lark, not the other way around. Your very existence depends on me," she hissed, any rational thinking nearly evaporating as an overwhelming possessiveness took her over. "You belong to *me*."

Lark stood a bit taller, her chin raised in unprecedented defiance. "I work for you, Sally, that much is true." She swallowed, seeming to gather her courage before she said, "I belong to—"

Sally tossed the heavy brush to the vanity top, which landed with a jarring sound and stepped around the padded vanity bench seat toward Lark. "You belong to who?" she pressed, her voice low and angry. A small voice inside her head was screaming at her to calm down, that she was being unfair, but her fear of Lark abandoning her was too strong, pushing all reason down with that warning voice. "You belong to who?" she demanded again.

Lark swallowed again but stood her ground, even as Sally had left little more than six inches of distance between them. "I don't belong to you, Sally," she said, her voice weak and small.

Like a match to a fuse, Sally blew up like a bundle of dynamite. Not that this was unusual for Lark to witness or catch shrapnel from, but somehow, this time felt different to Sally. Her rage was coming from a deeper place—fear.

"You'd be on the streets if it weren't for me!" she raged, moving away from Lark toward the center of the room. "You'd have nothing!" She turned to Lark, who looked back at her, her expression seeming to be upset mixed with sadness. "I will have no liars in this house!" Sally shrieked, no longer even sure what she was talking about, the words vomiting out of her mouth. "No liars!" Face hot, neck throbbing with her increased heart rate, Sally was surprised to hear a timid knock on the outer door of her apartments. "What?" she roared.

The door opened, and a moment later, a beautiful black woman stepped up to the open doorway to the bedroom. Though she was in her late forties, her eyes said she'd seen the lifetime of a woman three times that age.

"Liberty," Sally said, her anger instantly draining away at the unexpected sight of Tomlin's beloved sister and a dear friend to Sally.

Liberty looked from Sally to Lark, then back again. "Sheriff Cook is here," she said. "They're gathering supplies to help those hurt in last night's tragedy on the train. He wants to know if you have anything they can take to the masses."

Sally felt her blood run cold and drain from her face, replaced by icy shame. "The train derailment?" she said stupidly. At Liberty's nod, Sally mentally shook herself to think and respond to the request. "Of course, Liberty. Any and everything they may need. Please tell Tomlin to take them to our storage. There should be foodstuffs and sundries."

"I'll help," Lark said, hurrying over to Liberty. She glanced back at Sally. "You were saying?" she said softly, then turned and left the room.

Chapter Four

With two wagons loaded with supplies, one belonging to Sheriff Cook, the other to Sally, Tomlin mounted and prepared to follow the lawman into town. Sheriff Cook extended his hand for Sally's.

"I thank you kindly, Miss Sally." The sheriff gave her hand a delicate squeeze before releasing it. "I won't soon forget this."

She met his gaze and gave him a genuine smile. "I certainly hope not, Sheriff," she replied, a small smile behind her words.

He returned the smile and placed his hat on his head before climbing up to lead the short wagon train off the property.

Standing on the front porch of the large manor, Sally watched the two wagons head out and didn't look as she felt a presence step up beside her. The fact that her steps hadn't made a sound on the wide wood planks told her exactly who it was that joined her.

"Tomlin didn't tell me you were coming," she said.

"No, we wanted to surprise you," Liberty said, her voice just as soft.

Sally turned to look at the older woman's profile, a gentle smile growing. "I'm glad you're here."

Liberty returned the affectionate look. "Me too. Come, let us catch up."

An hour later, Sally and Liberty could be found in Sally's upstairs office, empty breakfast dishes pushed aside and Liberty galloping around the room like a lame horse.

"And I said," Liberty exclaimed, "slow down, chil'. You ain't no stallion like daddy used ta breed!"

Through her laughter, Sally managed to ask, "And how old was your granddaughter?"

"Three!" Liberty exclaimed, holding up the appropriate amount of fingers. Chuckling herself, she plopped back down in the seat she'd vacated for her story. "No idea how on earth that chil' can run so fast on them short little stubby legs."

Still smiling, Sally rose from her chair to pour her friend more of the special herb tea Liberty had brought with her, steeped to perfection. "It's so good to see you," she said softly, returning the delicate cup to the saucer where it had been. "I can't believe Tomlin was able to keep your visit from me," she added, amused, as she knew Tomlin wasn't great at keeping secrets from her.

"I told him if he talked, I'd add his stones to my oxtail stew." Liberty spared a glance at Sally as she squeezed a bit of juice from the lemon wedge that rested at the edge of the saucer. She smiled at Sally's bark of laughter. She picked up the small silver spoon and stirred the contents of her tea as she eyed Sally.

"What?"

Without a word, Liberty reached across the desk and grabbed Sally's teacup, just a small amount of liquid at the bottom. She brought it back to her side and dumped the bit of liquid into the garbage can next to the desk.

Sally sighed as she sat back in her chair. "For

crying out loud," she muttered.

Liberty glared up at her with a raised eyebrow. "That is the worse pun I've ever heard." She gave her a small smile. "Scared?"

"No," Sally said stubbornly. "I don't believe in all that psychic voodoo mumbo jumbo."

"Precisely why you should be scared." Liberty looked into the teacup and the random design of tea leaves left behind.

Truth be told, no matter how brave a face Sally was putting on, she *was* scared. Liberty used her gifts sparingly, and she only grabbed a teacup or Sally's hand to divine a message when there was a message to be divined. The scary part was, she was always right.

Sally cleared her throat and shifted in her chair, feigning non interest as she studied her nails, noting out of the side of her eye that Liberty was moving the teacup this way and that, her gaze intense and focused.

"Your crops will do well this year," Liberty said at length, not looking at Sally. "No need to water them."

"Crops?" Sally said, confused. Then it dawned her on. She knew Liberty was speaking of her many investments. "Wonderful," she said, relaxing a bit.

"But," Liberty qualified, holding up a finger as she used the other hand to turn the cup a few degrees. "There are some weeds."

Sally let out a heavy sigh. "I knew that hotel was far too risky—"

"Not about a hotel," Liberty barked, near-black eyes boring into Sally. "This is not about money or business. No, no." Liberty shook her head, looking back into the cup. "You have a dark soul in your midst," she finally said. "They feel you've wronged them." Her brows came together in consternation as she mumbled to herself, almost as though trying to work out what she was seeing.

Sally's mind instantly went to a man in Philadelphia who had always been after her, convinced she'd stolen his wife, when the woman had desperately wanted to escape his abuse and had run away with Sally and the girls. She knew better than to voice that suspicion, however, as she didn't want to be admonished again and rile Liberty up.

The dark-skinned woman gasped loudly, the cup tumbling to the table and wobbling around until it settled on its foot. "It can't be," she whispered, staring off into the distance, mouth slightly open.

Sally felt icy fingers walk down her spine. "What is it?" she asked, voice barely above a whisper.

It took a moment, but eventually, dark eyes met green. "You have a traveler."

᠕᠕᠖᠖

Sally absently sipped from her flute of champagne. Her gaze roamed around the room, watching as the night's festivities wound down as the chosen pairs disappeared upstairs. She noted that the handsome young blond man Willard Tatum, she believed was his name, had arrived to spend time with Margaret once again. Watching the pair, she believed she was likely watching the beginnings of a couple. It happened rarely, but was not nonexistent. The question would be if the young, dashing man would "rescue" his lady love from Sally's grasp.

Amused, she turned away from the two huddled on the settee nearest the grand fireplace. She wandered over to one of the large front-facing windows, looking out into the dark night beyond. She felt restless and antsy, her conversation with Liberty from two days before still bouncing around in her mind.

"Wait," Sally said, trying to wrap her mind around what she'd been told. "Dark soul, you said. What is that, a demon?"

"If only that was your problem." Liberty scoffed, looking tired as she'd sat back in the chair.

"Aren't demons or whatever bad? Out to manipulate and corrupt mankind? That's what the preacher man always said," Sally added, feeling uneasy.

"Manipulate and corrupt mankind, yes." Liberty leaned forward, her gaze dark and intense and seemed to bore into Sally's very soul. "But what you face is not here to manipulate and corrupt mankind. It's here to destroy you."

"Miss Sally?"

Sally whirled to face the owner of the sudden voice behind her. "What?" she barked, hand rising to her heaving chest as relief washed through her. "I'm sorry, Tomlin," she breathed.

"You okay, Miss Sally?" he asked, concern in his voice. "You look like you seen a ghost."

She felt a cold thud in her gut, like a block of ice had been dropped. "Why did you say that?" she whispered, fear still gripping her throat.

Tomlin looked at her with wide dark eyes. "Well, Miss Sally, 'cause you white as a sheet."

Sally took several deep breaths to get her emotions under control. She gave him a brave smile and shook her head. "I'm fine, really. What can I do for you?" she asked, voice still a bit breathy, but far more calm, belying the war of uncertainty inside.

"Someone here to see you, Miss Sally," he explained. "Miss Lark took her upstairs the back way for you."

She nodded, giving him a smile as she finished off her champagne in one swallow before handing him the empty glass. "Thank you, Tomlin."

Sally made her way up the many stairs to her apartments, expecting to be met by Lark. She was nowhere to be seen, and Sally was bothered by it. Something had happened, a fracture in their relationship over the previous days. She felt the loss greatly but wasn't sure what to do about it.

Pushing aside those thoughts, which she knew could quickly become morose, she brought out her key and unlocked the main door, allowing herself inside. She was about to head to her office, where Lark would have taken her visitor, but stopped, surprised to find Rachel in her bedroom, naked and waiting for her on the bed, lying in a most inviting position.

༺ ༻ ༺ ༻

"How did you get started in the business of peddling pleasure?" Rachel asked casually, resting on her side, head cradled in an upturned palm.

Body relaxed and satiated, Sally glanced over at the woman she'd just spent the last two hours having sex with. She lay on her back, one hand tucked behind her head on the pillow. "My mother. Things got so tough after Daddy headed off to the war, then when he died..." She let out a small breath, still grieving for him all these years later. "After he died, she had to get serious about making money." She smirked. "I made her lots of it." She raised an eyebrow as she studied the sexy redhead. "Do you have any idea how much money a man will pay if he thinks he's the first to conquer the mountain? My mountain was 'conquered' for three years," she said, using her fingers to make air quotes.

Rachel returned the raised eyebrow, her free hand reaching under the sheet to run a fingernail along the rounded side of one of Sally's naked breasts. "You were sold off time and time again as a virgin?"

Sally grinned. "You'll never meet such an experienced virgin if you lived four lifetimes."

"That is deeply wrong."

Sally shrugged, a shiver going through her as Rachel's fingers wandered closer to her nipple. "It was a long time ago, and I learned a lot."

"So," Rachel drawled, "tell me about Lark."

Sally stiffened, about to move away when a soft hand gripped her wrist.

"Relax, Sally," Rachel said. "I'm only asking because she looked so sad tonight."

Sally let out a sigh and settled back into the softness, luxuriating in the feel of Rachel's hand on her flesh. "She's been very distant lately," she confided. "I feel like I'm losing her, to be honest." She gave a rueful smile. "Or I've already lost her."

"You love her then?" Rachel asked gently, no jealousy or accusation in her voice. If anything, her tone seemed a bit sad.

Sally studied Rachel's face for a moment before she nodded. "Yes."

"Have you told her that?" Rachel asked, her hand coming to rest on Sally's belly.

Defenses pricked, Sally glared over at her. "I tell

her every day."

"Do you?" Rachel asked, skepticism in her voice. "You tell her?"

"Yes. In my own way, I tell her." Sally was becoming more and more uncomfortable with the conversation.

"I'm going to guess that 'in your own way' doesn't include the three magic words," Rachel pressed, trailing a fingernail playfully around Sally's belly button.

Annoyed, Sally pushed the covers back and scooted toward the edge of the bed. "Words are meaningless, Rachel," she spat, feet hitting the floor. "Do you have any idea how many lovesick clients I said those words to in order to get a few extra pieces of silver over the years?" She slid her arms through the sleeves of her silk robe, which had been tossed over the back of a nearby chair. "Words are meaningless, Rachel," she said again, tugging the belt of the robe a bit tighter than was necessary in her irritation. "People lie when they open their mouths. Actions," she said, holding up a finger. "Actions say it all. People lie, actions don't," she reiterated, almost as though to convince herself.

"So, then," Rachel said, making her own way out of the bed. "You kiss her then? Touch her? Make love to her?"

Sally felt rage rise in her belly, starting a hot fire inside. "What do you care?" she said, voice low. "If you're so worried about Lark, why don't you kiss her? Touch her, make love to her—"She cut herself off as something dawned on her, bringing a gasp from her lips. "You have, haven't you?" She took a menacing step toward the foot of the bed, Rachel standing on the other side. "You seduced her," she accused, convincing herself as she spoke. "You seduced her, and you convinced her to pull away from me. Didn't you? Didn't you?" she demanded.

Rachel, who had been tugging on the various layers of her clothing, looked Sally dead in the eyes. "No. But I know what it's like to be that young woman who just wants to be loved, just wants to be accepted and is tired of being used."

Suddenly, and to her surprise, Sally felt hot tears of guilt and old hurts of her own prick the backs of her eyes. She turned away from Rachel and headed toward the door that led to her office. "Please leave once you're dressed," she said softly, closing her office door behind her.

⊰ ⊰⊱ ⊱

Hands on hips, Sally looked around the room, frustrated. She looked back to her desk, opening the drawers again, peeking under papers, books, and ledgers for a third time. Shoving the drawers closed, she walked over to one of her bookcases, looking through the shelves. That was when she heard a soft knock on the doorframe.

"What?" she barked.

"I'm sorry, Sally. You're busy, I'll come back."

Sally turned to see who had spoken, standing on her tiptoes to reach the topmost shelf. "No, Margaret, it's okay. You can come in." Giving up on her search for the moment, she turned to head back to the desk, flopping down in her chair. A long wavy piece of dark hair fell into her face, which she batted away. "What can I do for you? Are you excited for your weekend trip?"

Margaret gave her a small smile as she lowered herself into the chair on the opposite side of Sally's desk. "Yes," she said quietly. "That's what I wanted to talk to you about, if that's okay."

"Of course. Is there a problem?" Sally settled in for one of the many conversations she'd had with her girls over the years about love or personal issues. She secretly loved the fact that they treated her more like a mother figure than a boss. Even more secretly, she loved each and every one of them like a daughter.

"No, not at all." The sweet, love-stricken smile that spread across pink lips said it all. "He sent me another letter that arrived yesterday, in fact."

Sally smiled in return. "Mr. Tatum seems like a real gem, Maggie. What's the problem?"

"Well," Margaret said, hands fidgeting in her lap. "What if it's not what it seems to be?" she asked, earnest worry in her brown eyes. "What if he's not what and who he says he is?"

Sally nodded, a truly valid question. "But," she said, "what if he is?"

Margaret chewed on her bottom lip before looking down at her lap. "I'm afraid of that, too."

Like so many, Margaret was a young woman who had come to Sally with nowhere else to go and nobody to care. Sally pushed up from her chair and moved around the desk to sit in the twin chair next to Margaret. She reached over and gently took hold of pale hands.

"Maggie, you're young, but you've seen a lot in your short life. I know for a fact that you want a family, want to be a mother and a wife." She waited until Margaret met her gaze. She smiled encouragingly at her. "Maybe this is your shot. Maybe Willard Tatum is just the man you've been waiting for." She brought up a hand and brushed a tendril of brown hair out of Margaret's face. "I've been in this business nearly thirty years, both in your chair and in mine. I've seen the absolute ugliest side of humanity, but I've also seen true angels." She smiled at her own words, an image of Lark coming to mind. "If you're asking my opinion, I think you should take this opportunity and run."

Margaret was quiet for a long moment, seeming to consider Sally's words. Finally, she turned to Sally, her smile bright, voice assured as she said, "I will. Okay."

Sally, excited for her, slapped her own thighs before pushing to her feet. "Come with me." Sally led the way into her bedroom and over to her vanity. She pulled open her drawer where she kept extra money. "Over in that armoire, grab the blue clutch." She pointed to the piece of furniture in question. She counted out some money, and when Margaret returned with the clutch, she stuffed the money inside. "Here," she said, placing it in Margaret's hand. "A little spending money. Bring the clutch back when you return to collect your things," she said with a wink and a quick hug. "Do you need Tomlin to drop you somewhere, or is he coming for you?"

Margaret looked down at the blue clutch in her hands and took a deep breath, letting it out in what seemed a nervous breath. "He's sending for me."

❧ ❧ ❧ ❧

It was a beautiful day with spring-like temperatures, though it was only mid-February. Sally had tucked her veil back as she got closer to home, the single horse pulling her buggy after she'd taken care of business in town. She'd put in her orders for the house, as well as for the orphanage. The orphanage.

As she and her mare Myrtle jostled along, she thought about what she'd been told about the night of the train derailment many weeks before. She mulled it over, but Rachel's words also echoed in her mind. She'd never admit it to her former lover—she hadn't seen Rachel since their argument weeks before—but she'd made her think. On March 17, Sally would be forty years old. Maybe it was time to surrender and try to be the woman she'd always wanted to be.

That thought in mind, she slowed Myrtle with a tug on the reins and guided her to the side of the road, which led to the final mile to the house.

"Whoa, Myrtle, whoa, baby."

The mare brought the buggy to a smooth stop in the shade of a line of trees and vegetation. Sally climbed down, careful not to fall on her face. She lifted her skirts as she picked her way through the vegetation to the little island of crocuses, the tiny purple and white flowers colorful among the winter-yellowed surrounds. She figured a small bouquet would go nicely with the tulips she'd bought from Mrs. Alverstein in town.

Removing her riding gloves, she bent over as best she could and picked the mostly scentless flowers when she heard the thundering sound of horse hooves coming down the road. She stood erect, watching as Sheriff Cook, a man she recognized as his deputy but wasn't sure of his name, and a third man flew by on horseback, none of the three looking her way. Myrtle was slightly spooked from the sudden noise so close.

Concerned, Sally watched as they disappeared in a cloud of dust, which made her cough before she quickly gathered the flowers she wanted, then climbed back aboard to head home.

It was a mixture of relief and confusion that the sheriff and his men weren't there when she arrived, so she figured they must have headed on to the hill country beyond her land. She pulled the buggy into the circular drive in front of the house. Tomlin was waiting to help her down and to take care of Myrtle and the buggy.

"Thank you," she said as she was helped down. "Make sure you and your boys are ready just after breakfast tomorrow," she instructed, tugging off her riding gloves again before reaching up to grab the flowers bundled together in paper. "Supplies will be arriving around seven thirty."

"Yes, Miss Sally," Tomlin said with a nod.

Sally looked around one last time. "Did the sheriff stop in?"

He shook his head as he took the reins of the mare. "No, ma'am. Been quiet, just how you like it," he added with a smile before leading the horse away.

Sally made her way inside the house, immediately hearing light chatter and laughter from the great room. Glancing inside, she saw her girls sitting around relaxing, enjoying one another's company.

"Good afternoon, ladies," she said, stepping into the room. "How are we today?" she drawled with a grin as she breezed farther in. Getting various greetings and even a light hug from a couple, Sally asked, "How did Margaret's trip go?" She looked down at some of the girls who were gathered on a few of the chaise lounges. "Her letter said she'd be back this morning, right? Three days late," she added in teasing accusation. "How big is the ring?"

"She's not back yet," one of the girls said, looking up at Sally. "I went to her room before coming down here to find out how it went." She shook her head. "She's not there."

"Well," Sally said, turning away from her girls, "I hope she's having a wonderful time."

"Who are the flowers for?" another girl asked, a smirk in her voice.

Sally looked down at the small bouquet cradled in her arm. "None of your business." Sally rolled her eyes as the girls broke out in a chorus of a popular song of the day, a young man requesting the love of his sweetheart while others made bird sounds. "Keep it up, ladies," she called over her shoulder. "You'll all starve." She smiled at the round of laughter that garnered before the singing continued.

Sally hurried up the stairs to the second floor, heading to the end of the hall to Lark's door. Taking a deep, steadying breath, she raised her hand and knocked lightly on the wood. No response, so she knocked again. Still no response, so she turned and headed back the way she'd come, only to mount the final staircase. Entering her area, she heard the soft humming coming from her bedroom. Heading in that direction, she found Lark bent over her bed, body braced by a knee on the mattress as she stretched out as far as she could to smooth the fresh linens she was putting on the bed.

Sally studied her for a long moment, admiring the long, sleek lines of her back and arms, punctuated by the womanly curves of her hips and breasts. Her hands itched to reach out and run all along that body. Lark, the unwitting temptress.

Apparently sensing she was being watched, Lark

stopped humming and glanced over her shoulder. When she spotted Sally, she pushed away from her task, standing fully upright. "Good afternoon, Sally. Sorry I'm only getting to this now."

"No need to apologize," Sally said with the smile she reserved to charm and ease. "I got supplies ordered for us here at the house, as well as for the kids." She spared a glance at Lark, who had gone back to making the bed. Sally plucked lightly at one of the fragrant tulips she held. When there was no visible response from Lark at the announcement, Sally continued. "Pamela gushed about you," she said, setting the flowers on a chair to help Lark maneuver the heavy quilt back onto the bed after the linens had been expertly put on. "She said you were invaluable the night of the derailment." *She also said you were only there for an hour, so where did you spend the night?* "So," she continued, thoughts unvoiced as she walked over to the chair after their task was finished and grabbed the flowers again. "I brought you these." She handed the startled Lark the gift as she leaned in and left a lingering kiss to her cheek, close to the corner of full lips. "Thank you."

"These are beautiful," Lark said softly, looking at the flowers in her hands. She gave Sally a shy smile. "I've never been given flowers before."

"Oh?" Sally asked, eyebrows raised. "That's a crying shame." Sally stood in Lark's personal space, their breasts only separated by Lark's hands and the flowers. She could feel the warmth of the other woman, could smell her, could feel just how much she'd missed her. Lifting a hand, she trailed the backs of her fingers down a soft cheek about to tell her as much when one of the girls peeked her head in.

"Sally," she said, sounding out of breath. "Sorry

to barge in like this," she added at Sally's glare. "But that sheriff fellow is here, and he ain't lookin' too happy. Said he wants to talk to you."

Sally leaned slightly away from Lark, business now, pleasure later. "What about?"

With a shrug, the woman was gone.

Turning back to Lark, Sally gave her a small smile. "I want to talk later," she said softly, leaving a quick kiss to a startled Lark's lips before she hurried from the room.

Sally found two of the three men she'd seen earlier standing in the foyer—the sheriff and deputy. The unknown man missing. Sheriff Cook was talking to Tomlin, the conversation seeming to have just begun.

"How often you use that sledgehammer, Tomlin?" the sheriff asked casually, thumbs hooked into the thick holster belt.

"Every day, jus' about, sir," Tomlin said, dressed in his ever-present overalls with a rag hanging out of the back pocket.

"'Bout how heavy is that? Five-pounder?" Sheriff Cook asked, pulling a pre-rolled cigarette out of a small pouch tucked into the front pocket of his shirt. He lit the tip with a match as Tomlin responded.

"Ten pound, sir," Tomlin said, pride in his voice.

Sheriff Cook nodded as he lit his smoke. "Impressive. You mind grabbin' that sledge for me?" he asked through a cloud of exhaled smoke.

"Yes, sir." Without another word, Tomlin ducked out the front door.

That was when Sally decided to make her entry. "Sheriff. What can I do for you?"

He glanced over at her, one hand removing

the cigarette while the other came up as his fingers removed a few loose flakes of tobacco off his tongue. "'Afternoon, Sally," he greeted. "How long your colored man worked for you?"

"Years, going all the way back to Philadelphia," she responded, crossing her arms over her chest as she looked up into the sheriff's face. "What's this all about?"

He looked her in the eye. "The body of a woman was found on your land."

Chapter Five

Sally sat behind her desk, a cold prickle all over her skin. She cleared her throat before she spoke, her words quiet. "Who is she?" She was grateful Sheriff Cook had been willing to move the conversation to her office, as she had no desire to scare the hell out of her girls downstairs.

"We don't know, Sally. That's why I'm talking to you."

"Someone new to town? You don't recognize her?"

He cleared his throat, a large hand coming up as his fingers stroked his full mustache. "Her own mother wouldn't be able to recognize her, ma'am," he said softly.

She looked at him, eyebrows drawing. "What do you mean?"

"Um, excuse me, Miss Sally."

Sally looked over to the door to see Tomlin standing shy, his sledgehammer in his hands. "Miss Lark let me in."

"It's okay, Tomlin. What is it?" she asked.

He raised the heavy tool. "Sir?"

"Yes, thank you." Sheriff Cook reached out to take it from him.

Sally watched, eyeing the lawman as he smiled up at Tomlin.

"You can go now," the sheriff said, not unkindly.

Tomlin looked to Sally, a question in his eyes. She had no answers for him, so she gave him a small nod of acknowledgment to his confusion and said softly, "Go on now." He nodded, then ducked out of the room. Left alone once more, Sally returned her focus to the sheriff, who was checking out the heavy tool from one end to the other. He studied what looked to be a dark spot on the metal head for a moment before he scraped a bit off with a fingernail, bringing it to his tongue.

"Why did you want Tomlin's sledgehammer, Sheriff?" she asked. "What exactly are you looking for?"

Sheriff Cook glanced up at her. "How does your colored man get on with the girls?" he asked casually.

"Real good. He'd do anything for them," she responded slowly.

"And how do they feel about him?"

"They love him." She smirked. "Some have even come to call him Uncle Tom, their affectionate nickname for him." She studied him, gaze hard and accusing. "Are you accusing Tomlin of something, Sheriff Cook?"

"No." He shook his head as he gently set the tool on the desk. "But we've got a dead woman out there, and I need to know who she is and who killed her." He hitched a thumb in the general direction of the south part of the property. "Are all your girls accounted for?"

Sally nodded. "Yes, all of them are downstairs, actually. Well, except for Margaret," she added. "She's on some personal time right now."

"How long has she been gone?" he asked, again stroking his mustache.

"Handful of days," Sally said. "Why?"

He nodded and pushed up from the chair, grabbing his removed hat from the desktop. "Thank you for your time, Sally. I'll get with you when I have more questions—"

"I want to see her," Sally said, also standing. "I want to see this woman."

He sighed, tapping his hat against the side of his thigh. "Now, ma'am, I just can't do that—"

"It's my land, Sheriff." Sally raised her chin in defiance. "This woman was disrespected on my land. I owe her to see her for myself." Ignoring his objections, Sally brushed past him and out of the office, clearly expecting him to follow.

On the fresh steed Tomlin had prepared for her, Sally followed the sheriff on his horse through the patchwork of snow and dead wild grass while avoiding stands of trees. She saw three men up ahead. The one she didn't recognize was kneeling near a large fallen log, clearly focused on something on the ground while the deputy stood a few yards away with a man she recognized as a neighbor, rancher Buck Heaver, who was gesticulating wildly.

Sheriff Cook's horse came to a stop, and he easily dismounted before walking over to Sally's and taking him by the bit to steady him so he could help Sally to the ground.

"Thank you," she said softly, looking up at him with confusion as he reached into his pocket and withdrew a red bandanna with a paisley pattern.

"You'll need this" was all he said.

She took it and, with a mental shrug, followed him over to the kneeling man. The closer they got, the more she understood the need for the bandanna. Nearly wanting to vomit, she brought the material up to cover her nose and mouth, trying to breathe as shallowly as she could. It was a stench unlike any she'd ever smelled: sickeningly sweet rotting meat.

She took as deep a breath as she dared as they neared the man by the log, a bandanna tied around the lower half of his face. He looked more like a stagecoach robber than the doctor the sheriff introduced him to be.

"Dr. West," she acknowledged. The man with iron gray hair glanced at the sheriff with questioning brown eyes.

"She owns the property," Sheriff Cook said quietly.

Sally was guided to the other side of the log where her breath caught. Lying on her back was a woman, her dress a simple pattern, though filthy and tattered. Her skin was an unnatural color, as clearly time and nature had taken their course.

What nearly made her feel faint, however, was when she looked at the woman's face. Well, where her face would have been. The woman lying there had clearly been subjected to a horrible beating about the head and face, a mass of indiscernible flesh and bone remaining, let alone what nature and animals had done.

"Jesus, Mary, and Joseph," Sally whispered, crossing herself. It had been so many years since she'd been in any church for a moral reason that she wasn't even sure she was doing it right.

She turned away, gasping, taking in lungfuls of rancid air. She was grateful for the steadying hand on her shoulder. She squeezed her eyes closed, only to see the image of that poor creature all over again.

"I'd like to go back to the house, if you please," she whispered.

❧❧❧❧

"Drink this," Lark said softly, kneeling next to the chair Sally sat in before the lit fireplace in her bedroom.

Sally watched her, wondering if her eyes looked as vacant as they felt. "Thank you." She accepted the cup of hot tea. The lemon-scented steam was soothing before she even brought it to her lips.

"Are you okay?" Lark asked, moving to the twin chair, reaching across the small table between them to place her hand on Sally's arm.

Sally took a few deep breaths before blowing the final one out as she brought the delicate teacup to her lips, blowing carefully over the surface of the hot contents. "I will be." She could feel Lark's gaze on her. She looked over at her and could see a deep sadness in her eyes. In fact, her face looked much like she suspected her own did. She adjusted the teacup to be supported by one hand and held out the other, Lark taking it. They said nothing as they stared into the flames in companionable silence.

❧❧❧❧

Hugging herself, Sally looked down at the spot by the log, smelling only fresh, spring air, but she took small, shallow breaths anyway, still able to smell the ghost of the dead woman whose body had been removed days before.

"Just awful," Tomlin muttered, standing next to her. He'd insisted on coming along, not comfortable with Sally going back to the site alone, even as she felt the comforting weight of Rose hidden in her skirts.

Sally let out a heavy breath and nodded. "I'll see if I can get her a proper burial."

"You know her?" Tomlin turned to walk with her back toward the horses.

Sally glanced over at him. "Does it matter?"

He met her gaze for a long moment, then smiled, the two heading back to the horses in companionable silence. He helped her mount Myrtle before expertly heaving himself up on his own horse. With a click of her tongue, Sally and her mare led the way away from the spot where Buck Heaver had come across the woman's body while chasing down one of his calves.

As they began a steady gait, she glanced over at the man she'd known the lion's share of her life. Surrounded by women, many more than trustworthy, she tended to go to Tomlin for a lot of her deepest problems or worries. He was a kind, sensitive man, but he had a good head on his shoulders and never lied to her or tried to sugarcoat anything.

"Tomlin?"

"Yes, Miss Sally?"

She smirked. "After all these years, are you ever going to just call me Sally?" she asked, teasing in her voice.

"No, Miss Sally," he deadpanned, never taking his gaze off their path.

She shook her head. "Pain in the ass," she muttered.

"Yes, Miss Sally."

She saw a ghost of a smile curl the corner of his

mouth. She shook her head again, then grew serious. "Do you think I have it in me to settle down?" she asked. "Love someone? One someone?"

After a long moment, Tomlin cleared his throat. "Miss Sally," he began, their gait slowing to a casual walk for their horses so they could easily hear each other, the mounts taking a circuitous route of their own choosing. "We be knowin' each other a long time. I watched your mama, what she become after your daddy die." He looked at her, heavy brow furrowed. "I hope you don't get sore at me for sayin' this, but she turned hard, Miss Sally. Somethin' inside her went bad. What she done to you, forced you to do." He shook his head and let out a little whistle between his teeth. "She used to be so kind. I think she tried to make you what she was."

Sally glanced over at him, surprised to hear so many words come out of him at one time. She didn't say a word or make a sound, afraid he'd stop. He wasn't wrong on anything he was saying, and it was interesting to hear his perspective.

"You was always so kind to me and my sister," he continued. "No matter what. But I see you got hard, too, Miss Sally." He smirked. "At least you like to pretend you hard. You got a heart three times the size of any of us." He gave her a genuine smile, which oddly made her blush a bit, mainly because she knew he meant what he said. "You only got one shadow on your soul, Miss Sally."

She met his gaze, that ugly knot in the pit of her stomach that had resided there since that day made its presence known. She swallowed. "What's that, Tomlin?" she asked softly, though she knew what he was going to say.

"We ain't stupid, Miss Sally," he said gently. "We all know the real reason why we here in Denver, no matter what you like to tell folks."

Sally nodded. "Yes," she admitted, neither of them needing to expound further.

"So, you ask me if you got it in you to settle down and love? Without a doubt."

She studied him for a long moment, then with an evil grin, she took hold of Myrtle's reins. "Race you!" With a kick and a yell, she got the mare running free, gobbling up ground and leaving Tomlin behind in a cloud of dust.

Her heart pumping and hair flying back behind her as it came loose from its restraints, Sally felt free. She could hear Myrtle snorting beneath her, mane flapping against her powerful neck with each stride of those long legs. She could just barely hear Tomlin and his mount gaining speed. She screamed out in impassioned competition, determined to make it to the stream first.

She let out a whoop of victory as she slowed Myrtle, the mare sweaty and breathing heavy. "Good girl!" she exclaimed, slapping the muscular neck and rubbing it affectionately.

"Ain't no fair!" Tomlin exclaimed in good humor as he, too, slowed his mount. "You a cheat now!"

Sally grinned at him. "No, you're just a sore loser," she said sweetly.

His steed walked up to her, Tomlin giving her a hard look, amusement in his eyes. Sally met his gaze, hers filled with the mischief of victory. She noticed, however, that his gaze moved past her, so she turned her head to see what had caught his attention.

"What is that?" she asked.

In lieu of a response, he clicked his tongue and urged his horse to forge across the shallows of the stream, the massive hooves splashing through the cold water to the bank on the other side and the stand of trees that had caught Tomlin's eye.

Sally held a bit tighter to the reins as Myrtle made her way to the water's edge to drink, never taking her gaze off Tomlin as he jumped down from his steed and walked to the trees and the brown carpet bag nestled in the branches. He had to jump to reach it, but after a couple of tries, he was able to dislodge it, catching it as it tumbled down.

He hoisted himself back into the saddle before making his way to Sally's side of the stream again. Pulling up beside her, so they faced each other, he handed the bag to her. It was dirty and worn, well-used. It wasn't heavy, but clearly, there were objects inside from the hard angles she felt.

Placing it on the saddle horn, she unclasped the worn wood clasp and opened it. Inside was a basic assortment of women's goods: boar's hair brush with strands of long brown hair in it, a partial bar of soap wrapped in burlap, a coin purse with a few coins, a lady's handkerchief, and finally a folded piece of paper.

Withdrawing the paper, she unfolded it and read. The writing was small and had the slant of someone lefthanded. It was delicate script, likely from a woman. It appeared to be unfinished, as well.

"Here," she said softly, handing the carpet bag to Tomlin so she could read.

"What's it say, Miss Sally?" Tomlin asked, voice filled with curiosity. But it was a voice that fell on deaf ears.

"Oh, god!" Sally cried.

※ ※ ※ ※

"I'm nearly broke, so I met up with some people who told me they could help me. They said all I had to do was tell them stuff. Ginny, I told them what they wanted to know, and now I'm real worried. I think I'm in trouble." Ginny swallowed, her hands trembling slightly as she read to her audience of two. "I'm gonna come to the house to talk to you, I need your advice. May even need to talk to Sally, but don't say anything to her just yet. I'll send word when I'm planning to come. I don't feel very safe to leave now. I think they may know—" She turned the page over to look at the blank backside, then shook her head as she tossed the letter to the counter before turning away, tears in her eyes. "That's it," she said, voice hard, edged with emotion.

"You think it's hers?" Sally whispered.

Ginny nodded, not saying a word.

Sally brought a hand up, covering her mouth, her other arm wrapped across her body. She looked over to see Tomlin leaning against the wall of the kitchen, a large hand rubbing at his chin. He was staring down at his shoes.

Sally's eyes fell closed as she felt the lump of unshed emotion in her throat quickly fall to her stomach, only to come roaring back up. She quickly made her way over to the sink, her stomach revolting quick and hard. She felt a warm hand on her back, rubbing soothing circles.

"Miss Ginny?" Tomlin said softly.

"Yeah?" Ginny said from her stance just behind Sally.

"You have other letters from Miss Rebecca, right?"

"Yes, I do," Ginny said absently. "It's okay, honey," she murmured to Sally as she heaved again.

"Well, ain't it a good idea to maybe see if'n her writin' matches?" he asked. "This be serious."

"That's a real good idea," Sally managed, gasping as her stomach seemed to be finished. "Real good."

"Tomlin, go tell Felisha to get the letters out of my room," Ginny said softly, rinsing a rag with water.

Sally heard Tomlin leave the room as she was guided to sit on a stool tucked in the corner near the stove. She allowed Ginny to wipe her mouth and chin like she was a child. She met Ginny's deeply troubled eyes.

"The body had brown hair," she said. "It was caked with mud and blood and God only knows what else, but it was brown."

Ginny stopped her ministrations and studied Sally for a long moment before she asked, "Do you think it was her?"

"It never would have occurred to me had we not found this." Sally indicated the carpet bag and letter, both resting on separate surfaces in the kitchen. "But with that letter pointing us in a possible direction..." She took a deep breath. "Yes."

Ginny nodded, her expression deeply troubled as she rinsed out the rag and took one last swipe at Sally's face. "You okay?"

Sally hugged herself from her perch on the stool and blew out a long breath. "I don't know." She met Ginny's eyes, no doubt her own holding the same deep sadness and concern she saw in Ginny's. "I feel I'm responsible for this. If only I'd let her stay—"

Ginny waved her off. "If only that som-bitch hadn't infected her with his filth. If only my daddy hadn't choked my mama to death in front of me and Barny. If only them Southerns hadn't killed your daddy." She looked at Sally, hands on hips. "One thing I have learned in life, Sally, is that everything is a chain of events. All of us here," she said, indicating the house around them. "There ain't a soul here that isn't here because a nasty link in that chain put us all here. There ain't a woman here who saw this as her destiny." She pointed at Sally. "Including you. I don't care how much money you got hidden all over God's green earth. If you had your way, you'd a been shacked up with a real looker living a good life long ago."

Sally looked down at her lap, a small smile curling her lips.

"Don't you go blaming yourself for what happened to her. I don't know who these people are she mentioned, but maybe Sheriff Cook can shed some light on all this. Or maybe even some of these girls here got an idea."

They both turned when footsteps neared the kitchen. A moment later, Tomlin entered with three girls in tow, including Felisha with Ginny's letters.

"Thank you, darlin'," Ginny said, taking the letters. The group gathered around her as she spread one of Rebecca's known letters out next to the one found in the carpet bag.

Sally stood at one end of the table used often for kneading dough, Tomlin at the other. She met his gaze, easily seeing the sadness in his eyes as it seemed the two letters were written by the same hand. Her attention was grabbed by Lark's appearance.

"Lark," she said, walking over to her. The two

women had been such good friends, she knew that surely Lark could help. "Do you recognize this bag as Rebecca's?"

Lark took a quick glance at the bag, then turned away. "I've never seen it in my life."

Confused, Sally asked, "Are you sure? You used to spend a lot of time with—"

"I don't want to get involved," Lark snapped, emotion in her voice as she glared at Sally. Her expression softening, she turned away to leave. "It's too painful," she whispered.

꙳ ꙳ ꙳ ꙳

Sally tapped the arm of the chair with her fingertips, watching Deputy Blair, who was taking his time comparing the two letters. She would normally think that sort of attention to detail was a good thing, but with the attitude this man exuded, she wondered if he was simply counting words to see which letter was longer. All the same, she kept her mouth shut and waited.

"So," he finally said, leaning back from his position over the side-by-side letters. "You said your colored man found this?" He nudged the bag that sat on his desk with his knuckles.

"Yes." She nearly spat the word out between clenched teeth. The way he'd emphasized colored, she knew that Southern accent of his wanted to call Tomlin something very different. She swore if he did, she was going to grab that carpet bag and whack him upside the head with it.

"The same one with the fondness for sledgehammers?" He moved the letters aside as he went through the contents of the bag.

"As it was explained to Sheriff Cook, Tomlin uses the sledgehammer and a variety of other tools for his daily duties."

"Mm-hmm," the deputy murmured absently, opening the coin purse and peeking inside. "Convenient that he knew where to go, don't you think?" He didn't bother to look up at her.

"He spotted it, Deputy, but I was with him at the time," Sally explained, her irritation shining through in her tone.

He spared her a glance. "So, he led you to it then?"

"No," she growled. "As I said, we were out riding, and I led us in the direction of the trees it had been thrown into. Tomlin was just the one who spotted it there."

He tossed the coin purse to the desk. "So, Rebecca Banes was ejected from the property because she gave one of her gentlemen visitors a disease?"

"No," Sally drawled. "As I explained, one of her clients gave her the dreadful disease, and I had to end her employment, so she didn't pass it on to anyone else."

"I see." He opened a wooden box on his desk that revealed tobacco and wrapping papers inside. He went about rolling himself a cigarette. "It's quite possible your colored man gave her this dreadful disease. Or!" he exclaimed, eyebrows shooting up, "she gave it to him, so he smashed her head in in revenge." He eyed her. "What'cha think about that?" He ran the flap of the wrapping paper across his tongue to seal the rolled smoke shut.

Sally squirmed slightly in her seat, uncomfortable

with his attitude and growing angrier by the second. "Tomlin doesn't have relations with my girls."

He stared at her, a smirk on his clean-shaven face. "Miss Little, he may be a colored man, but he's still a man. You dare to tell me he's a saint around all them half-naked girls prancing around him?"

She glared at him. "My girls have more self-respect than you'd ever bother to give them," she said, her voice low and dangerous. She pushed up from her chair. "They trust Tomlin, and he protects them."

He looked up at her with equal disdain. "So much so that one of his sheep went to the slaughter."

Her jaw muscles bulged as her teeth clenched behind closed lips. Taking a deep breath through her nose, she said, "I'd appreciate it if you'd tell Sheriff Cook I'd like to speak with him regarding this case when he returns from Brooke View." Without another word—as she was afraid she'd curse him out—she turned on her heel and marched out of the sheriff's office.

≈≈≈≈

The flames may as well have not been there at all, as Sally didn't see their brilliance, didn't feel their warmth. She sat in one of the chairs before the fireplace in her bedroom, staring off into another time, her thoughts jumbled into a mass of images marching through her mind, every one of them cast with the people she'd lost in her life, including one she'd created in her mind over and over again over the years, updated, changed, longed for.

She absently brought her hand up, the wine glass it clutched coming to her lips. She took in a small drink of the sweet red within, the act of swallowing more automatic than because she made it so. The tears had long ago dried, leaving the flesh along their path feeling tight from all the leftover salt.

It was late, the day gone, sun tucked in for the night leaving behind a sliver of moon in its path. The firelight threw eerie shadows all over the room, as well as her face and body, wrapped in her robe.

Once she'd returned from the sheriff's office, Sally had gathered all the girls and her staff, breaking the terrible news. Though not fully proven, the circumstantial evidence was ugly, considering none of Rebecca's close friends in the house had heard from her in weeks despite promised letters to come and even a potential meeting between a couple of them to catch up.

There had been lots of anger and even more tears. She'd sat with them doing nothing more than playing a role in that moment, the mother hen of the house, when all she wanted to do was curl up and be alone so she could feel the cold, hard sting of guilt all by herself and cry all by herself. Which, after a while, she did. Now sitting by the fire, she felt empty.

She turned her head a bit at the sound of the doorknob to the main apartments turning. She was glad she left it unlocked in case she came. She took another drink as she listened to the soft, nearly silent footfalls. Lark was barefoot, which told Sally she'd likely changed into her bedclothes, too. She smelled her rosewater perfume before she felt the gentle embrace from behind, Sally's head cradled back against Lark's soft breasts.

Reaching up, Sally gripped Lark's forearm with the hand that wasn't holding the wine glass, her eyes squeezing shut as fresh emotion threatened to rise. After a long moment, a soft kiss was left to the top of Sally's head, her long hair long ago loosed and brushed.

"How are you?" Lark whispered, backing away just enough to run her fingers through the dark strands, Sally's head falling back in relaxed pleasure.

"I'll be okay," she whispered back. "How are you?"

"Okay, I suppose." Lark rested her hands on Sally's shoulders. "I'm sorry I wasn't any help with the bag in the kitchen. It was just too much."

Sally nodded, reaching up and taking one of Lark's hands in hers and holding it so she could leave a kiss in the palm. "I understand."

"Can I have some?" Lark tapped Sally's wine glass with a finger, still standing behind her.

"Of course."

"Finish what little is left, and I'll pour you a fresh glass."

Sally finished the last bit and handed her glass over. She watched Lark walk over to the small bar she had in the bedroom, her gaze falling to an incredibly shapely behind, unable to resist watching the way the silk of her robe embraced it with the subtle shift of Lark's hips with every step.

Feeling like a cad, she looked away, turning her focus back to the fireplace but this time actually seeing the flames within. She heard the cabinet door open and the slight *clink* of crystal on crystal as Lark got herself a glass, then the soft, unmistakable sound of poured liquid. A moment later, Lark padded over to her and handed her a fresh glass before taking the twin to Sally's chair. The two said nothing as they lightly tapped their glasses together and took a sip. She winced, looking at the glass.

"Ugh, that's bitter."

Lark looked down at her own glass before looking at Sally again. "I opened that bottle you bought from the winemaker in New York when we were there last summer." She gave her own wine an experimental sip, also slightly wincing. "You've been saying you wanted to try it."

Sally shook her head. "Won't buy from him again," she murmured before taking another sip. "Do you have any idea who she may have gotten mixed up with?" Sally asked at length, her voice quiet.

Lark didn't answer for a moment, but finally said, "Rebecca has always been a troubled soul. If you put her in a room filled with one hundred men, she'd always find the one scoundrel."

Sally glanced over at her, Lark's gaze firmly fixed on the fire. "You think she found that scoundrel?"

Lark let out a heavy sigh before sipping her drink. She nodded before meeting Sally's gaze. "I know she did." She took another drink, this time looking over at Sally. The orange light of the flames turned her bright blue eyes a strange gray color. "I wish I could have saved her."

Sally met that sad gaze for a long moment before reaching across the space between their chairs and taking Lark's hand, which was freely given. Their fingers intertwined as their hands rested on the small table. "I wish I could have, too." Sally took a drink of her wine. It was the start of her fourth glass, and she was feeling it. Between the wine and the weight of her emotions, grief, and guilt, she was feeling very tired.

"Are you okay?"

She glanced over at Lark, who met her gaze with concern. Lark smiled.

"You look like you're fading over there."

Sally nodded, taking a last drink of her wine before she reached across her body to set it on the table where she still held Lark's hand. She squeezed the hand before releasing it. Pushing to her feet, Sally was surprised when Lark was suddenly standing next to her, a hand on her arm.

"Let's get you to bed," Lark said softly, though there was an edge to her voice Sally had never heard before, an edge that made her heart skip a beat.

Taking Sally by the hand, Lark led them to the massive four-poster bed. Once up at the head, she dropped Sally's hand and turned the bed down. Sally watched, her heart racing as Lark's every movement seemed to be made with specific care to Sally's tastes in a woman's body.

With the covers pulled down and pillows plumped, Lark stepped back over to Sally and, looking her in the eye, reached down and swept the belt of her robe free. The silky ends fell open to reveal Sally's naked body, as she was never one to sleep in what were considered "proper" bedclothes for a woman. She found them entirely too restricting.

"Time for bed," Lark murmured, taking Sally's hand again and leading her the short distance to the bed. "Get in."

Sally did as she was asked, the wine kicking in all the more. She felt a bit woozy on her feet, the room seeming to breathe on its own. She definitely didn't feel right. But she did as bade and climbed up onto the high mattress, sliding her legs beneath the covers. She lay on her back, head cradled in the soft pillow.

"Comfortable?" Lark asked, a hand coming up from where she stood at the side of the bed, one knee braced on the mattress, and ran her fingertips down Sally's cheek.

Without thinking, her mind fuzzy and brain not working right, Sally took that hand and brought it down to cover her breast. Lark met her gaze for a moment before she leaned over, Sally's eyes sliding closed at the first touch of soft lips.

As the kiss deepened, Lark climbed onto the bed and, just before settling atop Sally, she shed her own robe, leaving her glorious nudity revealed. Sally didn't even have time to take her in before accepting her warmth on top of her own. Their kiss was deeply passionate, yet soft and sensuous.

Sally moaned into the kiss as one of Lark's thighs found its way between Sally's, pressing into molten need. Her hands ran down the soft strength of Lark's back until she cupped her behind, urging her movements as she slightly raised her own thigh, pressing it into Lark's desire, which earned her a soft sigh.

As they continued to kiss and move together, she knew she'd done this before, knew she'd been touched by this woman before, knew she'd made love with her before.

Her mystery lover held Sally to her as they continued to move together, their breathing too hard to continue kissing... She could feel and hear the quickening breaths and whimpers in her ear as the blond woman buried her face in Sally's neck.

Sally gasped first in surprise at how vivid the

flash of memory was, then again as Lark hastened her movements atop Sally.

She could feel and hear the quickening breaths and whimpers in her ear as the blond woman buried her face in Sally's neck...

Sally's eyes fell closed as she tried to push the images and memory away, wanting to focus only on Lark. Her hand came up to cup the back of her blond head, Lark's quickening breaths hot against her neck. Her own breathing was nothing more than constant moans...

Sally's nails dug into the woman's shoulders as a new wave of climax washed over and through her. She felt the other woman's body tense, her hips grinding against Sally's partially raised thigh before she went rigid, a loud burst of sound in Sally's ear marked the moment of her release...

Her foggy brain confused stolen moments in an abandoned building with those in her own bed, losing track of which was which. Sally's body exploded with her climax.

...blond woman wearing a mask, looking down at her ...

...Lark staring down at her, a soft smile on her lips ...

...soft kiss to the lips by the mystery woman ...

...Lark's lips, so soft as she brushed them against Sally's.

Sally responded, though it was more automatic as a dark fog clouded her movements, her limbs feeling as though they were made of lead.

"Thank you, Sally," Lark whispered against her lips. "I have to go now."

Sally tried to speak, protest, anything, but nothing happened. Her eyes closed, and her chest rose and fell in deep, even breaths.

Chapter Six

*H*eart racing, she ran, eyes wide as saucers as she tried to find somewhere, anywhere to hide. The halls were long, seeming never ending. Every door she passed was open, a person inside the small room, which only had a narrow bed with painted iron headboards, the bars chipped and stained. There were men, women, and even a few children. Some were handcuffed to those bars with chipped paint, others rocking.

Breathing hard and desperate, she came upon a room that looked to be empty, the bed nothing more than a bare mattress on the iron frame. She ducked inside, throwing herself against the wall just inside the doorway. She squeezed her eyes shut, trying to steady her pounding heart, but she knew he was out there.

"Mama?"

She turned slowly, her heart in her throat. Gasping, a trembling hand came to cover her mouth. "Chloe?"

"Look, Mama," the four-year-old said, holding up her stuffed animal. "I found Bear," she proclaimed proudly, a stuffed unicorn held in the other arm.

Footsteps, loud and coming closer. She hurried over to the child, kneeling to her height. "Listen, baby," she whispered. "I need you to be quiet for me, okay? Can you do that for me, hmm?" She raised a hand and brushed back strawberry blond hair. "I'll be back soon."

She gave her a quick hug, eyes squeezing shut as she inhaled the child's special fragrance, then she let her go, hurrying from the room.

Running. She was running again. Suddenly, at the end of the hallway, he was there. He was holding a baby, swaddled and still. She looked as though she were sleeping. As always, he was nothing more than a silhouette with no facial features, but she could tell he was looking at her. A little girl hid behind him, peeking around his back. Her hair was still wet, raindrops dripping to the floor.

She felt trapped. She couldn't move forward, but she knew going back would only start it all over again. Her heart still raced, but now she felt her hands itch, her arms empty as she stared at the baby he held, the little one she felt walking up behind her.

"Do you want to hold my unicorn, Mama?" Chloe asked softly.

Her eyes squeezed closed as her head was thrown back. "I'm sorry!" she shrieked.

"Too late for sorries," the silhouette growled. "Far, far too late."

"Don't touch me!" Sally screamed, scrambling away from the touch so far that she fell off the opposite side of the bed. Landing with an unceremonious thud, she looked around. Finding herself on hands and knees on the floor, she pulled herself to her feet to find Ginny staring at her wide-eyed, hands up in submission. "Sorry," Sally muttered, blowing hair out of her face as she decided to walk around the bed rather than over it. She nearly growled when yet again, Ginny's aim was right on, her robe flopping over her head like a possessed veil. "God, you piss me off,"

Sally muttered from beneath the silky material before she tugged it off her head and slid her arms into the sleeves, belting off the robe to cover her nakedness. She glared at Ginny. "Why are you here? And why the hell does my head hurt so badly?" she yelled, regretting it instantly as it made her head hurt worse. She had a horrible headache, as though she'd spent the night before drinking rot gut. She gripped her head, willing the band inside to stop banging on the drum and go to intermission. "Where's Lark?" she whispered, walking over to her little bar to clean up the single glass and bottle of wine she'd left open.

"That's why I'm here, Sally," Ginny said, voice firm, which caught Sally's attention.

"What do you mean?" she asked irritably, putting the stopper back into the bottle and putting the wine back on its shelf. "All sticky," she groused.

"Do you have any idea what time it is?"

Sally glanced at Ginny, smirking. "Are you my mother?" She stopped short, however, when she saw the deep concern in her eyes, not accusation. "What?"

"It's nearly ten thirty, Lark is gone, and she apparently took Myrtle with her, and you've got a houseful of girls who are scared."

Sally stared at her, mouth open. "What are you talking about?" she asked, nothing Ginny had just said fully absorbing. "Why, she was just here last night." She thought back to the previous night, though in truth, she felt like she was trying to see a gold key hidden behind a wall of molasses. "I had a glass of wine," she said stupidly. But that was all she could recall. She felt as though Lark had joined her, but the truth was, she couldn't remember. "Gone?" she said, as though a parrot repeating a command.

"Get yourself together while I clean up this pit," Ginny growled, walking over to Sally and lightly shoving her in the direction of the bathroom.

❧ ❧ ❧ ❧

Sally sat atop the closed lid of her prized baby grand piano that was played during entertaining evenings, the girls in the house seated or standing in a horseshoe shape around her. She looked into the eyes of each of her girls and the few men she had on staff, who stood back behind the ladies, Ginny among them.

"Many of you have been with me for a long, long time," she began softly but loud enough for the room to hear. "Many of you followed me halfway across this great country, all the way from the City of Brotherly Love out here to the wilds of Colorado. We came to gain our independence, out from underneath the thumb of that 'brotherly' love, and you all have done me proud." She took a deep breath and let it out slowly, her head still not fully feeling attached to her neck. "So, I know things have been strange of late. I understand Lark has left, and I'm going to look into that as soon as we're done here. I want to talk about Rebecca." She paused when she heard a few sniffles, her own emotions threatening to rise.

"Who killed her, Sally?" one of the girls asked quietly.

Sally met her pained gaze and shook her head. "Wish I knew. Listen, ladies, only Lark and Ginny knew this, but I gave Rebecca a train ticket to go back home to her mother, who she'd told me so many times she missed. I gave her that ticket and funds to start over." She shrugged, feeling tired and sad. "I have no idea why she was still here."

"And what about Lark?" one of the girls asked, anger in her voice. "Why'd she leave? Did you knock her off, too? What about Margaret?"

A chorus of voices erupted, demanding answers, voicing concerns, and some just outright crying. "Wait!" Sally held her hands up. "Hold on, everyone. Hold on!" As her raised voice rang out over the room, everyone quieted and looked up at her with wide, surprised eyes. "First and foremost, I did *not* hurt anyone," she hissed, glaring at the accusing woman. "I have done all that I can to protect you girls." She was hurt, and it came through in her voice. "I share your concern about Margaret, but there's not a damn thing we can do until we hear from her. As for Lark, I was awakened this morning with the news she'd left us." She paused dramatically, letting her words sink in. "Now," she said at length, "if any of you don't feel safe here, don't feel I've done all I can to keep you safe and protected, there's the door." She pointed a finger in the direction of the front door. "You're not chained here." She looked at the outspoken one in particular. "You're welcome to leave." The defiant woman held her gaze for a moment before she looked down at her hands, which rested in her lap.

When there was nothing more forthcoming, the group dispersed, leaving Sally alone with Ginny and Tomlin. She looked at them as she slid off the piano, no doubt the look of concern in their eyes matching her own.

"What happened, Tomlin?" she asked. "Where's Lark?"

He shook his head, thumbs tucked into the beltloops of his overalls. "Felix come in the house 'round six to let me know Myrtle had been saddled and taken. Didn't think nothin' of it, Miss Sally. Thought you was out early. We went on with our mornin' duties till one of the girls found Miss Lark's room empty, all her things gone." He shrugged. "We put one and one together and realized she'd left with your horse, Miss Sally."

Sally let out a heavy sigh and ran her hand over her hair, pulled back into a long braid down her back. Without a word, she headed to the stairs, taking them as quickly as her dress would allow to the second floor. The girls, many of whom had been gathered in one another's doorways as they talked, all grew quiet, watching as Sally marched down the hallway, her gaze focused on her goal of the last room on the left.

Pushing the door open, Sally stepped inside the room, now a sanitary shell. The bed was made neatly with hospital corners. The dusted surface of the dresser was void of anything that used to be there: hairbrush, framed picture, and the bottle of perfume Sally had given Lark for her first birthday at the house. All gone. Every scrap of personalization had been removed.

The unshed tears stung her eyes. She didn't know what to say, how to feel. Bringing a hand up, she covered her mouth and squeezed her eyes shut. Taking several deep, calming breaths, she turned and hurried from the room, a sea of stares behind her. It wasn't until she was in the safety of her own apartment that she let the emotion come. The sobs hit her hard and fast, taking her to her knees with their ferocity.

After several minutes and an even worse headache, her tears slowed, then dried up. Her eyes hurt, her head hurt, her heart hurt. She sniffled and ran her hands over the hot skin of her face. Getting to her feet, she made her way to her office and plopped down in the chair. She knew she had work to do, but she was so distracted by the events of the morning she couldn't concentrate on what that work was.

She groaned and rolled her eyes when she heard someone walking toward the room where she sat. A moment later, Ginny's head appeared around the doorframe. "What?" she demanded. "It's been a hellish day, and it's just barely lunchtime. What do you want now?"

Ginny didn't rail against Sally for her attitude, nor did she give her an admonishing look. Instead, she tossed an unfolded missive to the desk and sat. "I reckon word has gotten out," she said sagely.

Sally reached out and grabbed the page, leaning back in her chair as she read it. Anger and frustration rose inside her as she tossed it back to the desk. "So, I guess tonight's gala will be a smidge smaller," she said with a heavy sigh.

"Four clients backing out," Ginny said. "That's four girls that won't be getting paid."

"I'm aware of that fact," Sally said, eyes closed as she covered them with her hand. Her headache was returning. "I bet that rat bastard deputy opened his mouth." Her hand fell to the arm of her chair. "You would not believe how he treated me."

"There's more," Ginny said.

Sally met her gaze for a long moment before clearing her throat and straightening up in her seat. "What?"

"Do you keep laudanum in your bedroom?" Ginny asked, tone serious.

"You know I don't." Sally waved off the

preposterous idea. "You know how ill that devil's syrup can make me."

"Yes, yes, I do. So, why did I find a drop of it on your bar when I cleaned up your wine mess?"

Sally studied her for a long moment, her mind racing back to the night before, trying desperately to piece together any events that would have concluded in that vulgar medication ending up in her bedroom. At a loss, she said, "What are you saying?" Her tone held accusation in it that she hadn't intended. Deep inside, she had thoughts she didn't want to have and her well-conditioned protection of a certain blonde who held her heart on full display.

"I'm not saying anything. I'm simply telling you the facts," Ginny responded.

"You think she did this, don't you?" Sally spat.

"Sally, I'm going to be straight with you. Here are the facts as we know them: Rebecca Banes is dead, found beaten to a bloody pulp on your land. Meanwhile, days later, your beloved angel seems to have drugged you for whatever reason and vanished in the night, taking your horse with her." She raised a hand to forestall Sally's deluge, mouth opening to begin. "Now, I'm not saying for a hot minute that the two events are connected because frankly, we don't know. I know Lark and Rebecca were close friends, and perhaps she just got spooked and got the hell outta Dodge. But I'm gonna say this," she continued, pointing a finger at Sally. "You don't trust a damn soul on this earth, not even those of us you've known for decades. You question every goddamn thing we do and say in your house. I ain't finished!" she admonished when, once again, Sally's mouth opened to speak. "I don't know where she came from or where she belongs, but since that little filly waltzed in here, your head has been in the clouds. She can do no wrong, and God help anybody who dare question her. She's a beautiful young thing, and Lord knows you got a weakness for beautiful women, but this place is full of 'em," she said, indicating the house around them. "But for whatever reason, Lark managed to squirm inside that crusty ol' heart of yours, and I'm downright scared it'll be the finish of ya."

Sally blinked several times, stunned by the avalanche of words that had just rushed out of Ginny's mouth. "Can I talk now?" she asked hesitantly.

"Go on," Ginny said, waving her on with a flick of her hand.

After the lashing she'd just taken, Sally adjusted in her chair. "When you cleaned up the bedroom this morning," she began, "were there two glasses?"

Ginny nodded. "Yup."

"Do you think she did that? Put that stuff in my drink?" Sally asked carefully.

Ginny studied her for a long moment, head slightly cocked to the side. "Did she make you a drink, Sally? Pour you wine?"

Sally shrugged. "I don't remember. I know I had a glass of wine when she came in, but I really don't know beyond that." She drew her eyebrows down in frustration as she glanced out the window at the sunny, spring day beyond. "I feel like my head is full of cotton or maybe even coal." She placed a cool hand on her forehead for a moment before looking at Ginny again. "Do you think she drugged me?"

"Well, Sally," Ginny said conversationally as she slung an arm over the back of her chair. "You know you ain't feeling so hot today and don't look too hot, neither. You slept until near lunch and can't remember a damn thing about last night. That don't sound like a normal before-bed-glass-of-wine moment to me."

Sally chewed on her bottom lip. She knew damn well that Ginny was right, but damn it all, she didn't want to think it, let alone admit it. "Fine," she finally blew out. "So, why would she do that?"

Ginny shrugged. "So you'd be out and couldn't stop her from leaving."

Sally looked out the window again. "None of this makes sense," she murmured, more to herself than to Ginny. "None of this."

"I know. Tomlin took his boys out to see if they could track Lark down or at least your horse." Ginny pushed to her feet with a grunt of exertion. "I'll leave you be. I know you've got to get ready for tonight."

Left alone, Sally stared off into space, wondering how on earth her life had gone from relatively happy and manageable to a nightmare in just a couple of months.

༄ ༄ ༄ ༄

"Really now, Jack." Sally looked at the older man over the top of her wine glass. "You know better than to ask something like that."

The usually charming Jack Landon looked out over the room—thinned a bit, what with the four clients who backed out of the evening's events—his heavy brow drawn. "I can't have my name attached to a spotty situation, now can I, Sally?"

She turned up her own charm. "Come now, Jack."

His own returned with his smile. "I fully intend

to." He took her hand and left a kiss on it before walking away, gathering the two ladies he'd chosen for the night and heading for the stairs.

Chuckling and shaking her head, Sally was pleased that at least one less girl would be going without pay.

Turning away, she sipped her wine, hoping she was finished answering questions for the night. She learned there was talk in town, and many of the men who had shown up were a bit nervous. She'd tried to allay their fears as best she could, but the truth was, she had no answers to give them.

She took one more look around, and as the men were pairing—or tripling—up with the girls, she decided she could call it a night and head upstairs herself. With a heavy heart, knowing there would be no Lark for company and still deeply confused and hurt on that entire situation, she reached out to take the banister when she was stopped by Tomlin.

"Miss Sally, this man needs to speak to you," he said.

She looked past him to a fresh-faced young man who held his hat in his hands and looked around at the goings-on with wide eyes. "I'm Sally Little," she introduced herself, extending a hand.

He took it, bringing it up for a less-than-delightfully sloppy kiss. "Mark Tuttman, Mrs. Little," he said. "I'm here on business for Mr. Willard Tatum."

That caught her attention. "Oh?" She smiled. "Tell me, when's the wedding?" she teased.

The young man looked confused. "Wedding, Mrs. Little?" He looked around, then cleared his throat before lowering his voice. "Is there somewhere we can talk?"

"As long as you stop calling me missus, we can absolutely talk," she said, hand on hip.

Looking at Tomlin with pleading eyes, he turned back to Sally when no such help was forthcoming. "Yes, ma'am?"

Sally nearly burst into laughter at the question, the poor boy out of his depth. "Follow me, Mr. Tuttman."

Situated in her office, Sally looked at the young man seated across from her. "What's your business regarding Willard Tatum, Mr. Tuttman?" she asked. "And what has it to do with me?"

"Well, sadly, I was sent here by his family attorney to tie up some loose business ends in the Denver area for his estate."

Sally stared at him. "His estate?"

"Yes, ma'am. We lost Mr. Tatum in a house fire."

Sally felt the very breath leave her body. "What?" she gasped. "Was Margaret with him?"

It was Mr. Tuttman's turn to look confused. "Margaret, ma'am? Willard's wife, Nola, was there, but the last moments of his life were spent in pure heroics. He managed to get his wife and two of their daughters out of the house. Sadly, when returning for their middle child, both he and the girl perished. I don't know who this Margaret is."

Sally could only stare at him. "I hadn't heard. Where did this happen?" she finally managed.

"Back in Baltimore, ma'am."

"He didn't live here then?" Sally asked, her head spinning.

"He had holdings here, ma'am, and came down to tend to business here, but his main family home is, well, was, back east," he said.

She nodded, certainly not the first time she'd heard that. "When did this happen?" she asked, still trying to put the pieces together. None of it made sense.

"Near a month now, ma'am."

"No." Sally shook her head. "That's not possible, Mr. Tuttman. It wasn't but more than a week ago that he sent for one of my girls he had..." Here she paused. Clearing her throat, she continued. "That he had relations with."

The man looked at her as though she had a giant spider on her head. "Ma'am, that's just not remotely possible. Well," he amended, "we're aware of his time here, clearly, thus why I'm here, but he did not send for this young woman." He reached up and tugged lightly at his tie. "He could not have, madam, as he was already with his maker. Though, even so, he never would have taken her to Baltimore."

Sally stared at him, speechless. Finally, she shook herself out of it for a moment. "So," she managed. "What do you need from me?"

"We have no desire to dance upon a man's grave, Mrs. Little, uh, ma'am. So, I'm here to gather all records you may have pertaining to Willard Tatum." He cleared his throat and brought a hand up to rub at the back of his neck. "And, um, should he have any outstanding debts, I'll be taking care of those."

She met his shy gaze. "I see," she said softly. "No unpaid debts, Mr. Tuttman, but I can't give you his records. They're in a ledger, so if I give you one, I give you all, and that just can't happen. But," she said, holding up a finger for emphasis. "I assure you the utmost discretion. I'll remove his name personally from all ledgers. I, too, have no desire to hurt his

family any further than they already have been." She
was about to speak further but stopped when she heard
loud voices and footsteps getting closer and fast.

"Sheriff, I can get her—"

The office door slammed open, and Sheriff Cook
filled the doorway. He looked at Mark Tuttman, then
to Sally. Without a word, he tossed something heavy
and metallic onto Sally's desk. Startled, she jumped
back before focusing on what it was.

Gasping, she looked down at the ornate mermaid
dagger. "What, how..." She swallowed, getting her
confused emotions under control. "This has been
missing for weeks," she said, looking back up at him.
"Where did you get it?"

"It was sticking out of Margaret Milton's chest."

Chapter Seven

Sally closed her eyes, leaning forward so her forehead rested against the cold iron of the bars, which her fingers were wrapped around. "He never gave it to him?" she asked, her voice sounding as tired as she felt. She was soul tired.

"No," Ginny said, her own hand resting on one of the cross beams running vertically along the bars. "Sheriff Cook had no clue what I was talking about. That bastard deputy never gave him the bag, the letter, none of it."

Sally brought a hand up to swipe discreetly at a tear that had managed to slip out. She cleared her throat and looked at Ginny. "So, now what?"

Ginny shook her head. "I don't know. I told him all I knew about it, how you guys found it in that tree. I also told him more than half a dozen of the girls saw it that day back at the house. He's talking to that man who showed up regarding Willard Tatum now, then he and I are heading back to the house so he can talk to the girls who saw that bag and letter. I'll show him her other ones to me, too." She glanced over her shoulder at the empty doorway that led from the room the two cells were housed in to the main room of the sheriff's office. "He best be hurrying, too." She turned back to Sally, meeting her gaze. "Girls were packin' to leave, Sally."

Sally nodded. "Can you blame them?" She

smirked. "It's all become a nightmare."

"Miss Ginny, I'm ready to go if you are," Sheriff Cook said, suddenly appearing in the darkened doorway.

"Yes, sir," Ginny said, sparing him a glance. She turned back to Sally, giving her a brave smile before squeezing her fingers quickly and leaving with the sheriff.

Sally watched them go, true fear gripping her heart like nothing she'd ever felt. More than once in her life, she'd managed to get herself in what she called ugly trouble. This trouble couldn't be any uglier, but the stink of it was, she had done nothing wrong. She was confused and deeply sad. Things had happened so quickly, she hadn't even had the chance to truly absorb the fact that sweet Margaret had been deeply betrayed by somebody who, it would seem, was pretending to be the man she had fallen in love with. Then she had to face the ultimate betrayal as she was found floating in the river, Sally's knife buried deep in her body, apparently put there after the deadly sharp blade had slashed her throat.

Moving away from the bars, Sally walked the few feet to the hardwood bench that ran the length of the back of the rectangular-shaped cell, the front and back walls the shorter sides. Sitting down, she stared straight ahead for a long moment, not entirely sure what to do with herself. Her emotions threatening to fully take over, she curled up on the bench as best she could and let the tears come, washing her eventually into a fitful sleep.

❧ ❧ ❧ ❧

Sally started, eyes slowly opening. Unfortunately,

the nightmare she thought was simply that was real life as she woke in the cold cell. However, she found that she'd been covered by a blanket at some point, and a rolled-up jacket had been placed beneath her head. It took a moment to realize, however, what had awoken her.

Pushing herself into a sitting position, her body arguing with her the entire way, she blinked a few times to focus on Sheriff Cook, who stood just inside the open cell door, a steaming tin cup of coffee in one hand and a large lump of cornbread in the other.

"Compliments of my wife," he said, handing over the food, then the coffee.

"Thank you," she murmured, taking the offerings. As she slowly ate her breakfast, he squatted where he stood, looking at her. She met his gaze, question in her own.

"I spoke to the ladies back at the house last night," he began. "I'll be having a very stern talk with my deputy. My deepest apologies for his inappropriate and unprofessional behavior. I think you gals are on to something with the body found on your land. I'm going to look into Rebecca Banes. At least it gives a direction."

"What about Margaret?" Sally asked softly, the realization hitting her anew. "What about her murder?"

He let out a heavy sigh, reaching up to stroke his mustache. "I talked to everyone 'bout that, too. I have a firm belief that there ain't nobody in that house that could have perpetrated that murder, clear on the other side of Denver, and nobody noticed them being gone."

Sally's eyes fell closed as her head bowed slightly, a massive wave of relief washing through her. She could feel the steam from the coffee she held warming the skin of her face. "Thank god," she whispered.

"Also," he continued, garnering her attention. "I heard about your assistant, Lark, disappearing with your horse. The mare was found."

Her head shot up, eyes wide. "It was? Is she okay?"

He nodded, pushing to his feet. "The horse is fine. She was found tied to a tree near a church, a note tucked beneath her saddle claiming she belonged to the person who lived at your address. She was brought to your place this morning."

"But nothing about Lark?" Sally asked slowly.

"Nope." He hitched his thumbs in the gun belt that was buckled across his hips. "Eat up and I'll get you home," he said, turning and walking out of the cell, not bothering to close the iron bars behind him.

An hour later, Sally allowed herself to be helped down from the sheriff's horse until she was standing at the foot of the stairs to her front door.

"Here you go." He reached into a saddle holster and retrieved Rose, which he'd confiscated when arresting her the night before.

"Thank you," she said, tucking the pistol away in her skirts.

"I'll be back in a bit to take a look at Miss Milton's room, if that's okay."

"Yes, absolutely," she said with a nod. "Want to do it now since you're here?"

"Can't. I need to get to court." He extended his large hand, which Sally took. He squeezed with affection, then turned back to his horse.

She turned to the house and made her way up the stairs. She was exhausted. Her hips were screaming at her, and she wanted a hot bath and a decent cup of coffee, unlike the Mississippi mud she'd drunk with her cornbread.

Inside the quiet house, she stood at the center of the foyer and looked around. It was an eerie silence that met her, other than the tick tock of the grandfather clock in the corner. Even when the girls were upstairs, quiet in their rooms or asleep, the house still felt alive. Now, it felt as empty and dead as the grave Margaret would soon fill.

"Quiet, ain't it?"

She turned to see Ginny standing at the entrance to the great room.

Sally gave her a small smile. "Yeah," she responded softly. "I was just thinking that. Are they all gone?"

Ginny sighed and placed a fist on her ample hip. "Every single one. A couple were gonna stay, but the others talked 'em into leaving, too."

"I can't blame them, Ginny. Hell," she said with a sordid laugh. "Part of me wants to go." She hugged herself, feeling so cold and alone. "Did you get them some money?"

Ginny nodded, taking a couple of steps closer to Sally. "I did. Knew you'd whip me raw if I didn't." She gave her a weak smile. "Got it outta the stash in the flour jar."

"Excellent." An awkward silence fell between them until Sally said, "Ginny, you can go, too. I would absolutely understand if you did. Take whatever you need—"

"No!" Ginny rushed the fifteen feet between them until she stood in Sally's personal space, her hands on Sally's arms. "No way, kid. You're not gettin' rid of me, and you're not gettin' rid of Tomlin. He and

I talked about this already." She calmed a bit, her iron-like grip turning to soothing caresses up and down Sally's upper arms. "We started out together after your mama died, and we can rebuild again."

Sally nodded, too filled with emotion to verbally respond. Before she knew it, she was engulfed in a warm, comforting hug, which she returned. It was those times when Ginny knew all she needed was that mother figure to let her know it would be okay. She let the tears fall silently down her cheeks as she basked in Ginny's familiar warmth.

"Sally?" Ginny murmured into the hug.

"Hmm?" Sally hummed back, eyes closed as her head rested on Ginny's shoulder.

"Are you happy ta see me, darlin', or do you got a Colt .45 in your pocket?"

Sally burst into laughter, backing away from Ginny as she reached into the gun pocket of her dress to see that, indeed, the long barrel had gained a mind of its own. She pulled it out, considering she was about to head upstairs and take a bath and change anyway.

"Jesus!" Ginny cried out, hand to her chest as three loud hard raps cracked against the front door.

Sally, also startled, looked to Ginny, who seemed downright scared. Their attention was once again returned to the door when three more raps sounded. It sounded as though God himself were knocking with a brick.

Swallowing her nerves—and the bile that rose from the fright she'd taken—Sally walked to the door. She was pleased to feel the weight of Rose in her right hand, though she hid the gun behind her skirts so as not to frighten the person on the other side, as likely it was a benign caller.

Reaching for the ornate door handle, she pulled the door open. On the other side, looking every bit the dapper gentleman he had upon their last meeting, Mr. DeMarco was replete with his skull-topped cane. She realized that devil-eyed monstrosity was likely what he'd used to knock.

"Top of the morning to you," he said, syrupy-sweet accent firmly at play, reaching up a gloved hand to tip the top hat he wore, as he was dressed in his finest.

"Mr. DeMarco," she said, taken aback. "What can I do for you?"

He grinned, blue eyes sparkling and his handsome looks near-mesmerizing.

"Why, you already did that, madam." He stepped inside the foyer, surprising her by his brazen behavior. "You sent them whores scattering like cockroaches after a candle's lit."

She looked at his grin with disgust. "I think you should leave, sir."

"Do you now?" He looked around the foyer and lightly tapped his cane on the floor. "I don't think so," he said, meeting her gaze. "Starting to feel at home now. I mean," he added with a full-on, brilliant smile. "As empty as this place is now, we need to fill 'er up, don't you think?"

She opened the door wider in invitation for him to leave, only to be stunned to see Rachel standing there, as beautiful as ever in her vixen-like perfection. "What are you doing here?" Sally asked, utterly confused until, to her horror, she realized Lark was standing behind her. More to the truth, Lark was hiding behind her. She looked disheveled, her eyes downcast and one of them encircled by a deep and punishing bruise. She reached past Rachel and grabbed her, tugging Lark inside. "What did you guys do to her?"

Rachel laughed, sauntering inside the house and over to stand behind Lark. She ran her hands suggestively down the sides of the younger woman's body. "What did we do to her?" she repeated. "Perhaps you should ask her what she did to *you*."

Sally watched, stunned as Rachel's hands moved up to cup Lark's breasts from behind.

"You people get the hell out of this house!" Ginny boomed, indicating the open front door. She turned her ire to Lark. "You've been nothing but trouble since the day you walked through that door, missy," she fumed, her face red and vein straining down the center of her forehead. "The best thing you ever did was leave. Now do us all a favor and do it again. All of ya!"

Shocking Sally and, from the looks of it, Ginny, Rachel violently shoved Lark over to Montreal DeMarco, who easily caught her in his arms, holding her back against his body. "You stupid old cow," Rachel growled to Ginny. "You're in over your head, woman. I'd highly recommend you stay out of this before you find yourself joining your sisters in filth." She turned away from Ginny and turned to Sally. "Monty's little sister may be good in bed." She smirked. "But you know that already, don't you, Sally?" Her beautiful face twisted into one of spite, hatred, and pure ugliness as she stood no more than six inches from the stunned target of her ire. "But she couldn't manage the one thing she was tasked to do," Rachel said, her voice dropping to an almost intimate level. "To bring you to your knees."

"Why are you doing this?" Sally asked, fear

trickling its way down her spine, as her suspicions of the events of late registered in her mind. "You three are responsible for Rebecca and Margaret, aren't you?"

"Well," Rachel said with a smirk. "I'm not."

"It's amazing the sound made with a few good whacks," Montreal DeMarco said, slamming the skull of his cane into his palm a few times.

Sally stared at him, mouth open. She saw again the image of Rebecca's head and face. "My god," she whispered.

He walked over to her, skull lightly tapping his palm the entire way. "That's what she said after the first strike," he murmured.

Suddenly, Ginny turned and ran out of the house, skirts held up so as not to trip as she sprinted down the stairs.

"Call that bitch back," DeMarco said to Sally.

"It doesn't matter." Rachel stepped up beside him, glancing out the door before stepping back over to where Lark stood. "No doubt she's going to round up the coloreds that work here." She turned back to Sally. "You really should have just sold to Monty when he would have given you top dollar. You made this entirely too complicated and made him do some naughty, naughty things." She smirked. "For that matter, you made *me* do some naughty, naughty things." She reached out and trailed a fingernail down Sally's throat. "It was fun, though, wasn't it?"

"Don't touch me," Sally hissed, moving away from her. "This is all about my business?" she asked, her shock and grief turning to rage. She glared at Lark, who had yet to lift her head. "Lark, you infiltrated my home and my *heart* for my business?" When there was no answer, her rage grew. She hurried over to where

Lark stood only to be blocked by DeMarco.

"Don't touch my sister," he said sweetly, though the blue of his eyes had become electric, dangerous. "You had your chance. Now you get to deal with me."

"What do you want?" Sally asked, looking up into his eyes. "What do you want?" she asked again, voice louder.

The slow smile that spread across his face was pure evil. Without responding, he shoved her away from him. Sally grunted in startled pain when her back came into contact with the edge of the opened front door, which nearly knocked the wind out of her. She could feel the chilly early spring air on the side of her exposed to the day.

The raging bull coming out in her, she felt the weight and heft of Rose in her hand, the gun she'd nearly dropped when shoved. Her jaw muscles bulged as her teeth ground together. "The hell you say," she growled. She raised the gun, pointed at Montreal DeMarco. "You come into my house and spew your hatred. You murder my girls, and you *dare* to try and take what I've worked a lifetime to build. You're disgusting," she continued, even as her heart ached looking at Lark, who continued to stand there like she was made of wood. "The lot of you," she finished in a whisper, tearing her gaze from the woman who had more than broken her heart, she'd scarred her soul. "Get out." She cocked the gun to show she meant business as she focused again on DeMarco. "Get out!"

Sally noticed DeMarco looking over her shoulder, which took his gaze outside the house. He looked back at her and, slowly, the hand that wasn't holding the cane moved toward the pocket of his overcoat.

"Don't you move, you son of a bitch," she said,

voice low and dangerous.

"Or what?" he asked, hand still on the move, though at a slower pace.

"Or I'll give you far better than you gave Rebecca and Margaret, but you'll be dead all the same."

He smirked. "You won't kill me."

"Won't I?" She steeled herself to do just that.

She could feel the miniscule amount of pressure her finger applied to the trigger. In a nanosecond, Montreal DeMarco, using seeming superhuman speed, grabbed Rachel and nearly knocked her off her feet as she was put before him just as the deafening *BANG* of Sally's revolver rent the air.

She gasped as Rachel cried out, instantly a crimson spot growing on her dress just beneath her left breast. DeMarco barely kept his hold on her as she slid to the floor, he following to kneel next to her. He glared up at her, pure challenge in his eyes.

Though utterly stunned, Sally cocked the .45 again, ready to finish the job when she was startled to be grabbed from behind.

"No, Sally, no."

She stilled, recognizing the deep voice of Sheriff Cook.

❧ ❧ ❧ ❧

Sheriff Cook waited patiently while Sally wiped her eyes, the tears just not stopping. She sniffled, squeezing her eyes shut, willing them to stop. Taking several deep breaths, she was finally able to breathe and calm down. She met his concerned gaze, giving him a small smile.

"Thank you," she whispered. "Doubt you want this back now." She smiled as she held up the handkerchief.

He smiled. "I'll get it later." Sheriff Cook was quiet for a moment as he leaned his shoulder against the bars that separated him and Sally. "I was glad your friends were able to come by, Ginny and Tomlin. Seem like real good folks."

"The best," she said, feeling her emotions threaten to rise again at the mention of her dearest friends who had just left.

"Known them a long time, huh?" he asked. At Sally's nod, he pulled out a rolled cigarette from his pocket. He was about to put it between his lips but offered it to her.

She wasn't a smoker, but she decided, why not? Taking it, she tucked it between chapped lips and waited for him to light it before pulling out a second cigarette and lighting it for himself.

"Thought it may help calm your nerves," he said softly. He took a long drag before letting the smoke slip from between his lips a moment later. "I'll make sure they get back to see you from time to time."

"I appreciate that, Sheriff." Normally, she loathed the smell of any tobacco product, but she had to admit, in that moment, it was welcome.

"You know," he said, surprising her with how chatty he seemed to be, usually so stoic and frugal with words. "I've been a lawman for a long, long time, Sally," he began, eyeing her as he took another drag. "In all my time, first as deputy and now sheriff, I ain't ever questioned anyone I brought in, never felt there was an injustice left undone." He reached up and picked a flake of tobacco off his tongue before meeting her gaze. "Until now."

Sally gave him a small smile, blowing out the

smoke she'd just inhaled into her lungs, followed by a small cough of inexperience. "Yes, I was surprised when you said that to the judge, Sheriff," she responded softly.

"Nick."

"Pardon?"

"Call me Nick, Sally. I think by now titles are unimportant."

"Nick," Sally said, tasting the name on her lips. "You know, Nick, I think you'd be a great guy to have a beer with."

He chuckled. "You know, my wife once had the audacity to tell me that I can be fun."

Sally laughed at that, and in truth, it felt good to laugh. "How's her pregnancy going?"

He nodded as he took in a deep draw from his cigarette. "Good," he blew out with the smoke. "Thanks for asking. She's ready for it to be over, but she's doing well. The girls are excited for their new sibling."

Sally was quiet for a long moment as she considered her next words carefully. Finally, she said, "You're good at your job, right, Nick?"

He looked at her, nodding. "I like to think so."

"I want you to find somebody," she said, hope in her voice.

"All right. Who would that be?"

"My daughter."

He looked at her, eyes wide in surprise. "I didn't know you had a daughter."

"Not many do," Sally said. "She was born May 5, 1868." She smiled at the thought and at speaking aloud about her. "A young woman now."

"Where was she born?" Nick asked.

"Philadelphia. Most painful damn thing I've ever

experienced," Sally said with a small smile. "You owe your wife an extra hug and kiss, my friend."

"Was she taken?" He crushed the tiny stub of his cigarette against the stone wall that the bars of Sally's cell were bolted into.

"No. I met a wonderful couple, Virgil and Natalie Leyton. They wanted children, but Virgil had been hurt in the war and just couldn't..." She glanced at Nick, who nodded his understanding. "I knew they could give her the life I couldn't."

"Well, if that was at birth, do you know what they named her?"

"I named her," Sally said, her words a bit firmer than necessary. She couldn't help it, already feeling like the ultimate failure as a woman, as a mother. "I named her," she said again, softer. "I had her until she was nearly two."

"What did you name her?" he asked gently, readjusting his shoulder against the wall, arms crossing over his chest in a more comfortable position.

"Whitney," she said proudly, still able to see her sweet face. "When she was fifteen, they left Philadelphia. Natalie sent me a letter to let me know."

"And," he added, "they came here, and so did you."

She met his gaze for a long moment, then smiled. "That's what my heart tells my head."

"So," he said, pushing away from the wall. "If I find her, what do you want me to do?"

"Do you still have my gun?" Sally asked.

He looked a bit surprised but said, "I do."

"Give it to her. Maybe it'll save her life one day." She gave him a small smile.

He looked down at his hands, thumbs hooked

into his gun belt. Letting out a long sigh, he nodded and looked up at her. "All right." He brought up one of those hands, holding it out. Sally lifted her own and pushed it between the bars and into his. To her surprise, he brought it up and to his lips, leaving a lingering kiss there before gently resting it atop one of the vertical bars of her cell door. He gave her a smile of affection, then walked away, his footfalls echoing against the stone.

Left alone, she walked across the cell to the back wall where a barred window was just above the wooden bench where she'd slept for the past three nights. The blanket she'd been given was folded neatly at one end and the pillow she was using atop it. She ignored the blanket and pillow and looked out into the night beyond. The sky above was like a piece of black velvet, the stars like diamonds sparkling, begging to be looked at, admired, their one job to captivate.

"Now this is a very pretty sight."

She glanced over her shoulder. Instantly, her heart turned to stone as she slowly turned around. "Well," she nearly purred. "Look what scum has risen to the top of the pond."

He grinned. "Snappy comeback, my dear." He walked up to the bars, wrapping well-manicured fingers around them.

Sally walked up to meet him, looking into the twin blue pools of pure evil. "Where's your syrupy-sweet accent, Mr. DeMarco?"

His grin widened. "No need to keep that pretense up any further. You see, for some reason, the ladies fall over with their legs wide open for a Southern gent. But," he added with a shrug, "they're not quite so impressed by a railroad man's son from Topeka."

"You're a despicable bastard," she growled, hatred burning bright in her belly.

"And you, *Mizz* Little, are a murderess. How does it feel?" he asked, head cocked slightly to the side.

"You should know, you son of a bitch. Next time, I'll aim better." Sally gasped in surprise as his hand lunged between the bars and grabbed her by the throat. Sally was yanked at the bars, her chin hitting so hard against the cold iron she bit her tongue.

He leaned forward until he was so close that she could smell his breath. "You stupid bitch," he hissed, his grip on her throat tightening. "You bet your sweet little ass you should have aimed better. Because now I'm free to continue destroying you bit by bit, piece by piece."

She tried to pull free of the vise grip he had around her neck. Even with her nails digging in, he refused to release her. "What more can you possibly do?" She gasped.

"It doesn't matter what happens here anymore, Sally," he murmured, shoving her back into the cell where she landed hard on her behind, her head banging against the bench. "I'll continue to hunt you." He gave her a winning smile as he straightened his suit. "Yes, you really do need to work on your aim." With that, he walked away, whistling a lively tune.

࿐ ࿐ ࿐ ࿐

Sally could feel the firm, guiding hand on her upper arm, helping to keep her balanced as she took one rickety step at a time. It wasn't easy with her hands tied securely behind her back. When Nick had done that, she knew it was real.

All eight steps climbed, she found herself on the

platform. Not big on heights, she looked up into the bright blue spring sky instead, big and beautiful. She could feel the hard wood of the stage beneath her feet and saw the hundreds of pairs of eyes on her, some adoring, others filled with less-than-kind thoughts. That was just fine with her. Can't win 'em all.

At least, that was what she tried to tell herself as she was positioned where she needed to be and Nick released her arm and stepped away. She could feel the slight give as she took the final step she was nudged to make, a small step. A final step.

She took a long, deep, shaky breath as she looked back out at the crowd. She tried her best to ignore the glares she received. Some were yelling horrible things at her. Truth was, that didn't bother her. She'd heard horrible things aimed at her her entire adult life. What got her, though, were those who she knew were there to support her. She saw Mr. Wheeler off to the left, his hat held in his hands. She didn't dare meet his gaze, instead glancing to the right where she knew she'd find Ginny and Tomlin. She was touched to see a few of her girls there with them, all crying.

Quickly looking away, as she was determined to remain strong, she saw a figure at the center of the crowd, standing out as the small framed person was wrapped in a dark cloak. It was in that moment that two pale hands raised and the hood was lowered. Sally gasped as Lark stared back at her. Her eye was still deeply bruised, but the other was red and swollen, though it was clear that was from the tears that fell slowly from those bright blue eyes down pale cheeks.

Sally couldn't look away, even as she felt the presence of someone next to her and heard the crowd grow silent as words were spoken loudly, a prayer for her, a prayer for her soul. She didn't listen, she couldn't look away from Lark, who looked as though at any moment, she would burst into all-out sobs.

Her heart ached, a heart that she'd tried to come to terms with over the sleepless nights she'd spent in that cell. She'd done a lot of thinking, done a lot of crying, more thinking, more crying, and a great deal of introspection in between. Now looking at Lark, she felt as though she was looking into her very soul. She felt before her was a woman far more trapped than Sally had ever been when she'd been Lark's age.

"Are you ready?" Nick asked, unwittingly breaking into Sally's thoughts.

She glanced briefly at him before she looked back at Lark. A slow smile spread across her lips, a smile of forgiveness and a smile of peace. *I love you*, she mouthed, Lark nodding and mouthing the words back to her.

Turning to Nick again, she nodded. "I'm ready."

Nick reached up over Sally's head and brought down the black hood he held over it. She closed her eyes as the heavy material was put into place. Instantly, it was hot and uncomfortable. She took shallow breaths, as there was so little air available to her in the hood, especially as it was tightened around her neck as the next layer was added, the thick, braided noose, no doubt. It tightened more with a yank that made her choke a bit.

Silence, stillness. She held her breath, almost as though one last act of independence. She'd take her own breath even as they took her life.

She gasped as the floor fell out from beneath her, sending her falling, falling...a quick, sharp sting...

Chapter Eight

D arkness. It took Samantha Leyton a minute for her eyes to adjust from the spectacle that had her crying to the sudden darkness that filled the theater as the final curtain call ended. A moment later, the house lights came on, and she felt her friend's gaze on her.

"You knew I'd cry, Cary, deal with it." She dabbed at her eyes with the balled-up tissue she'd held in her hand for the entirety of the nearly three-hour show.

"You've been in love with this woman's voice since your seventeenth birthday yet, here we are, twenty-three years later, and you still get all misty-eyed when you hear her." He grinned at her. His Ken doll good looks still hadn't faded after twenty years of friendship. In fact, he seemed to get even better looking, which Sam thought was entirely unfair.

"Shut up," she grumbled, smacking him in the thigh with the back of her hand as she got herself under control. Taking a deep, cleansing breath, her emotions and adrenaline calming, she glanced over at him. "Thanks for coming with me. Seriously. It means a lot to me."

He met her gaze, hazel eyes twinkling and dimples threatening as a slow smile appeared. "Well, I figured since I got you the tickets for Christmas, I was kinda obligated to go with you since things didn't work out with what's-her-name."

She grinned. "Well, I appreciate it." She looked around to see the theater was clearing out. They were close to the stage, which she looked at longingly, wishing that curtain would open again. Letting out a final sigh, part contentment, part sadness that it was over, she pushed to her feet and led the way out of their row and to the aisle.

"Good lord," Cary Hume muttered from behind her.

"Okay, how many times did he text?" Sam asked, amused.

"Let's see," he murmured. "One, two…nine… twelve…"

"Good lord!" Sam gasped, glancing over her shoulder before turning back so she didn't do a faceplant into the back of the man ahead of her.

Finally, the pair made it out of the theater and onto the streets of New York. It was a cold January night, the heavy clouds above threatening more snow. Sam tried to shrug deeper into her puffy coat, adjusting her scarf before tucking her hands into her pockets. She saw the huge framed poster announcing that night's show *Maria Sonia*, with a twenty-foot-high picture of the singer who had captured Sam's attention, imagination, and heart the very first time she'd heard her angelic voice. Though now in her early sixties, the woman staring down at her in a gorgeous evening gown was as stunning as ever with her petite body, shoulder-length, deep auburn hair pulled back in an elaborate chignon, and makeup that intensified deep brown eyes.

With a sad smile as they walked away, Sam turned her thoughts to Cary. "So," she said, whipping her head to get dark brown bangs out of her eyes. "From what you're saying," she continued, "you're worried Brian may want to put you on a leash?"

Cary blew out a breath, which escaped in a white puff of steam. "He's trying. I mean," he added, glancing at her. "He knew I was with you at the show. What the hell? Did he think I was going to find some guy to fuck at the Maria Sonia show?" he asked with a dramatic wave of his hand. "I think I was the only guy there under sixty!"

Sam grinned, more than used to her best friend's flair for the dramatic. "I don't know, Cary. This guy sounds like a real dud. And," she said, moving closer to him as a crowd of loud teens headed their way, and it looked like the one closest to her planned to plow into her. Once they passed, she turned around, walking backward as she said, "Pardon me, no problem at all."

Cary chuckled. "You're gonna get us killed one of these days, Sammy."

"Yeah, if I don't kill those fuckers first," she growled.

"Are you still coming up for an after-concert-orgasm drink?" Cary asked as they came to a stop in front of his building.

Sam looked up at the large structure, then out at the street. "Nah." She reached up and took him in a tight embrace. "Thanks again. I'll see you at Tuesday's production meeting."

"Okay." He left a chilled kiss on her equally chilled cheek. "Catch a cab, will ya?" he called out, taking a few steps backward toward the door to his building.

"Sure thing!" she called back, glancing over her shoulder, walking toward the subway stairs. She laughed as he shook his head and waved her away.

She hurried toward the stairs, looking forward to the warmth of the subway tunnel. She slipped her Metrocard into the slot, then hurried toward the platform that would take her closer to home. The train was already there, so she ran the last handful of yards and barely slipped in before the doors whooshed closed. A few of the people already seated glanced her way, but most were buried in their phones or other electronic devices.

She hung on to the overhead bar for balance as she made her way to an empty seat. Sitting on the hard plastic seat, she quickly glanced around to see who her companions were for the short ride and settled on the woman who sat directly across from her. Living   off and on in New York, she'd seen all kinds, and not much surprised her anymore. It wasn't her favorite city to work or live in, but it was part of the job. The woman across from her had her complete attention. She wore a large-brimmed hat, so it was difficult to see her face, but from the state of the skin covering her hands, she seemed to be about Sam's age, late thirties, early forties. She wore a deep blue dress, simple, no adornment. It rose up to a conservative rounded collar, and the sleeves, though somewhat fitted on her arms, reached her hands. The length went to her feet, even seated, with the tips of white shoes of some sort peeking out. Sam found it peculiar that on such a cold day, the woman wore no jacket, no gloves, or even a scarf.

Her gaze rose from the woman's outfit to try to see her eyes in the shadows created by her hard-brimmed hat, but it was impossible. Even still, Sam knew the woman could feel that she was being watched. The energy coming off the stranger was nearly singeing. Sam felt that if she reached over to touch the woman's knee, before her fingertips ever found their target, there would be a blue arc of electricity that found them first.

Feeling uncomfortable and rude, as she was staring, she decided to focus on the train's location, so she didn't miss her stop. Even so, she kept glancing the woman's way, still feeling her gaze on her. She didn't feel afraid, but certainly, it was unsettling.

As her stop neared, she pushed to her feet and reached up to grab the overhead bar again to steady herself as the train rocked its passengers to and fro. Finally, the speeding train eased to a stop, the platform and waiting passengers coming into view. The doors whooshed open, and Sam shouldered her way out among the other disembarking strangers, as well as those trying to crowd in.

On the platform, she noticed the strange woman had also left the train. In the dense sea of humanity packed on the small platform, she was able to see the woman, as she was taller than average, as well as her unusual white hat. For reasons she couldn't understand, Sam followed her.

They headed with the herd to the stairs, the slick tiled walls reflecting the overhead lighting. The crowds of people between them and around them moved in concert up the stairs, though a few pushed their way past as they hurried to get to their next destination. Once they reached the top of the stairs and entered the long, dimly lit hallway that would lead to yet more stairs, Sam concentrated on keeping the woman's hat in her line of sight, as it would be easy to lose her as people spread out, quickened their pace, or turned off down other hallways, took other stairs, or disappeared into public restrooms.

Up another flight of stairs and a choice to go up one more onto the street or take a left to yet more maze. She lost her.

"Damn," Sam muttered, nearly knocked off her feet as someone hurried past where she'd stopped, ramming her shoulder in their haste to continue on.

Looking around again, even lifting herself to her tiptoes to try to see above the crowd, she didn't see what she was looking for. Knowing the street-level stairs would get her where she needed to go, she trotted up them and back into the frigid night. She reached into her pockets and pulled her gloves out, after she'd removed them on the train. Wiggling her fingers into the right one as her left hand tugged it on, she was startled and momentarily frightened when she felt a hand on her shoulder. Whipping around, she found herself face to face with the woman.

"*La foudre va tomber,*" she said in a soft, lyrical voice.

Surprised, Sam opened her mouth to respond and ask what that meant. The woman ducked into a cab that pulled up to the curb and was gone. Sam watched the car go, baffled. Shaking it off and freezing her behind off, she hurried toward her apartment.

Four blocks later, Sam rushed into the brick building, a tenement building of small affordable apartments built in 1914 and turned into large luxury condos in the mid-2000s. It was one of the first locations where she'd flipped condos and had made a tidy profit. Now she owned one on the seventeenth floor that she kept for when she was in New York working. Her roommate, Genji, lived there full time.

She kept the young financier on as a roommate for a little extra money but mostly to make sure the condo was kept up and not a target for crime since she was away so many months out of the year on other projects in her business with Cary, as well as filming projects for their show. It was a win-win for both women.

Riding the elevator up, she made it to her door and unlocked it, stepping inside and locking it behind her.

"Hey, Gen," she said to the Asian woman who sat on the couch with her legs stretched out and bare feet crossed at the ankle on the glass coffee table. Dressed in cotton pajama pants with snowmen all over them, she had her ever-present tablet on her lap while she watched some unknown movie on the huge plasma TV mounted above the fireplace.

"Hey," Genji said, her long, black hair pulled up into a messy bun. "So, how was the concert? Do you owe me twenty bucks?"

Sam grinned, tugging off her gloves and setting them on the wet bar before unzipping her jacket and shrugging out of it. "Yes, yes. She finished with *Ave Maria*."

Genji laughed, clapping. "I knew it. Since it wasn't on the CD but I found that amazing YouTube vid, I knew she'd sneak it in there."

"Hey," Sam said, tossing her jacket and scarf to the overstuffed chair. She plopped down on the matching ottoman. "You speak like eighty-four languages. Is French one of them?"

Genji chuckled. "Eight, but yes, I do fairly okay with French. I guess that one is like eight and a half."

"Well, good, 'cause I only know enough to get me in trouble." She explained the situation on the subway and the strange woman and did her best to repeat what the woman had said. From the look on Genji's face, she could tell she'd absolutely butchered it.

"Yeah, you can flip a house and turn it into a historic masterpiece in forty-five minutes, but languages clearly aren't your thing," Genji said dryly.

"And I have never claimed any different." Sam pushed to her feet and gathered her winter wear to put away. "So, what does it mean?"

"Well, in a nutshell, *la foudre va tomber* means the storm has built and now will break."

Sam stared at her, puffy jacket hugged to her chest. Dark eyebrows fell. "What the hell is that supposed to mean?"

Genji blinked at her a few times. "Why are you asking me? I'm just telling you what she said."

"True enough. Okay, I'm heading to bed. Early production meeting tomorrow so we can head out." Sam grabbed her gloves as she headed toward the hall that would lead to the bedrooms.

"Where to this time?" Genji called out after her.

"Colorado," Sam called back.

❧❧❧❧

The production team had rented two massive houses in an area called Highlands Ranch, a wealthier suburb of southern Denver. The house would serve as the production's headquarters but also would house the members of the crew, as well as Sam and Cary's team. A nearby warehouse had been rented to store construction supplies and for off-site work to be done.

Sam was in the house that would be shared by her and her company, standing at the French doors that looked out over a fenced backyard. Beyond, however, was where her attention was.

"Man, isn't that gorgeous?" Cary said, stepping up behind her.

"It is," Sam agreed, both taking in the gorgeous snow-capped Rockies, so close yet looking like they existed on another planet.

"Other than the altitude kicking my ass, I could totally live in Colorado," he said, stepping away from the doors.

Taking in a few more moments, Sam turned away and followed him where he'd gone to the chef's kitchen. She knew better than to get in his way, so she took a seat on one of the tall chairs placed at the marble-topped peninsula.

"Sandwich?" He stood at the opened fridge. At her nod, he took out the half dozen ingredients he'd use to make a masterpiece.

"So," Sam said, bringing up her email on her phone. "Lexi emailed me a history of this place, what she could find of it. I guess a lot of the records disappeared in the late eighteen hundreds. Okay." She opened the email. "Whitney Grove," she read. "Built between winter 1881 and 1888, it was one of the most beautiful houses in all of Denver at the time, though it had been built on the outskirts, surrounded by farm and ranch land. Built by a woman named Sally Little. I wasn't able to find any marital records," Sam's researcher had added in her report, "Nor any family records other than her father had been a war hero for the Union back east." Sam looked up from her phone to see Cary chopping a tomato in perfect slices.

"Maybe she owned a lot of land," he said, never taking his gaze off his task. "Rented it to tenant farmers?" He spared her a glance.

"Or maybe she was a horse wrangler," Sam added, amused.

"Oh!" Cary exclaimed, voice dramatic. "Maybe she was a madam!"

They stared at each other and at the same time said, "Nah."

Looking back to her phone, Sam continued. "After Sally Little was hanged for murder in March 1890, the property was willed to her longtime cook and employee, Virginia Bethel. Whoa," Sam muttered, absorbing that bit of information. She continued reading. "It was then deeded to Virgil and Natalie Leyton in 1883, whose daughter, Whitney, and her husband, John Forbes, took it over in 1903. It stayed in that immediate family, though went into disrepair."

"Wild. Any relation?" Cary asked.

"Doubt it. Never heard of any of these people," Sam muttered before she continued. "It had ultimately been sold to distant family members, Alan and Ruth Leyton, in 1965 where it was turned from a large single-family home into individual apartments. After a death in 1977, the following decade saw the decline in residents, and eventually, the house once again fell into disrepair. It was bought by its current owner in 2003." She put the phone down, as that was the end of the report. "Well," she said, watching as Cary constructed their sandwiches. "Looks like we've got our work cut out for us."

Cary glanced up at her. "So, the current owner is who contacted the show?"

Sam tossed her phone onto the island with a tired sigh. "Um, I'm not sure. Obviously, the owner signed off on the contracts, but that's been kept under wraps. I think someone else has stepped in to work with us and the show."

"This place is gonna take a minute to do," Cary said, using the same large knife he'd used to cut up vegetables to cut the two heavily stacked sandwiches in half, placing both on their respective plates. "Chips?"

"Yeah," Sam said, glancing at the bag of Ruffles. "That's why this is going to be a three-parter." She accepted her plate and the bag of chips that were slid her way. "You think our eight-month timeline will work, allotting for delays and whatnot?" she asked. "Considering how huge this place is. Hell, there have been times we've needed six months for a fifteen hundred-square-foot house."

He nodded as he chewed the slice of pickle he popped into his mouth. "I think so," he said at length. "We've got three times the normal crew at the ready, plus the locals."

She nodded and took half a sandwich into her hands, eyeing it to figure out the best way to get it into her mouth. "Well," she said, holding it out toward him. "Here's to a successful flip."

He tapped half his sandwich to hers. "Cheers."

❧ ❧ ❧ ❧

"Okay," Dave, the cameraman, said, turned around in the front passenger seat as best he could with his camera aimed at Sam and Cary, who sat side by side in the backseat of the sleek black Subaru Trek that had been rented for the project. "Location reveal reaction shot, take one. Action!"

Sam centered herself, knowing how important it was to get this part just right. The reaction of her and Cary would set the tone for the viewer when the episode aired. Before Dave had called for action, she'd glanced at herself in the rearview mirror. Her short dark hair was cut into a sporty, somewhat-meant-to-be-messy style that went well with her more laid-back nature. Though the intensity of her green eyes showed the spirit inside that warned against crossing her. Or so she'd been told.

The crossover made its way down an old street, lined with big beautiful trees, though the houses were neglected, some boarded up, others clearly well taken care of. All would have been higher society in their day, likely built in the earlier part of the twentieth century. Finally, the trees broke, and a massive structure came into view.

Sam gasped in surprise, but then her surprise melted into disgust and shock. The mammoth house was made of red sandstone, but it was horribly abused and neglected, windows broken out, the front porch sagging on one side. The circular drive, once big and spacious, was clogged with overgrown weeds and dumped trash.

"Wow!" Cary said, leaning forward slightly in his seat. Sam could feel him glance at her, but she couldn't take her gaze off the house. "Creepy, huh?" he said. "Huge."

She knew by his tone that he was trying to read what she was thinking. It was his way to toss out words that he thought might be on her mind, and when the right one hit, it usually knocked her out of her own head and into verbal action.

"I...I don't...I just..." Nothing would solidify in her mind. She was filled with irrational anger and grief looking at the state of the house, a state that so many of their projects were.

"Dave, let's take it again," Cary murmured.

"Lynne, go ahead and turn us around," Dave said from the front seat.

Sam heard all this, felt herself being jostled as the car slowed and pulled a U-turn in the middle of the street, but her mind was still in a different place, caught up in her first impression of the house.

"You okay?" Cary asked softly, lightly nudging the side of her thigh with his hand.

She squeezed her eyes shut and shook her head to clear it. She met his gaze, noting concerned blue eyes. "Yeah." She turned to the two other people in the car. "Sorry, guys."

"Okay," Dave said as the Trek got back to its mark. "Take two. Action!"

≈≈≈≈

Hugging herself, Sam wandered around the small foyer that led down either a hallway of doors or up the stairs. It was somewhat of a tight space, the light overhead a good twenty feet up. She glanced up at it. She had a few minutes to look around as they'd finished up their shots outside. Now the crew was setting up for the shots inside, as well as using a drone to get some B-roll of the grounds, neighborhood, and upper parts of the house.

"Can you believe this place?" Cary stepped up beside her. "This is going to be one helluva project."

Sam heard him and nodded absently, but she was deeply bothered. "This is all wrong," she said, eyebrows drawn in consternation. She walked over to the wall to her right, using both hands to push on it.

"This shouldn't be here."

"What are you talking about? There's probably an apartment or office space or something on the other side." Cary ran his hand down the shiny dark wood that covered the wall.

Ignoring him, she took the few steps to the open front door, bracing her weight with both hands on either side of the doorframe. "Dave!" she called, seeing him getting some equipment out of the back of the Trek. "Bring me my sledge."

He nodded his acknowledgment.

Moving back over to the wall, she knocked in various places, trying to see if there was a stud anywhere. It was all hollow. "Yeah, this has got to go," she uttered. "Who the hell put this up? It has no place here."

"Here you go," Dave said, the head of the ten-pound sledgehammer thudding on the worn wood floor as the long handle *thunked* against the wall.

"Aw, shit," Cary said, hurrying out of the way as Sam grabbed the tool and lifted the heavy head high in the air as she gripped the fiberglass handle. With an almost feverish determination, she swung with a grunt of exertion, the metal head slamming into the wood, forming an instant hole. She grunted again as she pulled the head of the hammer out before attacking a second, third, fourth and finally, fifth time. She was out of breath and her bangs were damp against her forehead, but she'd made enough space for them to kick their way through.

Glancing at Cary, she grinned. "That's how it's done."

"Um, great." He looked at her handiwork and shook his head. "Lexi texted while you were going ape shit." He held up his phone. "The owner's daughter, the artist, and art restoration expert are on their way."

She slung the sledge over her shoulder. "Why do we need an artist and art restoration person?"

He shrugged. "Guessing maybe there are murals or frescoes here."

Sam leaned the sledgehammer against the wall by the front door, and she and Cary made quick work of the wall, revealing a dark space beyond. She grabbed her phone from her back pocket and clicked on the flashlight feature, Cary doing the same.

"Holy shit," he whispered. "It's huge."

Pure satisfaction and joy washed over Sam, as well as a strange sense of relief. Beyond that horrible wall was a huge room, what would have been the great room. The windows in this room were either some of the ones boarded up from the outside or somehow obscured from the inside because it was pitch black.

"This is fantastic." Cary stepped in farther.

Sam gasped, jumping back startled as something small and quick buzzed by her work boots. "Jesus." She laughed, hand to her heart. She met Cary's concerned gaze. "Mouse."

The room was full of objects covered by dusty drop sheets, some pushed off toward the walls in groups, others scattered around randomly in the middle of the floor.

"Furniture?" Cary walked over to a square object and lifted up the sheet on one corner, which sent dust floating up in the air and him into a coughing fit. "Yup." He gasped. "Table."

Sam grinned, making her way around the room. She was drawn to the huge fireplace, the carved stone mantel so encrusted with dust and muck from who knows how long, it was impossible to tell what the carvings were.

"This place had to be amazing during its time," Cary said, joining her. Together, they shone their phone flashlights out over the space. "I can't believe they walled this off."

Sam nodded in agreement. "That's okay. We're gonna unearth this place."

Chapter Nine

"A im that light a little more this way." Sam used all her strength against the crowbar as she tried to wench loose some of the nails that were holding the sheets of plywood in place over the windows. "It's like a gift wrapped in paper, then wrapped in tape!" she growled between clenched teeth as she used the metal tool to pry the stubborn nails free.

"Hello?"

The sudden voice was so unexpected, Sam wasn't paying attention, and one side of the plywood ripped loose, which sent her face-first into the wall.

"Oh, shit, you okay, Sam?" Cary asked, a hand on her back.

"I'm so sorry," the unfamiliar female voice said, closer than she'd been a moment before.

Rubbing her nose and blinking rapidly, as she'd instantly seen stars and her eyes had watered, Sam focused to make sure her nose wasn't broken. Sure it wasn't, she turned to the newcomer.

"Are you okay?" the woman asked.

Sam smiled and nodded. "Yeah. No problem. Can we help you?" It wasn't uncommon for a random stranger to wander onto one of their project sites. Curiosity killed the cat, but satisfaction brought it back, after all.

"I'm Tandy Becker, the art restoration person

and artist," she said, extending a hand.

Sam took the soft warm hand and took the woman in. She looked to be in her thirties, perhaps just a bit younger than Sam. Her body was wrapped in a heavy jacket, but her hair, which seemed to be on the longer side, was auburn with stylish blond streaks, all of which was pulled back into a harried ponytail with loose strands framing her face, which was quite lovely. With the harsh artificial light of the flashlight their crew member Bud had brought in, it was difficult to determine her eye color, though perhaps a gray or a gray-green. She wore little to no makeup but seemed to be a natural beauty.

All that said, what got Sam, though, was the instant familiarity she felt to her. She studied her for a moment as they shook hands. "Have we met before?" she asked, head slightly cocked to the side as she searched her memories. "You didn't work with us on the Santos project in San Antonio, did you?"

Hand falling back to her side after it was released, Tandy Becker shook her head. "Nope. Never been to San Antonio." She smiled. "I'm pretty sure I would have remembered working with you guys."

Sam couldn't shake the feeling that she knew this woman but pushed it aside. "Well, welcome. We just discovered this gem of a room, and we're literally trying to bring it to light while we were waiting for you, and now that you're here, we're just waiting on the owner's daughter, and I guess she's our liaison."

"Oh!" Tandy held up a finger as if telling them to wait a second, then turned and walked away a few steps before returning to the circle of light created by the flashlights, hand extended. "Hi. I'm Tandy Becker, owner's daughter and liaison."

Sam chuckled, as did the two men flanking her. "All right. Well, let's get down to business."

🍃🍃🍃🍃

"Look at this." Tandy gently scraped off the first few layers of paint. She and Sam leaned on ladders in one of the second-floor rooms. The dirty white paint gave way to show some sort of darker paint underneath.

"What is that?" Sam tilted her head to get a better look. "Mold?"

"No, you see these tray ceilings?" Tandy indicated the entirety of the ceiling above them, the inner part seemingly scooped out as compared to the outer edges of the room. "It was a style thing in the latter nineteenth century for murals or frescoes or even a tin ceiling to separate the two."

Though Sam knew much of this information, she knew it needed to get on camera for the viewer, and quite frankly, she loved listening to Tandy explain it. Her passion for her work was evident in every word.

"So," Sam said, "why would people paint over this?" She reached up and lightly ran her fingertip over the tiny bit of exposed mural.

"Well," Tandy said with a sigh, meeting Sam's gaze. "Taste, the look they're going for in the home, lack of resources or knowhow to properly restore them. And I've even seen where people have an incredibly inaccurate view that to paint over these works of art is helping to preserve them."

Sam's eyebrows rose as she feigned surprise. "All righty then. Guess that's why we have you." The two women grinned.

"And cut! Okay, think we've got some good

stuff. Sam, we'll clear out so you gals can do some real work," Dave said. He and the production crew broke down the small amount of equipment they had in the room.

Sam climbed back down the ladder, grateful to be back on solid ground. With the high ceilings throughout the house, incredibly high ladders were required. "You know," she said, bracing for a moment on the ladder frame. "For what I do, it's a serious minus to be terrified of man-made heights."

Tandy chuckled, taking the final step to the floor, covered in a protective drop cloth. "Isn't that like a brick layer having issues with rough-edged objects?"

"Hey, be nice." Sam collapsed the ladder she'd been on and moved it to lean against a nearby wall. "You're doing great. Seem to have a natural presence on camera."

"Thanks," Tandy said, following suit with her ladder, as she'd be using a scaffold with a wooden plank across the top to lie down on and do her work Michelangelo style. "I'm a bit rusty, but it harks back to my days in the industry."

Intrigued, Sam crossed her arms over her chest. "You worked in TV?"

"I dabbled in TV, movies, lots of voiceover work, whatever my agent could get me."

Smiling and feeling relieved, Sam said, "Okay, so *that's* how I know you. I saw you in some movie or something, right?" She shrugged. "Maybe heard your voice in something?"

Tandy smirked. "Were you a regular watcher of *As the World Turns*?" she asked. "A crazed pre-teen morphine addict named Luna who was in and out of the insane asylum for a three-arc storyline in 1994?"

Sam stared at her a moment before slowly shaking her head. "Um, no, no, I can't say that I was."

"Well, that's the only thing of any real consequence I've done. Well," she added, a sly little smile on her face. "That is, unless you were a fan of a creepy little kids' show called *Miracle Mayhem* that aired for two seasons on PBS. I voiced Cockatiel Lu."

Sam chuckled. "You got me again, no." She leaned a shoulder against the wall, one ankle crossing over the other. She was amazed at just how comfortable she felt with this woman, apparently a stranger. "How did you get into art then? Strange leap, acting to the Sistine Chapel." She pointed up at the yet-to-be-uncovered mural on the ceiling.

"Art was always my first love," Tandy said easily, mirroring Sam's position on an adjacent wall. "Like any good parents, mine tried to get me to see what was as clear as the nose on my face, but like any teenager, I thought I knew better." She grinned, reaching up to brush a few blond-streaked strands out of her face. "So, at nineteen, I loaded up my blue Acura Integra with all my earthly possessions, including my stuffed monkey, Sprout, and headed west, all the way across the country from New York with a stopover in Manitou Springs, Colorado, to get a pep talk from my dad, then on to the big lights and even bigger dreams of the City of Angels."

"How long were you there?" Sam asked, fascinated. Looking at the woman standing a handful of feet from her, she couldn't imagine Tandy in the glitz and glamor or the cutthroat industry of Los Angeles. Instead, she could imagine her with a smudge of paint on her cheek that she hadn't even realized was there during a long, in-the-zone day of creating.

"Six and a half years. No," she corrected, a hand coming up for a dramatic pause. "Six and a half *long* years."

"So, one day, just barely old enough to buy a pack of cigarettes, you said, 'later gator,' and drove to Los Angeles? Alone?" Sam asked. At Tandy's nod, she shook her head and smiled. "You are your mother's daughter."

Tandy sobered. "You know my mom?"

Sam blinked, staring at her, confused. "Your mom?" Her head felt fuzzy, a slight headache tapping just behind her ears.

"Yeah, you said I'm my mother's daughter. I didn't know you knew her."

"I...I don't. I..." Sam shook her head, bringing up a hand and running it through her hair. "I'm sorry," she blew out with a nervous laugh. "I have no idea why I said that."

Tandy chuckled. "No worries."

The sound of an ice cube being tossed into a tumbler rent the air, and Sam looked at her phone as a text came in. Relieved for the distraction, she said, "They're bringing up your scaffolding."

"Oh, great!"

Saved by the ice cube, Sam headed toward the door. "I will let you get to it." Something caught her eye. She headed in Tandy's direction, again noting the glint of the small cross she wore. It was unusual. The front and back of the cross were silver, the sides, top, and bottom plated in gold with a tiny gold Christ figure crucified on it. It was unique and beautiful and was attached to a silver chain.

Uncharacteristically, Sam reached for the small

crucifix, invading Tandy's personal space, as it was only on a sixteen-inch chain. "This is beautiful," she said softly, transfixed by it. "Where did you get it?"

"My dad gave it to me," Tandy said, just as softly. "Story goes, sometime during or just after World War I, back in the Midwest somewhere, I had a cousin, I guess third cousin, who wanted to become a nun, but she gave it all up for love."

"Did she get married?" Sam glanced up into Tandy's eyes, so close as they stood little more than a foot apart.

"The love of a woman."

That got Sam's attention.

"So, the young woman, I don't know her name, had a baby, and they ran away with the baby. For reasons that aren't told in the story, the birth mother died, so my cousin took the baby on the run. I don't know who was after her, or maybe it was just the time in history and because she was a lesbian. But she ended up in Canada, and that's where she raised the baby. The crucifix has been in the family ever since, and my dad gave it to me on my thirteenth birthday." She gave Sam a soft smile. "It's never left my neck since."

"Wow." Sam realized just how close she was standing to Tandy, so she dropped her hand, the crucifix resting back against the pale skin just beneath the hollow of Tandy's throat. She took a step back from the other woman. "Well, quite a story." They both glanced over as Sam's team brought in the pieces of scaffolding to build it. "I'll get out of your way." She gave Tandy a quick smile, then hurried from the room, not entirely sure how to process all that she was feeling.

Stepping into the hallway and out of the way of

the men carrying in pieces of wood and metal, Sam walked to the window at the end of the hallway and looked out. The window was broken, so the cool air coming in was welcome. She took several deep breaths to clear her head, which still felt foggy. She felt as though she were only partially there, only part of her standing in that hall on the second floor of their latest project, while the other part of her was floating somewhere else.

Squeezing her eyes shut for a moment, she took a few more deep breaths to center herself before she began to feel somewhat like herself, but only somewhat.

❧❧❧❧

Agitated. Sam was really agitated. Letting out a frustrated sigh, she moved her fingertip over the screen of the tablet, the blueprints of Whitney Grove moving with her nudge. She was focused on the staircase that once upon a time sneaked up the back of the house from the kitchen, meant to be used by servants, the main grand staircase for the wealthy owners and their guests. Everything about these big, beautiful houses were meant to impress, the paid or enslaved staff meant to be invisible. But in the blueprints for the reno, they were in the wrong place, as was the kitchen.

The door to the production trailer opened, and Cary appeared. He stepped inside, closing the door behind him as he removed clear plastic safety goggles. "Hey, what's up?" he asked, his work boots making heavy steps on the floor as he walked to her desk.

Sam glared up at him. "When I call for you, you drop whatever the fuck you're doing and come."

He looked at her, taken aback. "Okay. We're rebuilding the basement stairs today, Sam, you know that. What did you need?" he asked, irritation in his voice.

"Who the fuck drew these?" She showed him the tablet. "Who the fuck put the back stairs in the wrong place? And do you know how I know they're in the wrong place? Because they go off the kitchen, and the goddamn kitchen is in the wrong place!"

He took the tablet from her and took a moment to look the whole thing over. Finally, he tossed the computer back to the desk. "You picked a good time to decide to change everything because we're still demoing the first floor," he said, sarcasm in his voice. He walked toward the door, slamming it open. "By the way," he said, glancing at her. "You're the one who put the fucking back stairs there and the fucking kitchen there."

"You're the fucking architect, Cary," she fired back.

"And you're the goddamn historian and designer who decides where everything goes!" He held her gaze, his blue eyes turning to the color of blueberries, which meant he was well and truly pissed. "And one more thing, Samantha," he added, hand holding the door open. "Don't ever treat me like the hired help again." With that, he was gone.

❧❧❧❧❧

Head hanging, Sam knocked again using the backs of her fingers. Finally, she heard his voice getting closer and closer until the bedroom door was pulled open. Cary, on his phone, glanced at her before turning away to walk back into the bedroom, but he left the door open.

"I have to go, Sam's here. We have tomorrow's plans to talk over—Seriously? She's dressed like a dyke...Oh, yes, Brian. Lesbian lumberjack chic is all the rage to make every good gay boy want to get his cock sucked. I have to go...Stop it...Stop. It. Good night."

Sam watched, both parts horrified and amused. She stepped into the room, closing the door behind her. Standing at the center of the room, she tucked her thumbs into the belt loops of her jeans and waited. Finally, Cary disconnected the call and threw his arm back, pantomiming throwing his phone against the wall but tossed it gently to the bed instead.

"I can't do this anymore," he said, voice tired. He turned and looked at her. "I really can't."

For a moment, Sam felt a sickening feeling walk its way into her gut, worried he meant their partnership, but after he let out a heavy sigh and ran his hands through his ever-perfect sandy blond hair, he met her gaze.

"What's up, Sam?" he asked, voice light and friendly. The only indication he was guarded with her was when he crossed one arm over his stomach.

She glanced past him to the nook near the window where stylish wingback chairs were placed with a table between. "Can we sit down?"

He followed her gaze and turned to lead the way, saying nothing as he took one of the chairs, Sam taking its twin. He got settled and looked at her, seeming to give her his full attention.

"You know," she began, sitting forward with feet spread and her forearms placed on spread thighs. Her fingers fidgeted between the space her spread knees created. "We do a lot of houses every year, or projects, as it were."

He nodded, crossing one ankle over the opposite knee. "Yup." He studied her, holding her gaze. "Is it too many? Do you want to slow down?"

She mulled over his words for a moment before shaking her head. "No. No, that's not it." She sat back in her chair, mirroring Cary's position as she let her wrists dangle over the arms of the chair. "I want to apologize for this afternoon, Cary," she said quietly. "Truly, I am sorry. We've had our doozies over the years, but never have you deserved to be treated that way. Nobody does."

He gave her the boyish smile that won her over the second time they met. The first time, she couldn't stand him. "I forgave you before I left that trailer. I just made a good show."

She grinned. "Yes, you did." She accepted his hand when he laid it palm up on the table between them. Once hers lay flush in his much larger one, he wrapped calloused fingers around it, giving it a squeeze. She responded, their code for all's well.

"This is a huge project," he said absently, rubbing the back of her hand with his thumb. "God, so much work to be done."

She considered his words, silently agreeing with them but said aloud, "There's something in that house. I don't know, it's...I don't know. Makes my head feel funny." She met his gaze as she rested her head back against the chair. "Have you noticed that?"

"Well, it can't be a fear cage, there's no electricity going to the house yet." He grinned. "You think it's haunted?"

She returned his grin. "Remember that place in Manchester?"

He threw his head back in laughter, tugging his hand free of hers as he clapped his hands together in amusement. "Oh, my god!" he breathed. "That bar. What was it, Healy's Pub? That new owner was so upset."

"Remember him yelling, 'I've brought in an exterminator, a fumigator, and now you're telling me I have to bring in a ghostbuster?'" Sam said, imitating the man's thick south Boston accent.

Coming down from his raucous laughter, Cary said, "And you looked at me, and we both were like, 'Yup.'"

They both kicked off into laughter, tears coming to Sam's eyes. After the long two weeks they'd been working on Whitney Grove, it felt so good to let go. "Lord," she said, slapping her hand on her stomach, which was sore from the laughter. She glanced over at Cary when she felt a touch to her arm.

"Tomorrow. You and me. We're going to take Saturday off and go check out Denver," he said.

"We've been here before." She chuckled.

"Doesn't matter. There's always something fun and new to do. We've worked thirteen days straight, fourteen-hour days, at best. Let's take a minute to breathe. Huh?"

She wanted to refuse, thinking of a hundred reasons they needed to get to work, even if maybe they started later so everyone could sleep in, but she knew it would fall on deaf ears. They were on track with the schedule, and there was no good reason she could say no. Finally, she nodded. "Okay."

Chapter Ten

S am sat back in her chair, hands on her very full belly. "Oh, my god, I love their burgers here," she muttered.

"Well," Cary said, scrolling through his phone, "I guess it was a wise move to call the place Hamburger Mary's then."

"Smart ass." Sam looked around the colorful place, which was a well-known Denver establishment known for not only great food, but also a fun, welcoming ambiance with colorful characters in the LGBTQ community as staff. "Find anything?" She smiled up at their waiter as he dropped off the check before sashaying his way to another table.

"There's a standup comic, but he's not on until tonight." He glanced up at her. "I know you want to be back to the house early so we can get an early start tomorrow. So…" His focus turned back to his phone, so Sam grabbed her wallet from the table and pulled out her credit card to pay the tab. "Hey, there's a fair of some sort not too, too far away," he murmured, gliding his finger across the screen of his phone. He read a bit, then looked at Sam again. "Wanna get a tarot reading?" he asked with a grin.

❧❧❧❧

"*Crystal Peak Metaphysical Fair,*" Sam read

from the giant sign mounted on the wall across the huge room in the Colorado Convention Center.

All along the outer walls of the room tables were set up, a person sitting in one chair while on the other side of the small round table a single person or, at times, multiple people sat across from them. A sign claimed various types of readings were available and said to sign up at the chosen reader. An aisle separated the two in a square around the booths and a crisscross aisle at the center of the booth area.

The booths held merchants and their wares, anything from jewelry to stones said to contain special energy, lotions and creams, and even one selling fudge. The two stood by the entry and glanced at each other.

"Shall we be metaphysical?" Cary asked, eyebrows raised in excitement.

Sam chuckled. "Let's do it."

They wandered past the various booths, stopping to touch this or that, Cary even purchased a basket of handmade bath bombs that allegedly contained healing properties. Sam could only shake her head, amused but not surprised. She knew how much he loved his long soakers while reading a book. Even for the five minutes they dated twenty years before, he had always been the girl.

"I haven't seen eyes that pure of color in a long, long time."

Sam stopped, glancing to her left at the man who she assumed had been speaking to her. Standing on the other side of the table that held a large assortment of jewelry made with an endless array of stones, as well as pottery pieces, was a tall slender man who looked to be in his sixties or so with long pure white hair held back in a low ponytail at the base of his skull.

His eyebrows were still the color his hair had likely been, a light brown, his trimmed beard the same color, though some of the white streaked on his chin. He wore a loose-fitting deep purple v-neck sweater that hung a bit on his thin frame and casual khaki pants. His eyes were brown, and though very kind, crinkled at the corners; they were intense. She felt as though he were looking into her very soul.

Not even realizing she had taken a half step back from the intensity of those eyes, she gave him a smirk. "My girlfriend said the same thing the first time we met." Well, it had been two girlfriends ago, and she was single at the moment, but she'd learned the language to use to shoo away male flies.

"Oh, I have absolutely no doubt." He gave her a kind smile. She relaxed, understanding he wasn't trying to be a pig, just a genuine guy. "Lovely color of green."

Stepping back up to the booth, Sam smiled. "Thanks." She looked over his wares. "Pretty cool."

"Thank you." He glanced at her again, studying her before he turned his back on her, walking to the backside of the booth that had a dark blue piece of material hung up. At that table was his money box and card reader machine, as well as a large water bottle. Sam watched as he opened what looked like a tacklebox.

"Look at this stuff." Cary picked up a bracelet with large brown stones on it that looked like walnuts. "So pretty. You gonna get anything?" He picked up another bracelet, this one a cluster of orange and brown stones at one end of a leather strap. "I want to check out those pottery incense burners. They look pretty cool."

"I don't know," Sam hedged. She did, however, think the stuff was beautiful.

The man returned, holding a necklace that was a thin sixteen-inch silver chain with a small round green stone about the diameter of a dime wrapped in a silver cage dangling from it. It was a color of green Sam had never seen in a stone before.

"This," he said softly, somehow the tone rising above the noisy venue they were in, "is called alexandrite, the green species." He held it up to Sam's face, the stone a few inches from her left eye. He smiled, seeming pleased. "Very close match."

Sam eyed it up close, bringing a hand up to hold the slightly swinging stone still. "It's really beautiful."

"Turn, please," he said, gently urging her with a touch to her shoulder. For reasons she could not explain, she did as he asked, his voice lulling her into a relaxed, almost trance-like state. "It's thought that this stone will bring good fortune and love," he explained. "The Russians believe alexandrite is a good omen, bringing its wearer balance between the earthbound world, where we are now," he added, clasping the necklace into place. The stone felt warm against the skin just below Sam's throat. "And the spirit world." He urged her to turn around again, facing him. "May it bring all to you, miss."

She took a moment to absorb how it felt to have the beautiful piece around her neck. She brought her hand up, cupping the silver-wrapped stone with her hand. She glanced up and met his kind gaze. "Sam." She extended her hand.

He took it, his larger, thin hand warm and soft. "Stormy."

"What a great name. Cary."

The older man shook Cary's hand. "A pleasure to meet you both."

Sam brought out her wallet from the hip pocket of her jeans. "How much do I owe you?"

He studied her for a long moment, then smiled. "Finish your path, Sam," he said softly, as though meant only for her ears. "We'll talk about it then."

Utterly baffled, she blinked. "I don't understand."

He reached out and lightly squeezed her hand before turning to Cary. "Let me show you these incense burners."

🙠🙠🙢🙢

It was early Sunday, earlier than everyone else was scheduled to arrive. Sam liked to be there alone, look things over without workers in her way or breathing down her neck or Cary shadowing her. He hated that she did it without him, given he was the contractor and architect, but that was why she didn't like him there. She needed to see it through the eyes of the designer, and a perfectionist one, at that.

She pulled her rental car up to the side of the house. They'd hired a landscaping crew to clear out all the weeds and trash on the grounds, leaving the front of the house looking plain and barren.

There were no tin types of the house available when it was built by Sally Little, which was the look and style Sam wanted to replicate, as did the owner. So, her training in history and design would come in. Sam thought as she parked her car and stepped out of it, walking until she was standing where likely a curved drive had once been. Remnants of bricks had been found, so it may have been created out of that.

Sam's thoughts were interrupted by something.

Ting, ting, ting.

She turned her head, looking to see what or who was making that sound. Most of the land had been sold off over the years, leaving the house on a scant bit of real estate outside of the footprint. Seeing nothing in the sleepy neighborhood, she turned her focus back to the house, forming a plan in her mind for the front portico.

Ting, ting, ting.

"What the hell is that?" she muttered.

Walking toward where she thought she heard it, she found herself standing near the production trailer, still closed and locked up. She knew there was nothing inside, no electronics that would be making that sound, especially not so clear and crisp.

"I guess he's fixing the stables again," she muttered. Sam looked around, startled to hear a voice, let alone to realize it was her own. She brought up a hand, running it nervously through her hair before it absently went to her necklace, hand wrapping around the stone. "Thank god I stopped for coffee."

She headed to her car to grab her venti mocha breve in its branded paper cup, as well as the box of doughnuts she'd picked up for the crew. Setting the box and cup on the porch, which had been braced until it would be repoured the following week, she dug out the right key and let herself into the house.

As the door swung inward, she leaned down to grab her things when something caught her eyes. "Son of a fucking bitch," she muttered, absently grabbing the food and coffee.

As the door opened and morning light was let into the foyer, she saw that someone had spilled red paint on the floor, in one spot. It took up maybe the size of a dinner plate, but she was furious.

Muttering curses as she stomped back to the table they had set up for when a random flat surface was needed, be it for foodstuffs or for house sketches, and set her goods down. Hands free, the hunt was on for cleaning supplies.

Ten minutes later, Sam was on hands and knees. She was nearly in tears in her frustration as she was making no headway. The harder she scrubbed, the more different types of cleaners she used, the worse the stain seemed to get.

"Damn it!"

"Hey, calm down, girl."

She looked up, bangs hanging in her face. Cary stood in the open front door with a tan plastic bag in his hand, the orange Home Depot logo printed on it. "You got it?"

"Yeah. Your text said to get the strongest stuff they had to get paint off wood floors. Sammy, aren't we taking these out anyway?"

"It doesn't matter!" she exclaimed, pushing up on her knees. "Look at this, Cary. How could they be so damn irresponsible? And where the hell is anyone using red paint in the first place? We're nowhere *near* ready for paint. Even Tandy isn't painting—"

"Sam, honey, what are you talking about?" He stepped inside the foyer and walked around the spot she was focused on.

Utterly confused, her eyebrows fell. "What do you mean, what am I talking about? I'm talking about careless workers and spilled paint on a multimillion-dollar project, Cary!" She indicated the stain she'd been scrubbing at. "This! It's not our money to fuck with. The owner gave us a strict budget to work with and—"

"Sammy, there's nothing there," he said, just loud enough for her to hear him over her tirade.

She blinked at him, his words not connecting. "What?" she said, irritation in her voice from being interrupted and the fact that he wasn't understanding the severity of the situation.

"There's nothing there," he said again, squatting across from her, the stain between them.

She looked down, gasping and falling to her behind in stunned surprise. All that met her gaze was the narrow planks of the wood floor, their only discoloration time and the dampness of the cleaning supplies she'd been using. "I don't understand," she murmured, getting back to her knees. "I swear." She looked over at Cary, who was looking at her with concerned blue eyes. "Cary, I'm not crazy. I'm telling you, there was a large red stain right here. It was this big." She used her hands to indicate the size.

Cary gave her a sweet smile, reaching over and placing his hand on her shoulder. "We've been working so hard this year," he said softly. "I think after this project, we need to take a break. Maybe go someplace fun."

She looked down at the spot again, hoping it would be there. Nothing. Absolutely nothing. Running her hand through her hair, she blew out a breath. "Yeah," she said, defeated. "I think you're right."

෯෯෪෪

Sam had brought her portable Bluetooth speaker, which was playing the playlist from her phone. At the moment, it was going through Maria Sonia's greatest hits album. She hummed along as she finished demoing a wall on the third floor. The layout had been strange, the smallest floor of the house cut up into three small apartments. Two of them had fireplaces, only one of them seeming to be functional. They were put in such awkward places in the rooms, she knew it wasn't the original layout.

Breathing hard after she kicked in the final bit of demoed wall, Sam cleared enough between her work boot and sledgehammer so she could start tearing it all out with her hands. She tugged off her leather work gloves and reached up to pull down the painter's mask she wore as drywall dust and other debris erupted into the air with each crash of her sledgehammer or foot. She slapped her gloves against the thigh of her jeans as she surveyed her work.

"Really brightened it up in here, didn't it?"

Sam glanced over her shoulder to see Tandy strolling into the room, one hand hitched into the back pocket of her jeans, which she couldn't help but notice fit her frame quite well, the other holding a large paper cup with a lid and straw, the name of a fast food place on the side. She wore yet another tank top, today's burnt sienna. Her black and white flannel was tied around her waist, and her hair was in its usual messy updo. Sam had to wonder how Tandy could look like she'd just fallen out of bed yet be totally and utterly put together to perfection.

"It did. Thanks." Sam accepted the ice cold drink and was glad to hear food was waiting downstairs. It had been a long day, and she hadn't eaten since the doughnut that morning. "After lunch, I'm going to attack this fireplace. I think it was a decorative one, which was extremely unusual, considering it was a large source for heat, even in the wealthy class," Sam explained.

The two turned and looked at the piece, which had been used and abused, the stone chipped, stained, and graffitied on.

"Such a shame. People have absolutely no care for anything," Tandy said softly.

"Nope." Sam glanced at her companion before she walked over to the spot she'd dropped excess equipment, her speakers, and the overhead fleece she'd shed earlier to work in only a T-shirt and her cargo pants. "We've found the most horrifying damage and vandalism in the houses we've done." She shook her head.

"You're coming down, right?" Tandy hitched a thumb toward the door that led out to the stairs.

"Yeah. Be just a second. Gonna round up all the stuff I used for demo," Sam said.

"Okay. Oh," Tandy added, backing up toward the stripped doorway. "I love this song. Personally, I think *Captive* is her best album."

It took a moment for Sam to catch up, but she realized Tandy was commenting on the music playing from her phone to the speakers. "You like Maria Sonia?" she asked, pleasantly surprised.

"Love her," Tandy said with a smile before disappearing out the door.

Sam stared at the spot where she'd been standing before rolling her eyes, amused at herself. As though she needed another reason to like that lady more than she should, she thought with a smile.

She reached down and moved her fleece jacket aside to uncover her phone to stop the music. The room was suddenly so quiet it was unsettling. She stood erect again and leaned back as far as she could, groaning as she stretched her midsection. She stopped midstretch when she heard something. Glancing at the fireplace, she swore she heard a breath, almost like a whistle.

Turning in the direction of the neglected fireplace, she stared at it. What she was looking for, she had no clue. Taking a few steps forward, she stopped, once again hearing a breathy whistle. It sounded like a combination of someone blowing air between their lips and the whistle of wind forcing air in through a crack.

Curiosity outweighing the fingers creeping down her spine, she walked over to the fireplace and slowly lowered herself to one knee in front of it. She looked up at the space where the mantel had been removed who knew when before, the holes where it had been mounted the only evidence it had ever been there. She reached out, running her fingers over the stone that remained outside of the mouth of the "business end" of the fireplace, which was all brick inside.

Hand dropping to the floor in front of the fireplace, she leaned forward, looking farther inside it, checking to see if there was any opening or space where that sound could be coming from. She reached her other hand in, waving it back and forth, trying to feel for any breeze. Feeling nothing, she lowered her hand, feeling the bricks that made up the floor toward the back, seeing if any of them felt cold. She was surprised when one of them moved under her touch.

Readjusting her position for better balance, she nudged the brick again, realizing that it was, in fact, loose. For a moment, she figured it was likely loose from time, the mortar giving way. She drew her hand back when she heard the strange breathy whistle again. She reached back for the brick when suddenly she had a clear vision of leather ledgers. A leather pouch. She knew as she knew her own name that they were underneath that loose brick.

With feverish movements, she reached in with both hands to dig out that loose brick that was buried with dirt and time. Finally, it came free, and sure enough, there was space beneath it, cold air coming up out of it. Another brick came loose, and she tossed it, too, aside.

"Wow," she breathed, feeling as though she'd just unearthed a pirate treasure.

Reaching inside, she was startled to feel cold metal, not soft leather. Face screwed up in focused concentration, her fingers did the exploring as she tried to figure out what she was feeling and how to get it out. It was a tight space, and not being able to see what she was working with, it took time to feel it all out.

It was a metal box, not very big, perhaps eight inches wide by three inches long and two inches deep. She got her fingers around it, and as though playing a life-sized game of Operation, she pulled it out. She set it aside, as she'd felt other things, so she put her hand back into the hole. There was another metal box, this one bigger, sturdier metal. That one took some more maneuvering, but finally, she pulled it out. It was about ten inches by six inches and heavy.

"What the hell is in there?" she muttered, looking at the two boxes placed side by side on the floor beyond the fireplace.

She reached back in to see if there was anything

else and felt something tucked against the side, something cool and smooth, though not metal. She realized they were record albums. Pulling them out, there were three Maria Callas records.

Chapter Eleven

"There is not a single coin or bill here later than 1976." Lexi held one of the dollar bills up closer to her bespectacled gaze to examine it better. The smaller of the two metal boxes lay open on the makeshift table at the back of the main level of the house. Inside that box had been a collection of bills and coins, adding up to forty-eight dollars in one- and five-dollar bills and then two dollars and thirty-eight cents in random coins. Lexi put the bill down on the stack she'd already gone through and grabbed one of the final few. "It all seems to range from the nineteen fifties to the late seventies."

"Nineteen forty-three!" Colten, one of the production assistants, crowed, holding up a dime.

"Fine. Not that *one*," Lexi growled, rolling her eyes.

"This puppy has got to be worth a shitload," Cary said, carefully handling the revolver that had been in the larger metal box, wrapped in a cloth.

Feeling a bit overwhelmed, Sam stood back, watching everyone marvel over her find. She and Cary had found a plethora of strange—and sometimes valuable—treasures during their renovations. But for some reason, this one made her feel deeply unsettled, nauseated even. Her attention was drawn to Tandy, who examined one of the record albums, her features tight, as though she were desperately trying to hold in her emotions. What those were, Sam had no idea.

Finally, Tandy set the album atop the other two that lay on the table and left the room, heading out the back door. Sam reached over and touched Cary's arm. Once he glanced at her, she gave him the look they'd exchanged many times during treasure finds. *Don't let this stuff out of your sight.* He nodded, understanding in his eyes, so Sam left, following in the direction Tandy had gone.

It was a chilly February afternoon that found Tandy sitting atop the weathered picnic table beside the house. Sam, hands tucked into the hip pockets of her jeans, walked slowly toward her, watching for any sign that her presence wasn't wanted. Getting no such sign, she walked to the table, stopping a few feet shy of it. Tandy sat, hugging herself. She looked so small and sad.

"Hey," Sam said softly. When Tandy glanced her way, she gave her a small smile. "How you doin'?"

Tandy shrugged and let out a sigh. "I'm okay." She returned the smile, though hers was tight. "You know, I've always been drawn to this house." Tandy looked up at the mammoth structure before looking back to Sam. "I don't know why. I've always felt this deep-seeded need to make things right here."

Sam took a couple of steps closer, the bench seat of the picnic table lightly touching just below her knees. "What do you mean? In renovation?"

"I guess." She let out a chuckle. "I don't know how else I'd mean. I don't really know. Yeah," she added after a moment of thought. "I guess renovation, bringing it back to life." She studied Sam for a moment, a serene smile gracing her lips. "I was so excited when you guys decided to take Whitney Grove on. Honestly, I didn't so much care about the show aspect of it, but I really wanted you and Cary on this."

Sam smiled and climbed up to sit on the table next to her, hands buried between her closed thighs for warmth. She wished she'd brought her fleece downstairs with her when she'd shared her finds with everyone after lunch. "Why? And you don't like our show?" she asked dramatically.

Tandy laughed and nodded. "Love it. That's how I knew who you were," she said, lightly bumping Sam's shoulder with her own. "No, I just saw how much you two love what you do, how good you are at it." She met Sam's gaze, almost as though searching it. "How much you care about the house you're bringing back to life."

Sam looked into Tandy's eyes, feeling as though she had done that a million times before. Again, that familiarity gripped her, like a hand around her throat. She cleared it a few times as she looked away, Tandy's gaze too intense for her to handle. "We do love what we do." Sam looked at the house, noting Cary was walking out to his rental car, the things she'd found in his hands. She was glad he was locking it all away so the crew could get back to work and nothing would go missing.

"How did you guys get started? Did the network throw you together?" Tandy asked, garnering Sam's attention again.

"No. Cary and I have known each other for years. We actually met for the first time at sixteen," she explained.

"Wow," Tandy said, eyes wide. "At school?"

"Nope, at Hardee's, when they were still every-where. We worked there. I could not stand that pretty boy ass," she added with a grin. "We only worked together for a few months before he got fired. He called off one too many times. Latah!" she said with a dramatic wave of her hand.

Tandy threw her head back in laughter. "Love it."

"So, zoom ahead three years, and we end up in a class together at WSU in Spokane. We had to work on a project together, and lucky for him, though still a pretty boy ass, he'd grown up enough I could tolerate him." Sam grinned.

"Did you guys date at all or just friends?" Tandy rested an elbow on her knee so her cheek could rest in an upturned palm as she looked at Sam.

"We tried dating. It lasted for about two weeks before I realized how utterly repulsed I was sexually by him, not that we ever had sex. The one and only time we tried to get physical, we made out on my couch and he took his shirt off. I mean, I've got Brad Pitt sitting in my living room half naked, and I wanted to be anywhere but there," Sam exclaimed, Tandy laughing. "I knew something was very wrong. Needless to say, within a month, I came out."

"Gold star then, I take it?" Tandy asked.

Surprised by the question and knowledge of such a thing from Tandy, Sam nodded. "Oh so proudly."

"I wish I could say the same. I actually got married."

Sam was taken aback, not wanting to assume, but she thought she heard Tandy say in an off-hand way that she wasn't as straight as she may appear. Rather than continuing that assumption, she said, "What happened? You kinda sound like you didn't want to, so why did you?"

"Because he made the mistake in saying I wouldn't," Tandy said simply.

Sam burst into laughter, clapping in delight. She also loved the shit-eating grin on Tandy's face and the fire in her eyes. "How long did that last?" she asked through her laughter.

"Until the first time he pissed me off." Tandy waited a beat. "Three days."

Sam was off and laughing again, this time Tandy joining her.

Their laughter apparently caught Cary's attention; he didn't head back into the house through the front door whence he'd come, but instead circled from his car parked at the curb around the side of the house to where the women sat. "What did I miss?" he asked good-naturedly, hands on narrow hips as he stepped up to the table.

Sam glanced at him, bringing up a hand to wipe at her tears of amusement. "We were laughing at our horrid attempts with the male species."

He grinned. "Oh, yeah? So, I'm assuming you told her about our romantic evening on your avocado-green couch then? I mean," he said smugly, "considering I was your one and only."

"Oh, yeah," Sam said through fresh laugher, which Tandy joined in with. "You taught me right quick that I found you outright revolting."

He nodded, jaw clenched. "Uh-huh," he said, before setting his gaze on Tandy. "Have I told you how incredibly inspirational she can be? Truly *amazing* when it comes to building up others' self-esteem," he said, even as he reached to playfully push Sam away with a hand to her forehead.

She batted his hand away, grinning as she accepted a kiss to the forehead instead and his arm, which he flung casually over her shoulders.

"It was horrible," he agreed. "But it worked out. I ended up dating her roommate Charles, and she fucked my sister. All good."

"So, how did you guys end up doing what you're doing now?" Tandy asked, clearly amused by the pair.

"Well, I got my degree in architecture, and she got hers in history. She went into teaching and hated it, I went into architecture and hated it, so we decided on a whim to buy an old clunker of a house where we lived, and…" He shrugged.

"We put our knowledge together and turned it into the gorgeous 1930 craftsman bungalow that it had once been," Sam continued.

"Didn't make a fortune on it," Cary added, he and Sam sharing a knowing smile. "Still too green to avoid costly pitfalls, but we made enough of a profit to realize that we were stupid enough to try it again."

Tandy chuckled. "I know that feeling."

"So, he got licensed as a contractor," Sam said, hitching her thumb in Cary's direction, "and we went in full tilt. We started flipping houses and selling them, but then as our reputation grew in our historic renovations, people started calling us to renovate their own homes."

"Four years ago," Cary said, picking up the story. "We were contacted by producers at the network, and our show was born."

"That's a great story. You guys are amazing together, like twins or something." Tandy looked from one to the other. "Even finish each other's sentences."

"Yeah, well, she's the evil twin." Cary tugged playfully on Sam's neck. Sam simply nodded in agreement. He squeezed Sam's shoulder before stepping away. "Let's get back to work, ladies," he said with an exaggerated lisp and sashay as he walked toward the house.

Sam grinned, shaking her head. "See what I have to put up with?" she asked Tandy. "The pesky brother I never had."

"Do you have sisters?" Tandy tugged her flannel free from where it was still tied around her waist and slid her arms into the sleeves.

"I do. I'm the middle one. I'm closer to the baby Lorne, but our oldest sister Theresa is aptly named, as she's married to her preacher husband and the endless stream of children 'God has given them' over in the Midwest. You know, a place where they like to wear their stupid red baseball caps that have even more stupid slogans on them," Sam said dryly.

"You mean like *Make Cheese Grate Again*?" Tandy asked, that same feisty fire in her eyes as before.

Sam burst into laughter. "Just like that, yes. What about you?"

"Nope. Lonely only. Well," Tandy added, "my dad was married for a while, and she had a couple of kids, but I was back and forth between Colorado and New York so often, I never really got super close to them. And," she said with a shrug, "they were younger than me. So, by the time he divorced Bonnie..."

"The bond just wasn't there to stay in touch," Sam finished, Tandy nodding. "And your mom had no more kids then?"

Tandy shook her head. "She was really focused on her career. She's a wonderful mother, though. I'm really close with her and with my dad. Love them a lot."

"Mind if I ask why you seemed so upset when I brought that stuff down I found today?" Sam asked gently. Tandy was quiet for so long, Sam thought perhaps she shouldn't have asked the question. She was about to change the subject when Tandy's soft voice rent the air.

"A woman was murdered here," she began. She met Sam's gaze. "She won't really talk about it, but she was my mom's best friend. Those are her things you found."

❧❧❧❧

Chewing on her bottom lip, Sam glanced at the serial number she'd written down that the man at the antique gun shop had given her. He gave her suggestions of where to go to find the history of the gun, who bought it, when, and where. The shop owner had told her the revolver was in remarkably good shape, likely still shootable and, in its current condition, was worth about twenty-two hundred dollars. He did, however, tell her that if there was anyone famous connected to the gun or if a famous engraver had made the fancy ivory grips with a rose carved in them, it may bump up the price.

Truth was, Sam wasn't looking for money out of the piece. Tandy had told her to keep it, as she detested firearms. She said she was going to give the albums and money to her mother. For her part, Sam wanted to trace the gun back to its rightful family. Tandy didn't know the name of her mother's friend who'd been killed, saying her mother said it was all too painful to talk about, and she'd not been able to find much about it online, which she found surprising. So, now at nearly eleven thirty, Sam couldn't sleep, so she was up doing research.

According to the records from the Colt manu-
facturer, at extra cost and upon the behest of the purchaser, the gun had been delivered to local engraver
Louis Daniel Nimschke for commissioned grip work
before being delivered to said purchaser, a Little, Sally
in Denver, Colorado, in 1888.

"Why do I know that name?" Sam muttered.

Rubbing her chin, she opened a new window
and went to her email, scrolling until she found Lexi's
email regarding the history of the house.

"Holy shit," she breathed. She glanced over at
the so-called Peacemaker, which sat on the bed atop
the metal box it had been kept in. "You belong to the
builder of that house?" she asked, clearly not expecting
a reply. "How the hell did Tandy's mom's friend get
hold of you?'

Now she was more than curious, she had to
know.

❧ ❧ ❧ ❧

Sam looked around, hitching her messenger bag
up higher on her shoulder. The place was seriously
sketchy as she climbed the stairs to the fourth floor.
The elevator had an *OUT OF ORDER* sign glued to it,
and the paper had yellowed, so Sam had to wonder if
it had worked since the building had been built in the
sixties.

From the looks of things, part of her wished
she'd taken Cary up on his self-invite to go along.
But alas, she was there and had to pick up her pace
and stop rubbernecking the various pockets of human
drama she'd passed or she'd be late.

Glancing down at the text message with the

address, she made note of the apartment number one last time before walking down the dimly lit hallway. The walls were covered in old cigarette smoke and time-stained wallpaper of a hideous design. The carpeting looked like what would be found in the worst and cheapest motels. She felt like she'd stepped into an episode of *American Horror Story*. Ironically, the weight in her messenger bag didn't make her feel much better, but she did take mental note of which pocket she'd placed her can of pepper spray in.

She found the corresponding door and stopped, pulling off one of her gloves to raise her fist to rap three times on the door. She glanced surreptitiously to her left in the direction she'd come when she heard a man's loud voice coming up the stairs. A moment later, his head popped over the top of the stairs followed by his body, replete with what looked to be a toilet bowl cleaning brush he was waving around as though conducting his own private orchestra. It became clear to her that he was involved in an extensive conversation with himself. She swallowed nervously and hoped her knock would be answered soon.

Finally, and to her relief, she heard footfalls on the opposite side of the door. As a litany of locks were undone—she felt like she was back in New York—the door finally opened. A woman stood on the other side, her hair clearly the victim of a terrible battle with red Kool-Aid and ratted into a beehive. Her makeup was heavy and caked into the crevices of her face, which looked to be aged far beyond her years, perhaps a life of bad vices had helped with that. Her eyebrows were painted on, giving her the frozen expression of constant shock and surprise. She was dressed in simple jeans and a satin blouse that made her bony shoulders look like the arms of a clothes hanger.

"Mrs. Martin?" Sam asked, hoping she was in the right place. She didn't want to have to turn around and leave as Mr. Chatty Man scrubbed a doorknob near the stairs with the toilet brush.

"Are you the reporter?" the older woman asked.

"I'm Samantha Leyton, ma'am. We spoke on the phone."

"Right, right, come in." The woman turned and left the door open, her steps slow and wobbly as she walked back deeper into the apartment. Assuming she was to follow, Sam closed and locked the door before following.

The apartment was lit about as well as the hallway, the tiny entryway opening up into a galley-style kitchen to the left, separated from the living room by a wall with a service window and bar cut out of it. The living room was to the right, small and square with a darkened hallway leading from it; Sam assumed the bedroom and bathroom were down that way.

The furniture looked like it had come directly from a Sears catalog in 1968, as did the carpet. Her hostess made her way to the couch upholstered in a horrid gold material that looked like it was once a Muppet. It was indicated by a flick of the woman's wrist that Sam should sit in the matching armchair, which she did, her messenger bag held in her lap.

"Don't know why you're here, Miss Leyton," she said, reaching over to the large glass ashtray sitting on the end table next to the couch. "It's been forty years or somethin'. Hell." She smirked, bringing the lit cigarette to red painted lips. "Not like you guys gave much of a damn back then anyway."

"Almost forty-two years," Sam muttered

absently, her gaze on the cigarette the woman was taking a drag from. "Thought you quit." The words were out of her mouth before she knew what she was saying. All she could do was watch the woman sitting to her right. When all she did was take a deep drag then blow the exhaled smoke out from between her lips and out her nostrils in Sam's general direction, Sam looked away, partially in dread of the disgusting smell headed her way. "I'm sorry, Mrs. Martin. I have no idea why I said that."

"Esther." When Sam met her gaze, the older woman continued, "Call me Esther, and you sound like my daughter." She smirked again, looking over to the ashtray once more as she used a finger to tap excess ash off the tip of the cigarette. "What do you want to know? You doing some sort of follow-up story or something?"

"I'm not a reporter, Esther," Sam said. "As I explained on the phone, I'm working on a renovation of Whitney Grove, and I found something that belongs to you. Well," she added with a small smile, "belongs to your husband, Harold Martin. I found him through genealogical records."

"*Ex*-husband," Esther corrected. "But," she said, bringing the cigarette back to her lips for a long drag before crushing the stub in the ashtray. "He's dead. Died of AIDS in eighty-six. Why were you looking for him? What could possibly belong to that son of a bitch? He left me for a man, did you know that?" Her eyes, which were already small, seemed even smaller wrapped in a thick band of eyeliner and fake eyelashes as she eyed Sam. "Abandoned me, abandoned his kid. Bastard."

Sam wasn't sure what to say for a moment, other

than she couldn't help but wonder why the woman wasn't over it yet, considering the guy had been dead for thirty-some years. She tossed those thoughts aside and unlatched her messenger bag, holding it open with one hand as she reached inside to grab the metal box that the gun resided in.

"I came upon a little hiding spot in a false fireplace on the third floor of Whitney Grove—"

"What the hell is a Whitney Grove?" Esther demanded, pulling a fresh cigarette out of the pack sitting on the coffee table.

"Oh, uh, sorry." Sam slowly slid the metal box from her bag and set the bag on the carpet at her feet. "It's the house we're renovating. Your daughter once lived there."

"She was murdered there, ya mean!" Esther exclaimed, shooting forward in her seat for a moment as she slammed her hand on the cushion beside her. "They questioned me about it," she said conversationally, lighting the fresh cigarette as she gave Sam a side glance. "Can you believe that shit?" she blew out with the exhaled smoke.

Sam stared at her, for reasons she couldn't explain, disgust bobbed in her belly, making her feel a bit nauseated. "Why would they question you?" she asked, her voice low and steady, a tone that sounded foreign to her own ears.

"Because that rat bastard told 'em about us," Esther spat, her eyes narrowing in anger and seeming hatred.

Sam studied her for a moment, not sure what to say. She had no idea who Esther was talking about or what she was talking about, but again, without her permission, words tumbled out of her mouth. "The secret."

Esther blew out more smoke, her eyes never leaving Sam. "Pardon?"

"She said you two had a secret."

Esther studied her for a long moment, taking deep drag after deep drag. "I know you didn't know Sonia, you're too young. You went to school or something with Chloe, didn't you?"

Sam looked at her, confused. She felt like she'd just left the room to go to the bathroom and had returned mid-conversation. "Chloe? I don't know a Chloe."

Esther blew out a long, slow stream of smoke. "Sure," she said finally, sarcasm in her voice. "What, is she still pissed at me for giving her to my cousin to raise? I mean, what am I supposed to do? A five-year-old kid ain't easy. They get into everything, and I'm trying to work, have a life..." She seemed to be waiting for some sort of sympathy from Sam, but when nothing was forthcoming, she looked away. "I knew Patti would do a better job than I could ever do." She snubbed out her second cigarette. "You know what really got me, Samantha? Here it was, *my* kid who got herself killed, her daughter left without a mother, so I stepped in to do what I could, and Sonia's own husband is rotting in prison to this day for it." She looked at Sam, eyes wide. "What about me? Where's the goddamn sympathy for what I was going through?"

Sam fought against her sense of repulsion. More out of politeness than anything, she asked, "How did Sonia die?"

Esther snorted. "Clearly, you're not a mother to ask something so asinine. I didn't ask, didn't wanna know. I mean, honestly, what kind of mother wants to have that image floating around in her mind until her dying day?"

Sam cleared her throat as she sat up straighter. "Well, Esther, I came by to give this to you. It belonged to Sonia—"

"Unless it's a stack of cash, I don't want it," Esther spat, pushing to her feet. Clearly, the meeting was over. "I have to live with all this as it is."

Stunned, Sam stared up at her for a moment, then pushed the metal box fully back into the bag and latched it. She got to her feet and hitched the bag's strap over her shoulder. "Okay." She headed to the door, followed by Esther. Door unlocked and standing open, Sam looked back at the older woman who met her gaze. "Take care of yourself," she said softly, then stepped out into the hall.

Door closed soundly behind her, Sam's eyes fell closed and her hands came up for a moment to cover her face. She took a deep breath, then hurried down the hall toward the stairs, trotting down the three levels to the main floor, where she nearly sprinted to the front door of the building.

The night was cold, and she was glad because she could feel rising emotion heat up her face and body. She hurried to her rental car, pressing the button on the small handheld remote and climbed in, locking the doors. No sooner had she set the messenger bag on the passenger seat beside her than the tears came, hot and fast. Her shoulders heaved as her sobs rent the air in the closed cab of the car. She cried for things she knew she didn't fully understand, but the emotions were strong and palpable. She cried out of confusion, and she cried out of a grief that made little sense.

She cried out in fright as someone tapped on the driver's side window. Eyes still heavy with tears, she looked to see the man from the hallway earlier standing at her window. He held his toilet brush in his hand, likely what he'd used to tap at her window.

"He's coming!" he said, voice muffled through the glass.

Sam said nothing, simply stared at him, feeling very afraid.

"He's coming!" he said again, his gaze boring into Sam's. He grinned, many of his teeth broken or missing. "He travels from afar." With those foreboding words, he turned, ranting into the night as he went.

Sam watched him go for a moment before she shook herself out of her trance and used the sleeve of her jacket to wipe the tears from her face. She got the car started and headed out.

Chapter Twelve

So, K&T, better known as knob and tube, is a type of wiring that started in these old houses around 1880, so not long after this gorgeous lady was built," Sam explained, indicating the room around her. "It was a common type used until just before the end of World War II. The problem is," she continued, "this place was loaded with it. So, we have to strip it all out and update it. Super expensive, but super necessary, so says the law." She looked directly into the camera. "I mean, hello, can you say fire?" She gave her signature grin. "So, K&T taken care of, plumbing ripped out and updated, to include and not limited to," she added dramatically, "heated floors in all nine bathrooms. New HVAC system, well," she grinned, "make that three of them, all cleverly hidden to retain the original charm and historic look of Whitney Grove." She clapped her hands before rubbing them together with an evil grin. "You know what that means."

"Okay, we got it!" Dave said, stepping out from behind the camera.

"Great. And this one will cut to Tandy and I shopping, right?" Sam pushed up from the seat that was set up in a room on the main floor of the house for the cast to do their interviews, where they talked about what project they were working on, interpersonal issues, or anything else the audience needed to know.

"Yes, ma'am," Dave said, accepting the boom mic from the sound technician so she could get her sound gear in order. "You heading out now with Little-Miss-Hot-As-Hell?" he asked, wiggling his eyebrows suggestively.

Sam rolled her eyes. She'd done her best to keep her rising attraction to Tandy under wraps, but the production crew knew her well. "Shut the hell up," she muttered, walking out of the room, followed by the laughter of the small crew that had just committed her interview to film.

Among the sounds of music, table saws, and people yelling to one another over the noise and distance of floors between them, Sam wandered through the main floor looking for Tandy. It was amazing, the difference of a month and a half. The house had been completely demoed, floors ripped out where they were going to be replaced, the original walls—best they could tell—framed and on their way to being drywalled. A rat-infested disaster was slowly blossoming into the beautiful flower she once was.

"Cary!" Sam called out, seeing him trot down the main stairway from the second floor to the main floor. He glanced at her, pencil tucked behind his ear and his project notebook in hand. "You seen Tandy?" she asked, hands on hips.

"You mean the woman standing right behind you?" He indicated her with a nod.

Sam glanced over her shoulder, and sure enough, Tandy Becker stood behind her with a grin and a little finger wave.

"Oh." Sam turned fully to face Tandy, shoving her hands into the pockets of her cargo pants, feeling shy. "Hi there."

"Hi, yourself," Tandy said, chuckling. "I think we were playing hide-and-seek. I was looking for you, too."

"Ready to go?" Sam reached up to rub the back of her neck as she felt her face reddening. *I am not twelve years old. This is ridiculous!*

"Sam, before you go."

Sam turned back to Cary to see him holding out something in his hand. She took it and saw it was a flyer for a security service.

"Maybe not a bad idea to give 'em a buzz," Cary said before hurrying on past the two women and farther into the great room.

Sam folded the paper and slid it into a pocket as she turned to Tandy again. "Sorry. Ready?"

"I am, but I wanted to show you something I found today." Tandy turned and led the way to what would be the formal dining room. There, at the center of the empty room stood a double-sided ladder with a two-foot-square platform dividing the two sides. Over weeks and weeks of painstaking work, Tandy had uncovered a marvelous mural painted on the dining room ceiling.

"Wow," Sam whispered, looking up as they walked toward the ladder. "This is incredible."

"Isn't it, though?" Tandy gripped the frame of one side of the ladder as she climbed one side, Sam climbing the other. The two spared a glance at the top over the platform before returning their attention to the mural just a few feet over their heads. "I've only gotten it cleaned, and I'll start any touch-ups or reworks next week."

"You've done such an exquisite job," Sam said softly, meeting those gorgeous green-gray eyes.

"Truly. I'm amazed how just about every day I walk into this place and in every room a new work of art is exposed, displayed, revealed once more. You know?"

Tandy nodded. "I do. This house was screaming for attention," she added, voice just as soft as she looked around the room. "She's been hidden far too long behind neglect and the shadows of secrets within her walls."

A slow smile spread across Sam's lips. "You know, that's always how I've seen buildings and houses, too. Doesn't matter how big or how small, how grand or how simple. There's a story inside each and every one of them, and it deserves to be told." The look that Tandy gave Sam made her feel unworthy of the attention of such a beautiful, amazing woman. The look was filled with wonder, excitement, and seeming affection. Sam cleared her throat and looked away, no longer able to look into those incredible eyes.

"What I wanted to show you in this beautiful scene of soul redemption is this angel." She braced herself on the ladder with one hand on the frame while reaching up with the other to lightly trace the figure with her finger. "Isn't that spectacular?"

Sam focused on it, her gaze zeroing in on the angel's face. Wide blue eyes looked back at her, so human in their expression. "She's beautiful. This doesn't seem like just the musings from a commissioned artist's mind," Sam said, glancing at Tandy. "You know?"

Tandy nodded, looking at her. "I agree. I think this was a homage to someone very special." She looked back to the angel. "I'm so drawn to it." They spent a moment studying the piece before finally Tandy smiled at her. "Okay, ready?"

≈≈≈≈≈

"Well," Tandy explained, driving her baby blue 1959 Ford pickup expertly through Denver traffic. "I spent a lot of summers here with my dad and his family or sometimes during the school year when my mom had a work thing." She slowed the old truck for a red light. "So, yes, I definitely have a connection to Colorado."

"Were your parents ever married? Do they get along?" Sam glanced over at Tandy, who was driving them back to the house after they'd spent the previous two hours at a variety of antique furniture dealers. The crew had gotten what they'd needed and had packed up and headed back to the house.

"They adore each other," Tandy said, her gaze focused on the road as she got them moving again, even as a peaceful smile crossed her lips. "They're best friends, really. They were never married, never even dated. Mom explained it that one night when he was there for her when she needed him most, things just crossed a line neither of them ever intended to broach."

"Uh-oh," Sam said, grinning. "Guessing you were the permanent mark of that line?"

Tandy chuckled and nodded. "Yup."

"That's amazing that after such an unexpected thing to happen between them, let alone a pregnancy, that they were able to remain friends," Sam said, finding the situation interesting.

"Dad said it actually brought them closer." Tandy was quiet for a moment before she spared a glance at Sam. "Can I show you something?"

Surprised by the question seemingly out of

nowhere, Sam nodded. "Of course."

The smile Tandy gave her was worth anything Sam had just agreed to. "You sure you have a few minutes? I know you're a busy girl."

"Yeah, let's do it."

Surprising Sam once again, Tandy turned the old truck so quickly into a parking lot to get them turned around, they left rubber on the road. In a world before *Oh, shit!* handles, Sam's hands braced against the dashboard during the erratic move. Tandy burst into laughter as she got the wheel straightened and the truck heading in the direction she wanted it to.

"Sorry." Tandy grinned. "Guess I'm a little excited." She glanced over at Sam, who was just releasing her death grip. "Believe it or not, I don't have a lot of people in my life who truly appreciate the personality of a home like we do."

"It's okay." Sam made a show of removing one hand at a time from the dashboard, making a suction cup sound with each hand, which sent Tandy into more delightful giggles.

Ten minutes later, Tandy pulled the old Ford into a quiet, older neighborhood with homes that looked to have been built in the thirties and forties. Most were well-kept and maintained with postage stamp-sized front yards. The trees were large and plentiful, giving the street a Norman Rockwell feel.

Finally, Tandy pulled into the driveway of a medium-sized brick house with a charming front porch and detached garage that sat a bit behind the house. The house was immaculate, the yard, which was mostly dead from the harsh winter months, was clearly well taken care of with planters and neatly edged lawn. Sam had no doubt that it would burst into beautiful colors come spring and summer.

"Whose place is this?" Sam climbed out of the truck and pushed the door closed.

"Mine." Tandy walked in front of the parked truck toward the side door to the house as she sorted through her keys.

"This is great," Sam murmured, her mind spinning with all the improvements that had clearly been made to the house, especially once they stepped inside.

A small short-haired black cat sat waiting for them, its green eyes seeming to glow against the black backdrop of its fur.

"Hi, baby!" Tandy exclaimed, picking up the cat and raining kisses on its head.

"Who's this?" Sam reached over to run her hand down the soft back.

"This is Cubed. Well," Tandy added, the cat jumping down from her arms and trotting deeper into the house. "Her full name is Prince Albert III." She grinned at Sam's look of confusion. "Long story."

Sam shook her head, amused, then turned her attention back to the house.

The kitchen was fully modernized with the latest appliances and gadgets, granite countertops, and updated cabinets. Even still, small touches helped keep its pre-war charm. The floors were original, she could tell, though they'd been refinished and stained a more modern darker color to add elegance to an already elegant, yet comfortable home.

"This is great, Tandy," Sam said again, following her through the home as she took in everything.

"Thank you," Tandy said, pride evident in her voice. "It's been a work in progress for about six years, but it's home."

Hands tucked casually in her pockets, Sam followed her down a hallway where they passed a bedroom set up as a guest room, a bathroom, a second bedroom, which was larger and looked more used, so Sam assumed it was Tandy's, and finally the room directly across the hall from that bedroom.

Stepping inside after Tandy, she gasped, looking around. It was a small room, square in shape, but what caught her attention were the walls. All four had been painted, transformed into a fairytale land, replete with rainbows, unicorns, and dragons in flight sending a stream of fire down at a suited knight with sword raised high overhead. A castle atop a hill took up a quarter of one wall, the detail remarkable, each stone carefully etched and carved to fit, all via the magic of paint and brushstrokes.

"This is absolutely amazing," Sam breathed, turning in a full circle slowly, taking it all in. The more she looked, the more details jumped out at her. She glanced over to Tandy, who stood back, a nervous smile on her lips. "This is extraordinary. What will you use this room for?" she asked, as it was empty, other than the stunning mural.

"The baby's room," Tandy said, hands on hips as she, too, took in her work.

Sam looked at her, for reasons she couldn't understand, feeling a bit disappointed at that information. "I didn't know you had kids," she said, keeping her tone as casual and friendly as she could. Tandy had never mentioned a spouse or significant other, so Sam had liked to pretend she was single. And available.

"I don't." Tandy met Sam's gaze, giving her

a shy smile. "I've always wanted to be a mom, but there was just never the right situation, you know? Thought I met the right person, but then she ended up having borderline personality disorder or liked to cheat or..." She smiled. "Just never worked out. So, after this project, once my part is done, I'm going to get inseminated."

Sam's eyes widened. "Really? You're gonna do it on your own, huh?"

Tandy nodded, hugging herself. "Yeah. I'll be forty in a few years, so I figure it's a good time, you know? I've got a home, settled in my career. So," she shrugged, "I guess it's just time."

"So," Sam said, looking around again. "This will all be for the baby?"

"Yup," Tandy said with that smile of pride returning.

"What a cool room." Sam's grin was large. "Super cool."

"Thanks. My dad is making a crib."

"That is really wonderful," Sam said softly. "I'm so happy for you, and I truly hope you get what you want."

"Thanks, Sam. Do you have any kids? Married?"

Sam shook her head, hooking her thumbs casually in the front hip pockets of her pants. "No. Single, and honestly, for some reason, I've always been so afraid of having kids."

"You don't want them, or...?"

"No, no, that's not it." Sam paused as she searched for the right words. "I don't know. It's like I have this feeling that if I had children, something would go terribly wrong." She met Tandy's understanding gaze. "Does that make sense?"

Tandy nodded. "It does. For the longest time, I felt like I didn't deserve to have them." She shrugged. "I don't know why, never did anything to a child, never been arrested. I don't know. Just always felt like I have a lot to make up for in this life."

"Like at the house?" Sam offered.

"Like at the house," Tandy agreed with a nod.

Sam grinned. "Maybe you were a bank robber in a past life, so now you feel the need to atone."

Tandy burst out laughing, throwing her head back and leaving the milky skin of her throat exposed. Sam forced herself to look away. "Come on, let's head back to the house."

～～～～～

Angry? Angry would be on a good day. Right now, Sam was *furious*! Unfortunately, vandalism wasn't unusual on a job site. More than once, things had gone missing, such as tools, once a claw-footed tub original to the house she'd intended to use in a different bathroom and even an HVAC had gone missing a time or two. But this? No, this wasn't opportunistic construction workers or even unethical flippers in the area cashing in. This was cruelty, plain and simple.

"Do you know of anyone who would have done this, ma'am?" the officer was asking, pulling Sam out of her thoughts as they stood in the entryway of Whitney Grove.

"No." She blew out a breath and ran a hand through her hair. "I don't know anyone here. Well," she amended, "I know some flippers and folks in the industry, but certainly no one that would do this." She indicated the direction of the dining room with a wave.

The young officer nodded, taking notes. He glanced up at her, pen still poised over his notepad. "What about any of your crew or the people working on this project? Enemies? Local issues?"

"I don't think so. We try to vet people pretty well, but I can't answer that. I can ask around, get you any information they may have," Sam said, hugging herself, desperately trying to keep her fury and upset under control. It wouldn't do to lose it with two police officers staring at her.

"All right, ma'am," he said, flipping the notebook shut. "We can step up patrols of the area, hopefully warding off any other attempts at vandalism."

She looked at him, stunned. "Attempts? Officer, I'm not sure that you realize this, but it was far more than an attempt!" *So much for not losing it.* "Some asshole came into *my* property overnight, not only busting out an expensive window to gain entry, but then they destroyed a work of art that had been painstakingly restored!" she exclaimed, once again indicating the direction of the dining room. "That's more than a hundred and thirty years old!"

"We understand, ma'am," the female officer said from where she stood near the front door. "We're only suggesting that with more patrols of the area, hopefully, we can dissuade anyone from targeting this property again."

Sam nodded, though not remotely mollified. From her experience, she knew there was nothing legally the police could do, as there was no video, no photographic proof of any kind of who had done the damage, but it still left her feeling angry and unsatisfied, as it always did.

Walking the officers out, Sam noted that Cary was pulling up as the two loaded into their squad car. She stood on the front porch, waiting as he parked and climbed out of the rental car, even as he watched them drive away, confusion on his face.

"What the hell happened?" He headed her way, his ever-present venti caramel macchiato, no whip, in hand and his notebook tucked under his other arm.

"Goddamn vandals," she responded. "Destroyed the mural in the dining room. I don't have the heart to call Tandy."

Cary stopped just shy of the steps. His shoulders slumped. "No fucking way."

"Way."

"Did they do this, too?" He raised his paper coffee cup in the direction of a small broken side window.

Sam nodded.

"Son of a bitch." He walked up the stairs and stood next to her. "Anything taken?"

"Strangely, no. It seems like it was purely about vandalism. Thank god Tandy took tons of pictures as she restored the ceiling." Sam led the way inside, Cary following to the dining room. The scaffolding that Tandy had been using had been rolled from the wall where she usually left it to the center of the room. Clearly, whoever had done the damage had used it.

Something had been smeared across the uncovered and cleaned mural. It looked like ketchup or some sort of sauce as opposed to paint. The person had also taken a screwdriver to stab at the mural, the tool left stuck in the ceiling, right into the head of the angel.

"Jesus," Cary murmured, standing next to Sam,

both focused on the ceiling. "Can this be fixed? I mean, look, even the medallion was cracked."

"I know," Sam said, taking in the decorative plaster plate that encircled the dining room light once it was affixed to the ceiling. "It's going to be costly, but yes, it can be fixed."

"Fuck," Cary whispered, letting out a heavy sigh as he took a drink of his coffee. "Well, what do you want to do?"

"I think we need to put up some cameras or something. I mean, the cops said they'd up patrols, but you know as well as I do that doesn't always stop these bastards."

"Want to try that surveillance company? Do you still have the card?" he asked.

Sam smirked. "What, a rent-a-cop?"

"If you have a better idea, I'd love to hear it. This is serious." He pointed at the ceiling. "This wasn't some jackass stealing tools. This was deliberate and malicious vandalism. Maybe somebody's pissed at Tandy or something since it seems her work was targeted."

Knowing he was right, Sam nodded. "All right. Let's talk to her and see what she says, then go from there."

☙ ☙ ☙ ☙

Sam stood next to Tandy, able to feel her anger like heat off a stove. She glanced at her to see her jaw set and arms crossed over her chest. Feeling her own anger build all over again, Sam turned back to watch Cary talking with Fred Carpenter, the security guard who had been assigned to the location. Earlier that day, the owner of the company Tandy's mother had hired, Sandra Rancor, had used her skills as a technology expert and had installed cameras and sensors where she and Cary decided would be best.

"This can all be fixed, right?" Sam asked softly, mostly for something to say than because she needed the knowledge.

Tandy looked at her, expression hard. "It can be fixed," she said, voice low. "But that's not what I'm angry about. Hasn't this house known enough damn betrayal?" she asked before storming from the room. Sam watched her go, feeling helpless.

"Hey."

Sam turned to see Cary walking over to her, the security guard leaving the room. "How'd it go?"

"Good. I think Frank will do a good job." Cary watched as the middle-aged man walked away, his dark blue security guard uniform identifying his profession. "He'll show up at eight and stay until five in the morning Monday through Friday." He shrugged. "Figure that gives us a good spread, you know?"

"Sure. What about weekends?"

"About that," he said, giving her a boyish grin.

≈≈≈≈

"We have plenty of crew members," Sam muttered, imitating Cary's voice as best she could. "We can all take turns." She grunted as she whipped out the folded sheet to cover the cot that had been brought in. "You can take the first night, Sammy," she muttered, making a childish face.

The electricity had been restored in the house, as well as all the gas and water. The "fake" fireplace had been converted into a working gas fireplace, and the small room it was in was the one Sam chose to stay in for the night. She knew it wouldn't be much to warm it up in there, and she felt a bit safer rather than in a huge, open room downstairs.

She had her computer with her, and it was hooked up to the cameras around the property so she could keep an eye on things. She only had to stay until the crew arrived to work in the morning around seven.

The fireplace was making the room nice and toasty on the chilly night as Sam finished making up the cot. She'd brought a book to read, a flashlight, and the Colt .45. As she was about to spread out the comforter, she noticed movement in one of the small squares on the monitor, nine of them in total, each showing a different view of the house, six outside, three inside. She saw headlights as a vehicle pulled up to the house. She grinned when she realized it was a 1959 Ford pickup.

Trotting down the endless staircase, Sam met up with Tandy at the halfway point, the redhead carrying bags from a fast food place. She held them up. "Hungry?"

The two sat facing each other on the cot, Sam straddling the narrow bed while Tandy sat cross-legged.

Sam crumpled up the wrapper after eating the last bite of burger, throwing the wrapper into the paper bag the food had come in. "Mya couldn't take me traveling so much," she said, after swallowing her food. She took a long sip from her fountain drink to wash it down. "I think she got lonely or jealous."

"Or both?" Tandy offered with a raised eyebrow, a ketchup-slathered French fry halfway to her mouth.

"From how you described her, she seems like the jealous type."

"You could be totally right," Sam conceded, grabbing her own French fry. "What about you? You said you've been single now for a few years. Why so long?"

"Honestly?" Tandy asked before tossing the fries into her mouth and chewing thoughtfully. She took a sip of her drink before responding. "I got sick of the bullshit. I got tired of women who don't know what they want, are codependent, stuff like that. I honestly thought by the time I hit my thirties, certainly mid- to late thirties, people had their lives together." She smirked. "Guess not. So," she added, tossing the empty carton from her fries into the paper bag followed by the wrapped last few uneaten bites of her chicken sandwich. "Now I just focus on my house and my career and keep a plentiful stock of double A batteries."

It took Sam a second to get the last part, but when she did, she choked on the drink of Coke she'd just taken, coughing loudly as her lungs burned. Grinning, Tandy slapped her back.

"Please don't die on me." She chuckled. "I need you to finish the house."

"Feeling the love here," Sam gasped, making Tandy laugh.

An hour and a half later, Sam walked Tandy to the door.

"You're sure you're okay?" Tandy asked, her hand on the doorlatch of the front door.

"Yeah, I'll be fine. At this point, it's only a handful of hours, you know?" Sam gave Tandy a reassuring smile, even as she was feeling a bit nervous. Truth was, she didn't want Tandy to leave for a whole host of reasons but knew she was part of the crew to arrive early in the morning to relieve Sam. "Thanks so much for bringing me dinner. I have to admit, a Whopper was a whole lot better than the peanut butter and jelly sandwich I'd brought."

Tandy grinned. "You can pay me back when it's my turn next weekend." She surprised Sam by taking her in a warm, lingering hug, which Sam returned. "If you need anything, don't hesitate to call. I can be here in, like, seven minutes. Thanks for doing this for me," Tandy murmured into the hug.

Sam's eyes fell closed as she nodded. The feeling of Tandy's warmth, the smell of her skin and hair, the sound of her soft voice in her ear all sent delicious chills through her. "Absolutely," she murmured in response. Her stomach did an entire flip-flop when a soft kiss was left on her cheek, then Tandy slowly moved away. Sam met her gaze, which held for a long moment before Tandy turned away, letting herself out of the house.

Sam locked up once she knew Tandy was safely in her truck, it had started, and she was driving away. Letting out a long breath, Sam closed and locked the front door, leaving the entryway light on, even if it was currently a bare light bulb. She planned to leave lights on randomly throughout the house, so it was clear it wasn't the dark target it once was.

She wandered throughout the main floor, marveling at all the work that had been done. The original house—as best as they could understand, imagine and, with her own strange visions that came to her—was coming to life. She walked through the main floor, running her fingers over the intricate figures carved into the beautiful—and huge!—mantel. They all got a nice, surprised chuckle when they realized what was carved into it. Kama Sutra, Victorian style.

She continued on, making her way back to what would be the kitchen. The owner wanted it modern, a chef's dream, so it had been plumbed and wired for all the newest and greatest. She flicked on the light over the back door and made sure it was locked before she turned to head up the back stairs that would take her to the second floor. Hand on the rail and foot raised for the first step, she stopped, something catching her eye.

Stepping back away from the stairs, she glanced through the kitchen and the hall that led toward the front of the house. She peered through the shadows created by the various lights she'd turned on. She saw nothing, but she heard something. It was a small thump, almost like if a rubber ball had been lightly rolled into a wall.

"Hello?" she called out, silently cursing as she realized her phone, flashlight, and gun were upstairs. She listened but heard nothing more, so she decided to head upstairs. There was no way someone could have gotten in without breaking a window, and she'd checked them on the main floor.

Walking back to the back stairs, Sam once again lifted her foot to take the first step when she nearly had a heart attack as a dark shadow darted past her, scrambling around the corner and across the floor to disappear in the shadows.

"Jesus!" she cried, leaning back against the wall, hand to her chest. "What the hell was that?" she murmured. It had looked like it was about the size of a cat and certainly had moved like one. The thought popped into her mind that perhaps Tandy had brought her cat with her, leaving her with Sam for company and didn't tell her. "Cubed?" she called out, pushing away from the wall, making kissing sounds. "Come here, girl. Cubed?"

She walked out of the kitchen, looking into every shadow she came to, calling out for the cat. She heard and saw nothing until she was near the open door that would lead downstairs to the basement and what had once been boilers. All the updating left furnaces and hot water heaters. The laundry room had once been down there, too, but at the behest of the owner, it had been moved up to the second floor.

Peeking her head in, she looked down the long narrow set of stairs. "Cubed?" she called.

Stepping onto the small landing that led to the stairs, she braced a hand against the wall as she reached down with the other hand to flick the switch for the stairwell.

Without warning, without a sound, someone appeared behind Sam and she felt a hand plant itself at the center of her upper back between her shoulder blades and push. She grasped desperately for the railing but couldn't get a hold before her body lurched forward. She turned, as she began to fall, gasping as she saw the darkest, blackest eyes she'd ever seen. It was just that split second before she lost any bodily control and fell down the stairs like a rag doll. All she could attempt to do was keep her head tucked in, as best she could, so as not to break her neck.

She hit the basement floor hard, landing on her back, her legs still up on the stairs. She groaned as she lay there, stunned. She took a nanosecond to take a mental note of her body and didn't think anything was broken. She gasped and scrambled and her eyes bulged when she heard a sharp intake of breath and saw someone go flying down the stairs, like she'd just done.

Sam scrambled away from the stairs, her heart racing. She crab-walked backward as quickly as she could, crying out in surprise as she backed into something, her head cracking against it, dazing her again. Distantly, she realized it was the brick wall they'd built around the furnaces and hot water tanks, but her gaze was focused only on the stairs, where from her vantage point, she could just see a profile of the last two that jutted out from the wall.

The tumbling body of a woman landed on the ground, where Sam had been mere seconds before. The woman had long dark hair, and Sam could tell she was badly hurt. Sam was frozen, couldn't move as she watched horrified as the woman began to crawl, the sound of heavy footsteps clearly heard walking down the stairs. Sam glanced to the stairs, but even as the footfalls got closer to the bottom, nobody ever appeared.

Sam cried out, hand coming up to cover her mouth as the woman's head was yanked back and as of its own accord, a knife, large and deadly and held by no one, sliced across her exposed throat.

Her heart was racing so fast, Sam felt faint. Blood. So much blood. It spread out in a slow flow across the floor. Sam watched as it inched its way toward her booted foot.

"Sonia? You down here?"

Sam gasped, looking up toward the wall that hid the majority of the stairs at the distant woman's voice, calling out.

"Sonia? You got another phone call." The voice

stopped at the top of the stairs. Two heartbeats later, a curdling scream rent the air.

Sam cried out again when she felt something rub against her leg. Looking down, she saw a large black and white cat rub against her, a purr rumbling from it.

Sam's head began to bob, her vision going from color to gray to black.

Chapter Thirteen

They're on their way."

"Okay, thanks, Lexi. Sam? Can you hear me, sweetheart?"

The voice was so soft, so close, as were the cool fingers to her forehead. It slowly lulled Sam back into consciousness. She took stock of her body and surroundings, no clue where she was. Cold, she was very cold, then she realized she was lying on a cement floor. Her head was pounding, and she felt incredibly foggy.

"She comin' around?" a male voice asked from somewhere above Sam.

"I don't know. Give her space," said the soothing female voice, fingers stroking along Sam's cheek. She found herself rolling her head slightly toward the touch.

After a moment, Sam concentrated enough to slowly open her eyes. She found herself looking directly into the face of an angel. "Lark?" she whispered.

"Sam, honey, can you hear me?" the angel asked.

Suddenly, Sam gasped, realizing where she was. She tried to sit up, heart racing as she remembered the dying woman lying at the bottom of the stairs. "Have to help her!" she exclaimed, her words coming out sloppy and slow, her mouth feeling as though her tongue was three times too large. "Can't you see the blood? She's bleeding!"

"Samantha! Stay still, sweetheart!"

Sam couldn't fight against the strength of the hand holding her firmly on the ground by her shoulder.

"I think they're here," one of the female voices murmured, followed by the sound of scrambling feet on cement before pounding up wooden stairs.

"Thanks, Lexi. Just stay calm, Sam," the soothing voice said. "An ambulance is coming."

❧❧❧❧

Sam's eyes blinked open. She found herself in a nondescript curtained cubical lying on a narrow, somewhat uncomfortable bed. She felt warm fingers holding hers, and turning, she saw Tandy sitting next to the bed.

"Hey," she said, for the first time noticing that Lexi stood behind the chair Tandy sat in. "Hey, Lex. Where am I?"

"Saint Joseph's," Tandy said softly, garnering Sam's attention again. "Dave and Cary are out in the waiting room."

"Why am I here?" Sam asked, no memory of what would have put her in a hospital.

"You went a little possessed on us," Lexi said in her usual snarky way. She cocked her head slightly, which made her short, asymmetric hairstyle that much more cockeyed.

"Something happened to you down in that basement, Sam," Tandy said gently, seemingly ignoring Lexi's words. "You have a concussion and a broken wrist."

It was only then that Sam realized she had a partial cast on her left hand, which rose to a few inches below her elbow.

"Once they release you, there's someone I want you to meet," Tandy continued.

"A priest?"

"Lexi, would you please go to the waiting room and ask Cary to come in?" Tandy asked, irritation in her voice at the other woman's flippant remark. Without a word, Lexi left the cubicle after giving Sam a small squeeze to the toe of her work boot. Once they were alone, Tandy turned back to Sam, concern in her eyes. "How are you feeling?"

"Very, very woozy." Sam blinked a few times to try to focus on Tandy. "Now and then, there are one and a half of you, but I'm working on it."

"Sam, what do you remember?"

Sam did her best to truly focus, not only visually on Tandy, but also focus her thoughts on what she'd been asked. Finally, she said, "I remember you hugged me." She looked to Tandy's face to see if she'd get some confirmation that had happened and hadn't simply been another of Sam's growing list of fantasies. When she got a small smile and nod, she continued her contemplation. "There was a cat," she said. "Yeah. A cat. I was trying to find it." Her eyebrows drew together in frustration, as her mind went into a fog, memory gone. She shook her head. "That's it." She looked away from the woman holding her hand, looking off into space as something was niggling at her. "Sonia!" she said, the name bursting out of her mouth. She looked back to Tandy, whose eyes were wide. "Somebody was looking for Sonia."

"Who was?" Tandy asked gently.

Sam could only meet Tandy's gaze, her own void of answers.

❧ ❧ ❧ ❧

"Okay." Tandy looked around, hands on hips. "You have your pajamas, fresh sheets, warm blanket, and quilt." Tandy hurried to the bed and grabbed both pillows, fluffing them to the point of looking like clouds ready to burst. "Fluffed pillows." She looked at Sam, who stood in the center of the room. Her eyes got big, and she put her hands up. "Oh! Hold on."

Sam watched her go, a blur of energy, only to return a moment later, a brown stuffed monkey in her hands with a big adorable face. He was about a foot tall and plush. "This is Sprout," she said, placing the stuffed animal on the bed, head on one of the pillows. "He's seen me through a lot of bad times over the years."

Sam looked from the monkey to Tandy. "Um…"

Tandy laughed. "He's just for good luck, good energy to get you through the night when you decide to go to bed."

Sam walked over to the bed and picked Sprout up, looking him over. "Where did you get it?"

"That was a gift from my mom the first time she went to Scotland for work. She brought him back to appease the tears of an upset seven-year-old who didn't get to go because it was in the middle of the school year," Tandy explained softly, closing the few feet of distance between them as she reached out and playfully tugged on one of the toy's dangling feet.

"Did it work?" Sam asked. Even as foggy-headed as she was, she was still deeply affected by Tandy's nearness. When she'd been released from the ER, she'd gone with strict instructions of staying with someone or someone staying with her the first day and night. The network had insisted, as well. Instantly, Tandy had insisted she come stay at her house for the weekend. Sam had tried to refuse, but who was she kidding? It was where she wanted to be, anyway.

Tandy grinned. "When I was that age, any stuffed animal would work. I used to have a huge collection." She dropped her hand back to her side while giving Sam a shy look. "I still have tons in storage."

"Well, I for one would like to see them." Sam's brow scrunched as her eyes closed and she teetered on her feet. "Whoa," she muttered, feeling nauseated.

"Let's get you situated," Tandy said, taking her by the shoulders and gently nudging Sam toward the bed.

Sam allowed herself to be tucked in, making them both smile when she pulled Sprout into a hug against her side. Tandy sat on the edge of the bed.

"When you came to in the basement, you called me Lark. Who's that?" Tandy asked softly. "Is that a person?"

Sam stared up at her, trying to remember that moment, let alone who that was. "I...I have no idea."

"Okay." Tandy leaned down and left a gentle kiss on Sam's forehead. "Get some rest."

❧ ❧ ❧ ❧

Sam let out a long, slow, sleepy sigh, getting a feel for her surroundings: she was warm, comfortable, rested, and had something lying on her stomach. She also found that her left wrist throbbed with every heartbeat. The moment she was fully awake, the throbbing went from a nice little jog on the nerves to tap dancing.

"Oh, shit." She gasped, trying to even out her

breathing as every breath she took made it hurt worse. Clearly, it was time for more pain medication.

Sitting up, she winced and sucked in a breath. This broken wrist thing was going to be a pain in the ass, she could tell. Truth was, she was deeply concerned about how it had happened. She had no memory of it nor any memory of how she ended up in the basement, let alone out cold and hurt. She had to snicker, amused to see Sprout lying in her lap. She grabbed it with her good hand and held it up to her face.

"You're a good cuddler, Sprout," she said to it, it's dark, plastic eyes fixed on her and perma-smile in place. "But I think I'd prefer your mother."

Setting the toy aside, she pushed back the covers and looked around the guest bedroom. Though the blinds had been closed, it was clear nighttime resided beyond, and she groaned, realizing she'd slept the entire day away. She was happy, however, when she noticed the bottle of prescription painkillers on the bedside table sitting next to a glass of water. It hadn't been there when she'd fallen asleep, so she figured Tandy or perhaps Cary had filled it and left it for her while she was out.

It wasn't easy getting the child-proof—and clearly Sam-proof—cap off the brown prescription bottle, but finally, she did. She dug out one round white pill and popped it in her mouth, followed quickly by a drink of water. Glass in hand, she opened the bedroom door and peeked out into the hallway. The other two bedrooms were dark, as was the bathroom across the hall, but looking to the left toward the rest of the house, she could see light.

About to take a step, she realized something was

looking up at her. Smiling, she leaned down and used the fingers sticking out of the cast as best she could to touch a soft head. "Hey there, Cubed."

The black cat rubbed her head against the edge of the cast for a moment before she darted off into the dimness of Tandy's bedroom.

Padding in socked feet down the hallway toward the light, Sam found herself in the living room. Tandy was curled up in an easy chair. To her surprise, the man Sam recognized from the metaphysical fair was with her. He wore a similar outfit to what he had the first time, his turtleneck making her just as uneasy as it had the first time. She couldn't stand things even close to being around her neck. The necklace he'd given her was as far as she could go, a necklace which she absently reached up and touched as she glanced at him. She couldn't remember his name, but she'd never forget that intense gaze of his. He sat on the couch, one long arm stretched out along the back. He was the first to notice her, as the couch faced the hallway that she appeared out of. He said nothing, simply sent her a kind smile.

"Hey!" Tandy said, un-pretzeling herself from the chair and getting to her feet. She walked over to Sam, taking the emptied glass of water that Sam extended toward her. "Are you hungry? If you took one of those pain pills, you probably should get something in your tummy."

Sam smiled internally. *Tummy. So cute.* "Uh, sure."

"My dad and I made muffins a while ago. Want one?"

"Your dad?" Sam asked. Just then, they were joined by the tall ponytailed man.

"Nice to see you again," he said, extending a hand.

"You two know each other?" Tandy looked from one to the other, confusion on her face.

"No. I met him at a metaphysical fair thing," Sam said. "I'm sorry, I forgot your name."

"Stormy." He slung his arm around Tandy's shoulder, who melted into the one-armed embrace, a contented smile on her face. It was easy to see she was very close to her father. "Tandy is my little girl."

Sam smiled, dropping her hand back to her side after the brief squeeze from Stormy's hand. "I've heard a lot about you."

No doubt reading the confusion in Sam's eyes, Tandy explained, "I invited him over to talk to you. I think he can help, Sam."

"Oh. Uh, okay." Sam gave father and daughter a small, tight smile. "You mentioned muffins?"

❧❧❧❧

"Sam? Do you like sugar, too?" Tandy asked from where she stood in front of her Keurig coffeemaker, Sam's freshly made cup in her hand.

"No, the sugar in the creamer is fine, thanks."

Tandy walked to the table, coffee mugs in both hands. She set one down in front of Sam, then her father before returning to the maker, which made one cup at a time. "I'll be out of here in just a sec, Dad," she said, preparing to make a third cup.

"Actually, honey," he said, raising his cup to his lips. "I'd like you to stay."

She looked at him, Sam looking back and forth between them as she picked the baking paper off her blueberry muffin. "Are you sure? Dad, I can easily go—"

"Stay," he said, his soft tone not unkind. There was something in the quality of it that brooked no argument.

Without a word, Tandy quickly finished what she was doing, then joined them at the table.

Sam, who had no clue what was happening, simply tried to focus on the ridiculously good muffin she was eating and warming cup of coffee, flavored by roasted marshmallow creamer.

"Samantha," Stormy said, getting her attention. "Tell me about yourself. Where were you born? Tell me about your family."

Sam would normally balk at such an intrusive question, but that damn tone of his, so quietly probing. "Well, my older sister and I were born in Oakland, California, but I don't remember that at all. My father worked for Walmart and was promoted into management, which got him transferred to Tacoma, Washington, which is where I grew up and my younger sister was born. Mom worked on and off, you know, LensCrafters for a year or two, floral place for a few years, homemaker for a few years." She shrugged. "When she got bored, she got a job. When she got sick of a schedule, she quit." She sipped her coffee, eyeing him, wondering if that was what he wanted to know.

Stormy studied her as he slowly sipped his coffee. At length, he set his cup down. "Are there any spiritual roots in your family, Samantha?"

"Spiritual roots?" Sam asked, taking another bite of the delicious baked good.

Stormy nodded. "Religion? Prayer? Particular spiritual beliefs? I have to say," he added with a smile. "You and your friend looked like fish out of water the first time we met."

Sam chuckled, nodding. "That's because we were. And no. My father's mother was very religious when she was alive. The last time I was in a church was last year when one of the folks on our production staff got married."

He nodded, taking another sip from his coffee before pushing the cup away. "Tandy tells me you remember nothing about what happened to you last night at Whitney Grove."

Sam sat back in the kitchen chair, the large muffin she'd been given gone, just the baking cup left. She shook her head as she finished the final bite. "Nothing."

"You feel a connection to that house, don't you?" He laced his fingers as he rested his hands on the kitchen table before him.

She considered his question before she nodded. "It's a strange familiarity, almost. I mean, I've felt that to a point with other houses we've done, and honestly, I think that's just the energy of an old place, you know?"

"But this is different," he prodded gently.

Sam considered his words and nodded. "Yeah. Though I'm not entirely sure why."

"I'd like to hypnotize you," he said. "See what happened, take your mind back past the fog to the events of last night."

Sam was admittedly intrigued, as she'd heard of such a thing, but was nervous. She glanced to Tandy, who'd been listening quietly to their conversation.

"Dad is a retired hypnotherapist," she explained. "He worked with police departments and therapists for years."

"Just curious," Sam said noncommittally, "why do you want to know what happened?"

"Don't you?" Stormy asked.

She studied him for a long moment, now seeing the resemblance between his eyes and Tandy's. Though they were a different color, the intensity was the same. Returning her thoughts to the question he posed, truth was, yes and no. She was afraid what would turn up, yet she had no idea why. So, in lieu of giving him a straight answer, she gave him a nervous quip. "You're not going to make me bark like a dog or quack like a duck, right?"

"No," he hedged. "Though tomorrow you may spontaneously start oinking like a pig."

⚞⚞⚟⚟

Sam lay out on Tandy's couch, her hands placed comfortably on her chest, head reclined into a throw pillow. As instructed, she was taking deep breaths in through her nose and releasing them through her mouth. She could distantly feel Tandy's closeness as she sat at the other end of the couch with Sam's sock-covered feet in her lap.

"Okay, Samantha," Stormy said, his soft voice even softer and close by. "Imagine yourself in a room dark and quiet and safe."

Sam let out a long slow sigh as she felt herself relax, mind clearing with Stormy's soothing voice and Tandy's comforting presence. She saw the room he spoke of, felt the comforting warmth of the darkness, smelled the calming lavender from Tandy's diffuser. She felt herself falling into that darkness, allowing herself to be swallowed by it.

"Now the curtain of darkness slowly slides open.

What do you see?" Stormy asked, seemingly from a million miles away.

"In the house..." Sam murmured.

"Which house?"

"Whitney Grove."

"What do you see, Samantha?"

"I see..." Sam murmured. "I see..."

She saw the up close and personal view of the basement floor. Lifting her head, she looked around, noting a black and white cat sitting close by, watching her.

"Hey, Prince Albert," she said, reaching out a hand toward the feline. He sniffed her fingers, then trotted off into the depths of the basement. "Traitor," she muttered, pushing to her knees, then her feet. Dusting herself off, she looked around.

"What's your name?" she heard asked, the voice distant, soft.

"Sonia Lucas," she said, though she didn't even remember speaking.

She walked up the narrow, rickety wooden stairs to the main floor of the old house, noting the line of closed apartment doors on either side of the hallway she found herself in. Distant sounds of life could be heard behind some of the doors.

She made her way toward the front door of the house, which opened as she neared it. A small figure appeared, and immediately, a smile came to her face.

"Mommy!"

"Hello, baby," she exclaimed, kneeling to accept the exuberant four-year-old who threw herself into her arms. "How's my girl?"

Rather than answering verbally, Chloe nuzzled

her nose against her mother's, the child hugging Bear close to her chest.

She got to her feet, Chloe's small hand in her own. "Ready?" she asked, looking down at the little one with the unruly strawberry blond hair and big, bright green eyes. The girl nodded.

Hand-in-hand, the two headed toward the door, even as another figure stepped into it. Richard walked toward them, a sneer on his face as he looked her over, saying nothing as he passed mother and daughter. Another figure appeared, her beehive hairdo giving her away even before her face could be seen.

"Mother," Sonia murmured, the older woman looking away as they passed each other.

Anger filling her, she bit her lip as she continued forward, yet another silhouette appearing in the doorway, though her anger instantly drained from her as she stepped into the hug that awaited her. Her eyes closed as she held her friend close.

"I've missed you" was whispered in her ear.

She felt tears sting the backs of her eyelids, finding so much comfort in the embrace of her most talented friend. "I've missed you, too."

"See you soon," her friend said softly, then moved away, heading in the same direction as those who had come before her.

Sonia turned, watching the young woman walk away. "Don't go, Daisy! Come with me! Please!"

Daisy turned, walking backward as she blew Sonia a kiss. "See you soon."

Tears running freely down her cheeks, Sonia turned back to the door, raising a hand to swipe at her tears as she continued forward. Just as she was about to reach the door, yet another person stepped into the doorway, though the silhouette never materialized into a person, rather, like a shadow brought to life, it lunged at her, through her, leaving Sonia shaken as a woman's laughter echoed throughout the hallway.

Tears continued to stream down her cheeks as she held on to Chloe's hand even tighter as she hurried to the door and out...

...of the kitchen and down the hallway until she reached the door. She was nervous, hand gripping and regripping the handle of her cart.

"You can do this," she whispered, sweat beginning to bead at her hairline.

"What's your name?"

She heard the distant voice, as though God himself had spoken. The thought made her smile, as she thought of Hope. "Sephora Lloyd," she responded. "My name is Sephora Lloyd." She blew out another breath and pushed herself and the cart forward, using the end of the cart to push lightly against the door, which swung outward into the room she expected to serve the ladies in.

The cart crossed the threshold, but the moment she did, Sephora's eyes flew open, nearly popping out of her head as she was slammed against the wall, a vise-like grip around her throat. Sephora clawed desperately at the hand, unable to breathe, unable to make a sound.

"It's not over," a voice growled from an unseen mouth in the pitch blackness that was the space she found herself in. "It'll never be over."

With the hand that gripped her throat, Sephora was thrown away from the wall, blindly flailing until she hit the floor hard. She quickly scrambled to her feet, eyes wide as she tried to see through the inky blackness around her.

Chest heaving with fear and confusion, Sephora got to her feet and reached out with her hands, trying to feel something, anything *that would lead to an out. A small whimper escaped her lips as tears lazily slid down her cheeks. She was nearly hyperventilating in her need to find the door.*

She yelped in surprise when her hand was grabbed. The fingers that wrapped around hers were soft and warm.

"Come with me," the sweetest voice murmured.

Sephora was led through the darkness until slowly, as though the sun was rising, the darkness gave way to the natural sunlight that poured in through the windows of the small room they shared, a bassinette tucked in the corner by the bed.

Sephora stared into the face of her love and her Hope. She smiled, relief filling her. "It's not over," she said softly.

Hope shook her head, hands coming up to cup Sephora's cheeks. "No. You have to go now. Stop it, stop it now, or it will never stop."

Sephora's eyes fell closed as Hope leaned in, their lips barely brushing....

...the slightest pressure before her lips were gone. She opened her eyes to see the beautiful blue of Lark's eyes looking back at her.

"What is your name?"

She looked at Lark, surprised that not only hadn't she asked the question, but didn't seem to have heard it, either. "I'm Sally Little," she responded, the slightest edge to her voice. "You should know that. You've taken over my house, after all," she said with a smirk.

She walked over to the fireplace, the flames warm and popping. She felt more than heard Lark join her.

They stood in silence for a moment before she spoke.
"Why?"

"Look inside yourself for the answer to that, Sally,"
Lark said quietly, her tone sad, sounding defeated.

"I trusted you," Sally said, her own tone flat, hurt.
"Did you?"

Sally turned to her, the angry words of arrogant
rebuttal dying on her tongue. Looking into those
sapphire eyes, she saw her own loneliness, her own
betrayal reflected back at her. Clearing her throat, Sally
moved to step over to Lark when she was yanked back,
her hands going to her neck.

Gasping, her hands shot up, fingers tugging
impotently at the biting, braided rope pulled tightly
around her throat. She could feel the unrelenting
hardness of a body behind her. She tried to say Lark's
name, tried to beg her to help her, but no words escaped
her lips.

Lark sidled up to her, her expression hard, yet
those eyes told of the turmoil inside of her. As the rope
was pulled tighter, Lark reached out and brushed the
backs of her fingers down along Sally's cheek...

...*"Sam!"*

Her lips twitched as her eyes popped open. Sam
gasped, gulping in air as she found herself face to face
with a very concerned woman. Mind still somewhere
else, she reached up and cupped the back of her neck
and brought her down until she forced a kiss. After a
startled moment, the lips against her own gave, and
her kiss was accepted, ending with the briefest touch
of a soft tongue.

"Don't leave me again," Sam whispered against
those soft lips.

Chapter Fourteen

Given a plastic trash bag and rubber bands, Sam was able to get a shower while protecting her casted wrist. But now she was struggling mightily to get her bra clasped.

"Fuck," she growled, frustrated and knowing great humiliation was just around the corner. She walked to the bedroom door and pulled it open. "Tandy?" she called, knowing the other woman was up and about, as she'd heard her walk by the bedroom door talking to Cubed. "Can I get your help for a second?"

"Be there in a second!" Tandy called from what Sam assumed was the kitchen.

Bra in place but hanging open in the back, Sam grabbed the towel she'd used to dry her skin and held it against her chest, bra cups held into place over her breasts. She felt nervous, stomach doing crazy flips as she waited.

"Everything okay?" Tandy asked, stepping into the bedroom. She, too, looked to be freshly showered, her hair damp and brushed back from her face. Sam was yet again stunned by just how lovely she truly was.

"Um, help?" Sam said with a crooked grin.

Tandy smiled and nodded. "Turn around," she said softly, a warm hand on Sam's bare shoulder to nudge her to present her back to Tandy, who gasped sharply when Sam did. "Sam, you have a terrible bruise here."

Sam's eyebrows drew. "Well, I tumbled down some stairs, right?" she said. "That's what you guys think happened."

"Yes, but this is...This is a handprint," Tandy whispered, her fingers lightly touching the skin of Sam's back, causing a small quake to thunder through Sam's body. "Hang on a sec," Tandy said, hurrying from the room, only to return a moment later.

Unsure what was happening, Sam waited. When she heard the click of Tandy's phone's camera, she understood. A moment later, Tandy's phone appeared over her shoulder, and she was able to see the picture taken. Sam turned so she was facing Tandy, the two women looking at the photo together.

"That looks like a hand," Sam admitted. "But is it possible that it was just a crazy bruise pattern?" She met Tandy's gaze; she looked as doubtful as Sam felt.

"Sam," Tandy said gently, lowering her phone before she set it on the nearby dresser. "Did someone push you?"

Sam let out a heavy sigh, holding the towel closer to her chest as she felt even more vulnerable as an icky feeling filled her. "I don't know. I was alone in the house."

Tandy urged Sam to turn around again and worked to get her bra clasped. "Does this hurt?" she asked, as the thick band of the bra would go directly across the bruise.

"No."

"Do you remember anything from last night?" Tandy hooked the bra together one clasp at a time. "You were so out of it when it was over. Dad had to help me get you to bed."

"I remember you guys getting me in here. I remember doing the breathing your dad told me to do. But that's about it," Sam said. Her bra clasped, she tossed the towel to the bed, intent on hanging it up in the bathroom once she was dressed. She grabbed the fresh shirt that had arrived whenever and by whomever had made her prescription pain medicine appear. As she stood in jeans and bra, she blushed, noticing that Tandy had been looking her over before quickly looking away. "Did I end up barking like a dog or clucking like a chicken or something?" she asked, a weak attempt to break the sudden tension in the sexually charged air.

Tandy smiled, grabbing her phone again and hugging it to her chest. "No. But you mentioned Lark again," she said. "You mentioned a few different names, including that of my mother." She hugged herself. "How did you know my mom's name was Daisy?"

Sam could only stare at her, mouth open. Just when she was about to close it, it fell open farther.

"And why did you kiss me?" Tandy asked softly, no anger in her words.

"I...uh...I'm so sorry. I don't know. I don't remember..." It was a rare thing for Sam to be left speechless, but her brain had ceased to work. Her gaze dipped to those gorgeous lips before she quickly looked away, feeling ashamed and embarrassed. "I'm sorry, Tandy. Truly. I have no idea why I would have done that."

"I think you thought I was someone else," Tandy said softly. "You were mentioning this Lark person, then sounded like you were in trouble. Like you were choking or something." Tandy hugged herself tighter. "I was trying to wake you up, snap you out of the hypnosis when you kissed me, then told me not to leave you again."

Sam felt sick to her stomach and deeply, deeply vulnerable. "Could you please hand me my shirt?" she asked, her words not much more than a whisper.

Tandy glanced to the bed where the shirt lay folded. She picked it up and walked over to Sam, stopping not more than a foot away as she held the garment out to her.

"Perhaps it was very wrong, but I returned the kiss," she murmured, sparing Sam a glance before she left the room, closing the door softly behind her.

❧ ❧ ☙ ☙

With extreme precision, Sam focused on the mantel, a very specific image in her mind of how it should look. After surprised greetings and hugs and endless questions, she'd made her way up to the third floor, *her* floor. She'd nearly claimed the entire thing as her own, done much of the work herself, and made just about every decision.

She sat on a stool in front of the fireplace that once held the secret compartment, the mantel she'd had specially made for the room was intricate and detailed. She didn't want one that was just stained and mounted. This one was painted an off-white, and now she was applying the color for the detail work.

Her focus was completely on her task, the paintbrush she held in her good hand lightly and expertly filling in the details of the tiny flowers carved into the wood. It was something she could do with one hand, and it was a great distraction that made her feel productive.

"One sec," she murmured, finishing up some leaves on a daisy. She heard the soft footfalls enter the room and knew it was Cary. They always did their best not to distract or startle when the other was working on something detailed or dangerous, like a table saw. Finishing, she lowered her hand and glanced over her shoulder. "Hey."

"Hey, lady." He walked up to her and set down the speakers she'd asked him to bring, as well as her phone charger. He set everything on the table where her paints were spread out and took her in his arms when she stood. "I was really worried about you," he said, leaving a kiss to the top of her head before releasing her. "You were passed out when I dropped off your pain meds and clothes," he explained. "So, Tandy wouldn't let me wake you."

Sam grinned. "Yes, she was a good mama bear while I was there."

"I'll bet." He snickered, receiving a smack to his arm in response. "Well, I spoke to Taz Barton last night and sent her that picture that Tandy texted of your back."

"Who's Taz Barton?" Sam asked, using a rag to wipe at some paint on her fingers.

"She owns the security company the homeowner hired. She's also a retired cop and said she's got some contacts that she can call in if we feel we need to have this looked into, what happened to you," he explained.

"But, Cary, we don't even know if anything happened. I mean, honestly, I probably just biffed it down the stairs and the bruise is just a coincidence," Sam said, feeling uncomfortable. Ever since Tandy had pointed out that hand-shaped bruise to her, she'd felt very uneasy about the entire situation. Something was niggling at her, a fear she couldn't put her finger on. Not usually one for avoiding situations, Sam felt this was one she needed to run far away from.

"Sam," he said softly, a hand on her shoulder. "This is serious. You could've been badly hurt. Or worse. Besides," he added with a shrug. "What if someone else gets hurt?"

She let out an irritated sigh, knowing he was right.

"Let's just see what she says, okay? Also, I ran into Tandy this morning. She said her mom is going to swing by. I guess she's concerned."

"Fuck, Cary!" Sam exclaimed. "Does she not like the job we're doing? Is she worried we're not being careful—"

"She's worried about you," Cary said pointedly. He left another kiss to the side of her head, then walked past her and headed out of the room. "Oh," he said, pausing by the door. "Dave wants to get an interview with you today, so be ready to explain the sudden cast on your wrist to the masses."

Sam groaned. "Goodie. Okay."

Left alone, Sam got her phone plugged in and charging as she searched through her music playlists to decide which one she wanted to listen to. There was no question it would be Maria Sonia, but it was just a question of which playlist she would choose. Settling on a favorite, she connected the phone to her speakers via Bluetooth, then got back to work.

Her mind wandered, thinking back to that morning in the guest bedroom she'd slept in. Tandy's final words to her echoed in her mind. If there was any time she'd do anything to remember a kiss, that would be the one. Why had she kissed Tandy? Well, she smirked at the internal question. Why wasn't exactly the question. She knew *exactly* why she would have kissed Tandy, but circumstances being what they were, why had she done it? What had driven her to that? Stormy had called her little more than an hour ago and told her that he would have her over for dinner the following night, as he wanted to talk about their session, as he referred to it. He said he'd compiled some information for her that he felt she'd find interesting. Sam had eagerly accepted the invite, hoping he could shed more light on what had happened at Tandy's house all the way around.

One of her favorite songs came on, so her thoughts dispersed, any unsettled concerns or fears gone. Maria Sonia's version of *Fleurs Du Mal* came on, an incredible mix of regular singing, soprano opera, choral backup, and rock 'n roll. No way in hell she could ever keep up with that gorgeous voice, so she relegated herself to humming along, her head bobbing with the hard, sharp, almost militant syllables of the choral backup. She was losing herself in the music, as she usually did, when suddenly it was as though she were hearing it in stereo. Maria Sonia's voice was not only coming at her from the speakers on the table to her left, but also from behind her, and that voice was growing louder than the accompanying music and choir.

Glancing behind her, Sam slowly rose to her feet from the stool, her mouth falling open and tears instantly springing to her eyes, though she had no idea why. She slowly walked toward her, the slight heels on her boots making soft sounds on the redone wood floor with every step, had to be a mirage. Her auburn hair was pulled back in a sleek ponytail, her makeup light and natural. Her casual dress of fitted jeans and a sweater belied the immensity of the talent that erupted in the final notes of the song as her coloratura was on full display in that moment just as it had been when she brought the house down at the concert many weeks before.

Silent tears rolled down Sam's cheeks as the sound went to her very soul, momentarily forgetting about her profound confusion. When the song ended, both on her phone and in real life, Sam clapped wildly, tears continuing to flow, and her face hurting from the smile that stretched it to its limits.

"Thank you, Sam," the mirage said, giving a dramatic bow.

Sam could only look on, stunned as the woman closed the distance between them. "You're Maria Sonia," she said stupidly.

The beautiful older woman smiled. "Call me Daisy." She stopped just short of Sam and looked her over, tears in her own brown eyes to add to Sam's confusion. "My daughter said you were a fan."

"Daisy? Your daughter?" Sam muttered, feeling like she was three days behind the conversation

"Tandy. My little girl." Daisy gave her a winning smile as she raised a hand and gently wiped away Sam's tears with her thumb before she took Sam in a warm hug, holding her close.

Sam was still fighting with her brain, wondering if she was seriously hallucinating when a comfort washed over her, a familiar warmth that she leaned into, returning the hug with this woman, her vocal idol for more than twenty years, though a complete stranger. In that moment, however, she felt as though she were coming home.

"It's so good to see you," Daisy murmured into the hug.

"I missed you," Sam responded, though she was startled by her own words, which seemed to have just tumbled out of her mouth. She said nothing more, in fear she'd say something else stupid.

After a long moment, Daisy pulled back and smiled at Sam, holding her by the shoulders. "You and me need to talk," she said softly.

꽃꽃꽃꽃꽃

"I love these old houses," Daisy said, her hand tucked into Sam's arm as they strolled around the grounds cleared of the weeds and trash but not yet landscaped. That would be done last, as it would be further into spring, heading into summer. "This house intrigued me from the very first time I was here."

"When was that?" Sam asked,

"Forever ago," she said, a smile on her face. "I was all of nineteen, just a kid." She led them to the picnic table where Sam had sat with Tandy weeks before. "Mind if we sit?"

"Not at all."

The two got situated on top of the old table before Daisy spoke again. "My grandmother had died, so it was just me. I decided it was time for me to go make it big in New York." She smiled over at Sam, who met her gaze, the awe of the woman sitting beside her very evident in Sam's eyes. "So, I was driving across the country from California, and my car broke down."

"Just like Tandy," Sam said, smiling at the memory of the gorgeous woman telling her the story. "The cross-country journey, that is."

Daisy nodded, returning the smile. "Yes, my stubborn, strong-willed daughter." She shook her head. "That girl. But yes, like her, I, too, struck out to claim my destiny. That is, until my car broke down here." She gave a little laugh, light and lovely, reminding Sam of the sound of wind chimes in the breeze, just like Tandy. "I was scared to death," she admitted, her smile fading. "Honestly, I don't think I've ever been so scared. But," the smile returned. "Sonia rescued me." She studied Sam for a long moment, so long in fact, it was making Sam a bit uncomfortable. "You know who Sonia is, don't you?"

"She was the woman who used to live here, who was murdered here. Right?" Sam asked, though she knew the answer.

"Yes," Daisy whispered, a soft smile returning to her lips. "But she was so much more than that." She met and held Sam's gaze. "But you know that, too, don't you, Sam?"

Once she got over the craziness that this woman she'd worshipped for her entire adult life had used her name, she felt a strange chill wash through her body, one she didn't understand. "I'm not entirely sure what's going on with all this, Mar—" She cleared her throat. "Daisy." Suddenly, something flashed through her mind, a snapshot of something: A memory? A dream? "You found her, didn't you?"

Daisy stared at the house for a long moment, hands tucked tighter between her knees. She seemed as though she were lost in a distant place. Finally, she nodded. "Yes. We'd been planning for our trip." A sad smile curled her lips, even as she continued to look up at the house. "She'd agreed to come with me to New York with Chloe. Start over. Get away from Richard," she added, her voice low and filled with a bitter hatred. "So, she was getting these crazy phone calls, crank calls, and that day, she got one that sent her out the door. She didn't come back. I don't remember why now, but for some reason, I went looking for her."

"She got another phone call," Sam said, startled as the words came out of her mouth.

Daisy seemed just as startled as she met Sam's gaze. "Yes. Yes, I believe you're right." She let out a heavy sigh. "So, I went looking for her and…"

"You found her."

"Yeah. I found her."

Sam shook her head, looking down at her own hands, which fidgeted a bit in her lap. "That must have been awful," she said softly.

"It was. Honestly, Stormy got me through it."

That caught Sam's attention, and she studied her companion, noting the change in Daisy's demeanor, a smile coming to her lips and a lightness to her energy.

"He was there for me the entire time. I stayed here during the investigation and then the trial. I had to testify," she said, sounding tired. "I'd heard Richard, Sonia's husband, tell her to her face that he'd kill her. My testimony was what got him convicted."

"Did that make you happy?" Sam asked.

Daisy shrugged. "It wasn't easy. I was so young, twenty by then, I think. He was so awful to her."

"Do you think he did it?"

"I have asked myself that a million times in the last forty years." Daisy met Sam's gaze. "The entire case was circumstantial. They never found the murder weapon, no real witnesses to speak of."

"Just your testimony of his treatment of her?" Sam asked, intrigued, and felt sad for the young woman who had such a horrendous burden to find justice for her friend.

"Exactly. I guess whether he was guilty of her murder or not, he was guilty of a lot of things. That comforts me. You know?"

"That took a lot of guts, Daisy. No doubt, Sonia is very proud of you." Sam gave her a winning smile, sure of every word she'd just said.

"You're the one who found the little treasure trove, aren't you?" Daisy asked, returning the smile. "In the fireplace?"

Sam nodded. "Yup. Tandy said you wanted the money and the record albums. Do you have any idea who those albums belong to? Were they Sonia's?"

Daisy's smile grew sad once more. "No, they're mine. I'd loaned them to her. After everything happened, they were nowhere to be found. Honestly, we thought maybe Richard had destroyed them or something."

"Wow," Sam murmured. "Really cool that you got them back. And a few bucks."

"Oh, no. That money will go to Chloe, if I ever see her again. It's not about the fact that it's fifty bucks, but it was truly blood money. Sonia was hiding that money to make a better life for herself and for Chloe."

"Esther Martin said Chloe was raised by a family member," Sam said, intensely curious.

"Ah, so you got to meet that crazy hag, did you? My condolences," Daisy said dryly. "I spent a lot of time with Chloe while I was still here, you know, took her to play at the park, get ice cream, that sort of thing. I knew that's what her mom would have wanted. I was livid, though I can't say surprised, to hear that

after I left for New York, Esther sent her packing."
She met Sam's gaze. "I never saw her again. She was
around five or six by that time." Daisy brought the
shoulder bag she carried up into her lap and unzipped
it, digging through it. "I knew I'd be seeing you today,
so I found this." She withdrew a Polaroid picture, the
colors long ago faded and turned into more of a sepia
color scheme. "I thought you might like to see it."

Sam took the picture. It looked to be set in the
backyard of an average house, certainly not Whitney
Grove. There were a handful of adults frozen in time
eating or laughing. To the top left of the picture was
a handful of little kids, all looking to be anywhere
from toddlers to around seven sitting in a group on
the grass, their attention on a beautiful young woman,
dressed much like the hippies Sam had seen pictures
of or in movies of the sixties and seventies. She held
an acoustic guitar and seemed to be strumming it as
she sang, her expression utter joy. Her long hair was
free and looked as though blown a bit by a breeze. She
brought the picture a little closer, studying the young
woman.

"Is this you?" Sam asked, glancing over at Daisy,
who was looking at the picture over her shoulder.

"Yup," she said absently. "It was Chloe's fourth
birthday party."

Sam returned her attention to the picture. Her
gaze followed where a young Daisy's attention seemed
to be, and it was to an adorable little girl sitting cross-
legged directly in front of her. Her strawberry hair
was long and flowing down her back, though it looked
like it needed a good brushing, as most children's hair
does after a day of play. Her little hands were caught
in midclap, as though clapping along with whatever

Daisy had been singing to her.

Heart swelling and emotion rising, Sam held the picture in the fingers of her casted hand and used the fingers of her other to lightly trace over the girl. Somewhere deep inside, she wanted to scream.

Forcing herself to look away from the picture for a moment, she looked up to the sky, taking several deep, cleansing breaths. She could feel Daisy's gaze on her and met it for a brief, meaningful moment before she returned to the picture.

She saw a young woman, her long, brown hair pulled back from her face. She stood to Daisy's left, only a third of her face visible from the way she stood. Sam felt her stomach roil, though she wasn't sure why. She quickly looked away from that woman, her gaze instead landing on the pair who stood to Daisy's right. The man had dark blond hair and looked scruffy, with too-long sideburns and shaggy hair. He was caught looking at his wristwatch. Instinctively, Sam hated him. Standing next to him was a tall woman dressed in black. Her hair was short and black or dark brown, hard to tell with the faded picture. Her face was a bit blurry, as though the picture had been snapped as she was quickly moving her head. It seemed, however, that her gaze was focused on the woman standing to Daisy's left.

Sam took in the entire picture again, the woman looking away from the camera, Daisy singing to the children, then the pair standing off to the side. A sudden wave of nausea washed over Sam, and she knew she was in trouble. She almost threw the picture at Daisy before she launched herself off the picnic table and ran to the bushes lining the property and lost her breakfast again and again.

Her stomach convulsing for the final time, tears came to her eyes and the emotional dam she'd been holding back for the past ten minutes broke. Standing up straight again after vomiting, she was surprised to find Tandy standing there, waiting for her, arms open. She fell into them, the sobs ripping from her throat and making her entire body heave.

Chapter Fifteen

T his is cute." Cary pulled the rental car up to the two-story house. "A little Cape Cod influence in the design." He parked next to the car in the driveway, which Sam recognized as Tandy's. Her stomach did a little flip at the sight. Cary turned the engine off and removed the key as he glanced over at Sam, who sat stock still in the passenger seat, seat belt still in place. "You okay?"

Sam nodded, though mostly as an automatic response, not because she was. She met his gaze. She still felt deeply unsettled about earlier that afternoon, her emotional reaction to the picture Daisy had shown her and her emotional reaction to Daisy herself. There was something to it she didn't understand, far beyond being a rabid fan. She felt like there was a cosmic joke at play, and she was the butt of it, clueless while everyone around her already had the punchline.

Cary smiled, reaching over and lightly squeezing the fingers of her cast-covered hand. "Let's go."

Sam nodded, unbuckling herself before climbing out of the car. She followed Cary up the driveway to the walkway that led to the steps of the front porch. Before they hit the top step, the door opened, and Tandy appeared.

"Welcome!" she exclaimed, taking Cary into a quick embrace before turning to Sam, her hold on her lingering. She released her, the two sharing a glance before Sam followed her inside.

The house was warmly appointed, as well as a comfortable temperature to combat the chilly evening. Wonderful smells filled the rooms as Cary and Sam were led to the family room where a fire was lit in the fireplace and Daisy sat, sipping a glass of wine.

"Hello!" Daisy exclaimed, setting her glass on the large square coffee table before getting to her feet, arms open for hugs.

Sam felt the twitter of excitement and awe as she accepted a hug, but also that same comforting familiarity as she returned the hug with gusto. She did, however, have to laugh out loud when Cary just stared at Daisy as Sam moved away.

"I...I got nothin'," he said, slowly shaking his head. "I have to admit, I've given Sam shi—I mean, crap over the years for how much she loves you and your music, but secretly, I really loved your stuff, too, and now I can't believe I'm standing here looking at you and about to get a hug from you," he finished, clearly out of breath from the run-on sentence of babble.

Sam glanced over at Tandy, who looked amused. No doubt she'd experienced this with her mother many times over her lifetime.

"Well," Daisy said, hands on Cary's shoulders. "Then we can be a mutual admiration society. I'm a huge fan of your show."

Cary looked as though he were about to faint as he accepted Daisy's hug. Sam had told him about Daisy before they'd arrived at the house, not wanting him to have the heart attack she nearly had.

"I thought I heard other voices."

Sam turned to see Stormy standing in the

arched entrance to the room. She smiled and raised a hand in greeting. "Hey, Stormy." She wasn't entirely surprised when he walked over to her and gave her a warm hug. She was learning that she was now among an affectionate bunch. It was a nice change in her life, if she were honest with herself.

"Hope you're hungry, all," Stormy said, beaming as he stood with his hand on Sam's shoulder.

An hour later, the group sat around the dining room table, very few bites left of the incredible dinner Stormy had made for everyone, which included baked chicken, scalloped potatoes with loads of cheese, and asparagus. Sam sat back from her empty plate, glass of wine in hand. She felt content, listening as Daisy regaled the group with stories of being on the road. She felt eyes on her and glanced to her left, where Tandy sat at the head of the table, opposite of her father. They shared a small smile before returning their focus to the story about a raucous trumpet player in Tokyo.

"I have to say," Cary added, stabbing the last of his potatoes with his fork. "I'm amazed how well Tandy has done with the cameras." He grinned over at her. "She's quite fetching on film."

"Probably her years as an actress," Sam suggested, sipping her wine.

"You were an actress?" Cary asked, eyebrows raised in interest.

Tandy opened her mouth to speak, but Daisy plowed on ahead of her. "Not *only* was my daughter an actress, and a damn good one, but she was also a drug dealer."

"Oh, geez." Tandy brought a hand up to cover her eyes.

"What, like in a movie or something?" Cary

looked from mother to daughter and back.

"Nope. She was pushing dope for Big Pharma," Daisy said dramatically, making the table chuckle.

"I did voiceover work for two commercials for an allergy medication," Tandy explained.

"Drug dealer!" Daisy stage whispered.

Sam grinned. She found the casual, loving, easy chemistry among Daisy and Stormy and Tandy so beautiful to watch. It was clear that there was a great deal of love and history there. She thought back to her own family, there was always so much tension, so much drama. She'd always dreamed of a family like Tandy's.

Sam's attention was turned to the front door when the doorbell chimed. Tandy, being closest to the short hall that led from the dining room to the front door, hopped up.

"I'll get it, Dad," she said.

Sam watched her go, her gaze falling to an extremely shapely behind before she heard Cary clear his throat from where he sat next to her. She turned her head and looked at him. "What?"

"Pervert," he whispered.

The voice of a woman could be heard greeting Tandy before Tandy appeared again, a woman at her side. She looked to be around Sam's age with short, somewhat spiked strawberry blond hair. She wore a dark blue polo shirt with a logo of some sort on the left breast tucked into a pair of jeans. In short, she looked the stereotype of a butch lesbian. Her gaze met Sam's, and the stranger gave her a small smile before taking in the rest of the group.

"Everyone, this is Taz Barton. She owns the security company we hired for the house."

"Hey, all." Taz raised a hand in greeting. "Sorry to bust in on your dinner, but Tandy said this would be the best place to talk to all of you at once."

"Welcome," Stormy said, rising from his seat. "What can I get you?" he asked. "A plate? We've got plenty. Wine? A Coke?"

"No, no, thank you. I've got dinner plans after I leave here." She took the seat Daisy pulled out for her, which put her directly across the table from Sam. "So, I just wanted to start by saying that I'm real sorry about what happened," she said, nodding at Sam. "Tandy texted me the picture of that bruise. Nasty stuff. I worked with our electronics expert, and we pored over every second of video for that entire night before, during, and after the incident." She shook her head, looking around the table. "Not a damn thing. Saw you come and go, Tandy," she said, indicating Tandy to her right with a nod. "And we saw you leave. There was no footage of anyone entering the house or the premises. We have the cameras on the three entrances to the house, as well as three taking in the grounds. Problem is," she added with a hand gesture, "we have none on the basement stairs or that area. If someone did in fact push you, Miss Leyton, it would have had to be someone already in the house. So," she concluded, lightly slapping her palms on the dining room table. "We can chalk it up to an accident, or as former Denver PD, I still have some contacts on the force that I can bring in to take a look at things. We can also beef up security during the day and on weekends, but that does come at a cost." The question was left hanging in the air as her gaze made the rounds of the table again.

"I think it was an accident, guys," Sam said at

length. "I probably just lost my footing." She looked at the woman sitting across from her. "Thanks for taking the time with the video."

"That's my job, Miss Leyton."

"I think we need to talk about that, Taz," Daisy said, getting to her feet.

"Understood," Taz said, also getting to her feet. "Apologies again for interrupting your evening," she said, then followed Daisy out of the room to the door.

Sam let out a heavy breath before taking a drink of her wine. Everything surrounding the circumstances of that night left her feeling uncertain and unsettled. In a way, she wished Taz had found something, but in another way, she was glad she hadn't, and perhaps it was just a coincidental bruise after all.

"Well, good news or bad news, depending on how you look at it," Daisy said, re-entering the room and taking her seat. She grabbed her wine glass and held it up in salute. "I want to thank Cary, Sam, and Tandy for the absolutely incredible job you're doing on Whitney Grove."

"I, for one, am excited to see it," Stormy said, raising his water glass. "I've had to force myself to wait until its completion."

Sam was so pleased to hear Daisy's words and the pleasure, almost emotionally so, in her voice. She, too, raised her glass as did Cary.

"For more than forty years, I've waited to see the soul of this house come to life, and I'm so grateful that this wonderful group of people," Daisy continued, indicating Cary, Sam, and Tandy, "are the ones who are making it happen. To Whitney Grove!" she exclaimed, echoed by everyone in the room.

"Are you planning to live there?" Cary asked

Daisy, reaching for the wine bottle at the center of the table and refilling his glass. He topped off Sam's and Tandy's. "One bottle down," he proclaimed, raising the empty bottle. "How many more to go?" he said with a grin.

"Well, sort of," Daisy responded to his question. "You see, there's a reason it was super easy to turn Whitney Grove into apartments in the sixties." She grinned. "The individual rooms were already there."

Cary leaned forward, eyes wide in excitement as he asked, "It was a brothel, wasn't it?"

"Yup, built by the incredibly successful madam Sally Little of Philadelphia," Stormy said with a lopsided grin.

Sam felt Cary's gaze on her and met it, even as she felt a little foggy in her head. She saw his grin and hand raised for a high-five, which she slapped.

"I knew it!" he crowed. "So, what are you going to do?"

"With the individual rooms already laid out," Daisy explained, "I plan to start a program for talented young voices here in Colorado."

Sam listened to Daisy's words, which began to echo slightly in her ears. She blinked a few times, trying to shake off the strange feeling that was taking her over, almost as though she'd had a little too much to drink or had taken medication to make her drowsy, none of which had been the case.

"I have a home here, but I'm mostly based out of New York. But," Daisy added, sending an adoring smile in Tandy's direction. "Now that Tandy is looking to *finally* make me a grandbaby, I'm going to make Denver my permanent base of operations."

"That's wonderful," Sam said, her voice slow

and slightly slurred.

"Sam?" Tandy reached over and placed her hand on Sam's arm, above where the cast ended. "Are you okay?"

Sam looked at her, shaking her head again to clear it. She grabbed her refilled wine glass, feeling utterly clear, clearer than she'd ever been as she met the gazes of those at the table, all looking at her. "You know," she began conversationally, "Sally built that house for love." She winked at Cary, who was looking at her strangely. "The oldest profession on earth, right?" She smirked, taking a sip of her wine, all attention still on her. "But you see, that house was built for an even older love." She raised her glass in a partial salute in Daisy's direction. "A mother's love for her daughter. You see," she added, sitting forward as she set her wine glass on the table. "Sally had a daughter." She met every pair of eyes looking at her as she continued her story, the expressions varying from confusion to surprise to Stormy's look of quiet pride.

"How do you know?" Cary looked decidedly uncomfortable.

"Let her finish," Stormy chided gently.

"She rolled the dice and gambled it all to come here to find her kid," Sam continued, as though nobody had spoken. She picked up her wine glass again and sat casually back in her chair, sipping the Riesling. "Kicker is, it found her before she could find Whitney."

"Who, Samantha?" Stormy asked, his tone hypnosis-soft.

She met his gaze. "The traveler. Son of a bitch found her and got her killed." She smirked. "Again." Another sip of wine before she continued. "House ended up going to her kid, though. Well, the kid's adopted parents, anyway. Whitney, that's the kid," she clarified. "She married a guy named John Forbes. He had the money, she had the house. Problem was, he liked to screw anything with two legs and tits. Embarrassed the hell outta Whitney. Especially when he started screwing a real hag named Agnes Venti. Italian bitch, lemme tell ya. Anywho, when she showed up, things got weird. Real weird," she concluded with harsh laughter before sipping her wine again.

"Sam? Have you lost your mind?" Cary asked in a whisper, his hand on her arm.

She glared over at him, gaze falling to his hand, which he removed. "I was talking," she said flatly. Turning back to her audience, she continued. "One night, mysteriously, Whitney disappeared. Never to be seen again, can you believe that?" She crossed one leg over the other, picking up a crumb from the dinner roll she'd eaten from the wood table and dropped it on her plate. "Three months later, Agnes moved in. Imagine that." She downed the rest of her wine before raising the glass in Stormy's direction.

Without a word, he pushed away from the table and hurried from the room, only to return with a new bottle, which he uncorked before refilling Sam's glass. "Thank you," she said. "Anyway, so Agnes is the new woman of the house, and a woman starts working for her as a cook. Sometimes, this woman brings her daughter, Sephora, in to help out." She looked at Tandy, snickering. "Target found, prepare to destroy." She looked over at Tandy. "They tell you you're a lot like your cousin Hope, don't they?" she asked softly.

"I've been told that yes," Tandy said. "That I remind some of the older family members of her."

Sam smirked. "Golly, wonder why." She took a drink of her wine before she continued. "You know where Sephora Lloyd is buried?" she asked, glancing at Stormy. "Check out the Pauper's Field at Ridgewood Falls." She gave him a sad smile. "Yep, forever at the loony bin." She let out a long, tired sigh. "It got 'em all, you know. But it started with Sonia Lucas. You wanna know how to get rid of this goddamn thing, look at her."

"How the hell does she know all this?" Cary asked, confused wonder in his voice.

Sam set her wine glass down before she dropped it, the object feeling as though it weighed fifty pounds. She brought her hands to her face, rubbing at it as she felt a wave of exhaustion sweep through her and an instant headache start dead center of her forehead.

"Sam?" Tandy said softly, placing her hand on Sam's arm, concern in her eyes. "What happened?"

"She's remembering," Stormy said, looking at Tandy, then Cary. "She knows this because she was there."

Sam's hands slid from her face as she looked at him. Truth was, she felt like she'd taken a little trip away from the table, no memory of the previous minutes and no idea why everyone was looking distinctly uncomfortable. "What? Who? Where?"

Stormy met her gaze, a small, knowing smile on his lips.

"What the heck?" Cary asked, upset confusion in his voice. "It was like she was possessed."

"Calm down, honey," Daisy said, reaching across the table as far as she could and touching Cary's hand where it lay on the table.

"The 'what' you seek," Stormy said to Sam,

who was nearly in tears herself, as her headache was getting worse and she was deeply unsettled seeing Cary as upset as he was. "Is the culmination of four lives, three of which were cut tragically short. The 'who' is you, Samantha. And the 'where' is the house, Whitney Grove."

Sam stared at him, trying to process what he was saying. "So, the lives of these women, guessing all of them died at Whitney Grove? I know Sonia did, but I'm part of this because I'm there renovating the place?" she asked flatly, feeling nauseated.

"The connection between all of you isn't the house, Samantha," Stormy said softly.

Sam got to her feet. "I need to go now," she muttered, worried she'd get sick.

"Yeah, let's go—"

"I'll take her, Cary," Tandy said, also getting to her feet. She gave him an apologetic smile. "If that's okay."

"Uh, sure. Yeah." He glanced at Sam, who simply nodded her acquiescence.

Daisy and Stormy stood, Daisy walking around the table to Sam. She took her in a warm embrace. "It'll all be okay," she murmured into the hug. "Everything will make more sense in the morning." She left a kiss to her cheek before releasing her.

Sam met her gaze and gave her a weak smile, not sure what to say to any of it. She accepted a quick hug from Cary, then Stormy was in front of her. He took both of her hands in his soft, warm ones.

"You're on the path now, Samantha," he said softly. "The tie between four women and four lives isn't one house, it's one soul."

All she could do was stare at him.

❧ ❧ ❧ ❧

Tandy pulled up to her house and pulled the car to a stop in her driveway. Car still running, she glanced over at Sam, who sat quietly in the passenger seat. "Is this okay? Or do you want me to take you to your house?"

Sam shook her head, meeting Tandy's concerned expression. "No. This is good." Truth was, there was nowhere else she wanted to be.

They made their way into the house, Cubed waiting for them at the door. She rubbed first against Tandy's legs, then moved on to Sam's.

"Hey, pretty girl," Tandy murmured, reaching down to run her hand along the length of the cat's soft fur before she continued on into the kitchen. Sam did the same, though she also gave the purring cat some loves under her chin before the feline skittered off

Sam walked into the kitchen as Tandy offered her something to drink. "Water?" she asked. Her mouth felt dry, and though her head had stopped pulsing, it felt like it was full of feathers.

"You got it," Tandy said with a smile.

Sam watched her go to the fridge and grab a bottle of spring water, twisting off the cap as she grabbed two small glasses from the cabinet.

"Your dad was talking about reincarnation," Sam said quietly, accepting the glass she was offered. "Wasn't he?"

Tandy nodded, standing close to her as she sipped from her glass. "He was."

Sam nodded, looking down into the cold, clear depths of the water she'd been given. "And," she said, her voice even more quiet, "you're somehow involved in all this, too. Aren't you?"

Tandy met her gaze. "My father seems to think so. And I know how deeply drawn to you and connected to you I feel."

"You trust what your dad says? I mean, with this stuff?" Sam took a sip, though more for something to do with her nervous energy than because she was truly thirsty, though she was.

Tandy nodded. "Always. Dad is very connected to things that I honestly don't understand. He's got the whole psychic medium thing going, but it's so much more than that. Mom once told me he was known as a mystic." She smiled. "Not entirely sure what that means. But I do know he knows things, senses things, just..." She shrugged, fingernails tapping lightly against her glass. "He has access to a knowledge and understanding far greater than you or I could ever grasp." She gave Sam a sad smile. "One time, when I was in California, I had been offered a job doing a photo shoot. Nothing major, you know, like four hundred bucks," she said, waving off the amount. "But back then, to a twenty-one-year-old kid, that was rent and a few groceries."

Sam grinned, nodding. She understood all too well.

"So, anyway, I hadn't said yes, hadn't said no, really wasn't sure. I really hated modeling, just not my thing. But..."

"The money," Sam finished.

"Yes. The money. It was honest money, especially compared to what some of the girls I knew out there were doing to get by. So, I had to give him an answer by the next morning, and my dad calls me the night before. Before I could even say 'hello,' he was adamant, 'Don't say yes, Tandy! It'll be the last thing you ever do.' What? I was so confused. Ultimately, he was right. I said no, and the girl who took my place was never seen again. Turns out, the photographer had raped and murdered her in the desert."

"Oh, my god!" Sam exclaimed, horrified. She shook her head. "That's awful."

Tandy nodded. "Yeah." She studied Sam for a moment before she set her glass on the counter reaching for Sam's and doing the same. She closed the scant distance between them, and in the darkness of her kitchen, she took Sam in an embrace.

Sam's eyes fell closed as she buried her face in Tandy's hair, which was down, as opposed to the usual messy bun or ponytail. She inhaled its scent, liking the little tickle of the soft auburn strands against her cheek. "It's been a rough week," Tandy whispered.

Sam nodded, strengthening her hold, their bodies flush. She let out a contented sigh as she absorbed Tandy's warmth, her softness, the smell of her. She felt fingers lightly running through the dark strands of her hair as her face buried deeper into Tandy, her lips and nose coming into contact with the fevered warmth of the flesh of her neck. She swore it was a sensation she'd felt a hundred times before.

As of their own accord, her lips left a small kiss on the side of Tandy's neck. She heard the softest gasp and felt the hand that rested on her back take a bit of Sam's button-up shirt into its grip. Feeling emboldened, Sam pressed her lips against Tandy's neck again, this time lingering, her hands on Tandy's back pulling her that much closer. Tandy's head fell slightly to the side, exposing more of her neck to Sam's lips.

Sam was quickly losing herself, utterly intoxicated by Tandy's skin, her very presence. She could hear the quickening breathing of the woman in her arms, her own heart rate jumping from the first taste of Tandy's neck as she lightly flicked her tongue at it.

The hand that had been in Sam's hair slid down to cup the side of Sam's neck as Tandy gently pushed Sam's mouth away from her neck, pulling it to her own mouth. Sam sighed into the kiss as it deepened, her hand sliding up into Tandy's hair.

Soon, the kitchen was filled with the sounds of their heavy breathing. Finally, forehead resting against Sam's, Tandy's hand slid from Sam's neck down over her shoulder and to her hand, which she curled her fingers around, Sam interlacing them. Without a word, the two walked through the dark house back to Tandy's bedroom.

With the flick of her wrist, Tandy switched the bedside table lamp on, sending a warm buttery light across her bedroom and the bed, which Cubed was sprawled out across. The tip of her tail thumped against the comforter like a rattlesnake, her displeasure at their appearance evident. She let it be known vocally when Tandy shooed her off the bed.

An apologetic smile on her lips, Tandy turned back to Sam. With the gentlest touch, she began to undress Sam, her fingers caressing skin as it was exposed to her gaze, which belied the gentleness of her touch, but looked as though it were devouring the sight before.

Sam reached for Tandy, cupping the back of her head to bring her in for a slow, deep kiss before she released her, her thumb running along Tandy's full bottom lip before she let herself continue to be undressed.

Naked, Sam watched as Tandy pulled down the covers, patting the mattress for Sam to climb on, which she did. She watched as Tandy undressed herself, those beautiful eyes never leaving Sam's. Sam was taken aback by the beauty that was revealed to her. As human as anyone else, with flaws and blemishes, but to Sam's eyes, Tandy was perfection. She was utter and total perfection.

Sam reached for her once Tandy had completely disrobed, Tandy allowing herself to be gently pulled onto the bed and over to Sam. They lay on their sides, facing each other. Sam couldn't take her gaze off Tandy, this beautiful creature who so enraptured her from the very first moment she'd seen her that day at the house. She brought up her cast-wrapped hand and used her fingers sticking out to brush soft strands of hair back behind Tandy's ear.

The words were verbalized from her mouth, but they came from her soul. "I've been looking for you," she whispered, knowing every word was true, even if she didn't fully understand them. "Waiting for you."

Tandy smiled, her hand reaching out to rest on Sam's hip, pulling her closer. "You finally found me," she murmured before taking Sam in a deep, exploratory kiss as she pushed her to her back.

Sam went willingly, reveling in the touch and attention. Her eyes fell closed and her lips open as Tandy worshipped Sam's body, using fingers, tongue, teeth, and all the passion that so easily came through. Her fingers entangled in Tandy's hair as soft, wet kisses moved from Sam's breasts farther down her body, her thighs urged to part.

Her groan was just as long and languid as the slow stroke of a fiery tongue through her desire. She gripped onto the hand that found hers as Tandy made love to her with her mouth, Sam's eruption imminent. Her breasts heaved with her heavy breaths, heart racing as her pleasure built. With a small squeeze to her uninjured hand, Tandy released her as she wrapped her arms around Sam's thighs, holding on as her tongue worked Sam into a groaning mass of pulsing, throbbing flesh. Finally, she cried out, her fingers claw-like in Tandy's hair, holding her in place as that torturous tongue pressed hard against that most sensitive place, sending Sam flying over the edge.

Hand going to cover her eyes, Sam tried to get herself back under control, her body trembling slightly from the intensity of the experience. She was surprised, and a bit ashamed, as she felt emotion build, tears threatening to break through the tenuous hold she had over them. To her horror, as Tandy kissed her way back up Sam's body, her dam broke and the tears flowed out of her eyes and slid down to tickle her ears.

"Baby," Tandy murmured, saying nothing more as she lowered her body to lay atop Sam's and held her close, leaving kisses to Sam's neck as they clung to each other.

Sam felt Tandy's closeness, being in her arms, and the tears slowed and then stopped, the confusion replaced by the deepest love she'd ever felt. She knew in that moment that she'd loved Tandy before, had loved her many times, and that empty feeling she'd felt her entire life was gone, filled, her soul complete.

That knowledge and understanding filled her with a passion so deep, she needed to share it. She cupped Tandy's face, bringing her in for a long, slow kiss, every ounce of everything she felt in that kiss.

She pushed Tandy to her back, careful not to put any pressure on her hand or wrist, as she lay next to her. She continued their kiss, hands running over the canvas of the incredible work of art that was Tandy's body. She touched the soft, warm skin of a shoulder, the rigid tautness of a hard nipple, which she lightly twisted and tugged on, eliciting a gasp from Tandy. Her hand continued to cup a full breast, so beautiful, so utterly womanly before moving down along Tandy's torso, fingernails trailing along the soft skin of her belly. She smiled into their kiss when she felt the muscles beneath the skin flutter at the move, which seemed to cause a ticklish response.

Finally, they reached their goal. She reached down and took one of Tandy's legs, wrapping her fingers under her thigh and urging it to rest over Sam's legs, opening her up to Sam's questing fingers. Sam groaned at the immense wetness she found there, Tandy's need so hot and swollen.

Tandy whimpered as Sam entered her with two fingers, easily sliding in. Her thumb moved up to find her hard and ready. She gently massaged her in rhythm with her fingers as they gently thrust inside.

Tandy's breathing was becoming too hard for them to continue kissing, but Sam stayed with her, murmuring words of comfort and encouragement as she increased her speed, little moans of sympathy leaving her lips as Tandy's hips moved with her, her gorgeous breasts heaving as her chest moved with her every breath. Suddenly, Tandy grew quiet, her face contorting in pleasure as Sam's fingers were locked inside of her. Tandy's orgasm swept through her, bursting out in a loud grunt, her back arching off the bed.

When she was able to, Sam removed her fingers, pulling Tandy's limp body to her, holding her as she attempted to get her bearings. She caressed Tandy's back, leaving small kisses on her forehead and lips.

After several moments, Tandy's eyes opened, looking directly into Sam's. She smiled, a hand coming up to caress the side of Sam's face. "I love you, Sam," she whispered. "I've loved you for a long, long time."

Sam's smile was big and happy. "I love you, too."

Chapter Sixteen

S am glanced down at the paper in her hand, a printed map with a yellow highlighted "x" scratched over the area she was looking for. She looked at the numbered marker on the corner and saw that it matched the one on the page.

"X marks the spot," she muttered, folding the map and tucking it into the back pocket of her jeans as she scanned for the specific one she sought.

Since two nights before, when she and Tandy had first made love, she'd been contemplating what she was about to do. It was time. It all had to come to an end.

She stopped, surrounded by a sea of names and dates. She turned in a slow circle, looking at each one she could; finally, she spotted it. Her heart was in her throat as she walked two rows over and down until she stopped. The plastic crinkled as her right hand clutched the wrapped stems of the flowers. A strange thing, bringing flowers for one's own grave.

Blowing out a breath, she looked down at the simple polished limestone headstone:

Sonia Anne Martin
March 23, 1953 – September 3, 1977
Loving mother

"Loving mother," Sam murmured aloud, reading

the stone.

Slowly lowering herself to sit on the grass, crisp from the cold winter and spring weather, Sam studied the stone's inscription for a long moment. It was surreal, very surreal, to be staring at a name that was slowly coming into focus for her over the last couple of days. If she gave it true and honest thought, it had been for the last couple of months that she'd been at Whitney Grove. The past two nights had brought her a flood of dreams, moving images of cleavage-filled soirees filled with lust. Those would flow into a lonely tour of a huge cathedral, priest in Roman collar watching from the shadows, only to find herself back at the bottom of the basement stairs. The one commonality among them all was the dueling feelings of betrayal and a deep, penetrating love, a love that had traveled across time and space, only to return to its roots, Whitney Grove.

Now as she tried to work it all out in her mind and in her heart, out of the many missing pieces, two haunted her the most: was Chloe still alive, and how could she end the cycle of violence and betrayal? Stormy called it a traveler. What was that, she'd asked, and he responded that it was evil itself, and at some point, she'd pissed it off.

She smirked to herself as she reached out, removing a dead leaf that had blown against the stone, wiping some dirt away. The situation was about as clear as mud to her, but to Stormy, it seemed all was falling into place. That was a bit comforting, she supposed, as he seemed to be the only one who truly understood everything.

She scooped out some dirt and debris from the bronze flower holder at the base of the stone before unwrapping the plastic from hers and lovingly fitting them into the cold metal holder. The bright whites and purples of the petals were a nice contrast against the slate gray of the stone.

Suddenly, a wave of emotion swept over her, and her shoulders shook as she was racked with sobs. Her hands covered her face, the cuffs of her jacket quickly saturated by her tears. It was as though she were releasing an entire lifetime of hurt and grief. Fact was, she was releasing three lifetimes of hurt and grief, all packed into the heart of Samantha Leyton.

Slowly, oh so slowly, the tears dried up. She dug out a wadded-up tissue from her jacket pocket and used it to wipe at her eyes and nose. She took several healing breaths of the cool, crisp air, glancing up into the sky, the blue just starting to give way to the soothing golds of the falling sun. It was then that she realized she wasn't alone.

Looking to her right, she saw a figure standing near a tree. The person was too far away to tell if it was female or male, and the bulky jacket didn't help. But from the width of the hips, she thought it might be a woman. The person wore a baseball cap and sunglasses, the two together making it impossible to see much of the face. All Sam did know was the person was looking right at her. She met the sunglass-covered gaze for a long moment before she looked away as she pushed to her feet. Once standing, she looked again. The figure was gone.

❧ ❧ ❧ ❧

"Are you sure?" Tandy asked softly.

Sam contemplated the question for a moment

as she readjusted her head and cheek where they lay against the softness of auburn hair. In return, Tandy tightened her grip across Sam's naked stomach, her head resting on Sam's shoulder. It had been a long, hard day at the house, but it was all worth it to be in Tandy's arms that night. "Yeah," she finally said. "I think I need to do this alone." She considered what she said for a moment before she amended her statement. "No. I know I do."

❧ ❧ ❧ ❧

"Put your arms out, miss."

Sam lifted her arms while the uniformed man behind her scanned her person with a handheld metal detector. She turned when he asked her to, noting his professionalism as he ran the machine all around her cast, careful not to bump it.

"Break your hand?" He indicated she could relax as he stepped back around the counter where her cellphone, wallet, and car keys rested in the provided plastic tray.

"My wrist. Fell down some stairs."

"A bit of a hazard with what you do, I imagine," he said. He spared a glance at her amused expression. "Um, my wife loves your show." He cleared his throat. "I do, too."

She grinned. "I appreciate that. Do I leave these here?" She indicated the belongings he'd had her remove from her pockets.

"No, ma'am, you may stow them in one of those lockers over there." He pointed to a bank of small cube lockers painted orange that were mounted to the wall on one side of the small lobby.

She smiled her gratitude and grabbed her items and did as he recommended. She followed the small group who had come to Territorial Correctional Facility to visit an offender.

The room wasn't huge, but it wasn't small. Round tables were strategically placed, flanked by plastic chairs with a thin padding on the seat. The brown carpet was aged Berber, worn from years of inmate and visitor tread. Some tables were already taken, one inmate per, easily indicated by their pale skin and inmate uniform that resembled kelly green scrubs, their inmate number on a thin white strip attached to the upper left chest.

Sam scanned the room until she saw an elderly man sitting alone at a table, his laced fingers resting on the table. Her heart lurched into her throat before it fell with a painful thud in the pit of her gut. Swallowing down her nerves—and some bile—she made her way over to him.

"Richard Lucas?" Sam asked, stepping up to the table.

He looked up at her, eyes huge behind the thick lenses of prison-issued glasses with cheap plastic frames, something in style from 1987.

"Yes, ma'am. Please, have a seat." He indicated one of the other three available chairs.

"Thank you," she said politely, choosing the chair across from him. She took a moment to gather her thoughts and emotions as she scooted her chair close to the table. Clearing her throat, she looked at him. His hair was thin and completely white, brushed back from his face. He wore sideburns and a goatee. His skin was pasty pale, a few age spots on his forehead, larger from a recessed hairline. "Um, can I get you something? Water? A pop?" she asked, indicating the vending machines that were against the wall several feet behind her.

Richard looked past her, then met her gaze, a smile coming to his lips. "You know, I'd give my right eye for a Mountain Dew."

She nodded and pushed away from the table. Truth was, she was grateful to get away from him for a moment. She waited for a woman to make her purchase, then pulled some coins out of her pocket that she was allowed to take in for just this purpose, inserting them into the machine. Neon green bottle for Richard, bottle of Coke for herself. She walked back to the table, setting his in front of him before retaking her seat.

"Bless you," he said with a genuine smile as he twisted off the cap and took a healthy swig. "Oh, goodness, that's good."

Sam couldn't help but let a little smile slip out. It was like watching a child taste chocolate for the first time. She set her drink aside, concerned that if she took a drink at that point, she'd throw it up.

"I appreciate you agreeing to see me," she began, lacing her fingers on the table, much as his had been when she approached him. "I know you had to agree to put me on your visitor list."

"Well, of course," he said happily. "I was thrilled someone wanted to visit me at all. Such a rare treat. Once in a while, my pen pal will come visit, but he's older now, and it's harder for him to get up to Cañon City." He looked at her, a small, content smile on his face. "What can I do for you...Forgive me, what was your name again?"

"Samantha Leyton."

"Miss Leyton. What can I do for you?" he asked again.

"Please call me Sam." She studied him. "Can I call you Richard? Or would you prefer Mr. Lucas?"

"Richard, please."

"All right. Richard." She looked down at her hands, needing to look away from his hopeful, expectant expression. Truth was, it was making her nauseated. She had a feeling of misogynistic, abusive narcissism from him, not the kind, gentle, and respectful fog she was being presented with. It was confusing and left her unsettled. "I'm here today," she began, "to talk about Sonia."

The smile froze on his face, and his gaze fell to the bottle of soda held between his hands. "Did Chloe send you?" he asked, his voice not much louder than a whisper.

"No. Does she have any contact with you?" Sam asked, hopeful that perhaps she could find her through him.

He shook his head. "No. No doubt Esther spent her entire childhood telling her what a monster her father is." Sam expected to hear petulant bitterness in his voice, but instead, she heard resigned and profound sadness.

"Were you not aware that Chloe wasn't raised by her grandmother?" Sam asked.

His head snapped up, eyes even wider than the lenses portrayed them to be. "What?"

"Apparently, raising her own granddaughter was too much for her, and Esther handed her over to a cousin to raise," Sam explained, the bitterness expected in his voice edging into hers.

He shook his head, jaw muscles bulging as he

seemed to be working to control his emotions. "You know," he said at length, clearing his throat before taking another drink of his pop. "I've been in here for almost forty-two years. Can you believe that? Spent a year in here, then got moved to CCF," he gave her a small smile. "Sorry. Insider talk. Centennial Correctional Facility, back in eighty, same year it opened. Opened for tough punks like I thought I was back then. Didn't give two darns about anyone but myself. Here's the rub, though, Sam," he added conversationally. "I was sentenced to twenty-five to life. Probably would have been out by now, but I got myself into a heap of trouble, and a man died because of it back in ninety-four. Life, no parole. I deserved that punishment. I didn't murder my wife, you see, but I deserved to be punished for it, anyway."

She was surprised by what he'd just said and studied him for a long moment. She saw nothing but truth, or at least the truth as he saw it, in his eyes. "You're saying you didn't kill Sonia?"

"As I'm sitting here, I did not kill my wife," he said firmly.

"Then, why do you say you deserve to be here for it?" she asked, head cocked to the side slightly as she studied him.

"Because I think I know who did, and I basically pushed Sonia at her," he explained easily.

"Her?" Sam was surprised. He definitely had her full attention.

"Diane DeMarco. Gosh, she was obsessed with Sonia," he murmured, grabbing his drink and taking a swig. "For a long time, I was suspicious that maybe they had something going on, but I never had any proof. Never really looked for any, you know?" He shook his head, sadness on his face. "Truth is, I just didn't care. I wasn't ready to be a husband, a father." He met her gaze. "Now I don't want you to take that as any sort of excuse for the way I was."

"How were you?" she asked quietly, pain in her voice and in her heart.

"Selfish. Stubborn. Sometimes, downright heartless," he admitted. Though the words seemed to flow easily, his tone was filled with regret. "Immature as hell. For a long time, I blamed Esther. You know, if only she hadn't seduced me, if only Sonia hadn't been so insistent I be home and responsible. If only Chloe hadn't made me feel so damn guilty about not being home enough, if only, if only, if only. Truth is," he added, looking Sam dead in the eye. "Truth is, there was nobody to blame but myself. Took me so long to figure that out, to really come to terms with that." He snorted. "Took me a long time to forgive myself. Again, the 'if onlys,' as my good buddy in here used to call them. If only I had been there, if only I had been a better man. If only I'd told Diane to leave her the hell alone."

"That had to be really hard," Sam said, her heart turning now from suspicion and anger to sympathy and respect for the man who sat across from her, the man who any daughter would be proud to call her father.

He nodded. "During the trial, I heard that Sonia was planning to leave, take Chloe and go to New York, I think it was, with her friend. I forget her name now. I think she wanted to be a singer, if I recall."

"Daisy," Sam said softly.

"Yeah!" he said with a snap of his fingers. "Daisy. I was thinking it was a flower, but Tulip didn't seem right somehow."

Sam smiled. "She did become a singer. Have you ever heard of Maria Sonia?"

"Isn't she an opera singer, Broadway musicals and stuff?" he asked.

Sam nodded. "Yep. That's her."

"She changed her name?"

Sam smiled and nodded. "Yeah. She honored Sonia in that way. They were very close when Sonia died," she whispered, emotion in her voice.

He looked down at his hands again, staying that way for a long time. Finally, he looked up, a sad smile on his lips and tears magnified in his eyes. "Sonia would have really blossomed in New York. Chloe too." His smile grew a bit. "You know, you kinda remind me of Sonia, in a way. Same kind of calm energy. Know what I mean?"

She nodded. "I do." Needing to be alone and to think, she said, "I thank you for your time today, Richard. Thank you for the answers."

He used his arm to wipe at his eyes, nodding. "Absolutely." He stood as she did, holding out his hand to her.

She looked down at it for a moment, then placed hers in it. His pale hand was larger, and it engulfed her hand, his other one covering them both in a warm, affectionate touch. She smiled at him, feeling a weight lifted from her shoulders, a bit of closure.

"If you happen to see my daughter, please tell her I love her," he said softly, releasing her as Sam gently pulled her hand away.

Sam nodded. "I will." She gave him a final smile and grabbed her unopened bottle of Coke and began to walk out.

"Sam?"

She turned back to see him standing where she'd left him, waiting expectantly for him to reveal the reason he'd called to her.

"You never did tell me. Who sent you here today to talk to me?" he asked.

Her smile widened. "I'm here for Sonia," she responded, then turned and walked away.

≈≈≈≈

"You know, I bought this house when Tandy was around eleven or twelve, I want to say," Daisy said, Sam following her from room to room as Daisy watered her many inside plants. "I love the big windows." She smiled over her shoulder at Sam. "In between albums or tours or shows, I'd come back here so Tandy could spend time with Stormy. Plus," she added, "it was so nice to get away from the city, you know?"

Sam nodded, as she was directed to water a hanging plant, which required climbing to get to. Once in place on the small ladder, she took the watering can Daisy extended to her. "I do. Thanks," she said, as Daisy took her hand to help her keep her balance. Sam climbed down from the step stool in the sunroom of the adorable little Spanish-style home outside Highlands Ranch, Colorado.

"After Tandy was old enough to be on her own, she lived here for a while as she figured out what she wanted to be when she grew up." Daisy grinned as she led the way to the kitchen where she turned the emptied watering can upside down to drain on a drying mat spread out next to the farm sink.

"You must be so proud of her," Sam said, an

instant smile coming to her face at the topic at hand. Her chest swelled, heart nearly jumping out of her chest as it exploded with feeling and love.

"I am. Lemonade?" Daisy pulled open one side of her double-door fridge. At Sam's nod, she pulled out the glass pitcher, setting it on the island where Sam had taken a seat. She went over to the cabinet to fetch two glasses. "Tandy has always been her own woman, so smart, so focused on just being..." She paused as she seemed to be considering her words. "On being *Tandy*, I guess." She smiled, pride of a mother in her eyes. "Ice?"

"No, thanks."

Daisy poured one glass and set it in front of Sam before pouring her own. "She really loves you, you know," she said softly, eyeing Sam. "I've never seen her look so, not sure what the word is," she murmured, bringing her lemonade up to sip.

"Complete," Sam suggested, the smile still not leaving her lips as she looked into the cool green-yellow depths of her own drink.

"Yes," Daisy agreed. "Perfect word." Daisy studied Sam so long that Sam felt her gaze on her and met it. "It's extraordinary," she whispered. "Sonia came back."

Sam still felt a little uncomfortable with all of it, found it confusing and against a lifetime of conditioning to think a certain way. "You believe all this?" she asked, already knowing the answer but needing to hear it anyway.

"Oh, yes," Daisy said, her smile wide and beautiful. "I see her in you. It's wild, to be honest. The way you'll say something, your mannerisms." She shook her head in wonder. "Even your eye color. Sonia had the most beautiful green eyes. Just like yours."

Sam let out a shaky breath, nodding. "Richard said something similar."

"Richard?" Daisy took a half step back to go along with the shock in her voice and expression.

"I went to see him in prison last week," Sam admitted, sitting back in the stool she sat on.

"Why on earth would you do that?" Daisy leaned on her forearms as she rested them on the granite top of the cooking island, her gaze boring into Sam's.

"I wanted to know the truth. I wanted to hear it from him. And," she added with a slight shrug. "I wanted to know if he knew where Chloe was. He doesn't. But he told me he didn't do it. He's not responsible for Sonia's death."

"And do you believe him?" Daisy asked, her voice hard.

"I do." Sam met Daisy's surprised gaze, her own steady. "He took full responsibility for how he treated her, the lackluster father he was to Chloe, but he absolutely denies hurting her."

Daisy sipped her lemonade as she seemed to mull that over. At length, she said, "You know, it makes sense somehow." She set her glass down and tapped manicured nails against the side. "He had nothing to lose if Sonia left him." She met Sam's gaze. "It wasn't like he was worth millions and would lose half. Hell, they didn't own anything. To be honest, I always wondered why he'd done it then. Sure, he could be a controlling asshole, but I thought he'd be far more relieved to be rid of the albatross around his neck when Sonia and Chloe left. Then, he'd be free to go on and live his life as he chose." She placed a hand to her forehead before running it back over her hair, which was pulled back in a messy bun, just like her daughter, and just like her daughter, she managed to look beautifully put together in a messy, casual way.

"No motive," Sam added.

Daisy nodded. "No motive. So, maybe it was just a random attack?"

"He mentioned his boss at the time. A woman named Diane DeMarco. Did you know her?"

Daisy nodded. "I knew *of* her. Met her once or twice, and I knew she and Sonia had a short-lived fling." Daisy raised a finger as if to say *be right back* and hurried from the room toward her first-floor master bedroom.

Left alone, Sam drank her lemonade, enjoying how refreshing the chilled tart/sweet drink was. She glanced over to the windows above the sink, the spring day beyond beautiful as everything was beginning to wake up after the long winter. The window overlooked the front of the house, and an instant smile came to her face when she saw Tandy's car pull up to the house that sat on five acres, away from prying neighbors.

She turned the stool around and stood, walking to the front door to greet the woman who had long ago stolen her heart. Her smile was wide as she opened the door just as Tandy was reaching for the doorknob.

"Hey, gorgeous," Sam said.

"Hey, yourself." Tandy grinned.

The two shared a kiss before a long, loving embrace. Sam's eyes fell closed as she breathed Tandy in, able to smell paint and turpentine on her clothes. She smiled, as that smell was becoming comforting to her, as it was pure Tandy.

"Sorry I'm late," Tandy murmured into the hug, her head resting on Sam's shoulder. "That ceiling in the upstairs bathroom took longer than I thought."

"Did you get it done?" Sam asked, her thumb running absently back and forth over Tandy's shoulder. She smiled at the nod and uh-huh, she got, almost like a child. "One more room to go, huh?"

Tandy let out a tired sigh as she pulled away. She brought up a hand and ran it through Sam's hair. "Yup. Almost there."

"Gonna miss you at the house," Sam murmured. "Gotten spoiled with you around all the time."

Tandy grinned. "Oh, I'm sure I'll find excuses to pop in."

"There's my girl!"

They both turned to see Daisy standing in the kitchen, a straight line of sight to the front door with the open floorplan of the first floor.

"Hey, Mom." Tandy grabbed Sam's hand and led the way to the cooking island where Daisy met her, giving Tandy a quick but tight hug. "Can I have whatever you guys are drinking?" She picked up Sam's glass and sniffed it.

"Coming up."

Tandy took a seat next to Sam, who reclaimed her seat at the island. "What do you think about all this, Mom? I'm assuming Sam told you about Richard."

"I'm not entirely sure what to think," Daisy said, sparing Tandy a glance as she poured her a glass of lemonade. "But I grabbed this again, Sam." She set the pitcher down and placed the Polaroid she'd left on the counter in front of Sam. It was the same picture she'd shared with her the day they sat on the picnic table. "You got pretty upset the first time you saw this, but I was curious now, after a lot has changed and is clearer to you, what your thoughts would be."

Sam took a deep breath before picking up the picture and studying it for a second time. The first time, she'd had a visceral reaction to it, but Daisy was right, much had happened since that day. She was comforted when she felt Tandy's chin rest on her shoulder, looking at the picture with her. Immediately, her gaze went to the woman standing to Daisy's right with the short dark hair, all dressed in black.

"That's her," she murmured, tapping the image with her finger. "That's Diane DeMarco."

"Yes, it is," Daisy confirmed, leaning on her forearms again on the cool granite countertop.

"God, she looks like an evil bitch," Tandy murmured. "Look at the expression on her face."

"Aimed right at Sonia," Sam murmured.

Chapter Seventeen

October 1, 1977:
At 5 p.m. Saturday, police were alerted to a yellow pickup truck parked near Stapleton Airport. Upon arriving at the scene, a woman was found slumped over in the cab with what was believed to be a self-inflicted bullet wound to the head with a .38 revolver. The woman has been identified as thirty-six-year-old Diane DeMarco. No further investigation is planned in the death, Police Chief Robert Gables said.

Sam read the article again, then sat back in her chair. She could feel three sets of eyes on her. To buy herself time as she processed it, she tossed a ketchup-drenched French fry into her mouth as they were taking a lunch break from working. Finally, she spoke.

"So, she committed suicide almost a month to the day after Sonia was murdered." She lowered the printout and glanced at Stormy and Cary. "If she did it, think maybe it was guilt?"

"I want you to read this one before I answer that." Stormy handed her a printout of another old newspaper article.

"Okay. And you said Lexi helped you find this stuff?" she asked, taking the sheet.

He nodded, sipping his milkshake. "Good little researcher," he muttered around the straw.

Sam smiled and looked at the article.

February 15, 1968
Funeral services for Stephanie DeMarco, seven,
were held at Riverside Cemetery today. DeMarco was
accidentally struck and killed Sunday when a fifteen-
year-old driver lost control during the heavy rainstorm
that hit the Denver Metro area. The minor's mother,
Esther Martin, said her daughter is distraught over the
incident. Stephanie's mother, Diane DeMarco, twenty-
seven, was too emotional for comment.

Sam gasped, a hand coming to her mouth. "Oh, my god!" Eyes huge, she turned to look at Stormy, the page seesawing its way to the floor where Cary reached down and picked it up, reading it. "Oh, my god," she whispered again. Somewhere, deep in the recesses of her mind, she could hear the squealing of tires and the pounding of overworked windshield wipers. Her eyes squeezed closed, and the tears came, the distant scream echoing in her head.

"I don't think she killed herself because of guilt," Stormy said softly, his hand rubbing comforting circles on Sam's back.

"Then why?" She sniffled, looking over at him.

He studied her tear-streaked face for a moment, absently reaching for a napkin from the fast food place they'd gotten lunch from and handing it to her. She wiped her eyes and nose. "Because she was on the hunt."

"Whoa! Wait, wait, wait." Cary popped up from his chair, the page still in his hand. "I'm so confused here, guys." He walked around the card table they'd set up on the third floor and were using to eat their lunch on. He faced the other two. "So, I'm guessing, because of the name of the two moms, this is the Diane from the picture, from the first article, the one who Sonia Lucas was having a fling with. Right?"

"Yes," Stormy said.

"Okay. So, then the other mom," he glanced at the page in hand, "Esther Martin, that's the same Esther Martin you went and talked to, Sam, right? Sonia's mother."

Sam nodded, blowing her nose.

"So then, that means the minor here," he said, slapping the page with the backs of his fingers from the opposite hand holding the paper, "the one who accidentally killed the little girl, Stephanie, was Sonia?" At dual nods, Cary looked back down at the paper in his hands. "Whoa," he muttered. He chewed on his bottom lip a minute before he met Sam's gaze again. "Wait, Stormy, you're saying all this got started here, right? With Sonia?"

"I believe so, yes." Stormy dropped his hand from Sam's back as he sat back in his chair. He crossed an ankle over the opposite knee.

"Okay, solid. But if this all began with Sonia Lucas and this crazy Diane bitch, that was in 1977. You said all these lives in our little Sammy here go clear back to the lady who built this house, right? So what, 1888? Why would she and the other one, aww hell, the one with the nun..." He snapped his fingers as he appeared to be trying to remember her name.

"Sephora," Stormy provided.

"Right!" He slammed the page on the table, though Sam knew not in anger but in passion to understand. "So, Sephora, why would those two have issues with this bad thing killing them, even if it is all one soul, since they came before Sonia?"

Sam glanced at Stormy, wondering the same thing.

Easy as you please, Stormy responded, "Who said a reincarnated soul has to live chronological lives?"

"What?" Sam asked, confused. She was curious what he'd say, and clearly, Cary was, too, as he moved back to sit in his abandoned seat.

"We all have a path," Stormy explained, positioning himself so he was looking between the two. "It's a path decided partially by our own soul before we're ever born into this life. A path, however, is determinant on all the expected factors and players coming together. Sometimes, though," he said, pausing dramatically as he looked at Sam. "Sometimes, an unexpected event can happen. In this case, a dark soul happened."

"A dark soul?" Cary asked, seemingly transfixed by what Stormy was telling them. "What's that? Like a demon?"

"If that's your belief system. But it's not sent by some grand wizard of evil. A dark soul has one purpose and one purpose only, and that is to cause harm and chaos simply for the sake of causing harm and chaos."

"And," Sam said slowly, "you think this Diane DeMarco woman is the dark soul in this story?"

"She started it all, yes. See, with Sonia's murder, her entire path was disrupted, which disrupted the paths of those who were part of it." He held up a hand, ticking off his points on fingers. "Chloe's path, Daisy's path, Richard's path, Esther's path, and so on. When this happens," he continued, dropping his hand back down to his ankle, which still rested on his other knee, "things must be righted. Almost like a past history, a backstory, if you will, has to be created to bring the original path around full circle. Or," he said, looking Sam in the eye, "to stop the cycle."

Sam felt the weight of his stare and felt nailed to her seat by it.

"The traveler began here, followed you through time and space, leaving destruction and carnage in its path," he said, lowering his voice, almost as though only for her ears. "You have to stop it, Samantha."

"I don't know how," she said honestly.

"You will. It's coming, if it's not already here."

⚜ ⚜ ⚜ ⚜

Sam sat behind the wheel of her rental car, Tandy in the passenger seat. They'd arrived at Colors, a local LGBT dance club where the night's event would be held. She'd parked toward the end of the parking lot so getting out would be easier. They waited for Cary to show up, coming separately in case, in his words, "He came across a cutie he just couldn't live without for the night."

"How are you doing?" Tandy asked, her thumb rubbing the back of Sam's hand, which she held on her own thigh. "I know Dad can be pretty intense in how he explains things."

Sam smirked as she met Tandy's gaze. "He's a good guy. Yeah, I'm rattled, I won't lie, but we'll get through this."

Tandy smiled. "I'm proud of you, Sam. Tonight is about you and Cary. That's one of the reasons I loved your show, the fact that in each episode some LGBT spot was highlighted in some way." Her smile grew into a wide beam of affection and adoration. "You're my favorite lesbian on HGTV."

Sam threw her head back and laughed. "I think I'm the *only* lesbian on HGTV."

"Yes, well, a mere technicality." Tandy leaned forward and initiated a deep, promising kiss. "Come home with me tonight?" she murmured against Sam's lips.

Sam nodded. "You bet."

The two glanced at Sam's window at the tap upon it to see Cary waving.

The club was like any other, lots of crazy lights bouncing over the walls, a bar with cute bartenders ready to fulfill your every beverage fantasy and pulsing music manned by a charismatic DJ.

As per usual, the network had provided security for Sam and Cary, as people could get a little crazy at their events, especially one at a large club where it was a dark, large population, target-rich place in an era of lunatics with far-too-easy-to-get guns.

They were escorted to a back room, which from the looks of it was used for drag queen and king shows if the empty, darkened stage had anything to do with it. There were tables clustered together around the phallic-shaped bit of stage that jutted out, much like the runway for a fashion show, where a performer could come out and mingle with the audience.

"Samantha, we'll get you and Cary set up on the stage with chairs and microphones for the Q&A, then you can sign copies of your book at that table over there," the manager of the club explained, pointing at a long table already set up with taped-up boxes of their coffee table book just released a few weeks before. She and Cary had done one for the show with their favorite flips along with tips and dos and don'ts. "Sound good?"

Hands on hips, Sam looked around at the area that she knew would soon be swarming and nodded. "Let's do it."

꙳ ꙳ ꙳ ꙳

"So, she's looking at me, like, get away as I'm all excited, a new idea for landscaping in my hands!" Cary crowed, on his feet and moving around dramatically, the crowd rolling in laughter at his story. "And I'm like, what? What did I do? 'That's poison ivy, you dumbass! We can't landscape with fucking poison ivy!'" He raised his hand in the air in a dramatic gesture. "Well, how the fuck was I supposed to know? It's free, green, and prevalent."

Sam's head flew back as she sat in her chair, laughing right along with them at the memory of one of their earliest flips.

"Remember that one, Sammy?" He looked back at her from where he stood toward the end of the stage that jutted out.

She brought the microphone up to talk, but words failed her as more laughter took her over, sending the crowd into even more laughter themselves.

"See what I gotta work with?" Cary asked the audience, hip jutted out and hand resting on it.

꙳ ꙳ ꙳ ꙳

"You are so welcome! Thank you so much for coming." Sam handed the book over, signed to the woman on the opposite side of the table. "Have fun out there."

There was a lapse in the line, which Sam was grateful for. There were only a certain amount of books to be bought, and after the hundreds of people she and Cary had just spoken with, met, shaken hands with, signed books for, she *had* to think they were nearly done. She was tired, but she promised Tandy they'd hang out for a while and dance and have a good time after the event.

"Lordy, my hand hurts worse than it did after my first gay porn marathon."

Sam glanced over at Cary, the two left alone other than the camera crew that was packing up. "That's gross."

He grinned at her, flexing his hand and fingers, the black Sharpie dropped to the tabletop. "Huge crowd tonight."

Sam nodded, flexing her own hand and fingers. She glanced toward the stage, their two chairs still sitting there, microphones laid in the seats. She stared as she saw a figure in the shadows. It was a man, it seemed, though in a club like this, anything was possible.

She pushed back from the table and grabbed the bottle of water that had been provided. "Be right back," she murmured, gaze locked on the area where she saw the lurker. She felt drawn to the person.

As though in a daze, she twisted off the cap of her water and took a swig, walking toward the shadowy figure. As she got closer, she heard a soft, slow tapping: *tap...tap...tap...*She walked around the runway section of the stage, her gaze locked on the figure. As she got closer, she could tell he was wearing a hat, a top hat, perhaps.

Nervous energy filling her, she brought the water bottle up again, the cool liquid slowly entering her mouth as she took a few more steps toward the shadows. Something caught the corner of her eye, and she lowered the bottle, following the downward motion of her hand until she saw the glint of light off something metal. It was moving up and down, seemingly part of what was making the tapping sound. As she focused on it, she made out a round object. A silver ball? Was that a skull?

"Sam!"

Gasping as she whirled around, she saw Cary standing at the table, looking at her. When he saw he had her attention, he waved her over, nodding toward another crowd of people entering the room.

Turning back to the shadows, she was alone.

꿍꿍꿍꿍

Sam could feel her blood running warm as Tandy moved in close, her hands on Sam's hips as they moved together as the slow song played loud over the huge crowd. Sam couldn't have described one person around her as Tandy was her entire world in that moment. They shared kisses and caresses as they slowly ground together. She grinned when the woman in her arms murmured in her ear what she was going to do to her later, once they'd gone back to Tandy's house. Sam was on fire.

As the song came to an end, Tandy left a lingering kiss on Sam's lips. "I love you," she murmured before pulling away with a smile. "Let's get a drink."

Sam allowed herself to be led by the hand through the throngs of people to the bar where Tandy continued to move to the beat of the new song that played, a dance beat. Being the driver, Sam opted for a Coke while Tandy ordered a cocktail for herself.

"Figure I should drink this while I can," she said into Sam's ear, loud enough to be heard over the heavy beat.

Sam grinned. She knew what Tandy wanted more than anything, and that was to have a baby. She and Tandy were working on building their foundation, though they hadn't had the discussion that Sam knew was necessary. Once the house was finished, which was only a few months away, what then? She knew she wanted a future with Tandy, that wasn't a question. She'd found her and wasn't going to lose her again. But still, there was much to be discussed and decided.

For tonight, however, she was going to have a good time. As Tandy spoke with the bartender, a young woman with half her head shaved and the other half buzzcut pink turquoise hair, Sam bobbed her head to the beat and looked out over the crowd. She had long ago outgrown her dance club days, but it was fun to spend time in one with Tandy, who loved music, loved to dance, and looked amazing doing it.

Something caught her eye, and it wasn't the two bodybuilder guys who were making out, but the very top of a top hat that was moving, the wearer shorter than the two human mountains, so the flat top of the hat bobbed along just over the tops of their heads.

A lump fell into the pit of her stomach, and Sam moved her body to watch the hat, which moved behind a dense crowd of revelers. She waited with bated breath for the person to come out from behind them over by the DJ booth, where the crowd thinned out.

"Come on, come on," she whispered, waiting on

pins and needles as the top hat slowed its movement as it got closer to the end of the crush of people.

"Babe!"

Startled, Sam whipped her head around to see Tandy looking at her, a blue something or other in her hand with a thin slice of orange wedged on the lip of the glass. "What?"

"What are you looking at? I called your name like four times," Tandy said, confusion in her eyes. "Anyway, this is Kai. She wants an autograph."

Mentally shaking her head to clear it, Sam looked past Tandy to the bartender with the asymmetric hair. "Hi!" she said above the music, instantly turning on her professional charm.

"Hey!" The bartender grinned, which made her many facial piercings move. "I'm a huge fan of your show. Would you be willing to sign a napkin for me?"

On automatic pilot, Sam took the cocktail napkin and pen she was offered, asked who to make the autograph out to, and accepted a quick hug over the bar, all the while surreptitiously scanning her surroundings. She felt deeply uneasy.

Fan moment finished, Sam turned back to Tandy, who was sipping her drink. Tandy let the straw slip from her lips. "What's wrong?"

Sam shook her head, accepting the bottle of water from the bartender that had been ordered for her. She smiled her thanks before twisting off the cap and taking a long swig. She was going to just not mention to Tandy how unsettled she was feeling, but seeing the concern in her eyes, she finally said, "I just have this weird feeling. I feel like the traveler is here." She shrugged. "Like I'm being stalked."

Tandy reached out and rubbed Sam's arm.

"Baby, I know my dad really shook you up. If you want, I'll talk to him and ask that he simmer down with all this."

Though tempted, Sam shook her head. "No. He's just doing what he thinks is right." She didn't know Stormy well, but she felt that in her gut. He was concerned, and that had her concerned, on top of her own unsettled feelings about things.

Tandy leaned forward and placed a loving, lingering kiss on Sam's lips. "We're fine, Sam. There's nobody here but us." She smirked. "And hundreds of rabid women who want you to sign their breasts."

Sam burst into laughter. "Hey, only two asked for that. Everyone else just wanted their book signed."

"Well, it's still intimidating, but I can handle it." She set her drink on the bar, reaching around Sam to do so. She brushed her breast against Sam's arm in the process. "Besides," she said, voice dropping to a sultry level as the song that had been playing ended, another about to start. "I'm the only one taking you home with me tonight."

Though it hadn't been long since they'd found their way back to each other, it had been long enough for Sam to know good things happened with that tone of Tandy's voice. Her water bottle was taken and placed next to Tandy's drink before she was once again led back to the dance floor.

They found a spot as the keyboard intro to the next song began. Sam had heard the song before, *The Sun* by Parov Stelar. It was a fun dance tune without the heavy *thumpa thumpa*, and she tried to just enjoy it and enjoy Tandy. She grinned when Tandy turned and began to grind her very shapely ass into Sam's crotch, Sam taking hold of her hips.

As they moved together, Sam was desperately trying to lose herself in the music, lose herself in Tandy's body and in the energy of the pulsing club, but she just couldn't. She found herself looking around again as the song launched into its chorus. She tried to ignore it, squeezing her eyes shut as she felt the wings of panic batter at her ribcage.

Balancing on the razor's edge of control, Sam started when she felt someone grab her shoulder. Thinking perhaps another dancing patron had bumped into her, she ignored it, instead trying to focus on Tandy. A moment later, she was grabbed again, this time with talon-like fingers.

Turning her head, she came face to face with Diane DeMarco. The top hat she wore was in place, and she raised her hand to the brim, tipping it in greeting. In her hand, she held a walking stick, the top of it a silver skull with red, menacing ruby eyes.

Fight or flight instantly kicked in. Sam pushed Tandy away from her and pushed her way through the crowd, blindly looking for the exit. Distantly, she heard someone yelling her name, but she was on a mission, and that mission was to get the hell out of there.

It wasn't until she'd reached her rental car that she stopped, her lungs burning from the run and the chilly spring night air. She rested her hands on the roof of the car, resting her forehead against them as she tried to calm herself. She was trembling, the terror of moments before still lingering.

"Sam!" Tandy cried out, her shoes slapping against the paved parking lot as she ran over to the car. "What happened?" she gasped, reaching her.

"I'm sorry," Sam said. "I'm sorry. I just got..."

She didn't know what to say, as she knew Diane hadn't truly been there, but good god, it had been so real! How on earth was she seeing such a crazy thing?

"Did you see something?" Tandy asked, a hand resting on Sam's back. "Did someone hurt you on the dancefloor?"

Sam shook her head, allowing herself to be embraced. "I'm sorry," she said again, feeling better in Tandy's arms. "I think I just let myself get a little worked up."

Tandy pulled back from the hug, concern evident in her eyes. She reached up and brushed dark bangs out of Sam's eyes. "Let's just go home, okay?" she said softly. "I don't think anyone's here tonight. I think you just got a little spooked."

A lot spooked! Sam nodded, not wanting to argue. "Okay."

"Our jackets are still inside, so why don't you get the car started and warmed up for me while I go grab them?" Tandy suggested with a sweet smile.

Sam grinned. "Yes, ma'am."

She watched Tandy jog back toward the building as she pulled out her car keys from her pocket. She glanced down at the key fob. She was about to press the button that would start the engine when someone caught her attention.

"Samantha!"

She turned to see a tall woman hurrying toward her from an SUV parked closer to the building. The woman had shoulder-length dark hair and sky blue eyes. She reminded Sam of the title character from the old TV show *Xena: Warrior Princess*.

"Oh, my god, I'm so excited I caught you before you left!" the woman gushed, a huge smile on her beautiful face. "My wife, Abel, and I are here on vacation from Maine, and when she heard you were going to be at this event, she went nuts. We got here too late for the book signing, and she's pretty upset."

Sam grinned. "Well, here I am." She was grateful for the distraction from the earlier events.

"Would you do me the absolutely enormous favor of signing our book for us? It's in my car over there." She indicated the dark-colored SUV with a hitch of her thumb. "Abel's inside using the restroom before we head out, so..."

"Sure. I'd be happy to." Sam followed the woman to the SUV and waited while she opened the back passenger-side door and brought out the coffee table book. "Got a pen?

"I do." The woman produced a Sharpie from her pocket, handing it over. "Brought for this very purpose."

"Excellent thinking," Sam said with a chuckle, removing the cap and opening the large book to the page she'd been using to sign all night, holding it against the side of the black Ford Explorer. "And what's your name?"

"Zac," the woman said. "Spelled Z-A-C."

Sam glanced up at her. "That's different."

The woman snickered. "So was my father. And my wife is Abel, like the biblical character."

Sam nodded, scratching out a short message to them both. She closed the book and handed it back to Zac before recapping the Sharpie and handing it back, too.

"Wow," Zac murmured, hugging the book to her chest. "Thank you so much. I'm really grateful. I'd ask for a picture, but Abel would kick my butt because she didn't get one, too."

Sam grinned, giving Zac a quick hug instead. "You guys take care and safe travels back to Maine."

Always glad to be able to make a fan happy, Sam headed back toward her rental. She again pulled out the key fob, glancing down at it before pressing the button to get the engine started. Before she could think, before she could react, before she could breathe, the night was filled with a deafening sound as the car exploded, sending a fireball filled with debris into the air and outward.

Sam was launched backward from the huge concussive wave that leveled out over the parking lot, sending her flying back into a parked motorcycle, she and the bike tumbling to the asphalt.

Chapter Eighteen

The night was aglow with flashing red and blue. Sam gritted her teeth in pain as she was moved off the heap of motorcycle, yelling out as her wrist was touched. She cried out again as pain shot through her left leg as she was moved again.

"One more time. On three. One, two, three!"

"Fuck!" Sam gasped, white hot lightning slicing through her leg and wrist. "Stop! Make it stop!"

"One more, Sam. Hang on, baby," Tandy said, standing out of the way of the paramedics.

Tears were flowing down Sam's cheeks as she was moved onto something hard and flat. She was panting from the pain, eyes squeezed shut as she tried to take as deep a breath as she could to ease the pain.

"I'm sorry, hon," a woman said, hovering over Sam. "Just hold tight. We're waiting on a second ambulance."

Sam nodded but didn't open her eyes.

"Can I touch her?" Tandy asked someone, perhaps the same woman who had just spoken to Sam.

"Yeah, but don't move anything. I don't think her neck or back is broken, but that leg and her wrist are in bad shape," the mystery woman said.

"I'm here, baby," Tandy said, suddenly right beside Sam, who opened her eyes and glanced at her.

"What happened?" she asked.

"A car bomb," Tandy said, her eye makeup mixed

with tear streaks down her cheeks.

Sam looked at her, stunned. She remembered being thrown but not why. "What? Where? Was anyone hurt?" She smirked. "Besides me? My leg hurts so bad."

"I know. It's broken. The way you were thrown and landed, the bike was laying on your wrist, too," Tandy responded.

"Anyone hurt?" When Tandy still didn't answer after she asked a second time, she did her best to look into the upset face of the woman she loved. Panic was beginning to settle in. "Tandy? Where's Cary? Is he okay?"

"Excuse me, ladies."

Sam looked up to see a woman standing on the other side of her from where Tandy knelt. She wore a tailored women's suit and short blond hair cut in a bob and tucked behind an ear on one side and dark-rimmed glasses. She looked like she belonged behind an anchor desk, not in a crime scene.

"I'm Detective Stuart," she continued. "Ms. Leyton, I'd like to ask you a couple of questions if I can, okay?"

Sam nodded as best she could. She noticed the woman's badge hanging around her neck. "Okay."

The detective lowered herself until she was squatting next to Sam, kindness in her eyes. The color was hard to gauge will all the colors painting the night. "I appreciate you talking to me," she began. "I know you're in pain and you're scared. They'll have another ambulance here in just a second." She clicked a pen to life and poised it over a small notebook that she'd flipped to a clean page. "Did you notice anything strange tonight? Anyone hanging out inside that looked out of place? Hear anyone say anything crazy?"

Sam instantly thought about the dead woman stalking her all night but wasn't about to share that. Instead, she said, "No. I was out here in the parking lot when it happened, obviously." She smirked. "But there were very few people out here. I spoke to a woman and signed her book for her, and I think I saw one of the security guards who'd been here with me tonight heading out, but not positive on that."

The detective met her gaze from scribbling a few notes on her notepad. "What was that person's name?"

"Joel Kobayashi." With that, she heard soft crying to her left. Glancing at Tandy, she saw her trying to wipe away tears. "What?"

"Mr. Kobayashi didn't make it," the detective said softly. "Did you see anyone by your car?"

Sam closed her eyes again, swallowing several times as she tried to keep down the tears that threatened. She didn't know Joel, in fact that was the first she'd met him, but still, somebody had lost his life, and he'd been there because of her. "No," she managed.

"Sam," Tandy said. "What freaked you out so bad in the club? Was it a person? Maybe they were involved with this."

Sam wished Tandy hadn't said anything, but she knew Tandy had to. She had no idea what had happened to Sam, and of course, she would try to put two and two together. "I kept thinking I was seeing someone, but it wasn't her," she finally said.

"Is this person dangerous? What's this person's name? How do you know it wasn't her?" Stuart asked, pen ready to write more.

"Yes, she was dangerous, and I know it wasn't her because Diane DeMarco is long dead."

Stuart spared her a glance before nodding, and she scribbled something down and closed her notebook. "Looks like they're ready for you." She pushed to her feet, moving out of the way as emergency personnel hurried over to them rolling a gurney. "I'll be in touch," she said, nodding at both women before disappearing into the red and blue lights.

❦❦❦❦

Sam's eyes opened slowly, and she looked around to find herself in a hospital room. She could feel a dull ache in her left arm, left leg, and her head. Her back was also making its presence known.

"Hey."

She slowly turned her head, as any movement made her feel nauseated. She was so happy to see Cary sitting in a chair next to her bed. He looked terrible, unshaven, eyes puffy and red. He was wearing the same clothes she remembered him wearing the night of the event at the club.

"Hey," she responded. "You look like crap."

He smirked, setting aside his phone, which from the angle of the screen she could see, looked like he'd been playing a game. "So do you."

She gave him a small smile. "Well, good 'cause that's how I feel." She studied him for a long moment. She couldn't remember seeing Cary with such deeply troubled eyes before. "Why do you look like crap?" She tried to continue the levity for a moment, not quite ready to dive into the serious stuff.

"Because for some reason, the hospital denied my request for a California king and rainfall showerhead." He smirked again.

Sam grinned. "We'll sue." Sam watched as the smile slid off his face and he scooted forward in his chair, one of his hands resting on the raised railing of her hospital bed.

"I'm so sorry," he said, voice an emotional whisper. "I should've been there." Tears flowed out of already red-rimmed eyes. He sniffled. "I never should've gone off with that guy."

"Hey." Sam reached out with her right hand to cover his fingers that gripped the top rail. "Cary. Cary, look at me." She waited until he met her gaze, his tortured. "Hey, you're a gorgeous, newly single guy who is as entitled as anyone to have a good time. You're not my babysitter." She smiled, squeezing his fingers as much as her limited energy would allow. "Nobody in a million years would have expected what happened to happen, and," she pointed out, "what if you were there and had gotten hurt? Or worse." She took a breath for a moment, remembering the fact that another man didn't return home to his wife from the club that night.

He nodded, clearly not appeased. "Yeah."

"How long have I been here?" she asked. From the state of his facial hair growth, she knew it hadn't happened the night before. She had little memory of anything after reaching the ER. "Where's Tandy?"

"She left an hour or so ago. She's been here the entire time with me, but she had to head to the house. Something about the art that only she could deal with. Not entirely sure. I know she intends to come back as soon as she's done. You've been in and out for two days. Doctor has had you on a nice little cocktail of pain medication and Valium after they did surgery on your wrist."

"Valium?"

"Yeah. You had a few pretty bad freak-outs. Doc says PTSD. Horrible nightmares. You kept screaming out that Monty was coming. Who's Monty?" He turned his hand so he was holding hers.

She studied him, though not really seeing him as she contemplated his words. Coming up blank, she shook her head. "I don't know a Monty. No clue."

"Well, you seemed pretty terrified of him." Cary released her hand and sat back in his chair. "They're calling this a hate crime," he said with a sigh.

"Against the LGBT?" Sam asked, eyebrows drawing.

Cary shook his head. "Against you. Or me." His jaw muscles were pulsing as anger flashed through his eyes. "The explosion originated from the rental car you were driving."

"Could have been an accident. Defect in the gas tank or something," Sam said, grasping at straws.

Cary shook his head. His phone sounded an alert that he had an incoming text. He grabbed his phone from the same table he'd placed his tablet moments before. Looking at it, he groaned. "I have to step outside and call Weber," he said, pushing to his feet. "I put him in charge while I've been here. Told him to call if he needed me. Apparently, some supplies have disappeared again, and nobody can get a hold of Dave." He stood next to the bed and looked down at her. "Cop said it was some sort of planted device." He leaned down and left a kiss on her cheek. "I'll be back in a few minutes, or I may have to go to the house."

"No worries. See ya, buddy."

"Bye, doll," he said as he breezed out of the room.

Left alone, Sam glanced back over to the table where Cary's tablet still sat and smiled, noting the vase of beautiful daisies. She didn't have to read the card to know who they were from, as they were as bright and cheery as their namesake. She was about to settle in to try to take a nap when the room door opened again, Taz stepping inside.

"Hi," Taz said softly, raising a hand in greeting.

Sam met her wave with a small, polite smile. "Hey."

"Sorry to bother you here." Taz carried a laptop under her arm as she made her way to the chair Cary had vacated. "I wanted to get your opinion on something before I get back with Detective Stuart."

"Sure, no problem. What's up?" Sam grabbed the bed remote to raise herself into more of a sitting position.

"Well," Taz said, running a hand through her spiky hair as she let out a sigh. "Someone was lurking around the house the other night, the night before the incident at the club, actually. I got them on camera and wanted to show you to see if the person looked familiar to you. I'm asking you since it seems the, well, *blast*, was aimed at you," she said, seeming uncomfortable with the topic. She met Sam's gaze, sympathy in hers. "I'm so sorry about what happened. That takes some hatred to do something like that."

Sam nodded. "Yeah, no kidding. Cowardly lunatic."

"How are you doing? Are you in pain at all?" Taz asked, closed laptop resting on her lap as she sat forward in the chair.

"A little, but nothing I can't handle." Sam studied Taz for a moment, noting she was wearing a mint green polo this time. "So, you mentioned you're retired Denver police. Aren't you a little young to retire?"

"Yes, only thirty-nine at the time. I was shot on the job." She held out her left arm, showing a scar and a divot in the underside of the pale, freckled flesh. "Busted my radius and ulna, rendering the arm fairly useless for the street with the nerve damage it caused." Her arm fell back to her lap where she gripped the laptop again. "I had the option of indefinite desk work or early retirement." She shrugged. "Figured there were better things I could do to help people besides pushing paperwork."

"Oh, that sucks. Sorry to hear that," Sam said, shaking her head. "Taz was your name, right?"

"Yup. Since I was a kid," the woman said, a smile of pride on her lips.

"What was it before that?" Sam asked, amused.

"Dunno. Well," Taz qualified, "the foster mom I was with the longest insisted on calling me Denise, but somehow, that never felt like my real name. No idea what it was, but that wasn't it." She chuckled.

"Foster mom?" Sam asked, surprised. "You were an orphan? Parents in jail?"

"Dunno," Taz said again with a shrug. "Nobody would tell me what I felt was the truth, you know? Had kids at school say horrible things to me. You know, the typical, 'Your mom is dead,'" she said, imitating the tone of a bratty kid. "'Your dad is a serial killer.' Nonsense like that. But I know nothing about my history." She crossed her arms over a heavy bosom and sat back in her chair. "Went real wild for a while, got stupid. Finally, this guy talks me into going into the Army, you know, one of those recruiter types."

Sam nodded with a smile. "Yes, I remember them haunting the halls of my high school."

"One and the same." Taz chuckled. "Figured I had nothing else anyway, so I joined. Became an MP and fell in love with law enforcement. Got out, joined the force, and the rest is history."

Sam slowly shook her head. "I have so much respect for those who serve, be it the police, EMS, military, whatever. I never had the guts to do that. Thanks for your service."

Taz smiled, studying Sam for a moment before she let out a sigh and slapped her hands on the closed laptop. "Okay, let's get down to business, shall we?" She stood and carried the laptop the short distance to the bed. Resting the computer on the narrow mattress beside Sam's leg, she lowered the rails. "Apparently, they think you're a toddler." She smirked.

"I guess I've been a bit of a lunatic. Had to give me sedatives and all," Sam explained, getting herself settled a bit more comfortably as Taz set up the laptop. "I guess some nasty nightmares and whatnot."

Taz nodded, sparing Sam a glance as she logged in. "Understandable." She turned the screen so Sam could see it. It was obviously the feed from one of the cameras mounted outside of Whitney Grove, showing the back door. "Okay, so this was Friday night, around one twenty in the morning, as you can see with the time stamp there."

"Okay," Sam murmured, eyebrows drawing as she focused on the screen. Taz tapped a key on the computer, the footage coming to life.

Everything was still for a long moment, the only indication it was a video and not a picture was the movement of a tree branch in the camera's view range, newly sprouted leaves shimmering from time to time with the breeze that seemed to be sweeping through the night. Then, from the lower right corner, a figure appeared. The picture was grainy, and details were hard to discern, but Sam could see the person was wearing a jacket with a hood. The form looked tall and slender as compared to the height of the greenery and house features near it, leading her to believe it was possibly male. It looked like the jacket may be a hoodie, and there was a logo of some sort on the back, which looked to be in a circular design.

Sam leaned forward, trying to make out what the logo was, but it was too grainy. Her focus was taken off the logo when a second person emerged into the frame. That person was shorter but also wore a hooded garment. The person seemed to be wearing a baseball cap beneath the hood, the bill just barely poking out from where the hood hung over the face.

"Okay, it's going to freeze here," Taz explained.

Sure enough, the scene froze as the taller of the two turned his head, his face now in profile to the camera.

"Do you recognize him?" Taz asked quietly.

Sam didn't respond for a moment as she studied the frozen image, her mind trying to work out what her eyes just couldn't quite organize in the black and white image. He seemed to be Caucasian or of light-skinned ethnicity, but beyond that, nothing. Finally, she shook her head. "No."

"Damn. Well," Taz said, slapping the laptop shut. "Worth a shot. I'm going to drop by the police department when I leave here and show this to our girl and see if it's worth looking into."

Sam nodded, her eyes getting heavy. "That

sounds like a great idea," she murmured.

Taz smiled down at her. "I'll leave you to rest. Hope you feel better."

"Thanks," Sam managed as she drifted off.

～～～～

The rubber on the tires squealed as they gripped the polished wood floor. Sam's heavily casted wrist rested in the sling around her neck, her cast-covered leg on the raised footrest while her uninjured foot sat on the other footrest in its normal position.

"Man, it's so beautiful in here," Sam said, voice echoing in the massive expanse of the great room.

"It really is," Tandy agreed from behind the wheelchair, which she was pushing. "The acoustics are amazing in this room," she added. "It'll be great for Mom's students."

"What a tribute to this place," Sam said, the first time in days she'd found a reason to smile, other than when she'd been released from the hospital two days before after a four-day stay. "It's seen so much tragedy and death," she murmured, looking around. They'd done so much work, putting their hearts into bringing the true heart out of the house. She'd personally made sure all the details were there, everything to take it back to 1888. "So beautiful."

"I want to show you something." Tandy turned the wheelchair in the direction of the formal dining room, companionable silence between them. "As you know, I got this ceiling fixed, and the boys helped me patch it after the damage done by the vandals. But she's finished, and I wanted you to see it."

From where she was seated in the chair, Sam

looked up in awe at the beauty that was the mural spread across the entirety of the ceiling. She knew Tandy had done her best to simply fix and clean the original artist's work. But after the vandals had done their handiwork, she'd had to re-create an entire section of it. Her skills and talents were incredible, and Sam loved that they were forever on display in the house.

She scanned the scene, her gaze finally resting on the angel, which seemed to have been largely targeted by the vandal. She gasped when she saw her own image looking back at her. Where once the angel had been a faded and somewhat damaged beautiful blonde, now it was a mirror image of herself.

"Wow," she murmured, not sure what else to say. "Absolutely beautiful."

"So are you." Tandy moved around the wheelchair to squat beside it. She smiled up at Sam, who looked down at her. "Do you like it?"

"I love it. You should have painted yourself, though." Sam grinned. "Somehow, I think your mom would rather look at you forever far more than me."

Tandy grinned before she leaned up and initiated a long, slow kiss. "Too bad," she whispered against Sam's lips. After several moments, Tandy pulled away, easing back to sit on the floor next to Sam's chair. "You know, everything is done now, except for the second floor, and," she added with a shy shrug, "even that's getting close."

Sam looked into Tandy's eyes, studying her for a long moment. She knew this conversation was going to need to be had and hadn't brought it up herself, as she didn't know what to say. She was not an impulsive person by nature, rather allowing her logic and practicality to guide her decisions. Even so, though she and Tandy were a very new couple, she knew they'd been waiting for this moment for far more than anything so simple as a lifetime. Nothing about them was simple, other than the ease of loving the amazing woman who met her gaze in that moment.

Reaching out a hand, she cupped Tandy's face. She took a deep breath, ready to speak her soul when the moment was shattered by the ringing of her phone. Groaning in irritation, she gave Tandy an apologetic smile and grabbed her phone, which rested on her thigh, looking at the screen. Noting it was Lexi calling, she answered the call.

"Hey, Lex, what's up?" Sam listened to what Lexi said, her mouth falling open with each word. "Oh, god." She gasped, a hand coming to her mouth.

❦ ❦ ❦ ❦

Eyes huge and hands covering her mouth, Sam watched. Though truth was, she wanted nothing more than to slam down the top of Lexi's laptop. She felt disgusted, disappointed, and very worried about what it would mean for them.

"I can't believe someone would film this with their phone," Tandy murmured from where she sat next to Sam.

"Are you kidding?" Lexi said, eyebrows raised above the dark rims of her glasses. "They're celebs. People film them doing shit all the time."

"Which is why he should've known better," Sam whispered.

The front door to the rental house burst open, Cary hurrying inside. "This better be good. Do you guys have any fucking idea how busy I was? I was at the warehouse ordering the last of our supplies, especially since some of them have gone missing yet again! Speaking of, where the fuck is Dave? I know he finally sent a text that he had to go deal with some issue with his ex-wife and kid, but this new guy taking over for him is a moron."

Sam would normally be sympathetic with Cary's emotional outburst, as she knew how stressful the final weeks of a project were, but in that moment, all she felt for him was ire.

"What the fuck are all of you sitting around watching a goddamn Facebook video for?" Cary continued his rage. "We've got a job to—" Cary's words seemed to freeze midair, his face going deathly pale as his eyes nearly popped out of his skull. "Oh, my god!" he shrieked, nearly pushing Lexi off her feet in his haste to get to her laptop, slamming down the lid. "Oh, my god," he said again, words muffled behind his hands.

"I hope the blowjob was good," Lexi muttered dryly. "By the look on your face, it was."

"Shut the fuck up, Lexi!" he roared, hands flying away from his face.

Sam watched as he moved away from the gathered women, her own rage building, no doubt her face as red as his. "What the fuck were you thinking?"

He whirled on her. "Oh, because you're such a fucking saint, Sam? Remember Dallas?"

"Someone took pictures of me holding her *hand*, not her fucking pussy!" Sam exploded.

"Okay!" Tandy exclaimed, a hand on Sam's shoulder and one held out toward Cary in a gesture of supplication. "It's happened, and now it's out there plastered all over the internet. That video alone already has thousands of views and shares. No doubt it'll be forcibly taken down, but the cat is definitely out of the bag." She looked from Sam to Cary and back again. "Yelling at each other and pointing fingers isn't going to solve this."

"What the hell are the network guys gonna say?" Lexi ran her hand through her hair as she let out a heavy sigh.

"That I'm fired," Cary said, emotion in his voice. "We all are."

Sam glanced over at Lexi, who was looking at her phone. The room fell silent as, not even looking up, Lexi began to read.

"*Popular HGTV renovation show,* Flipping Out, *has been canceled, network executive Ted Riley said Friday. He said it was a culmination of injuries on set and a video of openly gay star Cary Hume, who was engaged in a sex act during an event at a Denver LGBT nightclub Saturday night, spreading across the internet. The event was followed by the explosion of other* Flipping Out *star, Samantha Leyton's rental car, which killed one and sent two to the hospital, including Leyton. No comment from the show's stars at this time.*" Lexi flipped her phone around to flash the screen and online article she'd been reading before her hand fell to her side.

A heavy silence fell over the room. Sam buried her face in her hands, her heart sinking and emotions rising. Even the feel of Tandy's fingers running through her hair in a comforting caress couldn't help.

"Fuck!" Cary yelled, startling Sam, his exclamation followed by a loud crash as he threw his phone across the room.

Silence returned until Sam's own phone rang. Dread in her gut, she looked at the caller ID to see Dave's number. Sniffling back threatening tears, she answered the call and put the phone to her ear. "I'm assuming you heard, Dave?" she said into the device.

"Seems like you've hit a bit of bad luck," the voice on the other end of the line said. It wasn't Dave's voice but one that was electronically modified.

"Who is this?" Sam said.

"Two down, three to go."

Sam pulled the phone away from her ear as the line went dead.

Chapter Nineteen

They sat, the silence heavy and uncomfortable. After Tandy had left to speak to Daisy about the events and what it would mean for the renovation, Sam and Cary had gone into his bedroom in the rental house to talk. Thus far, they'd sat for nearly ten minutes, neither saying a word. For Sam, she didn't know what to say. She was still in shock.

Sam sat in the wheelchair, hating the fact that she was so immobile. Her doctor had told her that after six weeks or so, she may be able to be fitted with a walking boot. Because of her shattered wrist, which was on the same side as her broken leg, crutches weren't an option, so the wheelchair had to do the trick. She'd been forced to stay at the rental house instead of Tandy's place because the doorways were wider, in tune with the modern tastes.

Cary cleared his throat from where he sat on the end of the bed. "Are you uncomfortable? Want me to get you to the bed?" Though his tone was quiet, almost shy, his voice boomed like thunder in the stillness.

She shook her head, looking down at her hands, which rested in her lap. "No."

After a long moment, Cary spoke again. "I don't know if it would be pitiful and even disrespectful for me to say I'm sorry, Sam," he said, legs spread with feet on the floor and hands dangling over his knees at the wrist. "I guess all I can hope is you'll find it in your heart to forgive me."

Sam swallowed, hearing his words, though not entirely sure what to think of them. It was a strange feeling, how she felt. Sure, she was angry at the stupidity of what he'd done, he knew better, and they both knew it. But with everything that had happened since so early on in the renovation, she thought she understood.

Clearing her own throat to try to organize her thoughts, she glanced over at him. She was about to speak when he inadvertently cut her off, speaking first.

"I don't get it." He looked up from his hands to the wall-mounted TV across the bedroom. It was clear he wasn't even seeing it. "We've never had this much trouble on a project." He finally glanced over at her, meeting her gaze. "You know? Now I'm not talking about what I did," he added, hand going to his chest in self-acknowledgment. "I did that, and I knew better. But the article Lexi read talked about the injuries here, then your car..." He looked like a lost boy. "I feel like we've been set up to fail."

"Because we have," Sam responded simply. "We absolutely have." She used the wheels of the wheelchair to get herself turned to where she was facing the side of the bed and Cary's body in profile. "It's trying to destroy me, Cary."

"Oh, god." He groaned, slapping his hands on his thighs before pushing up from the bed. "Sammy, you know I love you. I adore Daisy and Tandy, and though he's a strange dude, I even like Stormy. But don't you see that all this is bullshit?"

"It's not bullshit," Sam protested.

"Sam," he blew out, sounding exasperated. "This is real life." He turned to look at her. "This isn't some crazy novel or something. Real lives are being affected by all this. You could have been killed!"

"I was supposed to be, don't you get that? It didn't work with the stairs, so it tried again with the car."

"It?" He smirked and shook his head. "What is this, the newest edition of *Aliens* or something?"

"The traveler," she specified. "And, yeah," she added, her mind becoming clearer as she spoke. "It was stupid as hell what you did. Why you didn't just go home with the guy first before getting into something, I'll never know, but what's done is done. Who's to say you weren't set up?"

Cary suddenly stopped his pacing. Sam thought that if he'd been a cartoon character, there would have been an accompanying screeching sound. "What? Andy?" He shook his head. "No way."

"How do you know? Other than spending a night with him, how do you know he's not a lunatic or part of something dark?" Sam asked, eyebrows raised in challenge.

Cary met her gaze, a war of wills until finally he broke first, looking away. He said nothing as he ran his hand through his hair again. "So, what about the creepy phone call?"

She recognized it for the dodge that it was, but it was a valid question, all the same. "I have no idea. And it was Dave's phone."

"Lexi's looking into that now, right?"

"That's what she said. The only thing I can think of is he's messing around, playing some stupid prank or one of his kids got a hold of his phone, maybe." Sam shrugged. Suddenly feeling very tired, she looked up at him with sad eyes. "We've got to finish this house.

Just because the network is going to fuck us over, I can't and won't fuck Daisy over. Or Tandy."

He nodded. "Yeah, I know." He crossed his arms over his chest and leaned back against the wall. "How?"

"I don't know. We'll lose all our sponsors, so no more free stuff in materials. We'll lose their construction crew, and we can't do this with us and our few guys. We'll have to hire a local crew to finish up."

"Does Daisy have enough left in the budget for that?" he asked, doubt in his voice.

"I don't know. We'll have to talk to her." Sam glanced past Cary to see Lexi hovering outside the opened doorway, seeming to wait for a break in conversation to make her presence known. "Talk to him, Lex?" she asked.

Lexi entered the room, plopping unceremoniously down on Cary's bed. "He's not there. Never was."

"Wait, what?" Cary asked, incredulous.

Lexi nodded, looking from him to Sam. "Got his ex-wife's number from HR. Get this, she said she hasn't heard from Dave in two weeks, which isn't entirely unusual since their kid has her own cellphone. But get this," she said again. "The kid's birthday was three days ago, and he didn't so much as text to wish her a happy fifteenth birthday." Again, she looked back and forth between her audience of two, wide-eyed. "The ex-wife said, and I quote, 'He may have been a twat for a husband, but he's a good dad and wouldn't miss Kelsey's birthday.'"

"Are his things still here?"

The three turned to see Daisy and Tandy standing in the open doorway.

"Why don't we go through his stuff, see if we can

find a clue to where he's gone?" Daisy continued.

Sam felt an energy shift in the room and turned to see Cary's head fall. She knew how much he loved and respected Daisy and could see the shame burning bright in the flesh of his neck and ears. As though she too understood, Daisy entered the room, everyone watching as she took him in her arms, whispering something in his ear before leaving a lingering, motherly kiss to his forehead. She pulled away and smiled at him, earning a small, watery smile from Cary in return.

Sam couldn't help but smile, and she saw a matching one on Lexi's normally cynical face. After a caress to Cary's hair, Daisy moved on, doling out hugs and kisses in greeting as she went, Sam accepting hers with vigor.

"I think that's a great idea," Lexi said, pushing up from the bed.

Like a little train, Tandy pushing Sam's wheelchair making up the caboose, the group walked to the other side of the house where Dave's bedroom was. The door was closed, though not locked, so Daisy turned the knob and pushed it open.

The bedroom was the master, given to him because he had so much camera and production equipment he liked to keep with him. The sturdy black Pelican cases were stacked neatly on one side of the bedroom, which was messy. Clothing was tossed everywhere, the bed unmade with blankets lying halfway on the floor.

"Yikes," Tandy murmured.

"It's always like this with him," Lexi muttered, stepping over a pile of clothing toward the dresser where a mountain of paperwork sat in disarray.

"Here," she said, stepping back over to where Tandy had left Sam's wheelchair. She put a large pile of papers in Sam's lap. "You go through these."

Sam looked down at the mess dropped in her lap and raised an eyebrow. "Oh, boy." She felt a presence near her and saw that Tandy had returned to her side, Dave's laptop in hand. "What are you going to do?"

Tandy spared a glance at her as she found a spot on the floor, back against the side of the bed. "Look to see who he's been communicating with," Tandy responded easily.

"Isn't that snooping?" Sam asked.

Tandy looked from Sam to the rest of the group. She wasn't leaving a single drawer unopened before returning her gaze to Sam.

"Good point," Sam muttered, turning her attention to the papers on her lap. She looked through several pages, realizing they were old production schedules. She was surprised to see a few of them were from two productions ago. Shaking her head, she tossed them to the floor so as not to get them mixed up with pages she hadn't gone through yet.

"Damn. Password protected."

Sam's attention was once again grabbed by Tandy. "Mom?" Tandy called out, Daisy turning from where she'd stood at the open closet. "Can you please grab my purse off the table in the kitchen?"

"I'll get it," Cary said, as he was closer to the bedroom door. A moment later, he returned, handing her the accessory. She smiled in gratitude at him before he went back to his task, and she dug through it.

"What are you looking for?" Sam asked, intrigued.

"A key," Tandy muttered absently. Finally, she withdrew a thumb drive. She uncapped it and inserted it into the laptop's USB port. After a moment, Tandy was typing something, then grinned. "Success."

Sam's jaw fell open. "So, you're a drug dealer *and* a hacker?"

Tandy grinned at her.

"Is there anything else about you I need to know?" Sam gasped.

"I love you," Tandy said in a silly voice. "Nah, Mom used to constantly get locked out of her phone and computer, so," she shrugged with an impish smile, "I had to get me some skills."

Shaking her head, Sam smiled and went back to her own task.

"This man seriously needs to find a washing machine," Daisy said with a light laugh, using her fingertips to toss a soiled shirt to an existing pile of clothing.

Sam watched, equally amused and disgusted. All that went away, however, when she saw Daisy pull out something that looked as though it had been haphazardly hung on a hanger and about to slide off. As Daisy carefully straightened the garment, Sam gasped.

"Wait," she said. Daisy stopped as she was about to rehang it in the closet. She looked at Sam with a question in her eyes. "Can you turn that so I can see the back of it?" Daisy did as asked, turning the light gray hoodie until the back was facing Sam. "Please lift the hood." Once it was done, the logo on the back was in full view. It was a bit faded, but it looked to be the name of a video game, the letters in a flaming circle.

"What's wrong?" Tandy looked at Sam before she lifted to her knees to crane her neck to see her mother.

"Daisy, can you toss me that hoodie?" Sam asked,

unable to move her wheelchair through the bedroom, as the floor was littered with obstacles. Daisy did, and Sam held it up, studying the logo closer.

"What is it, Sammy?" Cary walked over to her.

Looking up from the hoodie, Sam realized that all eyes were on her. "When I was still in the hospital, Taz came in to talk to me." Noting the confusion on Lexi's face, she explained. "She owns the security company watching the property. Anyway, she had some footage for me to see. The night before the explosion at the club, two people showed up at the house in the middle of the night, caught on camera. She wanted to see if I recognized either of them."

"Did you?" Daisy asked.

Sam shook her head. "Nope. Too hard to see them. But," she added, again looking at the hoodie she held. "One of them wore a jacket that had a very similar thing on the back."

"Do you think it was Dave?" Cary asked. "You think he was skulking around the house?"

"No clue," Sam murmured. She tossed the hoodie to the bed.

"Does anyone know if Dave goes by another name?" Tandy looked up from the screen of the laptop to the others in the room.

"I think he was named after his grandpa Frank," Lexi offered. "But he goes by his middle name. Why?"

"This email is to Francois Davis Byron. Just in case you've forgotten," Tandy read. "Then there's a copy of a newspaper article." Tandy's eyebrows drew together as she read silently, then shot up. "Holy shit," she whispered. "According to this news article from November 1998, in Franklin, Tennessee, a sixteen-year-old boy was arrested and charged for the rape of his eleven-year-old cousin. Obviously," she added, "both being minors, no names are included." She looked up at Sam. "Did Dave do this?"

"Who's that email from?" Lexi asked.

"Justice_Sees@gmail," Tandy said with a shrug.

"Did Dave respond?" Cary moved to stand next to Sam's chair.

"I think we should call the police," Daisy said, slowly lowering herself to sit on the bed.

"Dave responded, asking 'who is this', and the response was, 'Your conscience.' Jesus," Tandy murmured. "Then this person threatened Dave with telling his daughter what a 'sick fuck,'" she read, using her fingers as air quotes, "her father is."

"We need to call the police," Lexi said, echoing Daisy's words.

☙ ☙ ☙ ☙

Sam tapped her thigh absently with her phone as she waited, Tandy sitting in a chair next to her wheelchair. They'd been shown to Detective Stuart's desk, surrounded by the hustle and bustle of a busy police department.

Sam noticed the desk was tidy, even though there were several files and stacks of paper on it, the desktop computer sitting on one side of the scarred wood desk. A woman's midnight blue blazer was hung over the back of the desk chair. She noted a light pink coffee mug that read *WORLD'S GREATEST MOM!* in big red letters. That made her smile. Her gaze drifted to the framed picture on the ledge that ran along the wall.

She recognized the detective, though her hair was longer, surrounded by a good-looking man with dark brown hair and a goatee, two young sons, both

under the age of ten, and a baby in her arms, the little
one with a head full of dark hair and big, bright green
eyes, she realized, much like her mother.

"My family."

Sam's gaze was grabbed by the sudden voice
above and behind her. She craned her neck to see
Stuart standing there, hands on hips. She smiled at
Sam, then walked around the two seated women and
the desk to plop down in her chair, tossing a pad of
paper and pen to the desk. She looked tired.

"Nice to see you're doing well, Miss Leyton." She
smiled at Sam before nodding a greeting at Tandy.

"You recognize me from the night of the explosion?" Sam asked, surprised. Truth was, she was surprised she recognized the woman from that horrible
night in the picture and now sitting in front of her.

"Well, of course I do." She smirked. "It's because
of your show that my husband finally agreed to
renovate the downstairs bathroom."

Sam grinned, nodding. She'd heard similar
stories a lot. "Glad to help."

"That being said," Stuart said, taking in both
women. "How can I help you gals? They told me
you asked for me specifically to talk about a missing
persons case. I'm homicide, ladies. You want the
Missing Persons Unit."

"We've put in a report with them," Tandy said.
"We wanted to talk to you, too, though."

"Okay." Stuart grabbed the pink coffee cup and
took a sip. Her focused look let them know she was all
ears.

Sam watched and listened as Tandy began their
tale, starting at the beginning as they knew it, which
was that Dave had last been seen during the day of

the explosion, and moved on down the timeline, producing the printouts of the emails.

"Plus, there's the footage our security person and your former colleague Taz Barton dropped off to you, footage from the security cameras around the property at Whitney Grove," Sam added.

"Okay." Stuart removed her glasses as she sat back in her chair, the printed pages in her hand. "I mean, all this is definitely compelling for a missing persons case," she acknowledged. "But again I ask, why talk to me and not someone in Missing Persons?"

"Because I think Dave is dead," Sam said, feeling as startled by the words that had tumbled out of her mouth as Tandy looked.

Keeping her poker face, Stuart said, "That's a big statement. Why do you think that?"

Sam glanced over at Tandy, not sure what she was looking for in her eyes, but finally she said, "It's a gut feeling. I've known Dave for the three years he's worked on our show, and this behavior isn't him. Production shut down for almost two days after the explosion at the club, and for him to take off during that time wouldn't be a big deal, but it resumed before the show was canceled. We had to go without him. The only two things we were able to surmise that he took with him were his wallet and his phone. He left behind everything else, including his camera equipment. His personal equipment were his babies." She shook her head to emphasize her next point. "He'd never just take off without them. And, I got a very strange phone call from his number."

"But it wasn't his voice on the other end?" Stuart asked, pen poised over the notebook she'd been using, taking notes the entire time.

"We don't know," Tandy said.

"It was someone using one of those weird electronic thingies that alters the voice, you know?" Sam explained.

Stuart nodded, jotting more notes. "Okay. How many calls? When? What was said?"

"Just the one," Sam said. "It came in yesterday…" She looked at her phone's call log. "Two forty-one in the afternoon."

"And it said?" Stuart asked again, glancing up at Sam from her notes.

Sam was about to speak when her phone rang in her hand. A glance at the screen showed Dave's number. "It's him!" she loud-whispered.

"Answer and put it on speaker," Stuart advised.

Doing as asked, Sam answered the call. "Dave?"

"*Sure,*" the same electronic voice muttered, followed by a bit of laughter. "*You can believe that if you want.*"

"Who is this? Where are you?" Sam asked, a chill shimmying down her spine.

"*Somewhere awfully pretty,*" the voice said. "*So green, well, except for the blood. That's red, as you know. Right, Samantha?*"

Sam swallowed, every hair on her body standing on end. "What do you want?" she asked, knowing who was on the other end of that line. She may not have known who the person was by name or face, but she knew the why.

"*You know the answer to that question, and there's not a damn thing anyone in that building where you're hiding right now can do to help you. You were a fool for even trying.*" With that, the line went dead.

⟨❧⟨❧⟨❧⟨❧

Hands wrapped around the mug of coffee she'd been given, Sam stared into the flames of the firepit in the backyard of the rental house. She absently blew over the hot surface of the liquid, comforted by the smell of the Irish crème that had been added to the brew to help calm her nerves.

"Here, hon," Cary said softly, resting the requested jacket over her shoulders where she was seated on a patio chair.

"Thanks," she murmured. She followed him with her gaze as he took the chair to her left, the artistic stone firepit before them both, the empty third and fourth chairs finishing out the circle.

Cary opened the bottle of Shake Chocolate Porter he'd carried out with him, taking a deep, long sip. He let out a long contented sigh as he propped his feet up on the stone ledge around the firepit. "How you doin'?"

She nodded and shrugged as she took a sip from her coffee. "Really nice to be out of that damn chair," she muttered, Cary having picked her up out of the wheelchair and placed her in the chair where she sat. "It'll be so nice when the doctor can put that walking boot on."

"When will that be?" he asked.

"Another month," she said with a heavy sigh. "At least."

Cary nodded, looking into the dark brown glass bottle. "Crazy about the show, huh?" He glanced over at her. "First Riley tells the media it's done, then Elizabeth says hold the phone."

"Yeah, but Ted Riley hated you and I and the

idea of us on the network since day one. I'm sure for him, being head of programming, it was like Christmas when shit hit the fan. But you can't argue with the president of the network," Sam said with a chuckle. "And the show isn't back, just on hold until they decide what to do."

"And see what the hell is going on," Cary said sagely. Sam met his gaze, noting she could see the reflection of the flames in his eyes. "I'm glad you and Tandy went to that detective lady," he continued, taking another sip. "I like her, good energy."

"Agreed. She told me she's working with Dave's cell carrier to triangulate where his phone is, follow the ping, you know? Also to track down the IP address on those emails."

"You really think he's dead," Cary said quietly. "Don't you?"

Before Sam could respond, her phone alerted that she had an incoming text message. Looking down, she saw it was from Dave's phone. Her heart lurched, making her nauseated.

"What is it?" Cary asked, feet falling to the patio as he glanced over at her.

"Dave," she whispered, looking down at the freeze screen of a video she'd been texted. It was his face.

She heard Cary scoot his chair around until it was next to hers, his denim-clad knee resting against hers. She was shaking so bad, she couldn't move. She allowed him to remove the phone from her hand, his thumb pressing the play arrow on the video.

Dave seemed to be seated, the barest bit of rich wood wainscoting on the wall behind him. There were many shadows around him, the scene seeming to be lit by a flashlight or a handheld lantern. From the quality of the video, Sam figured it was a cellphone camera, not one of Dave's expensive, fancy ones.

Clearing his throat, Dave looked into the camera, then down, clearing his throat again. Finally, he looked up into the camera once more. His eyes were clear, though their expression seemed to be anxious, stressed.

"Um, not sure who will see this, but I just want to begin by saying that I'm sorry," he said. "I've done some things in my life that I'm not proud of. Truth is, I'm worried my daughter will find out what I really am." He swallowed hard and looked down, and Sam got the distinct feeling he was incredibly uncomfortable.

"That looks like the wainscoting in the third-floor sitting room. And is it just me or does he seem like...I don't know...like those aren't his words?" Cary murmured.

Sam nodded. "It does." She felt emotion threatening to push its way up, no matter how hard she was trying to keep it at bay. "It does," she whispered again.

"I want my daughter to know how much I love her. She's the best thing that ever happened to me." Dave's smile seemed genuine, though brief. His eyes spared a glance up, as though looking at someone standing in front of him. Quickly, however, he looked back down, then to the camera. "I'm sorry," he said softly, then the video went dark.

Sam nodded, looking at the screen of her phone, the frozen image of Dave again with the start arrow over his face. Tears silently ran down her cheeks. "I do," she said, Cary's earlier question in her mind. "I think he's dead."

Chapter Twenty

I think...uh..." Sam glanced up from the swatches to the three officers searching Dave's room. She forced herself to look away, giving her attention back to Tandy. "I think the deep blue with yellow accents will be gorgeous."

Tandy nodded, chewing on her bottom lip. "I like that one, too."

Sam ran a hand through her hair. Tandy had come over with options as they were entering the final stages of the renovation, which was the interior design part. She had no idea she'd arrive to a house full of uniformed officers and Detective Stuart going through Dave's things after Sam had alerted the detective of the video Dave had made. Though she and Tandy were upset, they knew there was nothing they could do but stay out of the way, so they did the best they could to make some work decisions.

"I know, baby," Tandy said softly, a hand on Sam's knee as Sam stared off into space, losing her concentration. "Do you want to stop?"

Sam swallowed, taking a moment to get her emotions settled before she shook her head and looked at Tandy with a brave smile. "No. Let's keep going." She accepted a new batch of swatches Tandy handed her when her phone rang. Noting it was Lexi, Sam answered. "Hey, Lex. Did you get all the footage?"

"I did," said Lexi, one of the last production

people still in Colorado, most being called to other projects until decisions were made regarding the show. "I found most of the security video and got it all cut and a rough edit to get it onto one disk per the detective's request," she explained. "I sent an email to Taz to see if I've got everything, so once I hear yea or nay from her, it'll be done."

"You're awesome, Lex. I appreciate it. Tandy and I will swing by and pick up the disk before too long. I know you're finishing up other production stuff, so I won't make you interrupt all that just to deliver the disk."

"*Muy apreciado.*"

Sam smiled. "Later." She disconnected the call and glanced up, noting that a very concerned-looking Detective Stuart was standing just outside of Dave's bedroom, her phone held to her ear. She nodded a few times before glancing over at where Sam and Tandy sat on the couch. "Wonder what's up."

"Almost afraid to find out," Tandy said. "Here she comes."

"Hey, ladies," Stuart said, reaching up to tuck some blond hair behind her ear as she sat on the sturdy coffee table in front of the couch. Feet set apart, she laced her fingers where they rested in the space between them. She let out a heavy breath before saying, "Dave's body has been found."

Sam felt the air knocked out of her lungs. She took a moment, trying to catch her breath.

"Where?" Tandy whispered.

"He was found in his rental car deep in the woods in Evergreen," Stuart explained. "We were able to pinpoint the pinging of his phone to that town but hadn't been able to locate him. A hiker found him."

Sam swallowed several times before she was able to ask, "What happened?" She met Stuart's gaze. "Was he killed?"

"Right now, it's looking like a self-inflicted gunshot wound," Stuart responded. "But obviously, we'll have to run residue tests and all that."

"I didn't even know he had a gun," Sam murmured. "He hated guns."

"Well, according to the responding officer, he had a great eye then or borrowed the gun from someone who did. An 1880s model Peacemaker in near mint condition is the suspected weapon used."

Sam stared at her, mouth falling open. "What?" She instantly felt nauseated, her ability to speak whisked away.

"We found a gun like that during the demo phase of the renovation," Tandy said softly, reaching over and taking one of Sam's hands in hers. "It had belonged to a woman who was murdered in the house. Sam ended up with the gun."

"Was Dave aware of the gun?" Stuart asked.

"Oh, yes. He was there the day it was found," Tandy offered.

"Was the gun kept here, in this house?"

Sam nodded. "Yeah," she whispered, her heart feeling as though it was breaking. "In my closet."

"Want me to show her, baby?" Tandy asked, her hand running over Sam's shoulders.

At Sam's nod, she was left alone with a kiss to her cheek from Tandy as the two women left her. Sam's head fell into her hands, the tears coming fast but silent as guilt and grief consumed her. After several moments, she got herself together, just in time for Tandy and Stuart to return, the metal box the gun had been found and stored in in hand.

"It's empty." Tandy sat next to Sam on the couch again.

Sam scrubbed her face with her hands before using the sleeve of her long-sleeved T-shirt to wipe her eyes and cheeks.

"We'll know more after ballistics," Stuart said, calling over a uniformed officer to hand the box off to, explaining what it was.

"Lexi called. She has the security footage you asked for," Sam said. "Tandy and I can go get it."

"Tell you what," Stuart said, hands on hips as she looked down at the two. "Why don't you and I head over to Whitney Grove, Sam?" she suggested. "I'd like to chat with you about something, anyway."

Sam nodded. "Okay." She looked at Tandy, seeing the pained sorrow in her beautiful eyes; no doubt, the same expression was in her own. "Be back soon," she murmured, sharing a tender kiss with Tandy. "I love you."

"I love you, too." Tandy gave her a sad smile as she briefly cupped Sam's cheek. "Let's get you to your wheelchair."

⁂

Sam brought up a hand from time to time to intercept a random tear before it could make its lazy way down her cheek.

"I'm really sorry about your friend," Stuart said, her voice quiet in the cab of the sedan.

"Thanks." Sam let out a long breath as the car made its way to Whitney Grove. "Just can't believe everything that's happening right now." She glanced over at Stuart. "You know?"

Stuart nodded, sparing a glance at her before returning her attention to the road. "In this line of work, sadly, there is no such thing as a 'normal' day."

"I'm sure. So, with this security footage," Sam said, wanting some distraction from her grieving for a moment. "Taz told you to get the rest of it? Did you work with her before she got hurt?"

"I want to tell you a story, Sam," Stuart said in lieu of a response to the questions.

"Okay," Sam murmured, waiting for more.

"Angela D. Yukor," she began, "was born in San Francisco on April 3, 1978, to Barry and Nannette Yukor. Older brother, Bradley, born in 1966."

"Wow. Quite an age difference," Sam said, trying to absorb all she was being told.

"Yes. Angie, as she was known, apparently was unexpected. Anyway, on December 23, 1991, a house fire erupts, killing Barry and Bradley. Unsolved. Angie and her mother, Nannette, moved to Maryland where some family lived. Nannette Yukor was killed three years later in a car accident."

"Jesus," Sam muttered.

"Suspicious circumstances," Stuart said, flipping her turn signal as she slowed the sedan to turn left. "Angie was questioned but ultimately cleared. Tossed into foster care at sixteen, arrested for petty theft four times, did eight weeks in jail off and on over the next year for various things. She ran away from her final foster family and then disappeared for four years until she showed up in prison for child endangerment. Gets out, falls off the map for sixteen years."

"Wow. Okay." Sam glanced from Stuart's profile out the windshield to see Whitney Grove coming up.

"What happened after sixteen years?"

Stuart pulled the car to a stop in front of the looming, dark house. She cut the engine and glanced over at Sam. "She's in charge of security for this property."

Sam was left staring at an empty driver's seat as Stuart climbed out of the car, briefly startling Sam with the sudden dome light. Shaking herself out of her shock, Sam pushed the passenger door open, seeing Stuart walking up from the trunk, where she'd pulled the folded wheelchair out. Slow and steady, Sam climbed out of the car, using her right leg to stand on as she shifted her weight over into the chair.

"Thanks," she said, getting settled.

In companionable silence, Sam was pushed to the production trailer where Lexi was working on the edits. Lights were on inside. The wheelchair was pushed to the foot of the metal stairs, which Stuart climbed. She raised a fist and rapped three times, waiting.

Sam tapped her hand on the arm of the wheelchair, yet again cursing its necessity as she looked around. It was late, and she felt uncomfortable. Even though a cop was not five feet away, she felt vulnerable.

"Not there?" she asked.

Stuart glanced down at her with a shrug. "I don't hear anything inside." She knocked again.

"She may have gone inside to use the bathroom," Sam suggested.

Stuart nodded and trotted down the stairs, taking her place behind Sam's wheelchair. I can try and get you up those stairs to the front door."

"Nah, go around back. No stairs." They reached the back door, and sure enough, the light was on above the door.

Stuart stepped around the wheelchair and opened the back door, pushing it open enough so Sam could be pushed through. They entered what was the kitchen once cabinets, counters, and appliances were chosen and installed, the back staircase disappearing into a dark stairwell just to the left of the back door, which Stuart closed behind them.

Sam peered through the darkness, looking down the hallway toward the front door. "Lexi?"

"Here!"

Sam was pushed through the kitchen and down the hall, past the closed door that led to the basement and into the entryway. She saw the light from the powder room that was just beyond the great room bleeding across the hardwood floor.

"You guys have done a remarkable job on this place," Stuart said. She'd parked Sam at the center of the large, open space as she walked around, never straying too far from the wheelchair. She ran her fingers over the mantel surrounding the fireplace. "Wow."

"Let me show you the mural in the dining room," Sam said, reaching down to turn herself in that direction then push herself. She could hear Stuart following just to her right. Looking up, Sam realized it was too dark to really get the splendor of Tandy's work and the artist before her. "Would you mind flipping that light switch over there, Detective? The one by the door."

"Absolutely."

Sam heard the soft steps of Stuart move away from her. A moment later, she heard a gasp before the unmistakable sound of an aluminum bat hitting something very hard. It was followed by the loud thud of something large and heavy hitting the floor and the clank of the bat dropped.

In panic and shock, Sam tried to turn her wheelchair around, feeling deeply vulnerable in the damn chair and in danger. She nearly burst into terrified tears when she heard someone behind her sing *Take Me Out to the Ballgame*, in the same electronically manipulated voice that had been on the other end of the line on Dave's phone.

Sam cried out and tried to push the person away. She was grabbed from behind, held firm with an arm around her neck, constricting her breathing as a cloth sack was put over her head.

"Fight me and you die," the electronic voice warned, arm tightening.

Unable to breathe, Sam stilled her movements, fingers still gripped around the arm that held her. After a moment, the arm loosened, the bag replacing it. A rope or something was then wrapped around her neck just tight enough to secure the bag, though it did not constrict her breathing.

Sam's eyes were huge as she tried not to hyperventilate. Her hot breaths were bounced back at her from the cloth, quickly heating her cheeks with humid, hot air. "Where are we going?"

The person pushing her wheelchair only responded by more singing of the old baseball tune.

Sam tried to focus, mentally visualizing where they were headed in the house. She thought perhaps they were headed through the entryway and past the stairs into the great room, judging by the louder echo of the person's footsteps.

"Who are you?" Sam asked, fingers gripping the

arms of the wheelchair with a death grip. "Lexi? Is that you?"

"It's a good thing that songbird bitch is so conscientious," the person said, again ignoring Sam's questions.

Sam's wheelchair was slowed to a stop, and she heard the telltale sound of the small elevator Daisy had installed for ADA capabilities should any of her future students need it, just past the bathroom off the great room.

The single folding door, which was covered by the same beautiful woodworking that covered the walls of the hallway and bathroom, whooshed open. Sam was once again on the move, pushed the few feet inside the small elevator car. The light above was on, and she could see through the tiny holes made by the thatched cotton.

The door that would open upon reaching the desired floor was at the back of the elevator, which was what Sam was facing. The inside of the sliding door was polished brass, the reflective surface showing Sam sitting in her chair, what looked like a black pillowcase tied over her head. Standing behind her was a person dressed in a dark gray hoodie, hood up. The black mask covering the face looked more like something Darth Vader or Iron Man would wear.

Finally, the elevator reached the third floor, the door sliding open and Sam being pushed out of the car. Her panic set in again as they left the comforting light of the elevator and entered the darkness of the hallway that would lead to the larger hallway that the two apartments that took up the third floor straddled. The apartments were intended for any instructors Daisy brought in for her girls who were from out of state or out of country.

As she was pushed down the hall, Sam's gaze was focused on the beautiful, round stained-glass window Daisy had commissioned at the end, wishing so badly she could erupt out of the chair and fly away through that window.

Her wheelchair was once again slowed to a stop as the door to the apartment on the right was opened. She was pulled backward through it. Sam wanted to cry but was too scared to do so.

"Please tell me why you're doing this," she whispered.

"What am I doing?" the voice asked.

"I don't know," Sam managed, her fear making her nauseated. She was worried she'd vomit in the sack over her head, then choke on it. She started and cried out when the door was slammed shut.

"Stop your whining," the person said, turning Sam's chair around. Sam knew she was now facing the fireplace that once held Sonia's hidden possessions. A lamp was placed on the floor in the corner, plugged into the wall and switched on. There was no shade on it, so the naked bulb sent sharp, eerie shadows across the room beyond its haze of light.

Sam's palms were sweating, making them feel slick and clammy. She rubbed them on the thighs of her jeans. She felt fingers working the tie around her hood, grateful as it loosened, then was gone. A moment later, the hood was removed.

Sam screamed, her hand coming up to her mouth, her chest heaving as her heart raced.

Lying on the floor off to the right at the doorway that led to the small bedroom in the apartment was a body. It was a man dressed in casual clothing. He looked to be no more than thirty, though there was so much blood, it was hard to be sure. His expression was forever frozen in shock, his throat slit from ear to ear.

"Meet Andrew, my computer guy," the voice said, then smirked. "Though you'd probably recognize him better if you saw the back of his head." The person walked over to him and nudged the dead man's leg with the toe of a shoe. "Last time you saw Andy, he was suckin' your friend's cock."

Sam gasped, a hand going to her mouth as tears gathered in her eyes. "I was right," she whispered, remembering her own musings about Cary being set up. She looked up at the figure who loomed above her. "Who are you?"

"And as for Lexi," the person said with a chuckle, nodding toward the doorway that led to the bedroom.

Sam looked in that direction, then up, a primal cry erupting from her throat as horrified shock washed over her. Her chest was heaving as she struggled to breathe. She gripped the wheelchair, desperately trying to pull herself out of the fuzzy state she was finding herself, darkness closing in around her.

≈ ≈ ≈ ≈

"Wake up. I said wake up, bitch!"

Sam gasped, sputtering and spitting out the freezing water that had been tossed in her face. She blinked several times, shaking her head. Wet bangs fell into her eyes, so she brought a hand up to brush them away. Looking around, she realized she was sitting on the floor, her back against the wall with her head leaning against the perpendicular wall to her left, which was the wall the door was on. To her right across the room was the fireplace wall and Andrew's body. Just beyond was the doorway to the bedroom. Though she couldn't see inside because of her angle, she looked away. The memory of the nightmare within came back to her. She couldn't help but feel like she was in some sort of sick Halloween fun house, mere actors.

The tears started again, the weight of the situation seeping in.

"You've always been weak."

A woman's voice cut through her grief and fear. Sam's hands fell away from her face only to see Taz sitting in Sam's wheelchair. One booted foot was on a footrest, her other foot lazily pushing the chair back and forth. The hoodie and mask had been tossed to the floor beside the chair.

When Taz saw she had Sam's attention, she grinned, waving a hand to indicate the room around them. "I thought it would be appropriate to bring you here for this. After all, this was the first place we fucked." She smirked, a facial expression so familiar to Sam. "Remember?"

Sam glared at her, so many emotions rushing through her, among them terror, confusion, and pure hatred. "You and I have never had sex." She growled.

Taz smirked. "Maybe not this go 'round, but," she leaned forward in the wheelchair, placing her other foot on the floor. "Doesn't mean it won't still happen before game over," she purred sweetly, making Sam's skin crawl.

"What do you want from me?" she hissed.

"Do you really need to ask?" Taz said, once again lazily pushing the wheelchair to and fro. "As many times as we've shared this dance?" She grinned, her gaze boring into Sam.

Sam remembered them being brown, but in that moment, they were black, nothing inside but pure evil. It sent a shiver down her spine. She surreptitiously took in her surroundings, trying to figure out how she'd get out of the situation, away from the lunatic who sat not ten feet away.

"I've chased you, following your stench," Taz continued, nearly spitting out the last word. The contempt for Sam was clear in her voice. "I've gotten stronger each and every time I've taken you down." The smirk that crossed her lips made Sam gasp in fear. "This time, you made it so easy to find you. You and your stupid show." She snorted. "Pathetic. But here we are," she added, again indicating the room around them. "Back where it all started, hmm?"

"What are you going to do?" Sam listened, waiting for the sound of wailing sirens or any movement below of Stuart. Anything.

"Well," Taz said, pushing up from the wheelchair, which she kicked back behind her so hard, it slammed into the wall next to the window across the room. The clang was deafening in the stony silence. "Since we're back here again and since I've decided to take things into my own hands this time," she said, her stance wide and aggressive, hands on hips as she looked down at Sam. "I thought we'd do something special, different."

Sam swallowed, feeling like a trapped animal. She knew there was no way she could get herself to her feet, let alone out of the room with her leg. Her left arm and wrist were all but useless. She was no better than a sitting duck. She mentally searched herself, trying to think if she had anything on her that would work as a weapon.

"You see, all I had to do was get in here. Your little friend the fairy made that happen when he convinced the old bitch to hire my company for our services."

Sam stared at her, mouth falling open. "You broke into this place, didn't you? Vandalized the art."

Taz smirked. "I always hated that fucking angel," she drawled. "Best twenty minutes of my life. Anywho, once I was in like Flynn, it was easy as pie. See, weeks ago, you, lovely Samantha, fell for it again. Damn, you have such a bad history with those basement stairs." She grinned, making *tsk* sounds with her tongue. "What a klutz. Your perverted cameraman took it on the chin for you guys in the car." She took a slow step toward Sam.

Sam's hand went to the floor, her gaze never leaving Taz's looming figure as she instinctually scooted away.

"You'd be surprised to know that there's a split second of incredible pressure, *painful* pressure, before that bullet explodes your brain. I don't recommend it. Then," Taz continued, bringing up a hand as she ticked off the deaths on her fingers. "Andrew here," she said, nodding in the direction of the body on the floor, "was a cut above the rest." She laughed at her own joke. "Be glad you only got the stairs this time, baby," she purred.

"Jesus," Sam whispered, head slowly moving back and forth as a vision of Sonia's throat being slit flicked before her mind's eye. "You are sick."

"You don't know the half of it." Taz took a couple more slow, lazy steps toward Sam. "And then, Lexi was good enough to hang around." She stood only a few feet from where Sam again began to scoot away. "Just like dear Sally. Ain't that right?"

Instantly, fresh tears pricked the backs of Sam's eyes. Though steeped in the shadows of the dark room, she knew she'd never get the image of Lexi's lifeless body out of her mind's eye. "Lexi was innocent," she whispered.

"So was my daughter!" Taz raged, using seemingly super-human strength as she grabbed Sam by her throat, sliding her up the wall and pinning her there until they were eye to eye.

Sam gasped for air, clawing at the vise-like grip around her neck. "She was all I had," Taz growled, her face within inches of Sam's. "You took her, so I've hunted you down to return the favor, again and again and again." Her lips cut into a cruel smile. "I watched as the very life was squeezed out of sweet Sephora's body. Now, in the revisiting of our very own fucked-up episode of *1000 Ways to Die*, there's only one left."

Sam's eyes squeezed shut as Taz's hand squeezed tighter. She could no longer bring in air, and her hand that clawed at Taz's hand reached out, trying to grab her hair, gouge out her eyes, whatever she could grab to make her let go.

"Oh, no, you don't," Taz said, moving her face out of Sam's reach. With her other hand, she grabbed Sam's injured wrist and slammed it against the wall above Sam's head.

Like lightning slicing from her fingertips all the way up to her shoulder, Sam tried to scream in pain, but nothing came out. She could feel her heartbeat pounding in her head and in her eyes, feeling as though her eyes would pop out of her head. Yet again, her vision was darkening, her grip on reality slipping.

The door to the apartment slammed open so

hard it buried the doorknob into the wall it slammed into, only a black leather shoe visible before Stuart appeared. The entire left side of her face was covered in blood, her left eye swollen shut and her blond hair matted. There she stood, feet planted wide and both hands wrapped around her 9 mm in firing position. Without a word, she squeezed off five rounds, three of which hit their mark.

Taz jerked with each shot, staggering backward until she tripped over her own feet and went down, just like Sam, like a sack of potatoes down the wall. She gasped for air as she fell to her right side, her cast-encased left leg shooting out straight to the side. She didn't even feel the pain as she desperately tried to bring air into her lungs. Her gaze went from Taz to Stuart, who stumbled into the room, a bloody handprint left on the wall before she collapsed to the floor.

Sam managed to do a combination squirm-army crawl over to Stuart. "Are you okay?" She gasped, noting the head wound was significant.

Both their attention was grabbed when a grunt was heard from where Taz lay on the floor, a puddle of blood forming beneath her. She lifted her head, pain radiating across her face as she began to push herself up into a sitting position.

Stuart gritted her teeth as she, too, tried to raise herself, her gun still held in her blood-covered right hand.

"No." Sam put a hand on hers to stop her. "You can't." She looked into Stuart's eyes, seeing the confusion in them. She gently took the pistol from her. "You can't," she said again. The gun felt heavy in her hand, the grip sticky from Stuart's blood.

She looked back over to Taz, who was fully sitting up now. Her gaze was locked on Sam, filled with determination as she gritted her teeth as she slowly moved to her knees. One hand was held to her side, which was bleeding freely, red ribbons streaming between her fingers.

"Sam," Stuart muttered, sounding out of breath. "Give me my gun back. I have to finish this."

"No," Sam murmured, lifting her upper body off the floor, gun in hand. "I have to."

Without even flinching as the single gunshot echoed in the empty room, Taz fell back with a thud, blood trailing across her forehead and into her spiked hair from the hole dead center.

Sam stared at her for a long moment until her eyes burned from not blinking. Her arm lowered, gun gently set on the hardwood beneath her.

"It's over now."

Sam turned to look at Stuart, only to see that she'd passed out. Looking to her right, she saw three women standing before her. The youngest smiled at her, the softest, most loving smile she'd ever seen. Her dark hair was pushed back away from her face, her simple dress showing the figure of a young woman just transitioning from girl to woman.

"Go, live your life now," she said softly.

"You better make us proud, you hear me?" the woman standing next to her and the oldest of the three said. Her hair was swept up in an intricate updo. Her dress looked like something out of *Gone with the Wind*. In her green eyes was a fire and passion for life.

The third woman, young and beautiful, was dressed in bell-bottom jeans and a flowing blouse. Her long dark hair was parted down the middle. She said nothing, simply walked over to the woman on the floor and knelt. Closing her eyes, she leaned down and left the softest of kisses to Detective Stuart's forehead. Slowly pulling away, she glanced over at Sam, who looked at her wide-eyed and mouth open.

"Thank you," the young woman whispered, then with one last look to Stuart, she got to her feet and joined the other two.

The older one winked, then the three of them turned around and walked to the open door of the apartment. Sam watched as they walked out single file. She was still staring, stunned as the distant wails of sirens filled the night.

Epilogue

Tandy's hand in hers, Sam looked down at the stone before them, fresh flowers replacing those that had begun to die in the brass vase. As Sam looked at the stone, she knew she'd been there before, remembered being there, but after the events at Whitney Grove three months before, she'd lost the reason it was so important. She knew the woman buried in the grave before her was murdered in the old grand house, and though it was a tragedy, she didn't know why they'd been asked to meet at her grave.

Feeling like they were being watched, Sam glanced up and over. Standing at a small stand of trees was a figure. The features were indiscernible, largely because of the baseball cap that shaded the face. Sam smiled, raising a hand in greeting. The figure raised a hand in return before stepping out of the shade and into the warm summer sun.

"She looks so much better," Tandy said softly.

Sam nodded, her left hand adjusting its grip on the handle of her cane. "Much better. She said the physical therapy is going well, too."

"Well, my god, fractured skull..." Tandy murmured.

"Beautiful day, ladies," their companion said, offering Tandy a quick, one-armed hug before she and Sam embraced, a full hug that lingered for a moment before she pulled away. "So good to see you, Sam."

"You, too, Detective," Sam said, returning the warm smile she was given.

Stuart raised an eyebrow. "After everything we've been through together, don't you think it's about time you start calling me by my first name?"

Sam smiled, feeling shy. "Yeah," she said, feeling like the first time you run into a former teacher and she asks you to call her by her given name. "It's so good to see you, Chloe," she said softly, the two sharing the knowing look of two people who had gone through hell together and lived to see the other side.

❧❧❧❧

"So, here comes Stormy, walking out of Whitney Grove *all* mysterious like," Cary said standing in front of those seated on the back patio of Sam and Tandy's house. Feet planted wide, fingers spread, he looked at each seated person, including the man named, who was clearly trying to hide his smile. "He's dressed in this bathrobe thingy," Cary continued, meeting the gaze of his husband, Ray, who was laughing at the story. "He's got Voodoo this in one hand, Wiccan that in the other," he said, shaking each hand jazz hands style with each mention. "I mean, the guy looks like he's been through hell and back, right?" He stands upright, bringing his palms together prayer-style and looks down at everyone seated, as though about to reveal a great ancient secret. "He says, 'This house is clean.'" His eyes closed and his head bowed.

Sam burst into laughter. "He did not!"

Stormy chuckled. "Though I do appreciate the Zelda Rubinstein imitation, I had to cleanse the place before Daisy brought those young women in for their musical education."

"Well, an incredible amount of crap went down in that place," Tandy added, her head resting back against the arm he had slung over her shoulders on the glider made for two where they sat.

"Okay, drama queen," Sam said to Cary before leaning over and giving Tandy a lingering kiss on the lips. She pushed up from her chair to head into the house and grab the pitcher of iced tea to begin refills. "Do you or Ray want another beer?"

Cary smiled at her, absolute contentment in his blue eyes. Sam had never seen him so happy, and it filled her with warmth and love for her dearest and oldest friend. "I'm good. Babe?" He turned to his husband of two years. Ray had served as Daisy's costumer when she did shows around the U.S. and the occasional overseas show, in between sessions at her successful school at Whitney Grove.

"I'll take another, Sammy," Ray said from where he lounged, Cubed purring contentedly in his lap.

"You got it."

"You know," Cary said, walking over to Sam and slinging his arm over her shoulders. "I just can't get enough of watching Daddy's little squirt run around."

They stood in silence for a moment, watching Sam and Tandy's three-year-old daughter, Elise, play with her BFF, five-year-old Isabella. The two were inseparable.

"You do realize that if you keep calling her that, there will come a time when you'll have to explain just exactly what that means and why it's relevant to her, right?" Sam murmured, glancing over at him. She could see the wheels turning in his head by the expression on his face, which she had to chuckle at.

There was a ton of Tandy in their little girl, but she definitely saw Cary's expressive eyes and dimples, as well.

"Well, shit," he finally said, grinning at her.

Shaking her head, Sam laughed and squeezed his side affectionately before moving away from him and to the back door of the house. She heard the strum of a guitar and stopped at the open French door, turning to look out into the yard.

Chloe sat cross-legged on the grass, Daisy beside her. Chloe's husband was manning the grill while their two sons played catch with a football, while tasked with keeping an eye on their sister, Isabella.

"Okay, remember this?" Chloe asked, strumming her guitar until it turned into a very recognizable tune.

Daisy smiled and swayed to the music, humming along until the intro was over, and it was time to sing.

Sam smiled. She'd had to be told all the stories of Sonia and Daisy after Taz had been killed, taking all of Sam's memories of anything before her life as Sam Leyton with her. The stories of Daisy singing *Me and Bobby McGee* to a very young Chloe had been the picture of the birthday party. Now to witness it was deeply touching.

When Daisy got to the chorus, Chloe raised her head and sang over Daisy's beautiful voice, "Me and little Chloe!"

Sam laughed, a tear of gratitude coming to her eye at the absolute perfection that was her life.

If you liked this book?

Reviews help a new author get discovered and if you have enjoyed this book, please do the author the honor of posting a review on Goodreads, Amazon, Barnes & Noble or anywhere you purchased the book. Or perhaps share a posting on your social media sites or spread the word to your friends.

About the Author

Kim has spent her life in Colorado and can't imagine living anywhere else. She's been writing since she was 9 and stumbled into her first book being published in her mid-20s. She's worked in the film industry as a writer, director and producer, but now enjoys the quiet, happy life of a professional author. She can be reached on Facebook and on her website at, www. kimpritekel.com

Check out Kim's other books.

Zero Ward - ISBN - 978-1-943353-19-4

Danny Felts grew up in the heart of the Midwest on a dairy farm, expected to follow in her mother's footsteps and marry a farmer and become a mother. Danny had other ideas. As World War II heats up, she makes a decision that will change her life forever as she becomes a lie, serving with the Seabees in the Navy as Daniel Felts.

Kate Adams is about to graduate high school in her prestigious and elite San Diego neighborhood when she's dragged to the USO for a dance with friends and servicemen. There, she meets the person that will catch her eye and her heart, only for jealousy and vengeance to tear her apart.

Are Danny and Kate strong enough to win the battle within and fight for their love?

Connection - ISBN - 978-1-939062-24-6

Julie Wilson lives a charmed life as a beloved teacher and aunt in the small town of Woodland. Close to her brother and guardian of two adorable Yorkies, she loves her life, the only negative being ex-boyfriend, Ray who can't seem to understand the phrase, "We're done." Believing that's her only problem, Julie has no idea what hell awaits her during a normal summer afternoon.

Remmy Foster is the quirky, friendly drifter who has

never found roots after a difficult childhood, as well as the difficulties her very special gift brings into her life. Though she may call it exploring, the truth is she's running from ghosts that haunt her every step.

After a chance meeting with Julie while hitchhiking, Remmy will be thrown head first into darkness she could never have foreseen, regardless of her abilities. As the clock ticks, life and death is on her shoulders to make the right connection.

Warning - Some scenes may be too intense for some readers.

1049 Club - ISBN - 978-1-939062-97-0

Almost two hundred souls, one plane, six survivors, endless heartbreak.

When flight 1049, headed from Buffalo, NY to Italy falls from the sky, a firestorm of drama, pain, angst and sorrow ensues. Can an author, a business owner, a teenager, good ol' boy, veterinarian and ruthless lawyer survive? Better yet, can those left behind?

1049 Club is a story of survival, love, deep regret and miracles. Can the living make peace with the presumed dead? Can the presumed dead make peace with the lives and loves they thought they had before?

Blinded – ISBN – 978-1-943353-53-8

After a horrible explosion sends local television news reporter, Burton Blinde reeling both physically and emotionally, she walks away from her life and the dream job she was about to start at a major news network.

For six long years she hides out in a small mountain town, working at the local library, though is haunted by the life she had, including mysterious messages and gifts she was receiving before her life was turned upside down, a veritable bread crumb trail leading to the unknown.

Unable to resist, Burton begins to follow the clues, which will lead her into the darkest places of human nature that she may not be able to return from.

Damaged - ISBN - 978-1-939062-45-1

Family. A group of people you are related to by blood or love.

Nora Schaeffer has come home to her family after twenty years working around the world as a photographer for National Geographic. She's welcomed into the open arms of her father and siblings.

Family. A group of people who support you, lift you up when you fall.

Shannon, the youngest of the four Schaeffer siblings, has vanished, leaving her five-year-old daughter, Bella, terrified and alone. To help find Shannon, Nora has no choice but to turn to the dark-haired specter who has haunted her for twenty years. Along the way, she finds her own long-dead heart and uncovers chilling family secrets beyond imagination.

Family. A group of people who will stick together to hide the rotten soul at its core at any cost.

Who will live? Who will die? Who will be the most damaged? And who will learn to love again?

The Gift - ISBN - 978-1-948232-47-0

The dead do speak. You just have to listen. Homicide Detective Catania "Nia" d'Giovanni is the only daughter in a large Italian family of six children. The backbone—a position not applied for nor wanted—she continues to create new glue to hold the dysfunctional group together. For Nia, family time feels more like herding cats than spending time with her brothers and feisty, aging parents. Her heart has always been in her career with the Pueblo Police Department, especially since it will never be okay with her very Catholic mother to openly give her heart to any woman, until she meets a secretive waitress who has her at, Can I take your order? And then it begins... Three murders that are so gruesome, so horrible, they rock the small town to its core. Nia and her partner Oscar are left to piece together a deadly puzzle to find the key to unlock the monster they hunt. Or, are they the hunted? As they dissect the murder scenes where not one shred of evidence is left behind, more bodies begin to show up, each cleaner than the last, the shadowy specter that is the killer vanishing without a trace, making the woman Nia loves disappear right along with it. When there is no evidence to follow, Nia must trust her instincts... or, is she being guided?

The Plan – ISBN – 978-1-948232-43-2

As the dark days of the Dust Bowl came to an end, the midsection of the United States tried to rebuild and revitalize. In the small, dusty farming town of, Brooke View, Colorado, teenager, Eleanor Landry and her mother were dealing with her father, a self-appointment fire and brimstone preacher to his congregation of two. A plan to survive.

As the dark era of the robber baron comes to an end, giants of industry and innovation emerged with fabulous fortunes manifested in the mansions that dotted the landscape across the country. Lysette Landon, the teen daughter of the wealthiest family in Brooke View, was everything a good, proper girl of privilege should be. Only problem was, she wasn't dreaming of finding a young man to raise a family with. A plan to be free.

One look, one touch, all plans are off.

Secrets deeper and darker than the grave would bring Eleanor and Lysette together, their families connected by a web of lies and broken promises. A plan to escape.

Be careful because, life has other plans...

The Traveler Book One: The Hunted - ISBN - 978-1-948232-91-3

A story so epic one book can't contain it.
BOOK ONE:

1977: In the era between flower power and the yuppie, Sonia Lucas is a young wife and mother, just starting out in life. Without warning, a strange presence and dark force enters her life, clouds building ....

1917: .... and a storm brewing as the world reeled from the horrific events of World War I just before it was ravaged by a Spanish flu epidemic that would kill millions. Sephora Lloyd is a 16 year old girl lost in the responsibilities of an adult world helping to support herself and her mother. A beautiful young nun-in-training enters her life, bringing love and hope with her. That is, until a force bigger than either of them threatens everything Sephora holds dear.

four women - three deaths - two words - one house

THE HUNTED

www.ingramcontent.com/pod-product-compliance
Lightning Source LLC
Chambersburg PA
CBHW020358260626
47156CB00007B/2171